THE BASTARD WONDERLAND

Lee Harrison

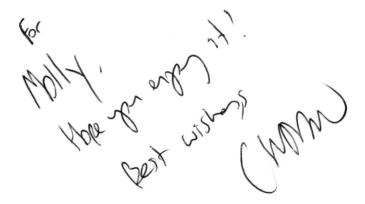

For
Molly,
Hope you enjoy it!
Best wishes

THE BASTARD WONDERLAND
Lee Harrison

ISBN 9781903110454
First published in this edition 2016 by Wrecking Ball Press.

Cover design by Lee Harrison and Owen Benwell
Typeset by leeds-ebooks.co.uk
All rights reserved.

THE BASTARD WONDERLAND

Part One

At journey's end, we look awed upon an endless coastline of silver, seeming both temperate and fair. The solitary, stooping mountain stands there as an emissary, respectful to the lands we have left behind, yet welcoming to a world of undiscovered wonderment.

— *1624 entry from the Journal of Captain Olaf Hagen, the founder of Aaland.*

1 SCRAPING THE BARREL

The *Call of March* bucked the waves, groaning against her anchor lines as she waited for port. Sun beams spilled through the rigging, etching a broken-nosed scowl across Mr. Warboys' face as he smoked sullenly against the gunwale.

He squinted at the churning city port that was supposed to be home. Coperny sprawled across the visible coast and half way up the mountain, the smog of newfound industry greasing the sunlight over the bay. The bow-backed shape of a half built viaduct loomed over the upper town, launching a glittering tramway over the city. Up through the haze, he could just about make out the weathered statue of Hagen the Founder on the summit of the mountain, crowned in flocks of shrieking gulls, his shit-striped arms open in welcome to the world's newest nation. The clamour of folk hit Warboys' ear intermittently through the roar of the wind, and away through the mesh of harboured masts he could see crowds gathering on the wharves, the facades of otherwise grim dock offices draped in arcs of red and black bunting.

A mob of deckhands gathered on the foredeck beyond Warboys, loafing with their smokes, jumpy with the anticipation of pay and shore leave, and made still giddier by the sight of the celebrations.

'Must be our welcoming party,' cackled one, scratching his scalp beneath a frayed woollen cap.

There was a collective laugh, but Warboys spat into oily, rainbow coloured waves, and did not crack a smile. They were getting on his nerves.

Through the ragged aisle made from awaiting vessels, a trade schooner – the *Katerina*, out of Nyssa – emerged at half sail. The deckhands leaned outward like wallflowers, eager to gather news.

'You're in for a right treat here, my lads!' grinned the *Katerina*'s mate, hanging from the rigging nets as she cut through the surf. 'King John's fucking abdicated! Stepped down he has, and gone off with his Jurman poofter! General Malvy's already sworn himself in and abolished the throne! We're a Nation State, now, he says!'

'Fuck off!' scoffed Warboys.

'Ha! Not a word of a lie, mate! And that ain't all. He's marching on Blackhaven! He's on about uniting the whole continent, Andamark, the Blacklands and all of it, right down to the fucking peninsula and across the islands! We're rousing for war, lads!'

He laughed as if this were a right scream.

'Give over! *Blackhaven?*'

'It's true! He's going to announce it now, in person. Why do you think you've been waiting so long for port? They're drafting every cross-eyed fucker they can catch! You'd better have your papers, lads, that's all I can say. Prove you're worth your salt, like!'

And off he went, laughing as the *Katerina*'s bow wave hit the *Call*, dipping Warboys' stomach. The deckhands exchanged nervous glances.

'What we invading the Blacklands for?' whined one. 'There's knack all down there but sheep and savages.'

'Say what you like about King John,' said a varnished veteran, 'he saw the sense in leaving the backward bastards to their swamps and bogs. Seems like Old Jonah don't see fit to honour the agreement.'

Shit, thought Warboys. The speculation began, and he wasn't much further on with his analysis of the situation when Jacky Biel, a gangly beanpole of a deckhand, appeared beside him.

'What do you reckon then, Warboys?'

Warboys squinted at Biel as if he were a stripe of seagull shit. Biel's mates sniggered and nudged one another in anticipation of fun.

'I bet you wish you'd finished that chartership, eh? Your old man can't help you now!'

'Piss off, Biel,' snapped Warboys. Privately, he felt a stab of anxiety at the mention of those two things – his chartership, and his dad. Like most work, the chartership had seemed like a waste of effort at the time. Now he didn't have the papers to entitle him to a berth as a seaman, he knew he was out of a job again. And the old man would be there outside the Dock Offices, waiting for him. Ready with an earful, like he always was when things went wrong.

'I've always thought you was the infantry sort,' said Biel. 'Here, you're a dab hand at taty peelin' aint you? An army marches on its taters!'

They laughed again, and Biel's pungent smoke smelled of his smugness. Warboys fumed privately, but shrugged.

'The infantry ain't so bad.'

'Yah, if you *survive* it's alright. Malvy won't last. He's a fucking lunatic. They'll find some new bastard for a king, and the sea'll still be there and it'll still want traversin'.'

'*You* might be 'appy comin' and goin' from this dump for the rest of your life, but I aren't. I still want to go somewhere. I want to see summat different. Make summat for myself.'

'Ah well,' shrieked deckhand Ives from among the mob. He was a young, pasty faced accomplice to Jacky Biel, and a gobshite to boot. 'You can make yourself some nice roasties once you get back among them taters!'

Warboys fixed Ives with a warning glare which the young lad was too giddy to pay heed to.

'It can be hard work though, taty farming. Musn't let it get on top of you...'

'Yeah,' added Biel. 'Ask Warboys' old lady!'

The laughter was uneasy this time. Warboys stiffened and straightened up, pointing his smoke at the two of them.

'Smile whilst you've got the teeth for it, you gangly fucker. We'll be off this tub soon, and I'll be seeing you.'

'Oh look, now Warboys mate, he didn't mean—'

'I know what he fucking meant.'

'Flag!' came a yell from above. 'We've got the blue!'

They scattered keenly, and were rousing to make port before the first mate could bark orders. Soon the *Call* was easing into the inner harbour, through boulevards of bare masts. The crew jeered as a tin-pot steamer waddled by, belching out clouds of white smoke to briefly swallow the scenery. More news and rumours were exchanged from ship to ship, but Warboys didn't listen.

He hauled rigging, feeling a gloom in his stomach. In this harbour he'd sat idly on jetties, smoked when he was too young to smoke, boasted of all the places he could go, the money he could earn, the women he could have. Yet here he still was. A nobody hard over the wrong side of thirty, still to-ing and fro-ing to neighbouring ports on chance commissions. Still bearing earache from his old man, even as revolution seemed to have arrived, and still the city toiled on, indifferent to him.

The *Call* came to dock, pulled instantly into the rabble as mobs of angry merchants and dock officials descended upon it, bawling at the captain with their quarantine regulations, contracts and hassle.

~ ~ ~

A checkpoint choked the wharves, packing alighting sailors together like livestock. Moustached conscription officers manned the gates in heavy greatcoats, calling for papers, herding men through a course of tents and holding pens. Glowering propaganda plastered every surface, promising the world for a bit of graft. Warboys had grown up with tales of the last war, in which General Jonas Malvy had made his name as the bulwark of Aaland. Old Jonah, that grounded, salt-of-the-earth figure at the throne's side. Now though, when it seemed the coup had won him the country, Warboys felt Malvy's poster-painted face glaring at him from every surface, and didn't feel so reassured. NO LONGER SHALL AALAND OBEY THE PAST, claimed one poster, picturing a great fist toppling a white castle. SEIZE THE FUTURE! The violent reds and blacks set the men as nervous as sheep.

Warboys craned to see that the line was being split into two. To the right went those with chartership papers, off towards Dock Street and freedom; to the left went the others, off to sign their lives away whether they liked it or not.

'That's you sorted then, Warboys,' sniggered Jacky Biel, his beany frame edging out of the mash of bodies. 'Least somebody wants you, eh?'

Warboys bristled at Biel's buzzardlike profile, but held himself, watching what happened at the gate. Before them, a ginger-haired deckhand named Calvert shifted anxiously, trying to slip through the gate unchecked. Without even looking, the officer slapped his hand on the lad and stopped him dead.

'Have you got your papers there, my lad?' asked the officer, puffing up so that the buttons on his greatcoat bulged like eyeballs.

'No sir.'

'Might you, then, be interested in a career in the forces?'

'No sir.'

'But you've got no papers? Might I remind you of the Public Responsibility Act of 1864?'

'I ain't 'eard of it, Sir.'

'Well, allow me. Passed *days* ago it was. It says that if you come through port without meanful gains, son, that's a criminal offence. And in these days of great need, it ain't practical to keep a grown man in a cell. We'd have to conscribe him into national service, like. Pay his dues. So I asks again, sir. Have you ever considered a career in the forces?'

'I ain't no fighting man, sir.'

'Listen lad. Our good General Malvy is scraping the barrel here. Every last man, barrel and duck is to be used. This country ain't no *respite*. It's a well oiled machine.' He leaned to growl in the boy's ear, pointing at the red and black Malvys as he did. 'If the duck can't fight, it wants to be shot and ate.'

With that, the officer collared the poor sap and shoved him off to the left

'Ho ho!' bellowed Biel, nudging Ives. 'Not so cocky now, is he? I reckon we'll be parting ways for a time here!'

Warboys considered. Part of him would rather be drafted, rather than have to explain himself to his dad. But fear blossomed once again as he saw Calvert make another weak run for it, knocking off the officer's hat. Biel and Ives guffawed again, heartily enjoying themselves.

Warboys saw his moment.

'Listen,' he began amiably, giving Biel a pally nudge, 'Jack, mate...'

Biel's big nose had barely turned before Warboys stuck the nut on him and mashed it across his face. Biel sagged where he stood, fingers relinquishing his papers as he fell into Ives, and Ives tumbled into the man behind him, causing a ruckus among the tightly packed sailors. Warboys backed off toward the gate, hands raised in a show of innocence. Ives managed to scramble from the brawl to catch Warboys with a jab, just as the officer – fresh from seeing Calvert off – turned back to his post. Warboys padded his eye, resisting the urge to fight back, holding Biel's chartership papers up and trying to pull as lovely a face as he could. The officer moved to set about Ives with his steel tipped Jonah, but then Jacky Biel squirmed his way from the cranked arm of a moustached man, squeaking 'He's nicked me papers! Check him! His name is Warboys, not Biel! *I'm* Biel! Check him!'

'Hang about, mate,' grunted the officer, beckoning to Warboys.

'Piss off!' yelled Warboys, indignantly, pointing at Biel. '*He's* Warboys! He didn't even finish his bloody chartership! He's got his name tattooed on his arse, look, case he forgets it.'

When the officer turned to see if this were true, Warboys ran.

Through the gate, he skittered over cobbles sparkling with oil and fish scales, and careered towards where the grand turrets of the dock offices loomed over the street. A line of deckhands curled out from the office like dirty dominos, waiting to claim their wages. All around them, women, children and old men crowded the street, doting on loved ones fresh through port. Some wore red flags or shawls, joining the spirit of General Malvy's declaration.

Then, amongst this merry throng, Warboys saw his dad.

William Warboys senior – Bill to those in the know – was a moustached man as thickset as Warboys, but with a more wiry, greyer head of hair. He stood frowning in his old charcoal jacket, puffing away on a paper smoke like a relic seeing out the last of the old days.

Bill's frown deepened, his smoke pivoting on his lip as he saw Warboys hurtling towards him. 'Now then!' he exclaimed, then, 'Oi!' as Warboys promptly hurtled past. Warboys said nothing, lest the officers collar his dad, but managed a constipated look that he hoped might express some kind of apology. He sailed by, letting Dock Street sweep him along, around carriages and guard troupes, past dockers shuffling from fish and dry docks. At the next junction, the muffled sound of a brass band pulsed unevenly from up the street. Armed infantry choked the road at a check-point, and Warboys slowed, seeing the crowd ahead arise in density until he could see nothing but people: soldiers, flat caps, glosswaxed ladies, all the masses assembling to hear the great General speak from Junction Monument.

Warboys turned to see the officer – now with a few burly grippers in tow – edging against the crowd to scan for him. He ploughed on, through deckhands spilling from Dock Street Tavern in rowdy, smoky groups.

A carriage clattered around the corner, earning a dull cheer from onlookers as it veered to avoid him, spilling mud-caked yams across the cobbles. One of the grippers chasing him had just enough time to point and exclaim 'Oi!' before the crowd closed in, opportune hands stuffing yams into pockets, blocking Warboys from view.

He fled into the vomit-spattered alley by the tavern, stumbling through overflowing bins. The alley bent sharply, and Warboys almost piled into a sailor having a topless hand-shandy with his sweetheart.

'Don't mind me,' he grunted, edging past. 'I ain't here.'

'Me neither, love,' croaked the sweetheart.

The alley ended at a boarding that glared with more propaganda. Warboys paused a moment, to see if he had been tailed, but could only see the sweetheart, her forearm beating away energetically, at odds with her stony face.

The boarding bent nicely, allowing him onto an alley partly obscured by a row of half-demolished buildings. Warboys picked his footing carefully, looking for some refuge among the gutted buildings. Sparks of light winked through gaps in the boards facing Dock Street, where the racket of the waiting crowds rattled through. Men coughed and blustered at one another over the sound of the band. A woman shrieked. A child nattered for a peg up.

There was a creak behind as someone shoved through the boarding. Warboys ducked into a doorway, expecting the grippers to come piling through after him. Then his dad arose, muttering curses.

'Bloody idiot! What are you...' was all Bill could manage before doubling over in a fit of coughing.

'Bugger off!' hissed Warboys, hoping to god the old sod wouldn't start ranting at him here. 'You'll get me caught!'

But Bill staggered obliviously toward him, cursing as he joined Warboys in the doorway.

'They've gone,' gasped Bill. 'Too busy today to bother for long with the likes of you.' Even as he said this, Warboys caught a fleeting glint of pride in Bill's eye – a look that always surprised him – and made his stomach tighten.

'How did you find me?'

'You ran down here that time the captain quarantined you for being pissed at the tiller. What have you done this time?'

'Dad, I haven't—'

Just then, the brass band faded into flatulent tones, and a hush fell over Dock Street. Bill nudged Warboys to shut him up. Then an officer could be heard yelling the order for quiet, and the two Warboys stalked toward the boarded windows. Quietly, they scaled a cracked staircase to crouch at a window overlooking the street, and settled there. Warboys sensed a reprieve, knowing his ticking off would have to wait whilst they heard what the Great General Malvy had to say for himself.

2 THE END OF HISTORY

Warboys had not seen so many gathered since the day Bill had brought him to see the first steam tram unveiled. A sea of humanity blocked the streets from Dock Street to Junction Monument, and from there all the way down to Nethergate. At the monument itself, flanking a lectern in the centre, the admiralty of the navy lined up on a raised stage opposite the generals of the army. Among a quietly apprehensive public, the posters that patterned the walls – AALAND UNITED! – seemed like the loudest voices. ASK NOT WHAT AALAND DOES FOR GOD, proclaimed the slogans, BUT WHAT GOD DOES FOR AALAND! Up on the peak, the statue of the founder could be seen, his arms raised in frozen apprehension.

With neither fanfare nor announcement, General Jonas Malvy climbed up to the stage and took the lectern. There was a general creaking of boots as everyone stood up on tip-toes to see this great figurehead. *He's actually quite a little man*, thought Warboys.

'Citizens of Aaland!' the General cried out, the amphitheatre curve of the monument's face making his voice resonate with surprising efficacy. 'I welcome, and salute you on this portentous day.'

The General took a moment to survey the gathering, as if he were doing a private roll call.

'*This day* marks the end of history. And so I present to you... its obituary.' Warboys here noted that Bill had begun tutting and muttering in disapproval almost as soon as Malvy had taken a breath. With practised effort, he tried to block the old man out so he could listen.

'Our history began when the great explorer Hagen crossed the western ocean to discover and claim this land for the Empress of Old Cory. He named it Aaland – the *New World*. Hagen saw the endless possibility, the great freedom to be found in what he called the *land of wonderment*. But the other great seafaring nations of the West followed – those who had long since colonised the Arricas and the Asiat, then squabbled in the southern seas like angry ducks ever since. And so came two hundred years of dispute, culminating in the Andwyke War, when the Empress bludgeoned a way to victory with an unprecendented display of naval might and heartless cruelty. Her son, King John the Tenth, was placed here as her Regent.

'I fought in that war, my friends. Like many of you, I fought to put John on that throne. Did we feel pride, my friends? Did we feel that the blood shed over the years had brought us to a glorious peace?

'No! We were rewarded with betrayal! And I was guilty, my friends. *I* stood by and saw Hagen's land of wonder treated as little more than a slave colony! Watched John Ten let *our* men struggle and die to cement the power of the West! Watched John Ten let *our* children starve and suffer to line the pockets of aristocrats in distant Imperial courts! We did not fight for independence, but for *their* monopoly! John was not a king, but a common fence for his old lady! A clothes prop! A chicken placed on a plinth ready for plucking!'

Here Malvy made a neck-wringing gesture, his rage giving way to savage humour. He allowed a pause to let the crowd laugh. Warboys smirked despite himself.

'My friends, on seeing this great land abused, I realised how weak monarchy is. How *decadent*. And so I saw fit to remove it. Remove the hold the history of the west has had on us all.

I declare now, that King John is no more. The old Empire no longer has a claim on us.'

There was a reserved cheer then, a conservative round of applause as Warboys sensed the same uncertainty he himself felt – *is this a good thing?* He stole a glance at Bill, but the old man remained stony faced.

Malvy raised his hand to speak again.

'With the monarchy, so history dies. *We* are not our history. *Our* time has come. We are not defined by the old nations. We no longer carry their rule, nor their religion. We cast off the shackles of the past, and we become what we will. Aaland will be first to claim the future.'

Another, more rigorous round of applause.

'But... The scar of the Andwyke War is still fresh. Though our brothers in Andamark, to the north, are now our allies, the south is still lost to history.

'The south was too *difficult* for the monarchy. Full of savages, they said. And thus, always more concerned with profit than national pride, John Ten left a convenient place to let rebels, and the defeated dregs of colonial forces flee, and there regroup. With this negligence, history keeps a creeping hand on us.

'Even now, Blackhaven, once a fine port, and our furthest great outpost in the south, is threatened by uprising. There, rebels seek to make a hostile frontier. To divide the Andwyke once again. They would threaten to pull Aaland into another power play between her own people, and so another Andwyke War. And I say *no*! Never again! *Unity* is the way.

'Already we lead the world in industry. Within six months, this viaduct will complete the great north south tramway, from Becohore in the north, down to the peninisula, and make Coperny the axis of the whole continent!'

Here Malvy pointed skyward.

'And if you still doubt, my friends, look up.'

There was a murmur among the crowds as all faces raised. Murmurs became gasps and exclamations. A woman squeaked as a great shadow spilled over the tops of the buildings and over the crowd. Warboys craned and saw the tail flukes of some great oval flying thing disappear over the roof. There was not a sound as several more loomed, great ships of the sky, with airscrews flickering in the sunlight. Airmen waved from the gondolas rigged beneath, showering the streets with fluttering handbills. Warboys caught the rising fever of the crowd as he stepped from one side of the stage to the other, watching the great air balloons wheel about overhead.

'As Old Cory were first to the seas,' cried Malvy, with triumphant glee, 'we are first to claim the skies! Soon our Eyrie – the world's first Air Station – will straddle the mountain. We are the world's first and *only* air power.

'The so-called Blacklands, the Wyvern peninsula and the many islands beyond, all these lay in waste because of the decadence of the royalty. We will reclaim Blackhaven, and the rebels – as any who oppose our freedom – will be swept away by the inevitable advance of progress. We will soar across the Wyvern, and unite those far flung islands! There will be no Andwyke War, but Andwyke United!

'I give you the chance – a chance of *Public Responsibility* that has never existed in history – for you to claim the fruits of your *own* labours. I bring you the chance at equality. Modern man is a soldier, no longer a slave. Aaland will lead a united Andwyke, and we will be freed, once and for all!'

Malvy hesitated, as if overcome with emotion. 'I thank you, my brothers, sisters, my *comrades...* I commend you.'

He stepped down. There was stunned silence. Warboys, not sure what he made of it, waited with bated breath for the public reaction. A thunderous applause erupted as the crowd seemed to take to Malvy's words.

'Yah!' objected Bill, a moment later. 'What's he on about? He's a fucking lunatic!'

And with that, he patted for his tobacco pouch and made for the stairs. 'Come on. We can nip off in the crowds.'

Warboys followed hesitantly, but as the cheering thundered on, he found couldn't be as dismissive. There in that applause, that shift of volume, he sensed that somehow, in some way he couldn't yet fathom, everything had changed.

~ ~ ~

It was a long time before they could speak freely. They forced a door further along the row, and barged out to join the dispersing crowds. An honour guard of glaring posters watched the people from walls and shop fronts, whilst volunteers lined the streets, handing out Malvy's little red handbook – the *Dictates*. Bill took one for appearance's sake, then dropped it once they were out of sight. A checkpoint had been raised at the end of the street, armed soldiers yelling to divert them along a prescribed route.

'I'm not going that bloody way!' moaned Bill. 'We'll have to march all the way out round bloody Rye Hill to get to Kingstown!'

He didn't raise this objection with the armed soldiers, and the two kept their heads down as they shuffled past. Soon they crossed a canal and left the city centre, passing lumber and dock yards, until the crooked chimney pots of the Kingstown district arose, forming faint battlements in the haze. The crowds thinned as folk turned off down this terrace or that, hurried along as dark clouds drawing in from the west began to spit. Abandoned flyers lay plastered across the cobbles and Warboys sighed, feeing the old familiarity of home usher away the grandeur of Malvy's rally. One last pair of soldiers watched them from horseback as they crossed a swing bridge into Kingstown and, finally, they walked unwatched, their pace easing some.

'I never did owt wrong, before you start,' began Warboys, deciding to get it over with.

'You ain't been fightin, then? I suppose that's girl's make-up round your eye then, is it?'

Warboys touched his swollen eye guiltily, recalling Ives' lucky jab.

'I told you, if I had to sail with that Jacky Biel, I'd be forced to deck him. Coming out with all the taty jokes about the old lady all the time. Gobshite, he is.'

'You got to be careful now, son! It ain't as if I never had a scrap in my time, but things is different! It's Malvy's world now! Have you thought about how you're going to get back on board, now? When do you sail again?'

'Listen. They already let me go. They're only taking on chartered seamen now.'

Bill was silent. Warboys fished in his pocket, found a packet of tobacco he'd saved, and passed it over. 'Here, I got you some blackleaf from Junkers...'

'You trying to sap me, boy?'

'Aye, maybe a bit...' Warboys cringed, ready for a lambasting. But fingering at his new blackleaf seemed to go some way to mellowing the old man, and he halted by a lamp post to roll a smoke, eventually exhaling disappointment in a silky plume.

'Don't suppose I'm surprised. This country's being whipped out from under our fucking feet. Homes, jobs, the lot. *Reallocation*, they call it.'

Warboys said nothing, happy to ride his luck.

'To be honest son, you're mebbe best out of it. In my years at sea I never seen such a shower of shite as what they're stackin' in boats these days. Some o' these bairns are no good for scrapin' dung off the King's road, nivver mind sailin.'

'Right. Thanks.'

'No, never you mind son. You carry on—' Warboys rolled his eyes, mouthing the old man's tired old phrase along with him. 'You look forward, and summat'll always turn up.'

Bill slapped his back. 'I'll get you sorted for summat, son.'

'Aye,' sighed Warboys.

Bill scratched his head. Warboys yawned, and tried to think of something to say. A haggard tomcat slotted slyly behind some bins and along the wall into shadow.

'Here, Cait Garron's been asking after you,' said Bill, eventually.

'Has she?'

'Aye. She's got a bit of a bump in the front of her an' all.'

'Oh aye?' Warboys managed to shrug innocently through Bill's scrutiny. 'What did she want?'

'She never said. Knew you were due home, though.'

'Oh well...'

'Hadn't you better go see her?'

'There's time yet.'

Bill waited, as if for some confession, and Warboys smoked through another awkward silence. 'Here, how's your allotment?'

'Not bad son. Keeps me fit. I've been expecting the bastards to take that an'all...'

'Aye?'

'Aye.'

'No stories to tell then?'

'Nah.'

The old man shrugged. 'Aye, well. Like I say. There ain't no more stories to be told.'

Rain sapped conversation as they trudged on through Kingstown. They crossed the swing bridge over the muddy river Jet, and Warboys glowered at the rows of terraces.

'Hang about,' said Bill, casting away the dog end of his smoke to nip off down a side alley. 'I need a piss.'

Warboys rolled his eyes. *Why does he always have to announce it?*

The rain hammered on. It made an orb of luminous spikes about a lamp-post overhead, and a struggling drain gurgled below. Warboys looked out over shimmering cobbles into the rain. Dim lights winked cosily from cramped houses, and he felt a bitter kind of nostalgia.

He remembered being outside the Blackwater Tavern, back when his mother had been alive, and Bill was home from sea, waiting outside with his mates, eating a patty butty whilst they had a kneesup. Nana Warboys' house was just across the road from here, beyond the tenement arch, and round the corner was the passage where he'd first copped a feel of Caitlin Garron. Over on the muddy green he'd scrapped for respect, and over on the corner was where he and Sykesy had ambushed the baker's boy and brayed him for his pies and pamphlets. Then, once he was old enough to drink himself shitfaced inside the Blackwater, came all the graft and queueing and misery. Now, revolution or not, he still faced the same lack of prospects, and felt a sense of hatred for all the potato fields, greasy factories, timber yards and mines he'd already done the rounds of over the years. Perhaps he should have let the draft get him.

Warboys' smoke dwindled.

Something bashed him about the back of the head.

He skidded on the cobbles and stumbled forward, then spun on his knees, expecting muggers, grippers maybe, perhaps Jacky Biel and his mates. He got ready with a punch in the nuts for starters. But there was only the empty street tittering with rain.

'Dad, did you...'

A clinking sound spun his attention toward the bridge, and he spotted something thin, jigging down the road towards town. It took a moment to recognise it as a rope, a *rig* of sorts, and trailing a curiously small anchor. He followed the line upward, just as a shadow yawned over him, a huge, oval shape that split the rain momentarily. He watched odd flukes flap from its whale-like form, until the rain tapped him awake again.

An airship.

He stared in disbelief as it swung away toward the bridge, entirely unmanned, loose rigs trailing alluringly along the cobbles like a tart's knickers.

Warboys turned, opened his mouth to shout again for Bill, but then felt suddenly loathe to let it go. He set off, stiffly at first, but as he broke into a run, a great foolish grin broke onto his face.

3 UNDISCOVERED WONDERMENT

Warboys caught hold of the anchor line and felt the ship dip for a few yards before hauling him up. His legs flailed in the air, as his weight tilted the ship to starboard, bringing it about in a wide circle over the street. Beneath the sound of the rain on the balloon, he heard Bill's voice.

'Where are you, y' bloody lummox?'

Bill trudged out as the ship's shadow slid over him.

'Alright Dad!'

'Here!' gasped Bill, sidestepping in pursuit. 'What... what are you doing?'

'What does it look like I'm doing? I'm off! To the land of undiscovered wonderment, and beyond! Ha!'

'Y' soft sod! You'll kill yourself! Get down here!'

Warboys laughed and the ship came about, heading for the river. Bill managed to catch another stray line, and sank on his heels to anchor the craft, steadying it enough for Warboys to scale the rope and haul himself over the gunwale.

'Here!' objected Bill – but, as Warboys flopped on board, he was too mesmerised to hear the old man's remonstrations. A cracked lamp swung over a deck somewhat like a small boat, probably less than twenty feet from prow to stern. The next thing he noticed was the *stink*. A warm, flatulent odour steamed up from the deck, and from a riveted stove-like thing in the midship. From the lid of this came a segmented pipe that fed directly into the balloon. A small raised deck sat astern, upon which lay a hooded array of controls. Compasses, gauges and meters blossomed from grimy pipes, their needles twitching inanely. A fine, pegged wheel had been installed, alongside various levers and pulleys that he did not understand. Various hatches patterned the deck. Other than a faint whooshing from the airscrews, there was no engine sound, and it was not obvious to Warboys exactly *how* they were being propelled.

Daring to stand up, Warboys reached for the great balloon, expecting it to be soft like a mattress, but instead finding it firm as muscle. He teetered over to the deck rail and followed it along, toward the prow. There, the only polished bit of her, was the ship's name – *A.S. Hildegaard.*

'Hilda!' laughed Warboys, remembering his dad trailing below. 'Here, Dad! She's named after Nana Warboys! What do you reckon to—'

Bill roared as the *Hildegaard* hit the wind off the river, and lofted into the sky.

'Oh shit!'

Warboys went to haul at the rope, trying to pull his dad aboard. Below, the bewildered bridgemaster came out of his box, spilling a steaming mug of tea. Over the river and down through a market square the Hildegaard sank. Bill's boots kicked at chimney pots, slithering on tiles and gutters as he managed to throw himself aboard the gondola. There he floundered into Warboys – and, as the two men fell heavily against the starboard rail, the Hildegaard leaned, turning hard about towards the city centre.

Warboys recognised Salt Row below as the *Hildegaard* swept down, nudging streetlamps out as she went. Both Warboys cowered as the balloon rammed a shop front, raking off the awning. The rebound dragged a gutter away as the aft ploughed through the canopies of deserted market stalls, overturning a covered spice cart, which smashed through the glass front of an office. Only then did the Hildegaard slow, sheltered for a moment between the two buildings.

Bill gaped at Warboys.

'Get off, you daft sod,' he yelled, 'whilst the wind's down!'

Lights popped on. Figures appeared in windows and doorways.

'Call the watch!' screamed a fearful lady, clutching at her night dress. The spice trader emerged to see what had happened, his mouth opening in silence at the mass looming over his storefront. Bill waved irritably at him. 'Oi! Numbnuts! Don't just stand there gawping! Come and help us! Catch one of these anchor lines!'

The spice trader yelled back, and before long Bill was in a heated argument with him. Warboys rolled his eyes, and suddenly felt a determination *not* to come down. With the ship still in a lull, he scoured the deck again, hoping for some control that would lift him up and away. In the shadow of the aft deck he spotted several soggy squares of paper. Edging toward them, he found a manual, face down and open, as if it had been dropped there.

Peeling it off the deck, he scooped up the loose sheets, glimpsing a jumbled mass of equations marked up with some strange foreign script. Didn't look like any normal sort of manual. Then the *Hildegaard* jerked to a stop, toppling him over.

'Here, son!' said Bill. 'They've set it fast!' Warboys staggered to peer over the rail. The bewildered spice merchant had recruited some passers-by and managed to set a tether to the overturned cart.

'Is there a windlass or summat about, son?'

Warboys sighed. His grip tightened on the soggy manual as he thought of potatoes and factories and allotments. He saw a cleaver down by the hold, and took it.

'Son?'

Warboys lifted the cleaver.

'Here, what are you doing?' cried Bill, as the blade thumped down and cut the rope. His cry was strangled as the Hildegaard was hooked away by a gust blasting down Courtway. The balloon expanded as if by sudden inhalation, and a bilious stench flooded the deck as the Hildegaard rose, its ascent yanking sharply at Warboys' stomach. Bill clung to the ratlines in terror.

Chimney pots passed them by, as they shot up through the layer of greasy smog that hung over town. The monstrous viaduct reared, scaffolds glistening in its flanks, but even this giant sank at alarming rate, revealing the warehouses and timber yards that sprawled beyond it. Warboys' eyes watered in the wind, and for a time he forgot the streets, rising high enough to see the fading fire of day still burning on the horizon. The light of the wider world beyond. He felt a moment of breathless freedom on sight of this luminous frontier, a feeling he'd not felt since childhood.

'Look at that bloody view!' cackled Bill, pointing north. There, the land rose steadily toward the border with Andamark, where the white tipped mountains of the Andavirke Pass hinted at the icy masses of the polar straits beyond. To the west, the vast plains disappeared into night, rising towards the Eldask – the great mountainous woodlands that spined the continent and, even now, defied incursion. Warboys had read legends of the Old Eldask as a boy, and now found himself thrilled to see signs of it for real. Their southern vista opened up into a churlish mass of grey sea, and even though he knew it was more than a thousand miles away, he imagined that the blurry, fragmented coastline showed hints of the curled tail of the Wyvern Peninsula, something he'd only seen on maps. All these places that had once just been names, idle blather, now suddenly seemed suddenly so present, so *available*.

For a time, father and son clung to one another in dumb awe.

Then there was a sharp snap, and a tiny flower of splinters appeared in the deck. The two looked from the mark to one another. A pop above, and a pock-mark appeared in the balloon. The Hildegaard hissed and began to sink, along with Warboys' heart. The viaduct reared again, the steeples and towers jabbing up, and through the wind Warboys heard a commanding voice. He peered over the deckrail to the cobbles below, where an infantry squad trampled into formation, dull green coats and rifles at the ready. A crowd of onlookers trailed along.

'Daft buggers are shooting at us!' said Bill.

'Take aim, lads!' bellowed the sergeant, forcing Warboys' heart into his mouth. They cowered, and the gasbag vented away, flooding the deck with that horrendous stench. It was slim consolation to think they might be gassed before they were shot dead. The Hildegaard nudged the steeple on the corner of Nix Steer, and swivelled, leaving Warboys within arm's reach of the chimney pots. He briefly wondered if they could make a run for it over the rooftops. Then another shot split the decking near his eye.

'Stop!' yelled Warboys, compelled by fear. 'Men on board!'

He stuffed the manual inside his coat before he arose, arms raised. Bill followed his lead, reluctantly.

'Oi!' bawled the sergeant. 'You up there! You'd better show yourself now!'

'Alright, son. Just stay steady, now.'

'Tether the thing,' commanded the sergeant. 'And get those idiots down. Arrest them.'

'What for?' Bill objected.

'Hijacking.'

'You what? We're no bloody hijackers! My son was just on his way home, like, and it... it *came* for him...'

'I was just trying to stop the bloody thing!'

The troops caught the trailing rigs, and the Hildegaard bobbed as she began to be hauled down.

'Get them down, and hold them. I want them and the ship searched.'

Warboys wondered what they were so desperate to find, if not just the ship itself. He patted the manual in his coat. *Is it this?*

'Bollocks to this,' said Warboys, turning and hauling at the first lever he could find.

'Don't—'

The *Hildegaard* issued a dull farting sound before lofting away down the row, dragging the troops through a stall and scraping them away.

Bill turned on Warboys. 'You bloody pillock! What the hell are you thinking?'

'You want to get arrested, do you?'

'No, but... what do we do now?'

'I don't know. Let's try and get her out of the way a bit. Pull levers. Turn the wheel about and that.'

They busied themselves with this. Bill loosened a valve and a quick burst of gas buoyed them as Warboys turned the wheel hard about. It was enough to bring them circling back over the river back towards Kingstown. They sailed in a big daft spiral, away from the streetlights to the dark spaces of the allotments.

The bow pushed a shed over, snapped the frames of someone's runner beans, and tipped over a water butt before ploughing a furrow through a potato patch. Warboys was thrown overboard acoss a compost heap, and the deflating balloon lolled over him, flattening several plots at once.

There was calm. Bill scrambled out and took a breath before assessing the damage.

'It's a bloody good job you didn't land it on *my* plot! I'd have wrung your fucking neck!'

'Thank-you, Father,' said Warboys, emerging dizzily. 'But don't worry yourself. I'm not hurt.'

'Aye, well. I should shut your mouth if I was you.'

Warboys teetered, still feeling the sensation of flight in his knees, and leaned against a fence. For a time, they said nothing. Then Bill looked at Warboys and, seeing his peaky face, burst out laughing.

'What?'

'Your face, when they put them muzzles on you! Saw your own arse then, didn't you? Ha! Fancied yourself as the captain going down with his ship, didn't yer? Ha! You big prat! Come on. Let's go, before they catch up.'

Warboys ignored him, looked around. A few dazed looking gardeners had gathered to stare, and the soldiers wouldn't be far behind. Warboys pulled out the manual and opened it. Each page showed wax rubbings of some ornate script, set in a language he couldn't begin to fathom. Only the inked annotations at the foot of the page indicated which way up the sheet went. He leafed through the pages filled with odd geometric patterns and arrays. The back of each leaf was stamped PROPERTY OF THE AERONAUTICS DIVISION. Some of the arrays resembled some kind of starchart, but he couldn't be sure – and even the annotations revealed little. Most seemed to list cross references of some sort, other volumes, page numbers and so on. But there were some vaguely mechanical notes – *cord masses, engine stems, anterior flukes, ventral valves,* and *airscrew housing tract, types A and B.*

Bill came staggering around.

'Come on! What are you looking at?'

'It's like a manual. For the airships, I think.'

'Leave it, daft lad! They'll be here any minute! Come on!'

'Alright, alright.'

Bill turned to leave. Warboys staggered after him, glancing

back at the bizarre scale of the airship now sagging over the plots. He grinned, broadly. Looking farther afield, he saw the chimneys and rows of the town all around yet again, at odds with that grand feeling of freedom that still fizzed in his legs. He couldn't, wouldn't throw that away. Not entirely. Slyly, he shoved the manual inside his coat.

'Come on!' demanded Bill. 'I need a pint.'

'Alright! Bloody hell!'

They fled into the streets. Warboys felt the manual's edge through the lining of his pocket, and wondered what he'd just nicked off with.

4 A LOVELY PAIR

Warboys had been giddy by the time they'd arrived at the Blackwater tavern. There was nothing like narrow survival and death defying flight to make a man thirsty. He'd figured a little celebratory drink would warm him up a bit before he got to wondering what to do with his fancy manual.

Too many pints later, Warboys awoke to the onset of pins and needles in his arse, and peeled his face up off the bar.

'Public Responsibility, my arse!' came Bill's voice. They'd agreed on the doorstep not to speak of the Hildegaard, and Bill seemed to have resumed normal service, having been droning on at his mates for hours now. 'Modern State! It's a bloody wilderness we're heading for, I tell yer, steam engines or airships or not!'

There were moans of agreement from Bill's mates as the taproom flexed before Warboys, congealing like a bad old memory: the Blackwater Tavern. His local. Thick as ever with smoke and the warm hum of beer, rain still tapping the windows, a hangover already throbbing, and old codgers setting the world to rights.

Just like the old days.

'"*Modern man is a soldier,*" he says,' continued Bill. 'Don't make me laugh!'

Through screwed eyes, Warboys sought the new barmaid he'd been eyeing before he'd lost consciousness – but she'd long since clocked off. Only Sourpus Jib remained, a shrivelled veteran sailor who worked the bar for free drinks. Jib gave him a nod and went on sucking at vinegary cockles with all of the three teeth left in his head. Belatedly, Warboys remembered the manual, the recollection echoing the giddy feeling of flight. He patted his coat, relieved to find it was still there.

'Book clutching Malvyites,' Bill went on, 'too busy with their high ideals to realise we're up to the knees in shite. Who the bloody 'ell *are* these Modern Soldiers?'

Warboys stood to attend the prickly fire in his backside. In the speckled mirror of an old tankard he saw his heavy brow collide with the long since broken nose, setting an angry looking knot in his countenance. The throb of a new bruise fattened one eye where Ives had jabbed him.

'And then you've got these lads,' said Bill, 'what can't see no further than the dregs at the bottom of their pint, as if the world's all found and finished doin' what it meant, and these kids just want stuffin' with bread and beer before the end of their days. Soft fucking heads they've got, ripe for drafting. Aye. Caught this country napping, Malvy has.'

There were more inarticulate murmurs of approval. Warboys braced himself.

'Is this a pub or a bastard lecture 'ouse? You're giving me 'eadache.'

Warboys turned round. Bill raised his glass.

'Here it is, look. The fruit of my loins! What a bloody sight. One hand on his beer, t'other on his arse.'

'Piss off,' moaned Warboys. 'I'm asleep.'

Bill drained his pint, whilst the other codgers stared as if Warboys were a caged ape on the menagerie.

'Anyways,' cut in Norris Hooks, a stubbly man in a tall-hat, keen to resume the issue of the day, 'it ain't proper war. I mean, everybody knows there's been upstarts in Blackhaven for years! The blacklanders hate us, and always have. That's nowt new.'

'You're not wrong, Norris,' said Bill. 'I don't believe there *are* any boody rebels. This is all just so Malvy can get everyone marching to his tune.'

'That's it, Bill. I mean, y'can't invade your own country, can you? He just wants a show of force, like.'

'Aye,' scoffed Bill, 'and a bloody show it'll be. Even if he gets Blackhaven back, and goes out to all them fiddly little islands down there – there ain't enough room to stick a fucking flag in some of 'em. It can't be done, and it ain't worth doin' anyhow.'

'It might be now,' grunted Rutger, a squat fellow with thick, soiled hands, 'what with all these new flyers.'

Warboys considered this a moment. Wondered just how valuable the manual was. Maybe he could fence it back to Malvy's aeronautics people. His mate Sykes had a few contacts out of town.

'Yah!' said Bill. 'Flyers! I've seen what good they are! Good for hangin' washin' off of!'

Warboys locked eyes with his father. He didn't expect the old sod to run off and enlist in the air force, but after their experience on the Hildegaard together, something about this public denouncement in front of Bill's mates got his back up.

'They could change the world, these airships,' he said, holding the old man's eye.

'Give over! They can't even steer them right. A fine fucking airforce that is, when you have your own troops running about shooting after your vessels.'

'Well, they haven't fixed it right yet, have they? You've got to be open to advancement, Father.'

'Advancements. Still got a draught in your skull, you have.'

'See, you're the one moanin' on about how the world lost its guts, and how no bastard wants to make an effort no more, yet you're sat knocking it all! There's all the world out there!'

'It's *Malvy's* world out there now. The Andwyke War was a fight for life. For our country and our livelihood. Now, we're just a load of engine parts. The world's gone backwards into slavery, and *some* silly bastards can't see it cos they're too busy *floating in the fucking clouds!*'

At this, the codgers took a step back, looking from one Warboys to the other as the tension became palpable.

'You've never 'ad any imagination,' said Warboys, dismissively.

'Imagination! What about you? All them jobs I had to find for you never came to you through imagination, did they lad? And was it *imagination* what's stopped you 'oldin down a single bastard one of 'em? Eh? Bollocks to your imagination.'

Bill tore away, and fumed privately a moment, whilst he rolled a smoke. Then he cleared his throat.

'Anyway. I was just saying to these gents about your work situation.'

'Oh you were, were you?'

Bill puffed himself up for his mates.

'You're going to have to watch yourself. They've drafted thousands already! New People's Infantry, he calls it. Fucking shambles I call it.'

'Aye,' snorted Rutger. 'A lump like him, with no papers? He'll be marching down on the Wyvern before long! Get yourself a sun-tan, boy!'

'He'll not get a tan in the Blacklands. Footrot, more like.'

'He will down past the peninsula, on the islands. They got terr-marters and all sorts down there.'

'Make a good batterin ram, he would!'

'Will you lot shut your faces? *I* aren't going down south.'

'Hark at *Lord* Warboys here! Well listen. No-one's safe. This Public Responsibility Act says if you haven't got a use then you haven't got a right, see? Even royalty, like you. There's been a raid a day at some aristocrat's house or other. There was a bloody *firefight* at the Duke of Bernigny's manor, and the next day, posters went up denouncing Bernigny as a traitor. So I'll tell you for nowt, your best bet's to get straight into some solid work.'

'Don't start on about them bloody taty fields again, alright? I'll sort me self out.'

Bill went red in the face, and Warboys' gut turned over again with the sinking feeling that the trip out to sea had never happened. 'Picky are you? I tell you what, son, the likes of us will just graft while you put your feet up, eh?'

'Don't start chowing at me. I'm just not going to work on that taty plant, and that's the end of it.'

Bill wielded his fist. 'Yeah, carry on. I'll give you another black eye in a minute, make a lovely pair. You can turn and jump back in the dock for me! Go on. Piss off in one o' yer precious flyers!'

Warboys did not reply. Bill glared, a mixture of concern and anger vying for him again. He took a breath, making a hard effort to compose himself.

'Listen. I'll go down the guild first thing. See If I can get you summat.'

'Fine, Dad. Just not the taties, alright?'

'Is it 'cos of your mother?'

'No, Father,' snapped Warboys. 'It's because I've eaten so much mash lately and I'm a bit fed up of it.'

'Oh, you're a clever little shit aren't you? You should have a bit more respect for your Mother's memory!'

'That's the point, isn't it?' snarled Warboys, slamming down his ale. 'I *do*!'

Warboys looked at them all gawping, heard Sourpus Jib's vinegary chuckling, the same old tankards gathering dust above the bar. A sickly, trapped feeling throbbed in his chest, and suddenly, he couldn't bear it any longer.

'Ah, fuck off, the lot of yer! Let me out of this shithole, for god's sake.'

And with that, he stormed outside, clutching the manual inside his coat.

~ ~ ~

Warboys marched out over shimmering cobbles into the rain, and was soaked to the skin in seconds. He tramped past a cart as it pulled onto the green, dropping off bedraggled potato pickers, who filed away in a tiresome, mud-caked procession. The smell of fresh, wet soil came with them, and with it, suddenly, the bittersweet recollection of his mother.

Lily Warboys.

He could hardly remember her face now. He could picture her wrestling into her grimy shirt and the old potato smock. No face, only the ruffle of the workshirt as she'd shaken it over herself, the whisper of her hair as she tied it back, and her hands, which he could remember best of all. Lily Warboys had rough, dry hands, strong hands. He recalled the row every morning, as old Martha Steeples and Izzy Corden came calling on the way, smoking heavily, cackling at the tops of their voices. He'd follow their procession past Kings Corner and down Salt Row, great regiments of women wearing the long, soiled uniforms of the potato fields. She'd leave him at the tall, arched iron gate, shoo him off on his way to Nana Warboys' house. And then she'd meet him there again in the evenings, thick with the smell of fresh soil, her hands lined with dirt.

He recalled the feel of her hand in his, caressing it with his thumb on the walk home.

He recalled the sandpaper slap of it on his face when she lost her temper.

He remembered the summers, when they'd go with Nana Warboys down to the horsewash on the Jet, wading in the mud at low tide, looking for flatties and winkles in the tidal pools left under the hulls of barges, and among the mops of bladderack on the pilings. Lily with her skirts up around her knees, mud caking her calves. Nana Warboys washing their feet in a bucket in the yard, barely able to crawl off to bed they were so tired.

Lily never let him go to wave the old man off when he sailed. She'd avoid Bill's eye, and carry on in her stiff-lipped way, as if it couldn't matter. But they always queued to await his return – Lily *always* acknowledged the old man's return – and Warboys remembered the nights when his dad was first home, singing on the back step, the sound of Mr. South's concertina drifting across the way. Fresh crabs for Nana Warboys, the crack as she laid into them with a claw hammer and sucked the flesh out with toothless contentment.

Bill came and went, and the time came when Warboys became too much for Nana Warboys to look after. He was taken with Lily, given a smock of his own, and queued outside the gate with the dusty smell of soil curling around him. Soil of his own in the lines of his knuckles. The spuds went from hands to pouch, barrows to carriage, and the carriage was walked by cart to a tramline that ran through the yards to the canal, ready to be pulled by horse. A great iron hopper stood there to load, ready for the steamer to come.

Sometimes the hopper would choke on the load, and someone would have to climb up and loosen potatoes at the neck. One day Lily went up there to free up a blockage, not realising that the hopper hadn't been sealed first. Down she'd gone, with the avalanche of potatoes giving way beneath her feet.

He remembered the clang as her head caught the side of the hopper, a resounding, final *gong*, and the ignoble tumbling of spuds over the tracks. They'd all seen her slide out, borne along on a rolling sheet of taters. Izzy Corden nudged Marta Biel, ready to wet themselves laughing.

But Lily didn't move, even as more spuds rolled down over her. The blow to the head had killed her before she'd hit the floor, and the potatoes lent the whole thing an indignity with which Warboys had never quite come to terms.

So there was another parade. Martha Steeples and Izzy Corden called, hanging their heads now, their shirts as clean and pressed as could be managed. That time, Lily Warboys lay in a coffin ahead of them, while Bill – fresh from sea to the news that very morning, and still awash with salt – gathered himself to bear the coffin. Warboys remembered the springy haired back of his father's head as he carried the box. The gaffer paid half her last day's wages, put against the cost of a headstone. Warboys remembered the feel of Bill's hands gouging in his hair, as if trying to recover some traces of Lily's form in the dust that had settled there.

He couldn't recall her face, even now. He'd stood and looked at the casket, but couldn't look at her face. His eyes had fallen to find those hands that were somehow more expressive than the face could ever be. There lay Lily Warboys, still with traces of dirt in the creases of her skin. He hadn't known at the time what upset him more: that they'd been careless enough to leave dirt on her, or that they'd tried to brush her up, change her, make her seem as if she'd never spent every day of her life smeared in soil. But either way, the anger stayed with him, itching like the soil in the cracks of his knuckles.

The procession, the waiting, the thick, humid smell as she went into the ground after her potatoes. Bill pawed at him in grief, vowed to give up his sailing as soon as he could. Come home and be together.

The day after the funeral, Warboys found himself queuing up for the fields again, angry at the audacious *continuity* of it all. When the gaffer's son came to usher him, all mouthy with thin authority, young Warboys broke from his stupor like a drowning man hitting the surface, took the weedy boy down to the soil, shoulder working like a steam piston as his blows rained down, to the shocked silence of the workers. And so Warboys ruined his first job.

He took his fighting to the green, the very same mudcaked green that lay before him now, where the aspiring hard men of Kingstown loitered about on a night. If you went on the green, either you fought or you got brayed. Warboys fought. Earned a place in the wrong crowd. Took to robbing and fighting some. Knocked about with some lasses already spoken for, lasses with other hard men for family. Even Nana Warboys – who'd first taught him how to make a proper left hook – came to worry. When the Garron boys broke in to get him one night, the old bird fired on them with her old Andam shotplug gun, and filled their arses full of nails and glass. She spent the night on the porch with a bottle of brandy and a tin of nails, like the last sentry from a dying age.

Bill quit sea finally, and was overcome with it all, the grief, the shock of a life on land, and caring for Nana Warboys, who'd faded some since her last stand on the porch. Bill was nothing if not practical, and well liked at that, and soon got in with the trade guilds. But Warboys resisted, resenting the fields and the pointless graft. The queues and the mud. Held out his cheek for a slap, so the old man said, but Warboys had never since managed to swallow it – how his father could work the fields after what happened to Lily. How he could bear to grow vegetables for a *hobby*, after all that.

Aye, it seemed to Warboys that all life in Kingstown came to this – we all queue up 'til it's time for the mud. And he thought of the Hildegaard, that terrifying, exhilarating freedom, and it fair near brought a tear to his eye – what would it have been like to take Lily for a flight?

He tramped over shimmering cobbles, veering drunkenly.

To have lifted her up, just for a while, up and above the grime and the graft. She'd never have believed it possible. But she'd have loved it, he was sure. Lily was never easily scared.

He walked on.

Soaked through and starting to shiver, old habit had Warboys musing on whether to give in and go see Cait, fancying the notion of the feel but not the talk. He turned about, making to cut back across the green towards her street.

As he approached the green, he caught the flicker of a lamplight across wet cobbles, and too late stepped out. A half dozen soldiers stood there, not far from the Tavern. Not your everyday grippers, but actual bloody *soldiers*. He hesitated – just enough to catch their suspicion before he hastened on.

'Here, mate!' called a voice he recognised. 'Hang about a minute.'

It was the same sergeant who'd chased out the Hildegaard.

Warboys' hand fell to the manual in his coat, and he ran.

'Here!' called the Sergeant. 'Halt! By order of – grab 'im!'

Warboys heard the clomp of boots coming up fast behind as he slithered around a corner into an alley. Old Ben Jaspar's pigeon coop still teetered at the end of the row, and thinking quickly, he flung the manual up onto the top before carrying on.

Buggered if I'll be caught for nowt, he thought. A hefty soldier slammed into his side as he emerged from the alley, slamming him hard into the cobbles. He lashed out with an elbow, but another pair piled on, mashing his face into the cobbles. The locals from the Tavern had gotten wind, and came drifting out to rubber neck at him.

'Oi!' came Bill's voice. 'Nasty bastards! There's no need to rough 'im up! Gerroff 'im!'

'Him, as well!' ordered the sergeant. 'Search them both.'

'What for? We ain't done owt!'

The sound of a scuffle cut Bill off. Warboys tried to speak up, to warn the old man, but couldn't lift his face. Bill chuntered and complained as he was slammed into the nearby wall and held. Warboys was dragged up and dumped beside him.

'Right,' snarled the Sergeant. 'Where is it?'

'Where's what?'

'There was a manual, on that flyer. Where is it?'

'Don't know what you're on about, mate,' snapped Warboys, feeling Bill's suspicious look boring into him.

'You didn't! You'd bloody better not have...'

Warboys' face set in a hard expression. He said nothing.

'Right!' barked the sergeant. 'You two've fucked me about enough tonight. You're under arrest, and lucky at that. I ought to've had the pair of you shot down!'

They were hauled roughly up to their feet. Bill glared at Warboys, shaking his head.

'You should've gone to see Cait!' he said. 'Should have gone straight to see her!'

'I will do!'

'Not now you bloody won't. Don't you understand what's going to happen?

As they stumbled along at rifle point, Warboys withered from his dad's glare, and found himself wondering if it might be better if he *had* been shot.

5 A MODERN SOLDIER

Warboys was ushered into a cell by a slablike retainer. By the lamplight, a young officer sat at a table. He was a smarmy looking little shit to Warboys' eye – blond hair swept across his brow, insincere smile swept across his chops. Didn't look like much – apart from the brawny, bearded gaoler standing ready with his Jonah behind.

'Mr. Warboys?' said the officer. 'I am Lieutenant Anders Sesaw. Take a seat.'

Warboys sat with a heavy exhalation, and rubbed his neck.

'It's a nice change of scene. I've been locked up with the old man all night, and I tell you what, the cold in my arse ain't half as bad as the earache.'

Sesaw said nothing. His smooth, unworked fingers rotated the rounded shape of Warboys' smoking tin.

'You've got lovely hands for a soldier.'

Sesaw's smile wavered for a fraction of a second, and he waited before withdrawing his hands self-consciously. He was no soldier, this one. The tin now stood alone on the table.

'Is that for me, or what?'

'I might have to ask a few questions first.'

'Oh, fucking hell, here we go again. I've already told them everything I know, which is nowt. You can do me, I don't care. Let the old man go, though. He's a grafter. Never did owt wrong in his life.'

'Out of my hands, Mr. Warboys.'

'You going to charge us, or what?'

'As I said, Mr. Warboys. Some more questions.'

'Can I at least have a smoke?'

Sesaw pushed the tin across the table, and Warboys' fingers made quick work of a fresh roll-up.

'As you may have heard, the former Duke of Bernigny was recently found guilty of treason. Troops raided his house and found stolen state property.'

'What's that got to do with us?'

'Yesterday, following the General's address, another agent of Bernigny's – who had been posing as a trusted member of hangar staff – stole a manual from the hangar archive, and tried to escape by hijacking the AS Hildegaard. He was shot dead just as the ship was set adrift – very dangerously, I might add – over the city.'

Warboys paused with his roll-up on his lip, not liking where this was headed.

'The Hildegaard drifted, apparently unmanned... until yourself and your father were seen intercepting her.'

'*Intercepting*? Give over! We were trying to anchor her!'

'Perhaps you were. But put together, you must understand how seriously all this implicates you, Mr. Warboys.'

'Look. I don't know anything about the Duke of bloody Bernigny.'

'Where's the manual?'

Excitement built in Warboys' chest. It was worth something to them, that was for sure. Could he work out some way to profit from this? He shrugged.

'What manual?'

Sesaw leaned back in his chair and exhaled. Looking over his shoulder, he dismissed the gaoler with a word, waiting until the door had closed. Those delicate hands spread on the table-top.

'I'll level with you, Mr. Warboys. It seems obvious to *me* that you're just a chancing dolt who's blundered into this. These are hard times, I know. Don't think *I* want to be here, in this uniform. I'm a student, did you know that? Only last month I was studying philology abroad, at the University of Old Cory.'

'I knew it. Lovely hands, see.'

'Do you know what a philologist studies?'

'The meaning of life? Arses?'

'No. Texts. Ancient scriptures. Inscriptions, runes, glyphs, that kind of thing. But when Malvy stepped in, I was recalled as an asset. Between you and me, I wish I'd run for it. But here we are.'

'Here we are.'

'The point I'm making, Mr. Warboys,' began Sesaw, 'is that we all have to have a state function now. We all have to earn our keep. Do you see? Even assuming you're innocent of treachery, you'll be sentenced to the gaoler's care. But the gaols are a waste of space and manpower. It's more worth our while to line you up and spend a bullet on you than it is to feed you and tend your slop. Still, you'd have company, eh? I'm sure you and your father would be a great comfort to one another in those last days...'

Warboys glowered at Sesaw.

'But – if you can oblige me at all, there might be an alternative career for you.'

'Conscription.'

'Yes.'

'They'll send me to Blackhaven.'

'Yes.'

Warboys felt a plunge in his guts as the inevitable was finally upon him. 'Fuck.'

'*If* you co-operate.'

Warboys chewed his lip a moment. Cursed inwardly, and couldn't see a way to wriggle out.

'You'll clear the charge on my Dad?'

'Well, if we can clear up your involvement and show your

willingness to aid a state investigation, I can hardly claim he was harbouring a criminal, can I?'

Warboys sighed.

'Tell me something, first. You're a philosopher—'

'—I'm a *philologist.*'

'Alright, whatever. What are they?'

'What are *what?*'

'The papers. The manual. Any fool can see from the notes that they're summat to do with the airships.'

'You're right. The airship schema was compiled from source texts called the *Datyas.*'

'The what-yas?'

'*Datyas.* It's a word that I suspect has some roots in Yevite languages. It means either *song,* or *whisper,* depending on your source. And buried in those scriptures is a kind of codex for the manufacture of new floatation engines.'

'But... where are they from?'

Sesaw sighed.

'Well, that's the thing. That's why I've been dragged back here. They... *we* don't know. I've got good experience of ancient languages of the Asiat, and I've never seen anything like it before.'

'Does it matter? The Airships are already up and running aren't they?'

'The airships were developed at a test facility on Havery Moor. But Bernigny's agents destroyed all the archives and materials.'

'Why?'

'To prevent Malvy from having them I suppose,' shrugged Sesaw. 'Only a few poorly translated examples of the Datyas remain.'

'And the manual I've got is one of them.'

'Yes. But these manuals are just one small fragment of an

overarching index. They barely scratch the surface. We believe that there are Datyas equivalent to thousands, if not hundreds of thousands of such volumes.'

'But you don't know where they come from originally?'

'No. So apart from the currently active ships...'

Warboys smiled. 'There aren't any more. And you don't know how to make more.'

'No. We need to find that codex.'

'Before Bernigny does.'

'Yes.'

'That's *if* the original *Datyas* even exist any more.'

'Yes.'

'Ha!' Warboys laughed bitterly. 'What a laugh. The world's first Air Force, held together with string and tacks!'

A bittersweet excitement whisked through Warboys' limbs, bringing his giddying flight in the *Hildegaard* back to mind, that strip of sunlight in the far distance. He'd sailed in just a nobody, ready for drafting. But he'd happened by such a lot, flown in an airship and seen a new horizon, brought *so* close to a lucky break. For a while, he'd been a nobody with the keys to the fucking world.

'I was right, then. They're worth a fortune.'

Sesaw acceded with a shrug.

'And here's the expert philanthropist who it turns out doesn't know any more than a chancing dolt.'

'I'm a philologist.'

'Not much of one, I'd say. Oh well. Never mind, eh? There's always the infantry.'

Sesaw's expression hardened.

'Mr. Warboys. Your part of the bargain...'

'Alright...' Warboys sighed. He didn't want to give up his newfound treasure, but he couldn't let them arrest the old man. He'd get to save Bill from gaol whilst getting away from the old sod into the bargain, and be absolved from his misdeeds with another necessary departure.

He told Sesaw about Ben Jaspar's pigeon coop.

'Right. Thank you. I'll check that out, and have the charges against your Father dropped.'

'Can I see him before he goes?'

'Oh no, he won't be going anywhere. I've cleared him of harbouring a criminal. But there's still the matter of harbouring an illegal entrant...'

With this, Sesaw pulled out a paper from his inside pocket and snapped it open. It was Jacky Biel's chartership paper.

Warboys felt the sharp old stab of futility burst his excitement, and anger arose thick in his skull. 'You *wanker...*' He kicked the table over as he rose. 'I'll give you some ancient language, you philandering twat!'

Two of the slablike gaolers lumbered into the room, blocking Warboys off.

'I'm a *philologist!*' protested Sesaw, already halfway down the corridor. Warboys was thumped back into his chair as a conscription officer replaced Sesaw in the doorway.

'Ha!' laughed Warboys, bitterly, recognising the very same officer he'd passed at the gate on alighting the *Call of March.*

'Have we met before, son?'

'Yah, don't *son* me. Get on with it, you tosser. Where do I sign?'

6 NEXT OF KIN

Late enough to see the night turn into grey, Voluntary Infantry Private Warboys, shaven and shorn, and wearing his standard issue military green greatcoat, stumbled into a wonky front door on a Kingstown terrace. It was his first and only free night since he'd enlisted, and he was very drunk. The door opened almost instantly. Caitlin Gorran stood there in a nightgown, greasy hair tied back, one hand on her hip. Grey, frowning eyes to match the hour. She was still, he reflected, a handsome sort of woman, if a bit hard faced.

'I was wondering when you'd turn up,' said Cait.

'The old man said you'd been asking after me.'

'Took your fucking time.'

Warboys' eyes dropped tactlessly across her, slipping into the cavernous pit trap of her cleavage, along the taut lines of the gown that spanned over her gravid stomach. The sight gave him a bit of a flush.

'Hell, Cait. Y'looking ripe.'

'Not bothered, are you?'

Warboys shrugged and shuffled clumsily into her. 'Not me.'

'Shurrup then. You'll have to be quiet.'

Edgear was faking sleep in front of the fireplace, his eyes gleaming under a blanket. A boy of nearly fourteen now. Warboys gave him an awkward nod, then burped. Cait shushed him, pulled him by the hand. The stairs creaked. The bedroom was dark, and the old cot was still by the window. Wilyam snored gently, a halo of frizzy ginger hair catching the lamplight from outside. Warboys sloughed eagerly over Cait. She pressed a finger to her lips as he set the bed creaking. Soon the headboard was banging against the wall regardless, Cait gurning and rolling her eyes beneath him, flinching as his stubble sanded her skin. *Too late to be effective now,* he told himself, and came gasping.

He slopped heavily off her. Wilyam's snoring resumed.

Irritably, Cait rolled him over and straddled him with her bulbous belly, hair sticking to her face as she tried to work him up again. But Warboys lay mesmerized by the shape of her, great heavy tits bouncing over the prow of her stomach, like a bulbous *Hildegaard* sallying forth. He goggled dozily at her for a time, then wilted. He felt himself beginning to snore, then started as Cait ripped a handful of his chest hair away.

'Ow!'

'Useless cunt.'

With some manoeuvring, she helped herself off and turned her back to him.

'Is it mine?' he murmured.

'So what if it is?' she snapped. 'Arsehole.'

He drifted off again.

In a heartbeat it was morning. His head felt like a sack of bricks, and his stomach protested as Wilyam landed on the bed, his freckled face framed by a mane of frizzy ginger hair.

'It's Mr. Warboys!' he yelled. 'Eady! Eady! Mr. Warboys is here!' He bounced on the bed until Cait appeared, a smoke hanging off her lip.

'Go and get washed, Wilyam.'

'Can I show Mr Warboys my pamphlets?'

'Show him in a bit. We're talking.'

Wilyam went thundering down the stairs. Warboys looked blearily at Cait.

'Why's he calling me Mr. Warboys?'

'Would you prefer him to call you *daddy*?'

Warboys sat up, the force of his headache multiplying. Cait loitered in the doorway, avoiding his eye.

'You know they came here, looking for summat.'

'Who did?'

'First I knew you was home was when a squad of fucking soldiers come stomping in here raking about for summat.'

Warboys said nothing. Sesaw would have wanted to make sure he didn't have any more Datyas stashed away.

'Wouldn't tell me what it was,' said Cait. 'Don't suppose I want to know, do I?'

'Probably not.'

'Hm. You're off to war, then.'

'Aye. To Blackhaven, to take it back off the rebels.'

'Oh. Right. Will it be dangerous then?'

Warboys wondered if she was worried about him. Through his hangover he felt a surge of regret for last night's wasted fumble.

'Don't know, love. Mebbe.'

She was quiet a moment, staring at a patch of mildew near the ceiling. Warboys watched her hand half-consciously smoothing over her bump.

'Cait?'

'What?'

'*Is* that one mine?'

She shrugged. 'I reckon. Why?'

He lowered his voice.

'You said that about Wilyam.'

'Hey, he's fond of you, that boy. Least somebody is. Don't upset him. Don't worry though. When this one's born, I shall tell her to call you *Mister Warboys* an' all.'

'How do you know it's a girl?'

'I can just tell. I'm going to call her Shandy.'

'Shandy? Fuck off. That's a foreign whore's name.'

'I tell you what, if you wanted a say, you'd have stuck around, wouldn't you?'

Warboys looked at Cait. Still a bit of alright, even when he was sober. 'Listen, Cait... Come here. Shut the door...'

'No chance, mate. You stink.'

Warboys sighed.

'Where's Helmet?'

'Don't call him that. He doesn't like it any more.'

'Where is he?'

'Downstairs.'

'Tell him to come up and see me now, if he likes.'

'Hark at you! Shall I fetch you some slippers whilst I'm at it? You'll be bloody lucky. Can't do owt with him these days. Moody bugger. Get up off your arse and have a word with him.'

'Why? What's wrong with him?'

'Takes after you, that's what. Scrapping on the green. Won't go to work. I don't know where he goes all day. Doesn't bloody listen to a word I say. I'm frightened *he* ends up in uniform. He's too young.'

'Nah,' said Warboys, though he doubted even as he spoke, 'they'll not take a bloody fourteen year old. Has Bill spoken to him?'

'Why should he? *You* speak to him!'

'Alright, alright.'

Warboys stood up and made his way down. Wilyam was yelling and jumping on the sparse furniture, waving a stack of old pamphlets, seemingly driven mad by the presence of the visitor. Warboys fobbed him off and went to find the elder boy.

Edgear Warboys was in the yard. It backed onto the green in sight of the Tavern. Along with all the other houses and yards, it formed an arena so every bastard could know every bastard else's business. In the middle of the green a few lads already milled around, some waiting for work carts, wearing boots and caps that were too big for them, others smoking and playing hard men.

'Now then, Helmet,' began Warboys, jovially rapping his knuckles on the boy's head, as he had last time he'd seen him. It'd been a while now.

Edgear flinched aside, scowling. 'Don't call me that.'

'What's up? Why not?'

'I told you not to call him that!' came Cait's voice sharply from within.

'It's just a joke.'

'It's not funny.'

Warboys flushed, yelled to Cait, 'Well, if you'd bloody spelt his name right...'

'If you'd *been there*,' she replied, 'you might have helped with the spelling and all sorts. I shouldn't argue. You won't win.'

Sullenly, Warboys turned back to the boy, who was staring with equal sullenness out at the green. Warboys kicked a pebble across the yard and started up a rolly. Edgear looked up.

'Do us one.'

'No, I bloody won't! You're too young to smoke.'

'Me Mam said you used to smoke when you was *ten*.'

'Don't mean *you* should.'

Edgear kicked the pebble in resignation. An awkward silence filled the gap.

'I'm off to Blackhaven,' said Warboys.

'Reckon there'll be fighting?'

'Don't know.'

'Can I have a look at your rifle?'

'I ain't got a rifle. We have to share one between five of us. Rest of us gets a steel tipped baton. They call it a Jonah stick, after Malvy himself. You can have a look if you like.'

'Nah. It's just a stick.'

The boy turned away, his eyes tracking the lads on the green.

'Look. Your mam says you been hanging about down there. On the green.'

'Yeah. So? There's fuck all else to do.'

'Watch your mouth. There's some daft bastards hang about out there—'

'Yeah, you'd know.'

Warboys took a step forward, showing the back of his hand. 'Aye, keep talking kid. You're not too big for a...'

Warboys faltered, lowered his hand, heard his father's words threatening to spew out. *You want to get yourself a job, go dig some taters. You carry on, look forward and summat'll always turn up, blah blah blah.* He choked on them.

'Ahh, fuck it,' he sighed. 'Here.' He passed a pouch of baccy over. 'Don't tell your mother.'

'Oh... alright. Cheers!'

'Just watch yourself, alright?'

'I will.'

Edgear edged off, making a cursory call to his mother. When it came to it, Warboys just couldn't be bothered to play the dutiful father. Not now. Not after all this time.

'Was that it?' said Cait, sticking her head about the door. 'Has he gone? What did you say to him?'

'What did you want me to say? Should have written summat down for me, shouldn't yer?'

Cait's mouth tightened in a way that made him flinch. She walked away. Pots clashed and chimed.

'You got any money for me then, or what?' she snapped, after a time.

Warboys smoked for a long moment, building himself up to answer whilst Cait simmered quietly.

'Look, love. I got collared straight off the fucking gangplank...

Soon as I get—'

Warboys ducked as the Jonah came flying at his face, missed him by a hair and spun off the wall to the floor.

'Useless *shit*! Least if I was on the game I'd get some fucking money off you!'

'But listen—'

'Stop! Stop before I come bat your stupid brains out!'

'Listen though, love...'

'Don't fucking *love* me!'

Her voice cracked, and Warboys froze. A whistle of guilt rang in his head, and he searched for some reassurance to give her. Even thought of mentioning the *Datyas*, claiming some cocksure quest to earn them a fortune. He cursed himself for an idiot, and wondered if he shouldn't just just hop it over the wall. There was a long, tense silence. Wilyam came edging closer with his pamphlets, making a show of stacking them, obviously desperate to show them off. Warboys opened his mouth to send the kid away, but recognised one of the covers, an inky, crosshatched illustration of a snake coiling around a struggling maid.

'Here... where did you get that from?'

'When the soldiers came, they went to your Nana's as well. These were all over the place.'

'These were mine...'

Warboys took the top copy and leafed through it. He'd treasured these stories when he was a kid. Daft old stories came back to mind, and he remembered some of his excitement for the far away lands in the tales. He opened the page on a twee little map of Aaland, drawn in ink, with little trees and mountains shaded in where the Eldask jutted down through the country. A curly, stylised dragon sat in the corner.

'Here, look,' smiled Warboys, pointing at the map fondly. 'That's where I'm going, near there. Past that dark bit. They call that the *Eldask*.' He smiled, remembering some of the corny old lore. 'An old Andam word for summat grown too old. Unclaimed in all the years that Aaland's been Aaland. Thick, it is, goes for 'undreds of miles through the middle of Aaland. What few attempts there's ever been to make inways have been abandoned as foolhardy.'

'Is it real?'

'Course it's real.'

'Will there be dragons like that one?'

'I don't think so, mate.'

Warboys' smile faded, and he put down the pamphlet, feeling the jaded weight of the years since he'd read these stories with eyes like Wilyam's.

There came a knock at the door. Cait, still flushed, composed herself quickly and went to open it. She seemed suddenly very pretty in the square of morning light, her face lit up by some pleasant sight. And then Bill walked in, all smart in his army greens. Cait sniffed back snot and whistled.

'Well, look at you in your uniform! If I was twenty years older...'

Warboys rolled his eyes, and watched as Bill swept in, just like he had when he used to come home from sea, there like a balm. Everybody always loved Bill. Warboys went and skulked in the yard.

'Has he given you owt?' he heard Bill say.

'You what? 'eadache, mebbe.'

There was some muttering. Warboys peeked around the door and saw Bill leaning close to say something to Cait. He caught sight of a few envelopes changing hands, Cait's flushed surprise. 'Oh, you don't have to do that, love...' he heard her say. *Don't let me interrupt*, he thought, childishly. A burning sense of shame knotted in his chest. Objection rollicked in his throat, some declaration of rights, but what exactly was he going to say?

What could he claim here? And so he said nothing, pretended not to notice, the way he always did. Best to keep out of it.

'Right. I'd best be off then,' announced Bill. He ruffled Wilyam's hair until it stood up off his head unsupported.

Cait all but fell into Bill's arms, seeming overcome. 'You go careful darlin'. Come back in one piece, won't you?'

'Aye, don't fret about me, love...' Bill's smile faded as he shot a meaningful look at Warboys. 'I'll leave you two to it then. You take care of yourself, eh? Say hello to the nipper from me when she comes.'

He turned to Warboys. 'I'll see you down at Nethergate,' he said dourly, then left.

Warboys wandered about collecting his stuff whilst Wilyam trailed around after him. Cait stood where she was, hand on hip, looking down. She wiped a tear from her eye.

'Alright?' he ventured. Cait said nothing. 'Right then', he went on. 'I'd better get after the old sod eh? Before he goes charging Blackhaven on his own.'

Still she said nothing. Feeling he didn't yet have leave, he faltered on the doorstep.

'When's it due?' he thought to ask.

'She's due next month.'

'Right. Well, go careful then. I'll see you later.' Wilyam tweaked at his sleeve pertly.

'Watch it you,' said Warboys. 'Look after y' Mam.'

'I will. Mind them dragons.'

'I will.'

Warboys had the awful feeling that Cait was going to cry as he backed meekly out of the door, his pack catching on the frame. 'I'll sort summat, love. You'll see. I'll get you out of here.'

'I don't want to *get out of here*. I just want a living, Will. Just a living and my family.'

And that was it. The door slammed shut and he backed away

from the battered old terrace, ducked the threadbare washing hung from tired lines. As Wilyam appeared at the window, he waved meekly. He'd done it now.

He turned and marched across the cobbles after the old man. Other soldiers mustered, some of them holding hands with their children, fawned over by their wives and mothers. Warboys swallowed and clomped up after Bill.

'Hold up there, old man. You alright?'

'I'll do. All sorted, are you?'

'I reckon so.'

'You *reckon so*. Done your form for your next of kin, have you?'

'Yeah, I think so. Signed a stack of things.'

'Who did you put?'

'You of course. Who else?'

Bill laughed humourlessly.

'Well I ain't put you.'

'What do you mean?'

'Some bastard's got to think on them bairns. I've put Cait down. And what's more, I've signed the deeds to the house over to her an' all.'

'You what? That's Nana Warboys' house! She'll be spinning in her grave!'

'Oh, you're a piece of work, you are. Can't see past your own arse, you can't.'

'Fucking hell, Dad! There'll be nowt for us to come back to!'

'We might not come back, shit for brains. That's the *point*, isn't it?'

Warboys opened his mouth to object, and paused. It didn't matter any more. It was too late. The meandering, reluctant recruits converged all along the King's Row.

'What did you do with your last night of freedom then?'

'Went down the allotment to sort me rhubarb out.'

'Fucking hell. You really know how to live.'

'I'd shut my face if I was you.'

Bill turned solemnly to shoulder his rifle, and, sighing, Warboys joined the ranks forming on Nethergate. As the barking officers rounded them up, Warboys wondered – not for the first time – if he really knew what he was doing with his life.

7 SHOWER OF SHITE

Daylight shimmered across the waterlogged fields as the 45th Infantry tramped across the plains, like a great bedraggled centipede skewered with rifles and banners. Warboys' strides slapped a rising tidemark on the coat of the man ahead as, equally, water was sloshed over him by the man behind.

He glanced over his shoulder and spotted his dad, marching a few rows behind. Bill had maintained a difficult, reproachful silence since their conscription – but the march had given Warboys some reprieve from his father's displeasure, and for a time he allowed himself to feel a bit of resplendence. In his military greatcoat, a soldier of the 45th Infantry, finally leaving Coperny under the red and black banner. The capital faded to the rear as they marched into the county outskirts, watched in awe by women, children and farmhands. He stifled child-like excitement on arriving at the tramway station to find a duck-steamer waiting to take them down the first stretch of the incomplete north south tramway.

Resplendence. That was the word.

Only when the entire 45th was loaded onto open top trucks for the long journey south, and hauled like cattle for nearly three full days, did he begin to feel far less resplendent. Along the way they stopped only to march to the next fragment of unfinished rail, herded off by thuglike officers who barked in their faces, with conduct more like that of a prison transfer than a military march. Then they were loaded up again, crammed aboard for such long stretches that men were forced to piss off moving carts. At least one fell off. When the tram stopped at a small station for rationing, food bundles were tossed up at them from parked up carts. Whilst the hungry men squabbled, Warboys saw one youngster snatch up a handful of rations and make a run toward the coast, only for a bullet to cut him down before he reached the breakers. Seconds later, officers whipped them back into line, and Warboys peered through the crowd to spot Bill, the two solemnly checking up on one another even as they pointedly avoided eye contact.

When dark rock jutted from the coastal moors near Port Havery, Warboys marvelled at the distance they'd covered, and at the foreign mugginess that made the air itself seem *different*. Past Havery, the track split and veered inland to the end of the line, where the sleepers finally faded into muck. Here the steamer clunked to a halt, and through the veils of steam that announced them, they were received by their command. Warboys glimpsed Colonel Linnaeus himself, that stern veteran of the Andwyke War, mounted on a sinewy black charger, whilst his ashen faced, bawling lieutenants manhandled the troops into line. Without respite, they were regimented and forced to march off their cramp and fatigue, sinking away east toward a featureless horizon.

Now, the damp crept steadily up his legs, and the black and red trimmings of Malvy's pageant began to seem much less grand.

'I've never seen,' came Bill's voice, as soon as the corralling officers were out of earshot for the first time, 'such a shower of shite as what they're wrappin' in these green coats nowadays. I reckon most of this regiment would get lost in a plant-pot, never mind a cross country march. Every daft lad in Coperny just thrown together and shoved away into the middle of nowhere. I tell you, this whole bloody world is on the drift.'

Here we go, thought Warboys. He turned to see Bill's face

flecked with mud, crazy coils of hair springing off his head.

'You make out as if we're just wandering about. We're being *deployed.*'

'Deployed!' spat Bill. 'Ha! Happy with it are you?'

'I don't have much bloody choice, do I?'

'Oh, you had your choice, lad. You had your choice.'

'How many times do I have to say sorry?'

'Don't recall you ever did.'

Biting his tongue, Warboys concentrated on hauling his boots through the mud. Like it or not, Bill had a point. The 45th was comprised almost entirely from conscripted criminals, drunks and outcasts. Some of them had never set foot out of the city before now. He noted his former ship-mates Jacky Biel and Ives marching ahead, both looking hapless and swamped by their coats. Both had been arrested and drafted on the dockside after the fight. Neither of them had set a foot past port, and neither had forgotten it. Not particularly inspiring warriors, but they looked like veterans compared to the wastrels that comprised most of the regiment.

It rained. Open plains became slurping mudholes, the wide skies great grey dispensers of miserable drizzle. The mounted command herded them onward, peeling away from the head of the column to pound up and down the line, screaming at those who fell out of step.

'Don't think much of these un-trammed reaches,' muttered Warboys. He noticed the old man was limping, and risked a glance. 'Well,' he muttered. 'I'm sorry.'

'Hm.'

'You alright anyway?'

'I'll cope. Still just working out a bit of cramp off. You?'

'Aye. I'll live.'

'Hm', grunted Bill. Warboys rolled his eyes again, even as he felt some small relief at hearing the old man's voice.

It rained.

~ ~ ~

The 45th passed the last waystation at Gallow Cross, from which the road vanished eastward. For three full days they trudged through marshland, halting only for short respites, during which the officers would make them join in readings from Malvy's book, the *Dictates*, with which every man had been issued. The winding silver line of the River Yew drew near, marking the end of civilization as modern Aaland knew it. Beyond there lay the Blacklands. As Warboys pressed into the congestion on the bridge, he looked across the misty east bank and felt a shiver of nerves.

Not long after, he began to notice strange rows of stones lining the countryside. They looked like waymarkers at first, jutting out of the marshy earth like teeth. But then they arose, and became tall, ominous monoliths overlooking them from knots of dry land.

'What are these things anyway?' said Warboys as one of the dark pillars sailed by. The mist drew silence with it, and Warboys felt glad of an opportunity to get Bill talking. Bill looked up from squelching boots, and checked that none of the officers was in earshot before he spoke.

'Them things is from before Aaland's founding. In the days before our colonies came to these shores, the natives used to lay all these stones out across the land.'

'What *natives*? There never was any natives. We're the bloody natives.'

'Well, who put all these fucking stones up, then, eh, clever sod?'

'So what are they for then?'

Bill shrugged.

'Buggered if I know. Reckon they must've been put there to mark summat or other. Used to be some round the farms when I was a lad. Most of 'em've been flattened now.'

Warboys considered it. 'There was one out at Petersen's orchard, wasn't there? Where we used to go conkering?'

'Aye, that's right. Come to think of it though—' Bill paused as an officer bawled at some poor sap further along the line – 'the first time I saw these was abroad, like. In the Asiat. I remember we was aboard the *Havery Anvil,* round the Blind Coast – just about holed her on the reef an' all – and we beached where these stones came out of the sea, like soldiers marching up the beach they were...'

Warboys scoffed at the recollection. 'The *Asiat?* That's the other side of the world!'

'I know it is, cloth 'ead.'

'Well, what are you on about then?'

Bill frowned and puffed himself up. 'I tell you what, in my *boring, unimaginative* life I might have visited a place or two, heard a story here and there, you know. There's more to me than bloody fruit and veg, y'know.'

'Oh aye? Like what?'

'For your information, I travelled a lot when I was young. Not just local to-ing and fro-ing through Junkers, like you did on the *Call.* Before you were born – before the war – I sailed merchant lines on a ship called the *Caravas.* Then we were requisitioned by the warship *Imelda,* sent north, holed on the shores of Andamark and all sorts. Ran for the border, enlisted in the land army... Then, after the war, I tried the silk lines, out for the continent, round the Asiat, like I say. But then your uncle Konrad was lost, and your mother begged me not to go out again. I took my vows of her, and made me promise not to go dazzling you with tales of high seas and foreign climates. Frightened to lose you, she was, like she lost her brother. Bit of an adventurer, Konrad was. Your mother thought you'd be safer closer to home. On a taty field, for instance. Somebody up there's having a laugh, eh?'

The monoliths cast long, probing shadows over the column, and Warboys looked at his dad in wonder.

'Bugger me. Descended from adventurers. And here I was, thinking I was a born spud picker.'

'You're a born lummox, is what you are. Part of me feels guilty telling you even now, for your mother's sake. But I figure the horse has bolted now. You're already in the forces, traversing the exotic Blacklands, eh?'

'Bloody hell. I never realised...'

'No, you never do. So you can shut your lip, clever shit.'

'Here, though—' began Warboys. Despite himself, he suddenly longed to know all about Bill's travels – but Bill waved him away, remembering his grudge.

'Don't talk to me. You're still in my bad books.'

~ ~ ~

Over the course of the week, a mountainous woodland loomed large and sudden in the north. It seemed to Warboys to attract and hold a weather system of its own, for whenever he looked, angry thunderheads were brewing over its rocky core, and constant mist smothered its edges.

'Is that the Eldask there?' Warboys eventually asked, recalling the map in Wilyam's pamphlet, that dark strip in the midst of the Aalandic mainland.

'Aye, that there is the *Eldask*,' said Bill. 'Unexplored as ever it was.'

'Did you never go there, then? The Eldask?'

'No lad. I'm intrepid, not daft.'

Warboys looked toward the Eldask again, feeling some of

his old childhood awe as thoughts of the *Datyas* flickered in his mind.

'What was that you said about all the world being discovered? There might be a fortune yet to be found in there.'

'Yeah, there might be worms in my allotment an' all. Oh no, hang on... it'll be full of slugs, cos there ain't nobody there to look after it!'

Warboys sighed, put in his place again.

He marched on, allowing himself to become transfixed on the incongruent loom of the Eldask. The land was mushy and damp in its shadow. Midges gathered, biting incessantly, and the riders gave out camphor bundles to try and smoke them away. It seemed to have little effect. At camp, tent-pitchers squabbled over the driest mounds. Campfires spat resentful sparks as soldiers collapsed , gazing listless at the fires. As rations were laid into and kettles boiled, most were quiet, introspective or empty headed with exhaustion. But Warboys' intrigue kept him alert.

He made as if to visit the privy in a nearby copse, where a broken monolith sat among the trees. Out of sight of the officers, he leaned against it to roll himself a smoke. This stone was the first of many that stood at regular intervals, leaving the trees to make a kind of highway toward the Eldask.

And there it occurred to him.

He'd been passing the freakish, battered stones for days – but only now, when he could see fully across the plain, could he make out the pattern: they were all heading toward the Eldask. Long lines of stones arced towards it from all directions. He fancied he could even see a certain tilt in nearby banks of trees, as if they too were somehow inclined to give way to these lines. Checking he was unwatched, Warboys walked over to the next monolith. It was about fifteen feet tall, worn smooth by the weather. But under his touch, Warboys could feel the remains of etchings in the rock. On the side leeward to the wind, he could even make out an odd geometric pattern – with a distinct resemblance to what he'd seen in the airship manual.

Warboys felt that flutter of excitement rising again, as he realised something else; all the Datyas bound into that manual had been wax rubbings, not originals. They must have been copied from an inscribed rock, just like this one. And here he was, standing at the beginning of a line of *Datyas* that led toward the Eldask.

'Bugger me...'

He felt himself bursting with the knowledge, a giddiness, just like the one he'd felt aboard the Hildegaard. Was it possible the originals might be somewhere in the Eldask? For a stunned moment he paced around, marvelling at the faded inscriptions, not knowing what to do with himself.

Someone pushed through the privy. Warboys quickly cleared his throat and made as if he was buttoning himself up, but it was only Bill.

'I got you a butty,' said the old man, passing his son a small packet. Before Warboys could object, he then set about pissing up the monolith.

'Don't mind me.'

'You shouldn't wander off near dinnertime. They're like vultures, y' know. Jacky Biel's eyes came out his head when he saw that lying spare. I practically had to put my arm down his fucking gullet.'

'Here, Dad, shut up a minute. Look...'

Bill buttoned himself up and Warboys pointed him toward the etched stone.

'See that, there? I swear, these same marks were on them blueprints.'

'What blueprints?'

'You know! The *Datyas*.'

'Are you still on about that?'

'Sesaw said they had no idea where the Datyas came from. They're looking to make an *Index*, he said. How about these? This might be what they're looking for! Look. Just *look* at all this lot, all heading up there...'

Warboys senior peered out at the distant Eldask. He shook his head. 'That's nice son... but, have I misunderstood, or are you in fact in the bastard Land Army at the minute?'

'So?'

'So? Did you think you could just swan off and—'

Warboys braced himself for abuse, but Bill faltered, chuckled to himself in exasperation, and pulled out his smoking pouch.

'Ah, balls. I'll not argue with you, kid. Not today. Least summat's given you wind up your arse at last. You do what you like. You will anyway. I'm past caring.'

Having gotten ready to impress his case, Warboys felt a little deflated at this unexpected submission. Why couldn't the old sod be more intrigued?

'Why? What's today?'

'Never mind,' grunted Bill, turning away. Warboys opened his mouth to object, irritated by Bill's reticence – but a clamour from the direction of camp halted him, as Captain Zander and his thugs came herding up strays for the nightly reading. Zander appeared in the clearing to thumb them back to camp and, not wanting to draw the captain's attention to the monoliths, Warboys suppressed his excitement and fell into step behind Bill.

8 THE PROMISE LAID

Patchy trees bore in around them toward the end of the day, and with visibility shortened still further by mists, orders were given to halt for the night. The 45th staggered to a halt and made camp in a clearing where a line of monoliths stumbled out towards the river from a nearby cluster of trees. Once relieved of his pack, Warboys wandered over to the stones – again making as if to piss – and found more faded inscriptions. He wondered if the stones would be more sheltered in the Eldask, leaving more legible inscriptions intact. He sighed. If not for the old man, he might have been tempted to make a run for the Eldask. The odds wouldn't be bad in this terrain.

Wearily, he trudged back to camp. Whilst the troops rested, the poster boy was out, lumping his rolls and paste-bucket along, slapping Malvy's propaganda across any standing stone he could find. Bill had begun to chunter about his knees to anyone who'd listen, and Warboys busied himself smoking and issuing competitive farts. He was all but drifting off when, in the corner of his eye, he saw a wiry figure burst abruptly from the cover of a copse. He sat up and saw it was an old man on a stick, growling as he hobbled forcefully toward the poster boy. A young boy, perhaps his grandson, trailed after the man, warily meeting the faces that turned to watch. Rowdy cheers went up from the 45th as the old man set about the bill poster with his stick, driving him off before ripping the posters away in obvious rage.

'Scurrilous northern *shite*!' he screamed. '*Ia tu t'na Datyas!*'

Warboys sat up straight, heart prodded into work by that last word – *Datyas*. Laughter subsided as Captain Zander was seen striding over, two Jonah-wielding thugs in tow.

The old man smoothed his hand reverently down the face of the offended stone, as if it were a horse he could soothe, then turned to meet the approaching soldiers. The grandson dithered behind him, obviously worried.

'Mahagat irin a Sun-Ivis!' screamed the old man, as if to issue a challenge to Zander and the whole regiment. 'Nef y cem bas Sun-Ivis!' His eyes gleamed hatefully out of the hollows of their sockets.

'Bloody hell' muttered Bill. 'The old feller's goin' to keel over if he doesn't calm down...'

At a command from Zander, one of his thugs cracked the old man about the head. The collective intake of breath from the watching troops was almost palpable as he fell stunned to the floor.

'Dirty bastards!' Bill called.

Warboys nudged him sharply.

'It ain't right though!'

'Dad!'

'For the sake of a shoddy poster? They'll kill him like that!'

Captain Zander turned to scour Warboys' section, and Warboys took a tight grip on his dad's arm, speaking through clenched teeth.

'Dad! For fuck's sake, shut your mouth before you get us shot! We'll try and help them later, alright? Keep your dinner packet for them.'

This seemed to placate Bill. Zander set the bill poster back to his work, and the two guards dragged the old man to the camp's edge, kicked and screamed at by the boy, until a hefty cuff about the head silenced him as well. Once they had recovered, the two crawled away into the darkening wood, and Captain Zander strode back to camp, his eyes considering Warboys' section as he announced the night's readings.

Through readings and rations, Warboys watched the wood, knowing that the pair couldn't go far. He used another falsified trip to the privy to spy a faint cookfire out in the woods, and then, after everyone had settled, he nudged his dad and the two roused to leave camp.

'Where you goin?' blared Jacky Biel, from his bedroll.

'For a piss.'

'What, both of you?'

'We're scared of the dark.'

They stole across the field into the cover of the trees, bumping into one another as they headed toward the faint cookfire.

The tear-stained boy was huddled by the old man, who looked barely alive. Seeing the intruders, the boy sprung to his feet, knife in hand.

'You go fuck off!' he warned. 'We won't bother you none! Done enough, you have now!'

Warboys held up his hands.

'It's alright there, son. We don't mean you any harm. We're not all bastards, look. Here...'

He threw his and Bill's dinner packets over. 'Save t'other one for your old feller. How is he?'

The boy hesitated, but Bill moved smoothly in, ruffling the kid's hair as he went to inspect the old man's blood caked face.

'Aye, it's a fair knock he's had there... Might be it's more blood than harm, though...'

Bill set about cleaning the old man's head wound, whilst Warboys crouched to work up the fire, glancing back towards the encampment to check they weren't missed. He saw the boy's exhausted defiance lapse in the warmth.

'Y'alright there, son?'

The boy shrugged.

'What's your name?'

'Steffyn Cambo I am, son of my Grandy's son.'

'What are you two doing out here?'

'Off to the *Gata*, we are.'

'Gata? What's that, then?'

'It's our festival, aye, out by Blackhaven Tor.'

'Festival?''

'Aye, that's right. Fuck you know, with that face on yer?'

Warboys opened his mouth to berate the kid, but saw Bill smirking, and took a breath.

'Listen, kid. I reckon your festival's going to be cancelled. Look. You've got soldiers comin' across your land.'

'Aye, my Grandy said you were comin'. He would say that's exactly *why* Gata will go ahead, aye! It... it's the healing of the land, he'd say. To cleanse this land of shite like you!'

'Going to sing and dance us off, are you?'

'You'll see. The elders are coming.'

'What elders? You got an army of these savage granddads, have you?'

Bill shot Warboys a chiding look. Steffyn shrugged and looked back to the fire. Warboys waited a moment, then changed tack.

'He's a bit protective of these stones here, isn't he? What are these *Datya* things he was on about?'

'What do *you* care?'

'Just so happens that I've been noticing these Datyas since we marched this way. All these standing stones. Been wondering, like. What they're for...'

'Well you won't find none you could read here. Even if they wasn't all worn, you couldn't read 'em. No one can read them any more. Even my Grandy. He says these are the songs of Sun-Ivis.'

'Sun-Ivis? What's that, then?'

'Do you have to?' groaned Bill, looking up from the old man. 'Ain't this boy got enough on his plate without you mithering him?'

'S 'alright,' retorted the boy. 'My Grandy would be telling you himself if he could. *Sun-Ivis* is the elders, our ancestors, the ones that farmed here first, before any of us. Farmed more than just land, they did. My Grandy says that when the ships landed and the killing began, most of our forefathers was pushed down south. But Sun-Ivis went back into the Eldask to wait for the day when they would rise again.

'He used to be a woodcutter, my Grandy, before his joints went, and proud, cos his grandy and his grandy's grandy done the same. He's seen 'em, the Elder-men of Sun-Ivis. Men that are part of the woods, in the soil and the wind. He's seen them in streams and branches. But you never see them away from the Eldask. They only come once a year, at the *Gata*.'

'What happens then?'

'They comes out to the Gata, to keep the land, lay their lines. And when they come, they got with 'em some bodyguards. *Janizar*, they call them. Like ghosts with blades they are. No man could get a stone's throw on the elders on account of these bodyguards – for they'd cut you dead soon as you set eyes on 'em. Came in secret they did. Every year.

'But this year, time has come. Your robber General has pushed too far. This year a king has risen for us among the Janizar, a warrior marked with the sign 'o the waning moon, to call on all the lost sons of his people, all us in the Blacklands that remember where our bloodlines owe. They say his mark augurs the end of the west, be it Malvy or some crooked Western half-king, the land back for our own, and a new beginning for Sun-Ivis. Fulfilling the promise laid long ago, that we would heal this land and have it back for our own, aye!'

'Listen, kid,' said Warboys. 'I don't take offence, but the mad bastards in charge might have you shot for talking that way. See these posters? There's more of these coming, kid. A lot more. Keep this stuff to yourself. You keep your head down and...'

Warboys caught Bill looking at him curiously during this speech, and petered out.

'Listen,' said Bill to the boy. 'You stay here and keep your old Granddad warm til the morning. Then you go back to the nearest farm and get help, you hear me?'

'No. We're going to join the king o' the waning moon. *Nef y com bas, Sun-Ivis!*'

'*Nef y com bas, Sun-Ivis!*' echoed the old man, lurching suddenly forward to send both Warboys stumbling together in fright. 'Time has come for you to go, northern shite. They're coming, aye! They're coming back! Time for you to go! The end is coming!'

The old man fell forward onto his elbows and started coughing, and the boy ran to his side. Warboys hovered nervously, looking back toward the troop encampment.

'I think we'd best get back.'

Warboys looked back at Steffyn, who cradled the old man in his arms, muttering vengeful promises into his shoulder.

'You take it easy, kid,' said Warboys and, looking back at the dark recesses of the old man's skull, he felt a sudden chill that made him prance along into the trees after his dad.

'Here, wait up! Dad. He said these Sun-Ivises are the ones wrote these Datyas.'

Bill shrugged. 'Could be, son. We might all be descended from fairies for all I know. But this is Modern Times now, ain't it? All that's gone now.'

'Sesaw reckoned the Datyas came from some lost Asiatic tribe or summat... but all this festival stuff... you reckon these Sun-Ivis people are really still about?'

'Nah, it's just a load of old folklore meant to make people feel better. Same as Malvy's bloody revolution is folklore meant to make us think there's a war to fight at all.'

'Don't mean there won't be trouble waiting. Did you see that old feller's eyes? I'd have feared for my life if he'd been more able.'

'Aye, well, can you blame him? You know, I caught you sounding all concerned back there. Thought for a minute you wanted to help that lad. But you just wanted to grill the poor bugger about your daft scriptures, didn't you?'

'Dad, that's not fair—'

'Fucking right it's not! You know the old feller might not survive the night?'

'*I* never coshed him, did I?'

'Oh, no, it's never your fault.'

'Dad!' hissed Warboys, but they were approaching camp now, and the old man wasn't having any of it. Warboys collapsed onto his bedroll, his head spinning with frustration. Guilt tinged thoughts of Sun-Ivis, festivals, the Elders, and the Datyas set him on a poor night's sleep.

~ ~ ~

Warboys eyed the standing stones even as the march took them south and east, veering steadily away from the gloomy lip of the Eldask. Broken monoliths appeared as scattered copses and rocky outcrops gave way to rolling green plains. Trails and waymarkers hinted at a decrepit kind of civilisation at first, until drystone walls segmented the land into pastures and cart-ruts. Watching the lay of the land as he was, Warboys noticed that the walls took bizarre diversions in places, swerving to evade the standing stones, defying the conventional patchwork shape of northern farmland.

Finally cart tracks emerged from the mud, giving way to

roads, along which small villages and farms clustered. The locals peered over walls, or stood limp on the roadside as the column marched past. Having envisaged a more barbaric sort of foreigner, the Blacklanders seemed a sallow bunch to Warboys.

'The enemy,' smirked Jacky Biel, as they passed a farmhouse wall lined by lank haired children. 'Right fucking slapped arses they got for faces, eh?'

'Yah,' Bill retorted, 'you want to talk. Anyways, all this bloody fog and drizzle might work to make 'em look a bit peaky.'

Many were pale eyed, and some had a certain hollow boned look – but there was not a lot else different to anyone they'd passed in the rural north.

'See?' said Bill. 'These are the raging rebels we're honour bound to defeat. What a joke.'

'Ah well,' sighed Warboys. 'We're all Aalanders now, eh? Whether we like it or not.'

The Colonel ordered his riders into every settlement, where Malvy's intentions were aggressively proclaimed before supplies were seized from terrified farmers. The riders left posters wherever they went, showing a white hand on a blood red map of the Andwyke with no borders. The puzzled looks of the locals suggested to Warboys that few people could read these messages of unification – but the vociferous slogans stood out rudely in the subdued landscape, so that no one could doubt their message.

The land took off into undulating hills, where more locals were spotted off the causeway in groups, all moving eastward on wagons or foot.

'Fucking bogtrotters,' smirked Jacky Biel. 'They don't know what's about to hit 'em.'

'You'd think they'd be running *away* from Blackhaven,' said Warboys. 'You reckon they're going to gather for the festival, like the old feller was saying?'

'Nah,' said Bill. 'They'll turn off soon. They ain't organised a toilet down here in two hundred years, let alone a rebellion.'

And yet, still more travellers appeared, heading east for Blackhaven. They camped, unperturbed, in sight of the 45th. Some carried banners, or weird, decorated effigies mounted on sticks, standing out starkly with their bright clothes and chirruping voices.

Bill enjoyed this with a cynical humour.

'Here, look, Malvy's red and black banner's in with the other fucking jesters where it wants to be!'

'Shut it,' said Warboys, ever wary of the officers.

'Yah! You shut it. I don't recall you ever minding what came out of *your* gob.'

The Colonel sent riders to challenge the travellers, and the troops looked on in collective curiosity as the riders returned, and the rumours of the festival – the *Gata* – began filtering back down the line.

Warboys looked meaningfully at Bill.

'So? No harm, is there? Don't mean a rebellion. They might as well have a party, hadn't they? Before us fucking spoilsports arrive.'

They watched troops sent to scatter the travellers into the night. That night's reading from the *Dictates* was a pointed retort – *esoteric public celebrations divide the people,* it read. *Let citizens gather for the sake of Aaland State, or not at all.*

But as the readings went on, the sound of singing drifted *defiantly* from the distance – and, as the revelry went on unseen, Warboys wondered what kind of lunatic place they were heading for.

~ ~ ~

An isolated stretch of railway embankment arose late on the last day's march before Blackhaven, ending at a long since overgrown platform. A defaced statue of the Founder stood to welcome them, Olaf Hagen himself, open-armed against a grim sky, waiting for a steamer that was yet to arrive. The regiment slopped down around him as darkness drew in. As meagre campfires sparked up all around, Warboys' section gathered to roll smokes, looking up at Hagen.

'Imagine having to wear a daft helmet like that,' murmured Ives.

'He probably only wore it for best.'

A rifleman by the name of Downes recited from the plaque. *'At journey's end, we look awed upon the silver coast... welcoming to a world of undiscovered wonderment.'*

'Undiscovered wonderment,' moaned Bill. 'The poor old sod. There he was, all full of pride and victory, a new world before him. *Now* look.'

Warboys frowned. 'What do you mean?'

'I mean, this land was all found and fought for before Malvy. *Journey's End*, see? The founders came here with trepidation, full of possibilities. The New World, it was. We were proud then. Came to make lives for ourselves. Some of 'em probably wondered if there might be dragons, beasts unknown and all that. Different now. A right bastard wonderland we got left now.'

'You're a miserable old sod. Who are you to say there's nowt to strive for any more?'

'Who said striving meant *war*? We been standing still in this country, sat on our arses and marvelling at steam toys whilst Malvy comes and snatches it off us and tells us we got to fight!'

'We're all still Aalanders, Dad.'

'Are we now? We've been fucking press-ganged is what. We ain't got homes to go to or jobs to go back to. We ain't got a King! We ain't even allowed god no more!'

Warboys saw a few eyes turn Bill's way. Across the field, one of the officers turned from his fire. Warboys saw the glint of his eyes, and recognised their company captain Zander.

'Dad...'

'We're marching to Malvy's tune. You think Hagen envisaged that? A nation of slack-jawed wasters too pampered to stand for what they had?'

'Dad!' hissed Warboys, as Zander stood to listen. The rest of the squad glared anxiously at Bill, prompting Warboys to pull him down out of the way. He waited until Zander turned back to his fire before he spoke.

'Fuck's sake, Dad! Don't rant like that. They'd shoot you for less.'

'Alright, son. Alright. I'm just a bit...'

Warboys watched his dad muttering as he rolled a smoke, all pale, sullen and dirt streaked. He was drained and exhausted, and not himself.

'Alright, Dad. Alright. I know.'

They sat quietly as cold set in. Warboys watched Bill, and felt a thread of worry he hadn't known before. Then Downes let out a mighty yawn, and crouched low to the fire. 'Flame's getting low,' he moaned.

'Chuck summat on it then,' replied Warboys.

'Like what?'

'How do I know? Here, shift out the way...'

Warboys set to the task, and managed to whip the fire up to a nice blaze. With that bit of warmth, things seemed better.

Then came the announcement that Colonel Linnaeus had ordered a reading to be made from Malvy's *Dictates*. A ubiquitous moan erupted from the Company. Each man reluctantly pulled out his little red handbook and turned as ordered, to *Chapter VII: On the resources of freedom*. Section leaders walked the lines, echoing as Linnaeus chanted the script in his booming voice, checking each man was huddled over his red book.

'What is the endeavour of Modern Man? The answer to this question has long been constrained by circumstance, by history, religion ...'

Everyone had their head down, eyes already glazing over. Warboys looked around sheepishly, and nudged Bill.

'Here, Dad. Can I share yours?'

'Why? What's up with yours?'

'I haven't got chapter VII. I used it on the fire.'

'Daft sod!' snorted Bill, stifling a laugh. His face appeared cheekily over a diminished looking copy of the *Dictates*. 'I haven't got chapter VII either,' he said. 'I wiped my arse on it last week.'

The section smothered its laughter until the sudden glare of captain Zander converted mirth into a mass coughing fit. The section sat sniggering as the reading droned into the haze of the night.

9 DISSENTING MEMBERS

'Look! It's the coast! We're here!'

The calls went out as the column gained the summit of the hill, craning their necks to see the glimmer of the eastern ocean.

From here, the land dropped steadily away toward the cliffs. Blackhaven itself emerged through the haze, etched in sharp angles by its walls and battlements. Looking down into the city from afar they could see the main road running on an embankment, splitting a sprawling residential area crowded with row upon row of winding streets.

'See those?' said Bill. 'I heard about them. They call them the Pits. You go *down* off the road into them. No streetlights or nowt. They reckon the city troops don't even go down there. They just patrol the main road, near the light.'

At the end of the main road arose tall warehouses, factories and silos, clustered around the shimmer of a dam. Lock gates fell away either side, down and out of sight toward the sea cliffs and Conlo Bay.

'Them factories is all derelict now. Got driven out of business after the war. The locals walked out, left the place with a load of deserted factories and no jobs. These Blacklanders, they hate us more than squalor, and that's for sure. They been choosing to rot ever since, rather than make money for the north. You've got to admire their nerve.'

Even from such distance, ruin was evident – towers ended in jagged brickwork, rooftops showed gaps in their slate, and tendrils of black smoke rose at random from various points across the Pits.

'Seems like a charming place,' said Warboys.

'Aye, son. This place makes the rough end of Kingstown look like a nun's shrubbery. They'll give us some grief, but there ain't no rebel army here, you'll see. We ain't here to soldier, we're labourers, here to tidy up.'

'I don't know, Dad...'

Warboys scanned the moorlands that spanned away to Blackhaven's north. From here he could see the lines again, and following the pattern over grasses and heath, saw them coiling toward a steep conical mound several miles out from Blackhaven's north wall. On the top stood a lone white stone, picked out by shafts of sunlight.

'That there is known as Blackhaven Tor,' said Bill.

In the fields overlooked by the Tor, a scattering of tents and caravans were dotted around. A few campfires burned, and stray bits of red and yellow bunting shivered in the breeze.

'Not much of a festival, is it?' muttered Warboys, watching the stone, and having the feeling it watched him back. 'Don't know that I care for that thing...'

Bil grunted in response. The descent was murder on their knees. As they levelled out for the approach to the city's western gate, the Colonel's black charger cantered by, glaring at the field of idlers. The fortified black walls of Blackhaven City rose up some thirty feet to meet them.

Colonel Linnaeus called a halt, and formed a flag company to bear Malvy's standard – a stark black star on red.

There was a hush from the 45th as the command approached the west gate. A handful of bovine Blacklanders slouched over the walls, and Warboys saw that they had each smeared a black crescent shape along one side of their faces. The gate showed no sign of opening even as Linnaeus approached, and the gatekeeper, a bristly, pot-bellied man, did nothing to rush. An impish slip of a boy let a long tendril of phlegm dangle down from the wall.

'In the name of Aaland State,' boomed Colonel Linnaeus, his voice hammering back off the walls and over Warboys' section, 'I demand to see the officer in charge! Where is Captain Danvy?'

'Danvy's not in charge here, and never was!' yelled the gatekeeper. 'This city belongs to Sun-Ivis! To Uparagha, the king of the waning moon!'

Linnaeus paused, conferred with his captains as to what all this might mean. Warboys felt a shudder of nerves and nudged at his dad to prove a point.

'Surrender the gate now,' began Linnaeus, 'and we can talk terms. This city will be glorious again, as part of a United Andwyke. I make this one offer. To you, and to this *Uparagha*, whoever he may be. The hand of Aaland is open to you.'

'Bollocks to you, Colonel!' came the reply, and with it, great masses of men suddenly sprouted from the length of the walls, wielding old muskets, picks, halberds and spears. 'We are the sons of Sun-Ivis! We want no part of your northern city state. We oppose the theft of this land by your Robber-General-Jonah! We oppose your advancement into these lands of old! There are forces here older and stronger than you. You shall not pass through here, and your ships shall not here see port! For Sun-Ivis! For the King o' the Waning Moon!'

'Sun-Ivis!' cheered the amassed army, unelashing a deafening, thunderous row from beyond the wall. 'For the Waning Moon!'

Linnaeus looked flustered, forced to steady his horse. He began shouting again, but the gatekeeper lifted his rifle and began to hammer it on the battlements.

Warboys nudged Bill repeatedly.

'See? Sun-Ivis. Rebel army. See?'

Bill looked pale. He said nothing.

Others joined the gatekeeper, banging with the hafts of pikes. More began. Old shields and sabers were battered, tools and makeshift drums, clattering together until the very walls thundered.

Linnaeus' orders were drowned out as the column disintegrated. Men stumbled back in retreat, and the crimson faced colonel turned his horse about, passing Warboys' section as he barked commands to his staff.

'Blockade all the roads in. Form a perimeter around the walls. When they quieten down, send an ultimatum: if this gate does not open to us, this Uparagha, these so called *Sons of Sun-Ivis*, whoever they may be, will see what happens to dissenting members!'

Warboys caught sight of Colonel Linnaeus' face. It seemed to Warboys that there was *embarrassment* there as much as anything. They hadn't been expecting this. Bill had been right: Malvy had expected little resistance from the people of Blackhaven.

The call went up to fall back, and the 45th, well and truly rattled, turned back on themselves, jeered and pelted as they went. Warboys cast a look back at his father as the rout swept them along, seeing Bill shake his head ominously. The shield-battering continued throughout the retreat, seeming somehow obscene against the muffled quiet of the Blackland skies.

10 NO MORE WARS

Over the next hours, a ramshackle siege was set in place around the city walls, and Warboys' unit spent a tense night tucked in behind a wall of crates, squinting at the dark battlements.

Then, as dawn began to seep out of the dark, he heard the low call of orders, and sensed upheaval in the ranks behind. He nudged Bill as he turned to see troops up and moving, flickering past campfires in droves.

'Oh shit,' quailed Bill. 'We're forming ranks!'

'You what? They're not going to send us at those bloody walls, surely?'

The clamour spread to the enemy, and the loutish defence force could be seen sprouting again from the battlements, silent, ready, determined. Warboys' heart sank as a runner approached their unit, and Zander came roaring among them, herding them off to join the ranks lining up to face the main gate.

'Arms at the ready, you slack dogs! Tight over the rifleman in front! Cocked and ready! Jonahs nice and loose!'

Warboys swallowed. That black wall suddenly seemed much more than its thirty or so feet in height. Around him, officers strode around the ranks, ordering the whole force down into a crouch. Murmurs of surprise were palpable on both sides of the wall.

'Stay down!' came the orders. 'Tighten down, and eyes front. Eyes front! Do not take your eyes off that gate!'

Whilst Aalandic officers waded around, hushing everyone, the Blacklanders rose guilelessly from their battlements like meerkats. At first, Warboys thought they were staring incredulously at the big daft kneeling army before them.

But then he noticed his own officers stepping back, their eyes drawn west, in the opposite direction from the walls. He couldn't resist a peek over his shoulder, and followed their gazes to what at first glance looked like a solitary cluster of clouds in the sunrise.

Then he realised what they were.

A fleet of airships loomed low and fast, slipping silently over the ranks of men. Almost no-one was watching the walls now. Warboys saw an officer stagger backwards, nearly tripping over the embers of a campfire. As the great oval shadows plunged them into darkness, Warboys gaped and recognised the AS *Hildegaard* among them. Awed as he was, he felt a pang of jealousy for the tiny crewmen peering down from her deckrails.

'Here, old man!' whispered Warboys. 'There you go, see? Told you they'd do it! Initiative. Imagination. Industry.'

'Aye, you did. Now watch what they do with it.'

Order was fast hammered into the gawping troops as the fleet approached, their long shadows stretching over the walls like slugs. A wild cry from the enemy defences ordered fire at will, and a volley of gunfire erupted from Blackhaven's wall. Gunsmoke swept from the walls, arrows and spears looped toward the gondolas – yet the airships drifted on with trancelike indifference. Then the lead ship *Andamark* crossed the wall, and deployed a small, cask-like object.

There was a blinding flash, a shattering boom, and the 45th all cowered as small pieces of the main gate rained over them. The boom echoed over the hills.

The bombing commenced in full, drowning out the cries of the defences. For what seemed forever the ships circled, and Warboys felt the explosions drum inside his ears. Flames lit the city, and the heat pulsed even from such a distance. When the bombardment ceased, clouds of ash reared up to veil the city, and the defences were gone.

The once impenetrable wall was now a flume of cracked bricks. Fires raged across the gatehouse and into the streets. Bill shook his head gravely.

'There you go lad. What did I say? We're just cleaners now, us. There ain't no more wars to be fought now.'

'You reckon?'

Colonel Linnaeus sat mounted on his black charger overlooking the ruin, bathing in the glow of the burning gate like some demon of the last days. His voice raised to his captains.

'Send five units in to secure the breach. Reserve another five to proceed along that main road to the industrial district. Locate any remaining members of the city infantry, and bring me Captain Danvy, if he still lives. And if you find this Uparagha, whoever he is, or anyone swearing to him and this *Sun-Ivis*, I want them hung by the neck in the square.'

The commands to advance echoed down the field. Warboys felt his bones rattle with fear. The troops dawdled toward the wall, officers barking behind them like sheepdogs.

'Form attack lines!'

Bill stepped up to lead his line, raising the old Entwick. A stripe of cracked blue paint on the butt marked it as one of the first batch of cast-off that the 45th had inherited from the proper military.

Warboys saw the old man's thumb fidgeting anxiously, peeling up slivers of blue. It suddenly hit home that the old man would lead them, and that he had no choice but to tuck in behind with the other three, so as to present a smaller target. If Bill fell, it would be his duty to pick up the rifle and move on. He stepped forward.

'Here, Dad. Give us that here. Let me go first.'

'No,' objected Bill, pulling away. 'I'm alright. Gerroff!'

The old man looked *terrified*. Warboys' heart began to pound, and he realised all of a sudden that Bill had been frightened for days. Weeks, even. He'd known this was coming, somehow, he knew this feeling. He'd fought in wars worse than this one. And he was shitting himself.

Warboys' stomach turned over, more than it had at any of the explosions. He suddenly couldn't speak.

'Take arms!' came the command.

He pulled out his Jonah stick, held it in a white knuckled grip. Behind him: a man named Seth, panting like a dog; pasty old deckhand Ives looking ready to spew; Jacky Biel, looking constipated, his hook-nose streaked with sweat and grime.

'Advance!'

The two Warboys jolted forward on limbs like juddering pistons, shunting one another forth. Waves of smoke billowed towards them, flecked with flying cinders. The old battlement now dropped into a jagged V of rubble. Bill let out an odd warble of fear and strode out of Warboys' reach to enter the city, whilst he staggered, bricks clopping as they fell. Blackened limbs jutted from the waste, and the shell of a gatehouse teetered before him, giving way to a road strewn with rubble that stretched away into the town. Warboys rushed after Bill. Smoke whirled across his father's shape, blending him with other fleeing figures. There came crying and shouting, distant women's voices.

'Onward lads!' came the officer's voice, shepherding them along. 'Press the advantage!'

Warboys charged blindly to catch Bill, and the others stumbled into them, pressing on again. Sweat prickled over every inch of skin as they edged along the rubble. Airships circled like vultures. A courthouse building lolled drunkenly at the end of the row, and there enemy Blacklanders flickered between pillars, dirty faces and ratlike movements. A shot zipped by, and Warboys hesitated – but 'Onward!' came the whiplash voice of command.

Bill froze, blocking the way. In the corner of his eye, Warboys saw a fellow soldier spun off his feet, coat twirling like a ball-gown in a fancy turn. The courtyard collected the wind, curling smoke around them so that he couldn't see the other lines beside him, let alone the enemy. Shots echoed, seeming to come from all around. One man whimpered as he rounded the stub of a brick pillar, and shot at his neighbouring column. Warboys caught hold of his dad and charged the courthouse, the two of them scaling another mound of bricks. A hooded rebel surprised them, wielding a spear, and Bill wailed, fired, missed, fell across the shaft of the spear – then Warboys raised his Jonah, and the others came stumbling over them both, Jonahs raised in a hapless avalanche of men. Warboys heard the sickening thuds of iron tips on skin and bone, and climbed to his feet. Bill lay prone, having dropped the rifle. Jacky Biel came crawling for it, but Warboys lurched over to shoulder Biel away, hauling the old man and the rifle up. They pressed to the nearest wall.

'You alright, Dad? Are you hurt?'

'No son, I'm...'

The mass of the infantry arrived behind them. Sergeants came, cajoling again. Warboys dragged Bill on, and they found themselves forming a kind of queue as they were harried down a side passage. The heels of the enemy disappeared around the corner as the alley opened onto a square. It was overlooked by a church with a vast stained glass window in a rainbow of hues.

'Alright lads,' came the officer's voice, again. 'Secure exits from the square and hold here!'

A shadow swelled overhead as they were bullied forth by the press of reinforcements. Moments later, something dropped from the sky, ricocheted from an adjacent rooftop and in through a hole in the church roof. Warboys looked up to see the airship *Lucidia* break the smog overhead, saw a crewman wave down, yelling between cupped hands.

Their sergeant realised the warning too late.

There was a deep, resounding thud so loud it silenced the world, seeming to shatter Warboy's collarbone with physical force. The pavement and church jumped up together in cracked segments, and the stained glass arose from its frame, a godly image holding almost intact in mid air for a moment before showering down in multicoloured shards. Bill fell into him, diving as a horrendous rumble chased at their heels.

Looking back through a veil of dust, Warboys saw that the church had collapsed entirely, splitting the courtyard, flattening all the men who had been herded inside.

In an instant, they had gone from an army to a pair.

The yelling of the officers was suddenly absent, and soon the low calls of the enemy arose with increasing confidence. Hooded Blacklanders appeared among the ruins, heads bobbing, casting around corners for survivors.

'We've got to move, Dad!' Warboys croaked, pulling Bill towards a nearby doorway. 'Come on!'

An enemy scout scaled the ruin of the collapsed church, his eyes fixing on them like a hunting dog. A dirty painted crescent was smeared across his face. 'To me, sons of Sun-Ivis!' he called, slapping his palm with the flat of an axe. 'We got some stragglers for hunting!'

The two Warboys piled through a doorway that still shivered from bombardment. Beyond, a broken stairway clung tenuously to a wall, creaking as they scrambled up to a balcony. From there they heard their isolation confirmed: the cries of the officers were fading away, shots cracking distantly as the skirmish moved up through the middle of the city, along the main road. Through columns of smoke and fire Warboys saw the accompanying airships drifting in the same direction.

'Shit! They're leaving us!'

He opened his mouth to call out after them, but Bill's hand slapped over it, hauling him out of sight. Another mob loped along below, baying to one another like wolves. Warboys crouched, watching the frightened twitch of Bill's eyes.

They waited.

Bill cleared his throat, straining to shake his voice out. 'Alright son, stay sharp. It'll be alright. Keep on.'

Then there was a creak, and they realised the mob was already scaling the staircase. Both stood to meet the enemy. Warboys saw his dad swing for the leader, the Jonah thumping dully on a hooded skull. Another came, axe raised. Warboys fired, Bill cried out, and the axeman fell heavily on the staircase. It cracked under the weight, and fell, dumping the rest of the mob.

Warboys pulled his dad along the balcony as more rebels gathered on adjacent rooftops, calling them out freely, pelting rocks and promising murder.

Warboys scoured the street below and saw a narrow stairway leading down between two buildings, down into the grime of the Pits.

'There. We have to get down there.'

He ducked out of sight into some sort of gallery, where paintings hung crooked and statues lay in segments.

There they waited, forcing breath down to listen. All was quiet. Warboys stood to look, wondering if a wave of friendly troops had driven the enemy away – and then another slow, languorous shadow passed the archway.

Warboys could only turn to look at his father as the bomb deployed. The floor lifted with a catastrophic boom, and Warboys was thrown towards Bill. The two hit the wall, cringing from debris as it clattered around them. The whistling after-effect of the explosion faded, and Warboys saw Bill's crutch darken. Bill met him with shameful, wet eyes, more vulnerable now than Warboys had ever seen.

'That noise! I can't stand the fucking *noise*, son! I fought in the Andwyke, but this...'

'It's alright, Dad. Don't—'

Bill's eyes shot up. Warboys looked up to see a jagged black line opening in the ceiling, then felt a blow to his back, the soft rush of spewed plaster falling over him, the floor rushing up to meet his nose.

'Son! Son!' came the old man's muffled voice. 'Will! William Konrad Warboys! Where are you?'

He grunted, felt the old man's grip, and came out gasping in clouds of dust. Bill teetered, eyes wide, his hair sprung out and all plastered white like a nancy. Coughing, they stumbled along and down some newly formed scree to reach the cobbles.

Warboys might have thought how hilarious they pair of them looked, with their powdered faces and pissy pants, clinging to one another like underfed monkeys on a sideshow. If he hadn't been so terrified, he might just have laughed.

'William!' came the old man's voice, like a dog barking in a yard. 'Will! Are you alright?'

'I'm alright, Dad,' he finally managed. 'Stop it! I'm alright. Stop shouting! You'll get us killed!'

'You what?'

'Stop *shouting!*'

Bill's eyes grew wide and wet, and he let go a shuddering exhalation as he slumped down beside his son.

'Oh fucking hell!' he wailed. 'I've gone deaf!'

Warboys gripped him, held a finger up to his lips.

'*Shush*. We'll be alright, Dad...' Warboys scanned about for ships, for friend or foe, but there was too much smog to be sure. He saw the stairway to the Pits, not far away.

'Come on. Down there.'

The old man poked fretfully in his ears, seeming dumbstruck

with fear.

'It'll be alright, Dad. We've just got to keep our heads down until our lot come back. Come on. You carry on, look forward, and summat always turns up...'

Warboys slapped Bill's back in reassurance, but felt little himself as they headed down into the Pits.

Part Two

What is the endeavour of Modern Man? The answer to this question has long been restrained by circumstance, by history, by religion, custom, and by economy. The truly Modern Man does not recognise these boundaries. He recognises that constraints must be fought against, both in the heart, and on the field. The duty of Man is to *soldier*, and the duty of the soldier is his endeavour. Man is not limited by his endeavour, he *is* his endeavour, and in fact, his endeavour exceeds him.

— *General Jonas L. Malvy, Responses to Hagen's Wonderland;* Dictates I – *1852*

11 BOMB DAMAGE

For hours, Warboys and his dad huddled together in a coal shed, listening. The sounds of conflict had long since dwindled, and the wind rasped through shattered and deserted buildings. Somewhere distant, a woman screamed in grief or perhaps in rage. Warboys strained for the sounds of marching boots and northern accents. None came. Then he felt a shudder from his dad, and the unmistakable sound of a quiet sob scratched at his heart.

'Dad...' he began, softly, not sure whether to admonish him or try and buck him up. But the old man cleared his throat, sighed, and collected himself with a sigh.

'Ah, don't mind me, son. Daft, really.'

'No it's not. I feel like it myself.'

'No, I mean... It was me anniversary. Just the other day.'

'Oh...' said Warboys. That hadn't been what he was expecting to hear.

'Aye. Thirty-seven years it would have been.'

'Well...' began Warboys, awkwardly, 'happy anniversary...'

'Thanks. That's nice, son. For shame, I forgot it meself you know. First time it's ever crept up on me, what with everything. It's 'cos I'm not at home, you know. Can't take her flowers this year, can I?'

'Bloody hell. I'm sorry, Dad.'

'You know what it was that reminded me? Them bloody bacon butties, on the road. Your mam used to make bacon butties like that.'

'What,' smiled Warboys, 'orrible?'

'Ha! Yeah. They reminded me of her. I used to think, how the hell do you get a bacon butty wrong? Never dared say owt though.'

'There was a talent there. Not sure what, but a talent. Demolitions, mebbe.'

'I can hear her telling me what a silly bugger I look in this uniform.'

'Oh aye? Do you often hear from her then?'

'Listen kid, you don't live with a woman as forceful as your Ma and not have a bit left of her in your head. She always had a level head on her, that woman.'

'Not always, Dad.'

'Aye, well, she did what she could, left with you lot on her own. She's a part o' my conscience now. I can hear her, what she'd think about things. F'r instance, I heard her this morning, telling me I'm too bloody old for this.'

'She can't be best pleased with me then.'

'Nah, don't be daft, son. It's all my fault, this.'

'How do you figure that? I landed us in this.'

'Long before that, son. Y' know, the day I married her, I said, I promised I'd look after her, keep her out of them bloody workhouses. Ballsed that up alright, didn't I?'

'What else could we do? Everyone was the same.'

'I should never have let it happen. I promised her.'

'Well, maybe you shouldn't have.'

'What else has a man got but his honest intention, eh? Tell you what, times like this, it's my only bloody regret in life.'

'Bloody hell, Dad. Don't get all maudlin.'

'I ain't maudlin, as it happens,' smiled Bill. 'I'm *resigned*. And, anyway, I've got some powerful memories to keep me warm... Ooh!' gasped Bill suddenly, digging his elbow into Warboys' ribs. 'Ah!'

'Aw, Dad, don't get upset. We've just go to keep... What's up? Be quiet! What's the matter?'

'Yah, shurrup, you daft bugger! Oooh! Aah! I've got to get out! I've got cramp in me leg...'

'Can't you—'

With a tremulous gasp, Bill pushed the coal shed door open with his rifle and tipped himself into the alley to rub his leg down. Warboys emerged warily and peered around. The crooked alley, barely a shoulder's width across, was just one of a mazelike spread. Bullied old tenement buildings stooped overhead, squeezing daylight through jagged spaces.

'Hard to tell what's bomb damage and what's not,' muttered Warboys. 'Here. It'll be broad daylight before long. We're going to have to move, get our bearings.'

'What? I can't hear you out here.'

'Get up higher. See if we can spot a Hilda or summat.'

Bill rummaged about in his ear. 'Eh?'

Warboys rolled his eyes.

'Up,' he said, pointing at the sky.

Bill nodded, then patted Warboys' arm.

'Here. A present for you.'

He unshouldered his rifle, and offered it to his son. 'We've got a few in our squad now. I don't need it.'

Warboys took the rifle hesitantly. 'You might want it soon enough. Just keep it.'

'Nah. I don't want the bloody thing...'

'Shush!' snapped Bill, taking poise with the rifle to demonstrate.

'Look here. Your cocking bolt tends to get stuck, *here*. It'll usually shift with a good hard slap. Hey, but if you get a delay, you have to be quick. The bloody thing near went off in my eye on the range.'

'Right...'

'Oh, and the sight groove is wrong. Bears to starboard. I scored a new one, but it's a bit harder to see.'

'Right, well... Cheers, Dad.' Warboys held the rifle warily before him. Bill nodded, satisfied with his briefing, and turned away.

'Here, Dad, are you sure about this?'

'Oh, I'm sure. I can't bugger things up any more for you, can I? I figure it's the best I can do, such as it is, to give you a gun and let you fight for yourself eh? Should've done it years a—'

Glass smashed nearby, and the two fell against the wall, awaiting attack. When, moments later, none came, they assumed it was just debris – and decided to move. Warboys fell into step behind Bill, anxious to be away. But he couldn't shake off a regretful sense of something left unsaid.

They ventured down the alley and out onto the nearest street. A bow-fronted inn leaned forwards precariously. They left the street by a stairway that became swamped by rubble about half way up, until it met an orphaned archway overlooking the ruins of the Pits. Below them a landscape of bricks and broken glass lay stretched out before a row of gutted houses. Great black dunes of rubble rose and fell through the district, and twisting coils of smoke further confused what little order and structure remained. Warboys stepped out to start his descent down the scree, but before he had gone two steps he heard a voice speaking in a thick Blackland accent.

'Not so cocky now, eh, you northern shite?'

Warboys froze, hands seizing his rifle. Bill barely stopped in time, his breath halting sharply in Warboys' ear. Ahead of them, the smoke cleared and, in the shadow of a collapsed wall, where fire smouldered in a bin, there loitered a gang of hooded rebels bearing sticks and knives. One, his face quite clearly smeared with the crescent, stood over a dead soldier who lay face down in a blossom of red. Realising he hadn't been seen, Warboys felt a mixture of horror and relief. Spotting that the gang had a lean looking dog, pulling on a chain, Warboys began slowly to tread backwards.

'Fucking ran like a rabbit, did this one,' gloated the speaker, twirling a stolen Jonah as others came pulling at the dead soldier, removing his boots, his pack, his coat. 'You see them run when the bangers went off, eh? Ha! Shitting themselves worse than we was!'

'You sayin' you weren't scared, Iren?' asked another.

'I weren't scared,' retorted the boy named Iren, twirling the Jonah. 'It don't frighten me.'

'Away! You was cowering with the rest of us, just so.'

'Fuck off, Kiery. I can't wait for them to send us some more. Take Uparagha some heads, so I will.'

'Aye, alright there, Iren Samsta. You ain't no Janizar, man.'

'Why the fuck not, eh? Our great Grandy's Grandys was kin to Janizar, weren't they? In our blood, it is. Uparagha says it's so, don't he? We're all the sons of Sun-Ivis now. Any road, I reckon I'm more Janizar than that Aaranya fucker.'

'Careful now, Iren. You get too cocky when you're drunk. Don't start that again...'

'I ain't drunk.'

'Alright, Iren.'

'Next time they come with the bangers,' came Iren's voice again, 'I'll take me bat out, eh? Knock the fuckers back at 'em.'

The others laughed.

'Come on, let's try down there. We get a few more, and Uparagha might let us—'

A slither of bricks gave under Warboys' boot, and went clopping down to the street. The dog barked. The hooded faces turned.

The Warboys ran.

Fleeing back down the scree onto the cobbles, they turned into the first street they found. A chimney stack sagged across the road, offering a makeshift stairway up to the second floor of a warehouse. Inside, they crouched low as the louts loped past after their dog.

'We'll find you!' Samsta thundered. 'You'll hang in Clover Square, you northern fuckers! You hear me?'

Warboys and Bill breathed into their coats so as not to steam up the air. For a time they waited, listening to the dog scamper about.

The hunters moved out of earshot, and Bill thumbed onward through the building. The other side was open to the air, as was the next block. Through that, they came to a great flooded crater that had once been a stretch of a canal. It took a moment to make sense of the mess before them. Canal boats lay scattered about like caught fish, one overturned completely, another jutting end up. A pair of ducks dabbled in the shallows by a pile of planks.

Warboys edged down the splintered mountings of a staircase and stepped into the water. He went to move into the shadow of the upright barge when, too late, something shifted above, watching them from the aft. A dirt streaked face snapped towards Warboys, a lean figure unfurling.

There was a foreign, almost Asiatic look about the young man before them – a subtle convexity to the bridge of his nose, the breadth of his cheeks. He had a smooth, fine-boned face, but his handsomeness went astray in one feral eye that stared slightly wider than the other. The lid of this eye twitched minutely, countering his motionlessness. Jet black, unevenly shorn hair stuck out as if it had been cut with a spoon. To Warboys' reckoning, he'd not yet reached his twenties. The handle of a long, elegantly curved blade jutted from his hip, ill-concealed by a split jacket that had seen better days.

Warboys readied his Entwick and increased his stride,

raising the rifle as he neared. Bill moved with him. At barely three yards from the hull of the narrow boat, Warboys halted. The kid made no move to draw his blades.

'Mornin',' ventured Warboys, with a nod. 'Bit foggy today, ain't it?'

Give him a bit of lip, thought Warboys. *See what he does with it*. But the foreign kid watched Warboys with eerie, lightning blue eyes that put Warboys in mind of a cat – they might equally have revealed either a savage hunter or a purring fuckwit, and he couldn't for the life of him decide which it was.

Warboys cleared his throat. 'Do you understand me, feller?'

'Ai,' croaked the kid.

'We're lost, son,' ventured Bill, more magnanimously. 'We don't want no trouble.'

'Hui, lower this, eh?' The kid gestured distractedly at Warboys' rifle. 'Questions are easier to answer without these arms pointing, nai?'

A brief, earnest smile broke onto his face, leaving Warboys unsure if he intended to seem friendly or not.

'It's alright son. We don't mean any harm.' Bill waved Warboys down, and he lowered the Entwick, if only a little.

'Alright then,' said Warboys, 'we're being nice. Who the hell are you?'

'I am the Janizar Nouzi Aaranya, once Jana Aasvina.'

He paused, as if testing the mettle of this name, then nodded, as if deciding it was right whether he liked it or not.

'Well that's funny,' snorted Warboys, 'cos I'm the great General Malvy 'imself.'

Bill gave him a shove. 'Are you daft? Don't say that to him! He doesn't mean it, son. I mean, he's not really...'

Nouzi Aaranya looked from Bill to Warboys, then another surprising smile opened wide across his face, as if humour – however facetious it may be – was something long forgotten and much lamented.

'Well now, it is a great honour to meet you, nai? Though I expected the great new champion of the west to be a much younger man...'

'Cheeky bastard...' muttered Warboys, nestling against the stock of his rifle. 'Wait a minute. Did you say *Janizar*? Are you Sun-Ivis? From the Eldask, like?'

'Ai,' nodded Nouzi Aaranya.

'You *are* real, then...'

'Ai,' said the Janizar, after a pause – and this time, as his eye twitched, his left hand joined it, making a sudden, anxious claw. The hand that had been touching the butt of the blade went to wrestle the twitch. If this kid really was one of the bodyguards of Sun-Ivis, he didn't look much of a ghostly killer.

'What are you... what's the matter with you?'

Nouzi Aaranya moved suddenly, jumping like a jack-in-the-box as some debris clattered down the deck behind him. Warboys barely held his nerve. An impatient streak itched to pull the trigger anyway, and be done with it.

'Ea-sy, lads...' cooed Bill, edging between them. Warboys shook his head, and shot an incredulous look at his father.

Bill's jaw squared. 'Will you stop pointing that fucking thing at him!' He patted the rifle firmly down.

'He's demented! I'm not taking my eyes off him!'

'Ask him where the barracks is.'

'How would *he* know? The barracks ain't even been set up yet!'

'Well, ask him where the front gate is then!'

'Shall I ask him for a piggyback an' all?'

'I'll give *you* a bloody piggyback if you don't frame a bit!'

Bill raised a calming hand as Nouzi Aaranya climbed down from the barge. Warboys kept the rifle sights tight as the Janizar's face peeled from the shade once more, stepping out onto the mess of planks that spanned the pool. He looked over both Warboys as they huddled together behind the rifle.

'Ai,' he muttered to himself, looking somehow forlorn, 'kaarya had us meet, nai?'

'Kaarya, right...' Warboys shot a look at Bill. *This kid is a few pints short of a cask.* 'If you say so. Well, now we're all friendly like – can you point us to...'

'Uparagha will be interested to meet you.'

'Hey now, just hold on a minute!' began Warboys, suddenly afraid at the prospect of meeting the upstart lunatic that had the locals screaming defiance from the city walls. 'We're just...'

'Why are you here?'

'We got lost! Those fucking bombs did as much damage to our lot as yours!'

'You look alike.'

'Eh? Well, all foreigners do, don't they? Listen, mate. I can see you're busy. If you can just point us in the right direction, we'll be out of your way.'

A howl of wind rushed in to fill the silence that followed. Nouzi Aaranya's eye flickered. His clawed hand shuddered.

'Nai. I think you come with me to Uparagha. You will be treated respectfully. Now please, accept kaarya, and lay down your arms.'

'Who's kaarya? Is he one of the Janizars?'

'Eh?' the Janizar frowned, perplexed. 'Nai. Kaarya is duty, *fate*, nai? *Destiny.*' He paused, and acknowledged the sound of a group approaching, a dog sniffing, footsteps through rubble.

Shit, thought Warboys. *Samsta's gang.* 'I am trying to politely suggest, General, that you have no choice but to follow me. Ai?'

Warboys opened his mouth to allow a measured response that was sadly missing. 'Ah, sod this for a lark,' he growled instead, and raised his rifle.

'Don't!' called Bill, slapping at the Entwick. The shot cracked away into the sky.

'Ahh, fuck! What did y—'

The Janizar closed in an instant, shouldered Bill off his feet and was square on Warboys before Bill had finished rolling in the rubble. Warboys was eye to eye with Nouzi Aaranya, and ready to swing – but with a quickness of hand that he had never seen, the Janizar flicked out his blade, a long and elegantly curved sliver of light, and cut the rifle from his grip. *Like ghosts with blades they are*, the boy had said. *Cut you dead soon as you set eyes on 'em.*

Warboys now found his throat against the blade.

'Now, this time,' grinned Nouzi Aaranya, blue eyes flashing, 'don't move. Or you die.'

12 DIVIDING EDGE

Warboys felt a sliver of blood trickling through the stubble on his throat.

'This is *dhas,*' Nouzi Aaranya said. 'Means in your language, *dividing edge.* Very sharp. Don't move.'

Gasping, Bill clambered to his feet, hands outstretched as if to coax the blade away. Warboys looked over the Janizar's shoulder to see the rebel gang arrive. Iren Samsta arrived, now clutching a bottle as well as the Jonah he'd scavenged. He glared from one newcomer to the next, and bewilderment gave way to indignation.

'Oi!' he barked, stamping his boot. 'What you doin, eh? *We* was huntin' these two cunts.'

Warboys realised Samsta was addressing Nouzi Aaranya when the blade shivered, stinging his throat. The Janizar frowned and addressed Samsta.

'Hui, Javani, be quiet. I am speaking here with the General of Aaland.'

'*Javani?*' echoed Iren, petulantly. 'Javani, he calls us? What's Javani, then?'

Samsta's dog set off barking again.

'Just let's all calm down!' Bill wailed. Nouzi Aaranya's eyelid started flickering like a moth's wing.

'Away, Iren,' hissed one of Samsta's mates, a shaven headed lad. 'Shut your mouth, so, eh? That's Nouzi Aaranya!'

'I know who it is, Sim.'

'He's *Janizar...*'

'He ain't *real* Janizar.'

Warboys saw another dainty flutter affect Nouzi Aaranya's eye, as if the idiot's words stung it directly. Warboys began to wish people would stop bothering the man.

'Hui! I'm speaking to you!' came Iren's voice, blaring out like a foghorn. He bickered and nudged with Sim again, but his blood was well up.

'Yah, I don't care. I'll tell him. Look, he can't even do that cunt. Uparagha would have taken both them heads for his fucken bedposts by now. This one here can't find his own cock!'

Nouzi Aaranya did not move, but Warboys feared the barely-contained turbulence in his eye. Infuriated by this lack of reaction, Samsta smashed his bottle on the bricks below. The rest of the gang lowered their heads humbly – but subtly peeked up to see what Nouzi Aaranya would do.

'Can't we just…' began Bill, but Iren blustered toward Nouzi Aaranya, flinging his arms in irritation. 'Oi! I'm talking to you, Aaranya! You better turn and look at me or—'

The demand was cut short. Warboys saw the Janizar's eye widen in shock. He seemed impelled as he whirled about. His dhas caught an arc of light, and so deft was his movement that Iren Samsta was still murmuring the end of his sentence even as his own finger ends began raining down on him with small thumping noises. His indignant, lemon-sucking expression collapsed, as did his knees, and he fell clutching at a hand which now ended in a wedge of bloody stumps.

There was a stiff silence. Nouzi Aaranya flinched a little late, as if he himself had just walked in on the scene. No one dared move. Warboys stood dumbstruck, until Bill came padding at his throat to see if it had been cut. Still watching the Janizar, Warboys patted Bill to assuage his fears.

Nouzi Aaranya had lost a shade of colour. His hand clawed involuntarily, shooting up to tug at the hair on the back of his head. He looked suddenly diminished: less swordsman, more dithering, apologetic tramp. The rebel gang lowered their heads. Iren Samsta let out a sob, jamming his stump under an armpit, and Nouzi Aaranya appeared to remember himself.

'Ai! I am Janizar, eh! Remember it!'

He turned on the gang, his face flushing with embarrassment thinly disguised as anger. They cowered, and Warboys saw that most of the gang were just cocky little kids like the ones you'd see on Kingstown Green.

'You!' barked Nouzi Aaranya, pointing at them. 'Javani! Don't just stand there! Help him pick these digits up! Your hunt is finished! Lift your fingers! Lend a hand! *Isht!'*

The Janizar's blade was still unsheathed as he paced around with uneasy aggression, and Warboys watched him incredulously, unsure if he was insane, or if he was making a hard-faced joke of it all. A pair of kids collected Iren and his severed fingers from the floor, attempting to stand him up until he leaned over and retched.

Nouzi Aaranya paused to watch Samsta's vomit slap down on the floor with all the sympathy of a drill sergeant, then turned to Sim.

'Well? You have captured enemy soldier, eh? Don't you suppose Uparagha might want to question him? *Murkha!'*

Nouzi Aaranya flung his arms for emphasis, and Sim – with everyone present – flinched. Nouzi Aaranya whipped the blade one last time for good measure, then sheathed it before turning to Warboys.

'I ask again. Who are you?'

'Warboys,' coughed Warboys and, still figuring that a bit of rank might do him good, he added, 'Captain Warboys.'

'You don't look like a Captain.'

Warboys felt Bill grip him, but nudged the old sod off.

'What does a Captain look like?'

Nouzi Aaranya shrugged childishly, as if he didn't care anyway. 'What is your mission here? Why did the Colonel send you?'

'Just to invade, like.'

Warboys met the blazing blue eyes for what seemed like a long time, and felt Bill tugging on his jacket in fear – perhaps to catch him when that blade came. Then Samsta retched again, and the Janizar wandered off to look. Bill nudged Warboys.

'*Captain*,' he quoted, disgusted. 'What did you tell him that for?'

'A bit of preferential treatment won't do us any harm.'

'Well, *Captain*, some orders from the war office. Shut your trap!'

'Hui, Captain...' came the Janizar's voice again. 'Do you know *Ausadha*?'

Warboys looked blankly back at him. 'Pardon?'

'Hui! Medicine! Do you have any surgeon's skill?'

'Oh, right... well... I've got half a charter—'

'Eh, keep that shite away from me,' snarled Iren.

'Oh, hey up,' started Bill without any sort of permission to speak. 'He must be feeling better, look. Started talking out of his arse again!'

And, with that, Bill bent to look. Iren made a show of shrinking away, but eventually gave over the bloodied stump of his palm.

'He'll probably bleed to death within the hour,' Bill said, flatly. 'You'd better get him off to a surgeon.' Despite his bravado, the boy's eyes moistened in fear.

'Avai!' grunted Nouzi Aaranya, wagging his finger. 'Let that teach you to yell and posture!'

Then Bill chuckled, and Warboys wondered if there was something in those bombs that had sent everyone barmy.

'No, son. You'll live. If we hurry about it, we might even get a few stiched back on. It's a very clean cut.'

'Ai,' muttered Nouzi Aaranya, patting the handle of his dhas, eager to have this fact emphasised. 'Forged in *Samagat*, eh?' He waved for them to hurry. 'Hui, dress the wound, then!'

Warboys dithered, then dropped his hands and stepped forward to help, only to find the Janizar's blade flash by again.

'Hui!' screamed Nouzi Aaranya. 'Not you! Arms rise! *Isht!*'

Warboys' arms shot up. He glowered at Bill, wondering how the old sod got to leap about wherever *he* liked. Soon, Iren got himself a red tipped bundle for a hand. The Janizar helped Bill up, nodded gruff thanks, and proceeded to have both Warboys tied up. This done, the Janizar stalked around to inspect his newly arranged party.

'To the *Sunken Pig*, and quickly. Perhaps we can save this fool's hand, if not his shame. And you, Captain. You can explain yourself to Uparagha.'

Warboys looked longingly at his Entwick. The Janizar followed his gaze, retrieved and shouldered it.

'Avai, Captain. I can only apologise for the poor manners of these *balegh*! Although, had you done as I asked the first time, we could have avoided all this, nai?'

He nodded persistently until Warboys nervously dummied him. 'He never bloody listens,' added Bill.

Nouzi Aaranya looked curiously to Bill at this, then back to Warboys, assessing him. Then, with a terse '*Isht!*' they were shooed on into the shattered town.

~ ~ ~

Between bomb damage and the growing Aalandic military presence, the route was tricky, but Nouzi Aaranya led a careful route through the streets and alleys of the Pits.

Aalandic troops had settled in the centre of Blackhaven, and were already taking tentative patrols along the main road. As the day brightened and the smoke cleared, Warboys managed to get his bearings a little more. Sometimes they'd come a little too close to the road, and Nouzi Aaranya would double them back. The Airships had taken sentry positions overlooking the city, and more than once they had to turn about to keep out of their lengthy view.

Crossing a timber yard on the canalside they could see the main road rising up to the industrial district, where factories and warehouses jutted up at the city's highest point. Aalandic troops swarmed and clattered beneath airships anchored at watch. Supplies were already being ushered in by cart, to the new headquarters: there overlooking it all, already flying the red and black, was a monumental slab of dead industry. The disused silos within peaked in a kind of turret, and a jagged staircase ripped up its side like a scar. The walls bore the title of the AALANDIC EXTRACTING CO. in flaking white paint, visible even half a city away. This was the colonel's new castle.

'Look at that!' scoffed Sim. 'What a shithole he chooses for his barracks, eh?'

'It's fucked, that AEC,' said Sim. 'A big toilet, that's what it is. Full of pigeons and shit. Right place for 'em.'

'I plugged your sister in there last week,' said one of the others.

'You watch it you. I'll pan you.'

'That'll be about right,' sighed Bill. 'Pick the biggest, most visible lump you can and lord over them with it.'

'No point crawling in and taking over politely, eh?' shrugged Warboys.

'Yah. Next thing you know it'll be caked in posters trying to talk 'em all into grafting again.'

'Hui!' barked Nouzi Aaranya. 'Quiet!'

He led them away, out of sight of the AEC. At last they reached a street lined with terraced houses that gaped from windowless portals. Nouzi Aaranya cut through a yard, up and over a wall like a territorial cat on his rounds.

As Nouzi Aaranya scaled a pile of bricks, a storm of black feathers erupted into the air. Warboys expected the Janizar to leap to cover; yet he froze, staring fixedly at the ground. As Warboys caught up, he saw a bare, colourless foot sticking out of the wreckage. A woman lay dead, one side of her face plastered with bloodied hair, empty sockets staring after the crows that had plucked from them.

Iren and the others bustled up behind, glancing over the corpse bitterly.

'Aye. That's old Mary Naster. And many more of 'em below the wreckage...' He turned pointedly at Warboys and spat. 'Women and children, eh?'

Warboys bristled. 'You can fuck off mate. I don't like it any more than you!'

'I didn't tell you to speak, shitpile.'

Iren shoved at Warboys, who looked to the Janizar for aid. But Nouzi Aaranya was still lost in the empty sockets of the corpse. Eventually sensing eyes on him, Nouzi Aaranya came to, looking shaky.

'*Isht*! Leave this for the *charya*, eh?'

Nouzi Aaranya turned and walked away, leaving everyone wondering what he meant. Warboys watched him move off uneasily, then halt. That clawed hand grabbed at his hair whilst some unintelligible stammer wobbled on his lips. Suddenly white as sailcloth, he halted the party with a palm and fled from the street. He disappeared into a sagging house without a word to his charges, leaving them to stare blankly after him.

13 SARPA

Crows cawed overhead, and Samsta's gang collected behind Warboys as the loud, obvious sound of vomiting could be heard echoing from the house.

'Here,' said Bill. 'Is he alright?'

Iren Samsta, still cradling his bloodied bandage, took a swig from a newly opened bottle.

'See? Them big booms bombed his box, so. Broken, he is.'

There was another violent retch.

Shit, thought Warboys. The Janizar was flaking out and leaving them with these murderous little sprouts. 'Oi! Isht!' he yelled. 'Nouzi Aaranya! Are you alright there?'

Samsta punched Warboys hard in the guts, pitching him over. Warboys rose, ready to fight, but Bill blocked his way.

'Oi! Give over now! Don't let them rile you.'

'Fuck off, old man,' snarled Samsta. 'He your boy, is he?'

'Just you step back, lad. No need for this.'

'You must have plugged some ugly sow to sire *that*.'

'Now look here,' growled Bill, suddenly scarlet. 'You've already lost your fingers. You talk to me like that again and you'll be shitting your teeth out an 'all!'

This time Warboys shouldered Bill back.

'Dad, come on! What happened to calming down?'

'Hui!' came a gasp from the house. 'Send the captain and his old man here. Just them, ai. To me. But if either runs... you can kill him.'

'Nouzi-Shah,' called Iren, pretending reverence through

clenched teeth. 'What's up, eh? Can't *we* help you?'

'You heard me,' came Nouzi Aaranya's voice. 'Send them.'

Amidst Samsta's cursing, Warboys found himself shoved off. Arms still tethered, he and Bill bobbed off up the ramp of rubble like ducks, grateful at least to be away from Samsta.

Inside the house, Nouzi Aaranya was crouching against the wall, sheet white and shuddering. He gasped for breath, arms wrapped about himself like a man in a strait jacket. He rubbed on his cheek repeatedly as his hand itched to claw in his hair. Warboys kept his distance – even as Bill shuffled straight over. The old man seemed more himself now.

'What's up then, mate?' Bill ventured.

'I can't feel my arms...'

'Fuck this, Dad. Leave him. Let's go. Out of that back window. Quick. We can make a run for that AEC thing.'

'Nai Captain!' croaked Nouzi Aaranya, more a plea than a command. 'Stay!' He shuddered, wincing as if in pain. The sudden movement startled the two Warboys.

'Is there summat in your eye, son?'

Nouzi Aaranya hid his face in the crook of one arm, holding the other up to belay them. Then he pointed off into the dark corner of the room. Warboys and his dad looked.

'What's he pointing at? There's fuck all there... dad, can't we...'

'Are you hurt, son?'

'I can't feel my arms... can't find my heartbeat!'

'Dad, let's *go!*'

'You're moving your fingers.'

'Am I?' Nouzi Aaranya held up a shaking arm.

'For fuck's sake...'

'Course you are, son.'

'I can't feel them...'

'You can, son. Just look. How could you move your fingers if you couldn't feel your arm?'

Nouzi gasped, feeling at his flexing fingers with his other hand. 'Here,' laughed Bill. 'Don't let old Iren Samsta see you doing that. He'll be jealous.'

Nouzi Aaranya managed a hapless laugh that rotted quickly into a sob. Another round of shudders shook the Janizar's body. He lost his breath again, and clutched at his chest, shooting forward as if he was convulsing.

'Shit! He's having a stroke or summat!'

'No, he ain't...'

The Janizar collapsed, limp and white across Bill's arm. Bill let him down gently.

'Dad. Let's go! Leave him! Come on!'

'I aren't leaving him. Fancy your chances without him, do you?'

'Dad, look at the state of him. He's going to die or summat...'

'No, he'll be alright.'

Warboys was of a mind to drag the old sod away even if he had to do it with his teeth – but then Nouzi Aaranya awoke with a groan.

'Here, let it pass, son. Just breathe. It'll pass... You're alright.'

'Yeah, don't worry mate.' Warboys mouthed an exasperated curse at the sky. 'It'll pass. Don't rush yourself. We don't mind... Got all the time in the world, we have...'

He cast look over his shoulder, wondering how the patience of the mob was holding. Bill hushed and eased the Janizar, who stared like some limp new-born.

'This happened before, son?'

'Many times. Since we left Gienha.'

'That your home, is it?'

'Ai. In the Eldask.'

'It was her set you off, wasn't it? Mary Naster. That lady lying dead out there.'

'Ai.'

The blue eyes began to focus on Bill.

'Seen summat like it before, have you? Lost someone?'

'Ai. Maia. I saw her face taken. Hollows in her skull where her eyes had been.'

'Maia? Who's that? Your mother, was it? Your sister? A girl back home?'

'Ai,' he said, without clarifying which. 'For twelve years I waited. When she was there in my *reach*... I couldn't see her face! And all the nightmares came again, snakes waiting to leak out. And they spit! Spit black clouds to take my eyes and my limbs...'

'When did she die, son?'

'Eh?' Nouzi Aaranya looked suddenly irritated. 'Nai, kitava!' he snapped. 'Maia does not *die*! Maia is born ever again with the sun!'

'Oh... that's alright then...'

Bill shot a bewildered look at Warboys, who shrugged unsympathetically. Nouzi Aaranya clawed at his head again. 'The snakes are *here*,' he whispered, banging vigorously on his head. 'Sarpa! Venomous, and always waiting in *here*...'

Warboys hovered, wary of approaching. But the old man beamed like sunlight, slapping a pally arm down on to the kid.

'Listen son. When was the last time you had a good night's sleep?'

The Janizar shook his head hopelessly, rocking on his haunches like the raggedy arsed people in the sanatorium yard on Chalk Lane. Warboys stepped back to peer out toward the street, and saw Iren Samsta ranting, flinging his good arm, trying to stoke the others up. Warboys turned calmly back, suppressing his urgency.

'Listen, Nouzi Aaranya,' he said. 'You're going to be alright. But you've got to get a hold on yourself and take us to Uparagha, or them fuckers are going to come and cut all our throats.'

'Ai.'

'Nah,' smiled Bill, and Warboys wondered how the old bugger could be so godforsaken genial at a time like this, as if he'd take his bloody time, come what may. 'Don't you worry. They've just got wind up their arses, is all. Listen, you've got by for this long haven't you? Isn't there something you do? Summat to calm you down?'

Nouzi Aaranya made a gesture that was a mix between a shake of the head, a sigh and a shrug. 'We practise *Resadem*.'

'What's that then?'

'It's a meditative practise used by the Sekhet,' he said, seeming a little comforted by reeling off an explanation.

'Oh aye?' said Bill, generously pretending he knew what that was.

'Ai. Sekhet are what the locals call the *elders*, nai? They are the founders of Sun-Ivis. Our Fathers and guides.'

'Right,' said Bill.

Warboys frowned. 'Aren't you supposed to be one of their bodyguards?'

'Ai. Janizar.'

'So where are they then?'

'Shut up with your daft questions, will you? Let him concentrate!'

Nouzi Aaranya keenly resumed his explanation to Bill. '*Resadem*. It means *playing listener*. Sekhet close off all the pollution of their bodily senses. That's how they learnt to sense the flow of the Lines. We Janizar have learned to appropriate it for combat training...'

'Aye, that sounds nice. You do that then.'

Nouzi Aaranya stood uncertainly whilst Bill waved him on. Warboys huffed and puffed and muttered to himself, looked to the heavens and wondered what in the name of God he'd gotten himself into. Nouzi stood, breathed deeply and took his stance.

When he drew his dhas, both Warboys cowered together before realising that it was merely a practise of motion. They stepped aside politely, and Nouzi Aaranya moved the sword over himself in graceful arcs, gaining his breath and composure.

Warboys leaned close to whisper to Bill.

'Here, Dad. How did you know what to do with him? I thought he was having a bloody seizure.'

'Well, it happened to your Ma a few times, just after you was born. She used to have these funny turns. Clinging to me in the night, convinced she was going to die. Doctor couldn't find 'owt wrong. Give her brandy, he said. Anyway, we worked it out ourselves in the end.'

'Eh? Well, what was it then?'

'Well, that's just it. It wasn't an *it* at all. See, your Ma was like him. Reckoned some evil spirit might have come to haunt her for being a bad mother. But the truth is, when you're already run down and one more thing goes wrong, sometimes your head just goes. Tells your body *that's* gone an'all. There were no spirits, no more than he's got venomous snakes in his skull. She was a hard working mother, she was on her own, with me at sea and all... and she was feeling a bit, *overwrought*, like. I reckon some mothers would find it easier to be shot at than raise kids.'

'Is that you glossing up family life for me?'

He gave Warboys another nudge. 'Nah, they're worth it. If you survive.'

'Well, you must be a saint, Dad.'

Bill shrugged. 'Nah. He's lost this Maia, he's a long way from home, wherever that is. And look about! This place doesn't give a kid much of an 'oliday, does it? He's just addled, I reckon, and behind all that shit and demons, there's probably a decent lad somewhere in there.'

'Pffff...' replied Warboys, shaking his head.

Nouzi Aaranya sheathed the blade, breathed normally, and

was calm.

'There. Alright now?'

'Better,' muttered the Janizar. 'Thank you, Captain. Old man Bill. I apologise.'

'Don't worry mate,' chirped Bill, tickled by the address. 'Should we go now? The troops are getting restless.'

Warboys ducked under the buckled archway to set off back, and felt the Janizar's hand on his shoulder.

'Hui, Captain,' said the Janizar, without turning. 'Do you think it'll be alright, Iren Samsta's hand?'

'He'll live. It's the face-ache I'd worry about.'

'Ai. Ha! Move along now, eh?' And with that, Nouzi Aaranya shoved Warboys on to rejoin the others.

Bugger me, thought Warboys, ready to tear at his own hair. *Have we made a friend, now, or what?*

The mob straightened up on the Janizar's return, offering wary nods of acknowledgement. But Iren Samsta's face stayed heavy with hatred and drink. When Nouzi Aaranya strode past, ordering them to follow, Samsta stood his ground.

'No,' he announced, smashing his bottle on the floor. 'I won't take orders off him no more! This fucking northerner and his grandy comes swanning in and this so-called *Janizar,* attends him like a rent-boy! Even the other Janizar don't like this fucker. No Sim, don't shake your head. You've heard about him. Uparagha's bugger boy, this one is. Heard them say it.'

Nouzi Aaranya halted. He looked curiously at Warboys before turning, and for a moment, Warboys thought that the Janizar might burst into tears. Then he turned to face Samsta.

'You!' he barked. '*Balegh*! Who speaks?'

The gang lowered their heads, but Samsta fumed on.

'I'll tell you who speaks. Iren Samsta of Blackhaven, I am. Son of Sun-Ivis, and loyal to Uparagha, the King o' the waning moon, and *proper* Janizar.'

Nouzi Aaranya sniffed.

'I have been courteous, nai? To disregard your insults. You mistake this for ignorance.'

Iren pointed his blooded bandage at the Janizar.

'Fuck yourself. You're not Janizar and everyone knows it.'

'*Iren*! Shut your face, so.'

'You can fuck off. I'll take you down, daft cunt. Fucken lot on you.'

Warboys saw drink swilling black and angry in Iren Samsta's eye. He braced himself, took a step toward Bill, ready to make a run for it. Up ahead, Nouzi Aaranya took root, dropping into a low stance, his fingertips a feather-touch on the handle of his dhas, as calm and composed as if he were practising his *Resadem* again.

'*Tchi!*' spat Nouzi Aaranya, and with guttural command, he called Iren to take his footing. '*Dhassama!*'

Warboys looked on in alarm as Iren took out his heavy old warehouse cutter, rocking on his feet. Only bravado kept either from running now. Warboys had seen the like on many drunken nights out, daft lads begging for a beating. He'd done it himself many a time. Daft lads on daft whims.

'*Inshie!*' barked Nouzi Aaranya, sliding forward.

Warboys braced himself. Where he had already seen a remarkable mishap of swordplay, he now saw a moment of violent grace. Samsta strode forth, raising his blade like an axeman. Before he could make his attack, the Janizar stepped clear through him with the smooth, inoffensive step of a ballroom dancer. The *dhas* darkened as Samsta slumped onto his backside, gazing down in horror at the glistening slit across his stomach. He looked from the sticky tips of his remaining fingers to his fellows, then fell flat.

With that one stroke, it was done.

Warboys felt Bill start beside him, and held him firmly as Nouzi Aaranya cast a challenging glare across his audience. The gang lowered their eyes as he paced back and forth, satisfied that they now knew their places. Only then did he clean and sheath his blade.

'Hui. Leave him to the *charya*. Wait with him. Kneel. Don't come near the *Pig* tonight, and learn a lesson from his stupidity. Claim to be Sun-Ivis, eh? *Kitava*.'

He spat. The mob knelt by their fallen fellow, and Nouzi Aaranya strolled over to the Warboys.

'Well now, Captain. Let us move on, nai?'

Bill lingered, watching the funereal scene, and had to be ushered on. As Nouzi Aaranya fell back into step, he immediately seemed composed again, as if they'd just come from tea in the park and not an execution.

'There you go,' muttered Warboys. 'There's your *decent lad*.'

Some time later, they came to a collapsed square where an orphaned bell tower stood. The Janizar stopped, and emitted a sharp whistle. Warboys saw a lookout move in the tower, and two more Blacklanders – painted with the crescent – emerged from archways to either side. The Warboys were shoved across the square, through to another cobbled row, which ended at an ancient looking building built into the city's north wall. An archway overlooked by two turrets was marked with a sign, identifying it as *The Sunken Pig*.

A pub.

They went inside, where a stone staircase dropped unexpectedly down into clammy darkness. Warboys heard Bill's laboured breathing, and regret corkscrewed into his chest. At the bottom, yet more Blacklanders awaited, each face smeared with the mark of the crescent. Nouzi pushed Bill through them to a door on the far side of the vestibule.

'Hui,' Nouzi Aaranya grunted, as the door opened to cast

dull light over Bill. 'Take the old man in there. The Captain stays with me.'

'Where are you taking him? You'd better not hurt him.'

'I'll be alright, son,' came Bill's voice. 'Stay calm. Do as they say.'

Warboys tensed at his restraints, thinly resisting the urge to try and struggle. Then the door closed, gates scraped and clanged, and Bill was gone.

'You would do well to obey your father, eh?' said Nouzi Aaranya. 'Now. You have your time with Uparagha. Use it wisely, eh?'

Another door creaked open and Warboys was shoved through.

14 KING OF THE WANING MOON

The warm, sour hum, and gentle gumminess on the boards below Warboys' boots confirmed that he was indeed in a pub. Lamp light blinded him at first, but Warboys still sensed eyes on him, a pause and presence in the room. He was in a low ceilinged bar lounge, ribbed with dark wood beams and struts. Tankards lined the walls, interspersed with dusty pictures of pig farmers, and heraldry depicting black walled castles.

A solidly built, savage looking young man sat at a table in an alcove, with a quiet air of confidence about him that belied his youth. Though he was more thickset, he was obviously kin to Nouzi Aaranya, with wild black hair, and similarly statuesque, foreign seeming facial features. A scything black tattoo cut through one side of his face. A copy of Malvy's *Dictates I* lay face down on the table before him.

'Sat Nam, Uparagha,' began Nouzi Aaranya, halting Warboys with a pincer grip on his shoulder, before bowing his head respectfully. 'We found two soldiers hiding in the Pits. This one claims he is an officer. Captain Warboys is his name.'

A terse grunt of acknowledgement came in response. Nouzi Aaranya shoved Warboys down onto a chair, opposite. Warboys met eyes dark enough that the pupils were indistinct from the irises, giving Uparagha an alarmingly inky stare.

'Sat Nam, Captain Warboys. I am Uparagha, once Jana Aasvina.'

Behind Uparagha, in alcoves cast into shadow by the glowing hearth, another three Janizar loitered. Sharp foreign faces with all the hospitality of a set of knives. All were dark haired, lean, sinewy and sprung. All half his age.

Warboys felt like a rabbit at the dogs.

'What are you going to do with us?'

'Well, that depends on what is said, nai?' Uparagha held Warboys' eye, as if to gauge his mettle.

Warboys noticed Nouzi Aaranya beside him, seeming no less anxious than Warboys; he looked stiff and awkward, unlike the others. Not daring to let his eyes linger anywhere too long, Warboys' attention wandered to the bar at the back of the room, where a barman with narrow eyes and a dodgy moustache worked at stacking up glasses. A normal Blackhavener by the look of him. These Janizar, it seemed, were indeed supported by the locals.

'Well... any chance of a pint?' Warboys eventually croaked. 'My shout.'

Give them a bit of lip, he thought. *See what they do with it.*

There was a pause, and Warboys felt a stab of regret in his heart, as if those knife like faces were already dissecting it. Then a smile tweaked Uparagha's mouth, splitting into a savage, toothy grin. With a cursory wave, he set the barman to work.

'You're him, aren't you?' said Warboys.

'Am I? Who is he?'

'The...' Warboys waved a finger over his own eye to indicate the crescent tattoo. 'The rebels are all wearing that mark. They call you the *King of the Waning Moon.*'

Uparagha laughed, showing those teeth again. Nouzi Aaranya suddenly flinched. The movement drew Uparagha's eye briefly, but he went on, as if he were used to it.

'Do you speak for your General, Captain Warboys? Or yourself?'

Warboys swallowed. 'To be honest, Malvy's snatched me off the street and slapped a rifle in my hand, so I'm just doing time, mate, same as all of us. I didn't get much say.'

'But you're *Captain*, nai? Does Malvy recruit his officers from street?'

'Look... I may have exaggerated rank a bit. A man has to try and negotiate his status in life, fit a little bit on the side, or else he finds himself dead at the end of his last shift.'

He waited fearfully for a reaction. One of the watching Janizar muttered in distaste.

'Ai,' said Uparagha with an attentive smile. 'Good. Then perhaps we can come to an understanding.'

Warboys nodded gratefully. He sensed it was the wise move to seem game, but even then, with no love lost on Malvy's new regime, he was surprised to feel a bite of shame.

'Go on.'

Nouzi Aaranya's hands jumped suddenly to wrestle with themselves. The faces of the other Janizar soured. Uparagha turned calmly to address him.

'Nouzi-Chai' he said, low and cold. 'Go and rest, ai?'

'Ai,' gasped Nouzi Aaranya. Warboys watched him rise, wondering if there would be nightmares and snakes again. But Uparagha stood and went quickly to his side, his bulky arm enshrouding Nouzi as he escorted him to the door, whispering something close against an ear. Whether it was some intimate reprimand, a forceful encouragement, or something else, Warboys couldn't tell. They were a bit foreign, after all.

Once Nouzi Aaranya had gone, Uparagha returned to his seat.

'Got problems, hasn't he?' said Warboys. 'No offence mate, but I think he's a few whiskers short of a kitten.'

There was a humourless, snorting laugh as one of the Janizar stretched out of his alcove, an outcrop of shoulders like a cliff side, a nose like the upturned prow of a gunship.

'Eh, this kukkura is right, nai? Nouzi Aaranya is a pathetic mess. When will you—'

'Avai, Goro Chai,' Uparagha interrupted, icily. 'I am aware of your opinion. You voice it so frequently and indiscreetly that we have every young knife in Blackhaven taking him for fodder, eh?'

The Janizar Goro grunted, and retreated with a barely perceptible nod of the head.

Uparagha turned back to his guest. 'Avai, Mr. Warboys. Our brother is child of the wilds, nai? Is his Name, given by the Fathers: Aa-ra-ny-a. Means *Wilderness Born*. This cramped-in city closes in on his mind, nai?'

'You're not bloody wrong. I reckon it's squeezed it out of his fucking ears.'

Goro snorted unkindly. Uparagha grinned, overlooking the slight.

'We were raised closely as *Asta*, Mr. Warboys – a brotherhood of eight. We all have our *eccentricities*, nai?'

'Lost some lass back home, has he? This Maia bird?'

Uparagha stared flatly at him, then slapped a palm on the table – making Warboys bowel do a pirouette – and laughed out loud.

'*Bird!* Ha! He misses his *bird*. Ai! Understand, Mr. Warboys. We are from what you call Eldask. We are made differently to people of Aaland, where you drink and copulate at will, dragging offspring through mud behind.'

Warboys opened his mouth to object, but recalled one or two nights out with Cait that matched that very description.

'Where we come from, we are kept from women, and women are secluded – *kardan*, nai? Because the Sekhet decree that Sun-Ivis has no *family*. It is an impractical liability. Breeds worldly attachments. We Janizar are raised to purpose, by nurses in Samagat until the age of six, then removed for training. Before this, our nurses whisper comforting tales, preparing us for those first nights when we lie in our cots with no nurses, tempted to weep and lament them, and shame our brotherhoods with weakness. To prepare us, they point to the stars, to the Maia constellation, and say, there is the heavenly mother of Sun-Ivis, always with us, always watching, and waiting for the day of our return! Look upon heaven, they say, and I will be there. *Maia* will be there.

'Most of us grow out of this, eh? We learn to fight and kill. Bitterness teaches us the lie of it all. Our khus drop, and we are shown the erotic aspect of Maia. We forget *mother* Maia, and begin to crave her in other ways, nai?'

Uparagha made a loose wristed gesture that Warboys understood clearly.

'Is part of maturity, of initiation as we go to our Naming. But some take the loss to heart. Our brother Nouzi Aaranya never overcame the pain of separation. He still thinks of Maia as a child would, not a man. You must view him with understanding, nai? He refuses to see *woman*. To him, there is only Maia, and Maia is truly *Devu*, nai? She is...'

Uparagha paused to lean over and check the definition with one of his brothers. 'Eh, Hazar, how do you say it? Spirit? Ghost? God?'

'Ai,' agreed Hazar, a wolfish Janizar, who fiddled with a paper smoke, not seeing fit to specify any particular one of those words.

'Ai,' smiled Uparagha. 'So kaarya has delivered Nouzi Aaranya a... *unique* path, nai?'

'Well, I'm sure he'll get by.'

The barman cast a derisory look over Warboys as he thumped down a churning pint of dark stout. Warboys frowned – was it not enough he had to brave these murderous Janizar bastards without the fucking landlord angling for him as well?

'Drink then,' said Uparagha.

Warboys watched the settling ale storm about the glass before taking a great, eye-watering swig. It tasted *good*. He sighed, composed himself and met Uparagha's eye.

'In answer of your question – ai. *Yes*. Here they call me the *waning moon*. They have need of me.'

'Not being funny, but do you still expect to hold on to Blackhaven? Even after that bombardment last night?'

'Nai.'

'What do you want, then?'

'All *I* want, Captain Warboys, is the *Gata* to go ahead.'

'What, this festival?'

'Ai. Gata has gone ahead here in secret for hundreds of years. It has always been legend to most of the people here, nai? But when your general sends his dictates to this oppressed people, sends his bans on ritual and public gathering... well then, there is nothing the people then desire so much as to make legend reality, nai? To enact Gata!'

'So you pop up, this legendary Janizar suddenly out from the shadows, and stoke them up nicely.'

'Ai! You have it.'

'So these Sekhet, they perform some ritual do they?'

'Ai. And warding the Sekhet is the work of the Janizar.'

'So are the Sekhet here, then? Upstairs?'

'Nai. They sit dormant, out on the fields, awaiting the time for Gata.'

Warboys scowled, dubious. Fucking lunatic rituals. He reckoned that Malvy's religious bans might be a good thing if they stopped people talking shite like this.

'Avai,' said Uparagha, shaking his head, 'you keep me talking, Mr. Warboys.' He patted the copy of the *Dictates*. 'You are *Modern Soldier*, nai? Don't concern yourself with superstition! Let us get to task.'

Warboys hesitated. He hadn't thought out much of a strategy

for this meeting. Staying alive would do.

'Task?'

'Nouzi Aaranya tells me you and the old man are family. He is *your* father, nai? You must protect him, as we protect our Sekhet.'

Warboys felt his throat tighten in fear.

'Don't involve him...' he choked.

Uparagha reached behind him and placed a sheathed dhas on the table. His eyes fell darkly on Warboys.

'There is an art we practise back home, called *Bijavata*. This means *Seeds to the wind*. Did you know, Mr. Warboys, that a man's head can be cut from his body almost bloodlessly. It can be removed so cleanly that the head will hit the floor a moment before the body feels it. Before the scarlet blossoms fall, nai? This is considered beautiful. Sometimes, practitioners resort to mild sedation to slow the blood pressure of the intended target. The Janizar Luaka – a master of the art – is said to have doped his victims, and sent them barefoot across the meadow before he came for them.'

Warboys dared not say a word. He swallowed hard. Uparagha gauged that he had Warboys' full attention before inclining his head toward the barman. 'Send another drink through for the old man,' he said. Then his eyes fixed on Warboys to watch the threat screw further in.

'You don't need to do this. I'm no Malvyite. We're just soldiers.'

'He won't be harmed. *If* you help me.'

'I'll help you, then. What do you want?'

'You have seen the Tor that overlooks the fields to the north of the city?'

'I know the one.'

'Ai. The Sekhet's rite takes place there. Tonight. Even as we speak, the revellers are gathering.'

'We saw a few tents set out on the way in.'

'By dusk there will be thousands more, on my invitation. Most have little idea what Gata really is, or that the real rite takes place miles away, up on the Tor. They gather for their own reasons, nai? But I want to use this rebel festival as a barrier, to ensure that the rite is uninterrupted.'

'The Colonel won't *let* them gather. Malvy's banned any sort of public gathering. He'll send troops.'

'Ai. I know. I have read this *Dictates*, nai? But I have many supporters. And my special, marked *Sons of Sun-Ivis* are among them, waiting to agitate, ready to engage your troops, so that true Gata can take place at the Tor. I want you to be my agitator on the other side. Help cause riot. Ensure Gata goes undisturbed, away on the Tor. Then you and your father both are free, and Gata is done for another year.'

'That's it?'

'Ai. Malvy can have his city and his port, and his war in the south if he wants it.'

'That's why you took the city? As a distraction? What about all your sons of Sun-Ivis? They seem to think they're at war with Aaland.'

'Avai,' shrugged Uparagha, dismissively, 'they will have had their Gata, nai? Their moment of rebellion. They can do it all again next year!'

Warboys wondered if there was more to this than Uparagha was letting on. He rubbed his face, thinking over the practicalities.

'It could be a right stinker to get done. All those people. What if it doesn't work?'

Uparagha smiled, eyes black and humourless.

'*Seeds to the wind*, Mr. Warboys. I'm sure you'll do your best.'

Warboys fought down frustration at the thought of Bill trapped here, guarded by those angry, crescent smeared lunatics. But he'd gotten the old man into this, in a round about way, and he'd get him out. There *was* a way out. That was what mattered.

'You'll let him go after Gata's done? On your honour and all that?'

'Ai. My word.'

'Unharmed?'

'Ai. I swear by mother Maia.'

Warboys thought it strange that Uparagha should swear on the name of Maia, after seeming to deride her as Nouzi Aaranya's fairy godmother. He wondered just how sacred Maia was to the man before him, and if his word meant anything at all.

'I'll do it, then,' he said, and took a moment's refuge in the last of his pint, draining every last frothy drop before slamming the glass down on the table.

I'll do it, you fucking arseholes.

There was nothing else for it.

15 TEA

Nouzi Aaranya sat cross-legged on the floor of his quarters, beneath a thin veneer of meditation. The room was dark but for a smoky wedge of light coming in from a small, cracked window. A tray lay beside him, arranged with a fine tea set. A fragrant green blend steamed up into the light, the last wisp of home, at odds with his surroundings. Upa's so called *Sons* – it rankled him that these Blacklander louts should claim the name of Sun-Ivis – loitered outside in the yard, their tobacco and murmuring only the closest of many distractions. Distant yells came from the soldiers now renovating the AEC, and somewhere an agitated dog yapped.

Nouzi Aaranya watched the silken steam and withdrew into himself, cast himself back home. Recalling the humid air, the bone deep warmth of the jungle.

You have to go now, little one.

Her voice he could remember as if it were yesterday, a soft chime in the dark. The kiss of breath on his ear. The smell of jasmine and fear. But, try as he might, he couldn't remember her face. He'd been five years old on the day of separation, and all he could recall of her face was the unwelcome glare of daylight on one cheek.

He closed his eyes, and put himself back in Maia's arms.

~ ~ ~

'You have to go now, little one.'

Nouzi Aaranya held tightly to his Maia, nuzzled against her body, listening to the thud of her heart through the midnight coloured fabric of her *dhapa*.

Taking a resolute breath, she lifted him up, carrying him through the nursery archway and down the corridor. Lamplight shimmered along the walls, illuminating the minute script of the Datyas etched there. The echoes of the other boys rebounded as they came from other passages, sobbing, whispering with their own Maias. This confirmation that separation was really happening shot panic through Nouzi.

'I don't want to go!' he moaned, writhing until she was forced to set him down. 'I'm staying here with you.'

She indulged him one last moment. Squeezed him. Over her shoulder, he saw the dizzying vaults of the Samagat's ceilings. Pillars and archways segmented the void above, channelling light and dark in angular floods, each surface overwhelmed with the scrawl of the Datyas. And there, over it all, hung the pyramidal ceiling that had been his lifelong firmament. Apart from visits to the secluded nursery gardens, these four vast, triangular planes had been the limits of the sky, the boundaries of his world.

There was a rumbling sound, and at the furthest edge of the vestibule, at the end of the world, a searing thread of daylight now appeared.

The end of *his* world.

Maia knelt, prising him firmly away to set him at arm's length. He was forced to meet her eyes a moment...

Through his meditation, Nouzi Aaranya could not picture her face – only the curls of black hair escaping a shawl to frame the vacancy of a face he couldn't recall.

...but the thread of light quickly widened, a blade glaring in his eye.

'I won't like it out there. I want you.'

'Out there, through that gate onto the glade, there are many wonders to see. Remember how I always said I would love to see the Samagat from outside? The emberweed fields! The very stars! *You'll* see them! Aren't you excited about that?'

He winced into the light, wary, wanting to believe her reassurances.

'I want you to come.'

'You know I can't. It is kaarya. You'll have brothers. *Astava*. You must go with them. Grow together into Janizar, eh?'

The other boys flitted past, tailing after the veiled figures of their own Maias. He didn't want to know them.

In the corner of his eye, he recalled, the other Maias' faces wormed, obscured by unsettling squirms of light.

The blade became a doorway, and daylight flooded in, casting long, probing shadows over the assembled boys and their Maias.

She gripped his arm tightly.

'Now. Do you remember what I told you?'

'No!' he snapped, petulantly.

'Three things.'

'No!'

'Repeat them to me.'

He struggled, as if to get away, faltering in the knowledge that getting away was the last thing he wanted. She shook him.

'Nouzi Chai! The first day of the Janizar determines his kaarya. Three things.'

'I don't want to be Janizar.'

'You were *born* to be Janizar, little one. You know this. There must always be Janizar to protect Sun-Ivis. The Sekhet created you, now you must protect them, nai?'

'I don't like the Sekhet,' he said, glancing at the other seven boys hanging from seven shrouded Maias.

'You mustn't say such things. Listen now. Go, and protect Sun-Ivis, eh? Protect... me.'

He paused. For this, he felt a shred of bravery.

He tried to recall her eyes, to hold them in memory. But above her lower lip the face was a scar rent in the air.

'We're only safe because of the Janizar – out there...'

Framed in the gateway by the daylight, a craggy figure stood in waiting, cradling a basket. 'And *they* were all little boys like you, once. And *they* all had three things to remember...'

His arms dropped, sullenly relenting.

'Obey Sukhanava at all times. Accept kaarya when the Father offers it. And...'

His head dropped again.

Maia gripped him, hissing through her teeth.

'In the circle, Nouzi Chai. You hit the other boy. You hit him with all your might and you don't stop until Sukhanava tells you, or you are dragged away!'

'What if he's my friend?'

'He's not. Not any more. You hit him. Ai? Do you hear? The way I showed you.'

'Ai.'

'Ai?'

'Ai.'

Her grip relented then. He saw her hands shaking. She cleared her throat when next she spoke, as if steeling herself for rehearsed words.

'Look to the stars, Nouzi-Chai. To the Maia constellation, where heaven awaits you. If you need—'

'But when can I see *you* again?' he said. At this, finally, the tear burst in her eye.

He knows this because he remembers it – the glint of light, but not the welling along the lashes, nor the eye itself. He can't remember her face.

'When you're a man, little one,' she whispered. 'When you're Janizar. Follow your kaarya, and it will show you the way back.'

'But when will that be?'

'When you're Janizar.'

A breeze came from outside, billowing the skirts of her *dhapa*. The Janizar Sukhanava stood fully on the threshold now, muttering some gruff verse as he scattered the blossoms from his basket, offered by ritual in exchange for the boys. Loose white petals fluttered around Nouzi's feet. He froze in fear, Maia stood back, away from him, her hand melting from his.

Just a step, but it took him to the end of the world. Suddenly he was one among eight nervous orphans. Nouzi watched the blossoms dance, circle pillars, flit away into the gloom. And when he looked back, Maia was gone. A chime of panic sent his heart thumping against his ribs.

'Hui!' growled Sukhanava. 'Come.' Nouzi hesitated, but remembered the first thing: *obey Sukhanava*. They marched from sanctity into the outside. The angular walls were suddenly gone, slanting away beside them as the whole world seemed to *invert* before their eyes – where the pyramid had once been the cover of everything, now it had suddenly receded, drawing away from them and up, into a cold, smooth apex. Its black, glossy walls reflected the uproar of the surrounding forest, and a new world blazed at Nouzi's senses – the bone deep heat and humidity at his skin, the earthy, perfumed scents bursting at his lungs, the lush green assault of the jungle smothering almost everything. Some beast ululated in the distance, and Nouzi staggered, feeling that this new world would swallow him.

With quiet gruffness, Sukhanava assembled them in the grasses before the Samagat. In the light of day he was a stony old Janizar, stiff against the breeze. He stood with his arms behind his back, grey hair strangely delicate against the rock of his face. Not a cruel expression exactly, but a cold one. A *necessary* one, and the sight of it made Nouzi afraid. He scanned the other boys, looking for one he recognised, for something to anchor his nerves. He saw only one – a taller, cross looking boy at the fore; Nouzi thought his name might be Kai. A dumpy, sickly looking boy stumbled near, and Nouzi recognised him – everyone recognised him, for his birthmark: a crescent-shaped scar through the eye. The mark of weakness, they said. The sickly boy seemed to implore him with wet black eyes just before vomiting violently, and for a moment Nouzi thought to move away, towards Kai. But he didn't. Having stumbled down into the grasses with a sob, the sickly boy pawed at Nouzi, taking a painfully tight grip on his hand.

'I'm scared,' he sobbed, quietly.

'Me too,' he whispered. 'What's your name?'

'Upa... Upa.'

'I am Nouzi.'

Nouzi's grip tightened on Upa's hand, and Upa's shaking trembled through them both. Then Sukhanava appeared over them, raising the fine whipping stick that they would come to know all too well, and severed their joined hands with a sharp crack.

'These are your brothers in arms now! Not your hand holding friends. An enemy overcome is more to Janizar than a friend retained. Remember this. Now. Come with me. *Inshie*! We go now to present you to the Fathers. Inshie! Move now!'

Nouzi and Upa were jolted into action. They followed like ducklings, down the trail, into the chaos of leaves and vines, away from Heaven. Upa snivelled behind him, whilst Kai took the lead behind Sukhanava. A lightning blue dragonfly zig-zagged erratically across Nouzi's path.

Sukhanava marched stiffly to a clearing where a circle of standing stones thrust from the undergrowth. He stepped forth, bowed low, seeming to mutter greeting to nothing but the canopy above, then ushered the boys in before withdrawing.

They edged into the clearing, and looked up. From a precarious perch at the top of the tallest stone a naked, emaciated figure loomed over them, bent double with the weight of unruly coils of matted hair that swung like loosened entrails. His eyes were a gleam in shadow.

This was Tetso the Stylite, a Sekhet father who had been there for as long as anyone knew. Though Nouzi had been raised to fear the Sekhet Fathers, this was the first time he or any of his new brothers had seen one. He seemed appalling, and yet Nouzi locked eyes on him in fearful fascination.

'Today is the eighth day of Aasvina,' came Tetso's voice, deep and sinuous like the tearing roots of a tipping tree. 'And so formed, you eight are now known as the Asta Jana Aasvina. Now, look, and look only once—'

He raised his hand to point back to the black pyramid of the Samagat, barely visible above the jungle. From here the view of the sky was vast, and Nouzi stared at the mountain of cloud that coiled over the Samagat, blue and white, tinged with pink, bruised depths with storms brooding. As they looked, this vortex seemed to pull twines of vapour from the clouds around it, and these in turn spanned the sky in all directions, following the stones that marched in lines through the jungle. Later he'd learn of the *Mahagat*, the great conduit of power focussed here through the Samagat; about the lines of power that purified the Janizar bloodline, strengthening them for their kaarya. In a dizzying moment, Nouzi imagined that he was tumbling toward that black triangle as if it were a hole in the ground. It seemed alien, now. He staggered, but Upa held him steady.

'Heaven is ever behind you,' said the Sekhet. 'Yet, ever ahead of you. See the work of Sun-Ivis! See the lines we draw back here, though sky and breath and stone. Creation originated in the Samagat, so all things must one day return! And so it will pass with you, Jana Aasvina.

'Mother Maia is behind you. Now you will learn to be Janizar.

Learn to protect Sekhet as we gather here these Lines. Soon they will ripen. Soon we will reclaim this world in a final blossoming, and you who stand to become Janizar will be the spearheads of our last effort. Ai. So then. Do you accept this kaarya, Javani?'

For a moment, though he didn't know the word at the time, Nouzi had felt resentful. What other answer could he really give? But he remembered Maia. The second thing.

Accept kaarya when the Father offers it.

'Ai,' droned Nouzi, along with the others, just as they had all been taught, 'we accept kaarya.'

The Stylite nodded appreciatively, as if he were enjoying the scent of sweaty fear emanating from the children below. Nouzi risked a glance at the Stylite's groin, his appalling sexlessness. This was supposed to make the Fathers inviolate, yet the boy had felt a stab through his own *khus*. Disgust, awe perhaps, something else that he didn't yet understand.

'Good. Go now with Sukhanava. He will teach you well. I will be waiting here, for those who return as *men*, to honour you with Names. Then – you will bring your seed to Maia.'

Nouzi stood shocked, giddy with the knowledge that he could do something to get back to her. What were these seeds? Could he find them in the forest perhaps, and come back sooner? He opened his mouth to ask, but Sukhanava ushered them away again. Nouzi glanced back, and the Sekhet seemed to hone in on him, the eyes just glints in the shadow of his tresses.

Sukhanava led the boys on a long trek, until they came to a clearing cushioned with leaf-litter. There, he stood the boys in a circle facing one another, and scrutinisied them. With a grunt, he picked out Kai.

'Hui!' he grunted, ushering Kai into the circle. 'In this circle, there are no friends, nor brothers. Only you and your enemy, ai?'

'Ai!' snapped Kai, a frown splitting his forehead up the middle. Then Sukhanava whirled around, his finger hovering over Upa before hooking Nouzi into the circle. As Nouzi stepped into the circle, seeing Kai's nasty sneer, he felt he might vomit.

Hit the other boy, came Maia's warning. But the warning made him think of her, a sudden painful yearning for those soft folds, the beat of her heart.

Kai edged up to him, that stupid frown still halving his forehead. Hit him. *With all your might.* And suddenly he felt a rage that surprised him. A sudden willingness to strike, that had always been there in hiding. He could do it. *Hit him.* Nouzi raised his fist.

Then Kai was filling his vision, and barely seemed to move before Nouzi felt a blow rupture his cheek. He'd been too slow. He'd barely had chance to fall to his knees before another came, and another, and he was there in the damp leaf litter, his whole being throbbing with outrage, shame and shock. Moments later, Sukhanava was hauling Kai away, leaving Nouzi to sob in the mush. Sobbing inconsolably even throughout the other bouts that Sukhanava ordered, not for pain, but because Maia was gone, heaven was gone, and there was no one to run to anymore.

He could barely make out the Janizar's barked command as the brothers Jana Aasvina, now blooded to the competition that would define their upbringing, were ordered to follow Sukhanava to their new home.

It was only when Nouzi felt a hand take hold of his that his grief abated. A soft hand in his. For a moment, he let himself believe it was his Maia. But the hand hauled him up, and there he found Upa, as puffy eyed and frightened as he. Sukhanava led the way, and out of sight, at the back of the procession, the two runts clung tightly to one another.

~ ~ ~

The door opened, and Nouzi Aaranya's eyes flashed open, hand rushing to his dhas. He sighed and relaxed when he saw Uparagha, who quietly leaned against the door to seal it. Outside, the dog barked itself hoarse.

'Samsta's dog,' said Uparagha. 'It thinks he is here still.'

Thinking of Iren Samsta and his episode earlier that day, Nouzi Aaranya dipped his head ruefully.

'Avai, this place is riddled with dogs, eh?' said Uparagha, gently. 'Filthy *kukkura*. In Gienha we would shoot them or train them but here they run wild, yapping, shitting and pissing, and sniffing each other's *khus*.'

Nouzi Aaranya took a deep breath.

'It is the bombs. They haven't stopped barking since those booms at the gate. The walls stand tight, sprung. The slabs seethe below our feet. The dogs sense the change in the air and it unsettles them.'

Uparagha settled with him on the floor, mirroring his posture a bow's distance away.

'Are you calm now, Nouzi-Chai?' The use of the informal, affectionate term *chai* did well to ease Nouzi's nerves.

'Ai, Upa-Chai,' he responded, venturing to return the gesture for the first time in what seemed an age. Upa smiled.

'Good. You look like *Sekhet*, sitting *sanyas* on the floor like that, listening to the Lines. Don't you like the comfort of modern furnishings?'

'*Furnishings*. They are clutter. All this place is clutter. I think the bombs have improved it.'

'Perhaps,' laughed Uparagha, 'if you tried one of the beds, you might gain your sleep. I don't think you've slept since we left Gienha.'

'How could I sleep, eh? Gutters crack and timbers creak. Every sound seems to be that of a gun-shot. Twice I have nearly sprung dressed from this embroidered cocoon they call *bed* and gutted the servant, eh? Sliced the cat in half!'

Uparagha laughed, and Nouzi Aaranya leaned to lay the tea set between them. He prepared the cups, poured, and presented one to Uparagha, bowing with both hands. Braving Uparagha's fond, cynical smile, he sipped.

'The ritual of tea. Order in the chaos, nai?'

'Ai.'

'Sukhanava would be proud.'

'Not proud,' said Nouzi Aaranya, and Uparagha joined him in amending, '*satisfied.*'

Nouzi Aaranya managed another fleeting smile, until he felt Uparagha studying him.

'It happened again, eh? The terrors.'

Nouzi Aaranya's confession blurted out.

'Ai. I lost composure, Upa-Chai. This place is smoke and dark and menace. I feel flawed. I feel eyes on me. I feel as if I am falling. Still falling, ever since the day we left Maia and Heaven, and hitting rocks all the way down.'

'Nai, brother...'

'After all we went through in those twelve years since leaving the Samagat, I failed. I have my own lack of resolve to blame.'

'Lack of resolve? Avai, I never knew a man so resolute in his will to torture himself! Look at me, eh? I see, and have always known your talent, and strength. The Sekhet will see it also. Your chance will come, Nouzi-Chai.'

'You are too kind, and too loyal. Forgive my self pity, Upa-Chai.'

Upa merely nodded his head, a slow smile.

'Remember what Sukhanava taught? An enemy overcome is more than a friend retained.'

'Ha!' spat Uparagha. 'Sukhanava said many things. You are too hard on yourself. This has worked out well. These War-boys were *your* capture. *Your* decision. They will prove very useful.

With their help the Gata will succeed, and the Sekhet will see your worth.'

'I worry, Upa-Chai. These *crowds* you have amassed! We have always worked in shadow, yet the Sekhet will rise this year to find an army of followers! Outlanders, calling themselves the *sons* of Sun-Ivis!'

'There are traces of our blood here in the Blacklands. The people here have always been loyal to us.'

'Perhaps. But these wretches are our descendants as piss is the descendant of wine.'

'The Sekhet have their eye on the last days, nai? They gather their Lines, whilst we see to defence. Is kaarya, as has always been. Don't worry, Nouzi-Chai. Your kaarya is coming soon, I promise. The War-boys are not the only thing the Aalanders left behind, eh? I have use for your talent in the days to come.'

Nouzi Aaranya did not share Upa's exuberance. The worry weighed on him that all of this would not lead him back to Maia. He sighed. Then Uparagha abruptly swept the tea set away and laid a rough hand on Nouzi Aaranya, fingers grasping his hair. Nouzi Aaranya bowed his head, knowing he should be quiet now. Upa slid himself up close.

Nouzi Aaranya knew it was coming, as it always did when Upa came smiling and kind with counsel. He felt the hot proximity of his breath, the outcropped muscle of Uparagha's shoulder. He watched a small teacup roll in an arc, painting a dark scythe across the floorboards, saw the head of Uparagha's *khus* tentpoling his clothes, helped hold aside the seams so it could twang unceremoniously out. With a relenting sigh he felt his own rise to join it. Quick and business like, they shifted and set to beating one another's *khus*.

The Destiny of the Janizar Named, thought Nouzi Aaranya, bitterly. Khus jangling like fruit in the autumn wind. Uparagaha's muscle like lead against his bones.

Through the gate onto the glade, there are many wonders to see.

A rush of images came to mind. He saw Maia's hand slipping away on the day they were separated. He felt shame to think of her now. She changed in his mind, as she had continually over time. Late at night, when he'd sobbed in his bed, she'd become a guardian angel. A shape in the stars that he'd talk to when no-one else would listen.

And later another Maia, the one that came with the dropping of his *khus*, and the merciless surge of concupiscence. The Datyas told of this one, a ripe, curvaceous, erotic Maia. He imagined *this* Maia now, her delicate hand beating him off instead of Upa's.

A pearly loop jumped across the muscle of Upa's shoulder, and Nouzi Aaranya gasped hot breaths, felt his cheeks flushing, feeling at once relieved and woeful. Upa followed, grunting and pulling at Nouzi Aaranya's hair as he came.

A silence grew as their breathing evened.

Uparagha stood and sniffed, pulling at his distended khus and stuffing it away before he turned about. He looked at the fading light of the windows, his aspect colder now. Nouzi Aaranya said nothing, lowered his head and waited formally for his departure.

'I think these War-boys will honour us,' Upa said. 'They fear for one another.'

'Are you sure you want to employ *both* of them, Upa-Chai?'

'Ai. They need not know.'

Nouzi Aaranya bowed his head.

'Ai, Nouzi Aaranya,' sniffed Upa, 'your time is near.' And with that he left, closing the door behind him.

At last, Nouzi Aaranya was alone. A lamp had been lit across the street, that guttering, orange light he couldn't quite get used to. He took a deep breath and began replacing the tea set, exactly where it had been laid out before, starting all over again.

16 CONJUNCTION

Uparagha came in person to release Warboys from his cell, and led him down through the flooded cellar of the Sunken Pig, past mouldering casks and racks to a grate that opened into an escape tunnel.

'Is older than the city walls, this place, nai? This passage will lead us onto the fields outside the city.'

Warboys held his rifle clear of the water, wading blindly through the dark. Ahead, Upa's hooded form caught a dim glow as they came to a place where light filtered down through a pothole. Grasping at weeds, Uparagha hauled himself up. Warboys followed, emerging onto a hillock, where golden light caught in the grasses, and music drifted on the wind. Muffled drums kept a constant beat against disjointed fiddling and bursts of rowdy song. Uparagha kept low, and led him to the summit to look down over the festival field.

When Warboys had last looked at the field, there had been a scattering of tents. Now, the sun was setting over a city of canvas. Hundreds of campfires had been set, and crowds moved into the middle of the field, milling around on rabbit tracks that now served as thoroughfares. Jugglers, dancers and food vendors had appeared, banners and weird effigies on poles wagged in the breeze, trailing ribbons and bunting. A man strode along on stilts, his shadow drawing long to the east. From here, Warboys saw the lines of stones circling the fields in swirling lines. Some distance away, the Tor overlooked it all through a cleft in the hills, its pallid white stone glowing in the sunset.

'There,' grunted Uparagha. 'The Tor. Keep your troops away from there.'

'Alright, alright. I know.'

It crossed Warboys' mind suddenly, now that he was in sight of the stones again, to ask Uparagha about the Datyas, but he thought of the old man – and how *stupid* his little quest now seemed – and swallowed it.

'Ai. Good,' said Uparagha, scrambling down the hill toward the crowds. Warboys followed, and at the bottom they joined one of the rabbit tracks. No one seemed to notice them, and they were soon lost in the crowd. Down here, the smell of roasting pork tied Warboys' stomach in knots. More aromas followed: freshly baked breads, the sickly sweet perfume of apple cider, heady smoking weeds.

Warboys scanned for his fellow soldiers, spotting several pairs milling around the fringes of the field, meandering with all the presence of flies on a cow's arse.

'They are waiting on orders from the city,' said Uparagha. 'It won't be long before reinforcements come.' He pointed back toward the black slab of Blackhaven's walls, where columns could be seen mustering.

They passed a circle of young revellers leaning this way and that like reeds in the wind, gathered around a barely dressed masseur who worked his bony fingers into the flesh of a pimply man lying on a fallen slab. Warboys nodded towards the masseur.

'Is that your Sekhet, there?' asked Warboys, only half joking. Uparagha shook his head.

'Nai. These people only *emulate* Sun-Ivis. He only *emulates* what legends there are of the rite.'

'Eh? So the Sekhet are going to rub the arse of the land? To dance and set fires on Malvy's backside and leave bread crusts in his privy?'

Uparagha laughed.

'There are certain contours in the body, nai? Can be smoothed down to increase the flow of blood or shift the knot. Is flow and a system in us, blood and air, bowels and bile.'

'Right... so?'

'So, Sekhet treat the land as same. Water flows and wind blows, and the land churns and changes. Tides, winds and earth, the moons haul at the tides, the sun pulls at the moons. There are channels, flows and systems. Sekhet press these, to irrigate flow, push to right cursus.'

'To the Tor?'

'Ai. And then to the Eldask.'

'How, though? Why?'

Uparagha ignored the queston, and hopped over a turnstile, nodding to a youth on the gate. Beyond, in a clearing around a large bonfire, more marked Sons of Sun-Ivis loitered, all casting things into the fire. Sparks showered down, accompanied by drunken cheers that broke the melodic beat of the festival. Warboys sensed their eyes taking note of Uparagha, wet with awe.

'These are my agitators, nai? When the time comes, work with them. Come to them. *Agitate.* Busy your troops.'

Uparagha marched on, making no effort to stay with Warboys.

'Oi! Wait!'

'Remember, Mr. Warboys. *Seeds to the wind.* If our fathers see out the night, so does yours.'

Warboys hurried after the Janizar, ducking along a row of effigies on tall poles billowing with streamers. Up ahead he saw other, more serene revellers, gathering to entwine a weblike mesh of ribbon around the lines of stones, around themselves, around one another. He scanned the stones for Datyas, but what few unobscured faces there were had been long since worn smooth. Bunting lay trodden in the earth like roots, winding up around pillars to wave in the breeze. Then a woman lolled into Warboys, spilling out of a burnt dress in a drunken twirl. He smiled awkwardly; she laughed and gave him a half smoked rolly and a wet kiss before floundering away. Warboys looked up, unsurprised to see Uparagha had vanished completely.

'Twat.'

Realising he was on his own, he took a drag, quickly taken aback by the strength of it.

'Shitting hell,' he wheezed. 'No wonder the silly bastards have all gone off to the wonderland!'

He suddenly felt nervous without Uparagha, standing there with his rifle and smoke like a dummy. He paced about a bit, unsure, nodding as more revellers came to wind ribbons around everything in sight. He had to wave one or two away to avoid being wrapped himself. They all seemed to be having a great time, not a care in the world, revolution or no. If Bill weren't in danger, with that wisp of weed in his blood, the music, the atmosphere, Warboys could almost imagine having a good time here. He tried to focus, spot other soldiers to orient himself by. Dusk drew on, and fires spiked in the darkness. As the clamour rose across the fields, he began to walk south, back the way he'd come, feeling nerves fizzing in his joints.

Firelight caught on the faces of the crowd as he walked along the rabbit track, and suddenly there came a great cheer from the crowd. A gout of flame silhouetted the mob of agitators, who were now stripped off to the waist, painted with the crescent as they danced around calling glory to Sun-Ivis, and death to Malvy. Warboys saw they'd been roused by a unit of troops that had formed nearby – but, as he approached, it was obvious the troops weren't the full reinforcements. He recognised a sergeant by the name of Mercer, calling the existing patrols together to prepare for the big rout. Crowds of revellers hung on the edge of the fiery clearing, uncertain of what to do as the painted Sons lined up. Warboys took another quick toke, then marched off to join in, feeling airship-light, as if gas were gathering in the top of his skull, lifting his boots from the floor.

Up ahead, Mercer cowered by a fire cart as if it were the last bastion of civilization, his face like an undercooked chicken as he barked orders. Unnoticed, Warboys slipped into the ranks.

'Right, lads!' Mercer was yelling. 'We've orders to hold, ready to sweep the lot of them away when reinforcements arrive. So just form lines, edge them back, nice and steady...'

Warboys joined an awkward forward line against the fire-eyed Sons. They came whooping and gesturing, pelting stones, but Mercer called for calm, and somehow, with the greater mass of the crowds hanging back, the line held. Thunder grumbled above, and Warboys looked back south to see reinforcements arriving under Malvy's banner, hundreds of riflemen marching up from the city walls.

At this, the onlookers began to move away, and Warboys cursed. If the reinforcements scared off the crowd, the Sons would never hold them back, and the troops would just charge through the festival and straight toward the Tor. The Sons edged forward, pelting more boldly now, but still Mercer would not be goaded. Warboys cast about, looking for inspiration. To the left of the bonfire, a wild violin started, its whine seeming to dart in and out of the drums. With it, a man with a painted face came screaming through the crowd.

'The Blackland is a crucible!' he yelled, fiddling coarsely between announcements. 'And it will burn! In the flame, and in the fall, we become one with the heavens!' He was drawing attention to himself, drawing folk north.

The first reinforcements were almost here now. He had to act, or this was a lost cause. Seeing his moment, Warboys broke rank. Another rumble of thunder shook the air as he shoved through the bystanding revellers toward the painted fiddler. Quickly, Warboys shouldered into him, and his chanting halted with an abrupt note.

'Fucking bogtrotter scum!' yelled Warboys, watching the poor sap stumble to the ground. 'Get down!' He lunged in with the butt of his rifle, then snatched away the fiddle and stamped hard on it. The sickly note seemed to sour the crowd, and they closed in, separating him from his fellow troops.

'Stop there!' he yelled, pointing his Entwick at them like an idiot. 'Halt, or I'll shoot!'

The column of reinforcements was almost upon them, tightening the crowd, increasing the pressure. Then a wild eyed Son charged and slammed into Warboys. He fired high. There was a sharp crack, a scream, and the Sons charged, the crowd with them. Warboys hit the mud, jarred by painful jabs to his side. Managing to swipe his Entwick across his assailant's skull, he rolled off through the muck. The oncoming 45th arrived, seeing the affray had already begun, and plunged without warning into the crowd, steel tipped Jonahs hammering down. What bystanders remained joined in out of outrage. Stones flew and waves of men shoved and heaved at one another. Warboys shouldered his way through the chaos, striking randomly at anyone in his path. A stray globule of liquid slapped his cheek, then another, and seconds later the air was alive with heavy rain. Around him, the fires guttered. Bodies slick with mud writhed and fought.

Warboys scrambled away. He'd done as much as he could here, and if this Gata was to go ahead, he was going to see the fucking thing for what it was.

Ignoring the chaos in his wake, he ran toward the field of tents, where rain clattered loudly on canvas, as if applauding the chaos. One tent shivered as a couple humped inside, the soles of dirty feet sticking out, toes clawing in the soil. Warboys snatched up a hooded jacket from the mouth of the tent, walked a little further, then kicked at another tent to see if it was empty. Diving in to strip off his coat and pack, he changed into the jacket and hauled up the hood. Then he bundled up his pack and rifle and stashed them under the groundsheet before making north for the Tor, leaving the riot raging behind.

Rain sliced the field into sizzling diagonal lines. Those who had avoided the fighting trickled over the lip of the hill into the field of the Tor, dragging a train of filthy ribbons and bunting over the hills. Some wound themselves up in it, others dragged trains of their own. Warboys fell in with them, snatching up a stray length of bunting to look the part. He helped his face to a handful of mud, just to help disguise him, should anyone be looking, and hurried to find the head of the train.

Uparagha led the procession, a wasted, elderly figure on his arm, veiled like a weak old lady. This, Warboys figured, must be the Sekhet. He didn't look like much, seeming barely conscious, and somewhat baffled as he peered over Upa's arm at the parade.

The Tor loomed, and the stragglers congregated around it, standing by one of the many barrows that circled the mound like numerals on a clock. Warboys spotted the two Janizar Goro and Hazar standing sentry nearby, and ducked his head.

Uparagha let go of the elder and stepped away. The gaunt figure teetered a moment, and tatty shrouds slipped away to reveal his sexless nakedness, with only a few wisps of hair framing the skull. The Sekhet suddenly took on an eerie stillness, as if he himself were a standing stone.

Suddenly, Warboys understood that the train of ribbons was symbolic. That it represented the Lines that Uparagha had mentioned. But he could feel something else here as well, something borne through that decrepit frame. Something that drew the hairs up from his skin, and lit the air with life.

The Sekhet took a quick breath, spreading his ribs, and what few torches and lamps remained blinked out suddenly. Warboys looked about in alarm. He saw Uparagha make a deferential bow before presenting a phial to the Sekhet, who promptly necked the contents. In moments, he collapsed, shuddering in the earth of the barrow, muttering unintelligible babble. Then, with a grunt from the Janizar, the audience descended upon their elder, Sons and revellers alike, and began to bury him, connecting those lines and ribbons – and whatever power that frail pile of skin and bones wielded – into the hill.

Around him, the silence lingered. Warboys saw Uparagha look up at the sky, then vanish into the dark. There were cries of alarm, and Warboys followed the gaze of the crowd to see an old barrow mound shudder. It shed a few mossy rocks, then the pile collapsed, and a second, emaciated Sekhet forced himself up from within, caked in rotten cloths. Rain streamed down a haggard face, and Warboys shuddered at what seemed to be a risen corpse. This Sekhet hauled himself out, his bony shoulders pocked with pits of shadow as he turned to face his audience. The crowd took a step back. He growled at them, tipping his head as if to shake off a fly – and Warboys felt the earth jolt below him. As one, the crowd fell to the floor, and screams of panic began. Wind and rain howled around the Tor. Stunned revellers backed away. Some fled cheering maniacally, others screamed or wept. Still others clung to the soil for refuge. The Sekhet ignored them all, and began to climb the Tor. Instinct told Warboys to run. He stayed put. An ominous pressure was building in the air, and Warboys looked up to see a low black cloud bulging like a fat gut. In that second, the Sekhet reached the peak of the Tor, and raised an arm.

The cloud spewed a fine white line of lightning, striking the Elder and flowing through him, into the Tor. The mess of ribbons were incinerated in a moment, scattering sparks and cinders.

Thunder boomed, so loud that Warboys fell to the ground stupefied. Heat bubbled from below as steam curled up through the soil. Another, more distant flash of lightning silhouetted the Tor briefly, and Warboys saw the Sekhet, still mounted up there like a withered conductor rod, and still *moving*.

A crushing sensation closed around his head, and for a split second he saw the pattern: felt the *Lines* themselves, rushing through the Sekhet, into the Tor and through the earth; trees and rocks herding them, a great relay of energy coming from all around, all of it bound for the Eldask. Wind rushed northward, force flowing in from every point of the compass, as if the Eldask were the plughole in a sink. Warboys sensed a great, abyssal void, drawing everything home. He felt himself falling, drawn towards this void in a sinkhole that enveloped everything.

He sat up, gasping in panic.

Dawn was already greying the horizon. Hours had passed. The air had changed, its charge gone. The rain had stopped. There was quiet. Fog obscured everything. All the revellers and Sons were gone, and the rioting on the southern field was long done. He heard a voice, and peered up to see the withered, charred Sekhet stumbling exhaustedly down the side of the Tor, scanning around. Warboys stayed in the mud, playing dead. The skeletal frame juddered off, and Warboys saw the silhouettes of the Janizar arrive to meet him, their breath clouding in the cold. Uparagha stood before the Sekhet, and bowed.

Warboys couldn't understand the language, but the guttural bite of his foreign speech chopped at Warboys' ears, leaving no doubt the Sekhet was not pleased. Uparagha bowed again, held up his hands in placation, lifted his head to try and get a word in, but the Sekhet raged on, driving Uparagha back to his knees. For a moment, Uparagha remained there, panting as the Sekhet passed him by, heading north towards the Eldask.

Then, Warboys saw rage sour Upa's face before he arose deftly in pursuit of his master. Moments later, he passed over the hill and out of sight. The sound of raised voices quickly faded away.

Warboys waited, holding his breath. He'd seen something here, something *arcane*, he supposed the word was. Sun-Ivis, *real* Sun-Ivis, dealt in more than dirty ribbons and etchings in stone. He cursed his stupidity. Regretted even more the fanciful search for the Datyas that had led him here, and a sudden, aching worry for the old man arose in his chest. He turned and slithered back the way he'd come, grateful to be away into the mist.

17 DIDDLED

The 45th had all but scattered the revellers by the time Warboys found the tent where he'd stashed his gear. Mist continued to roll in, making ghosts of the soldiers as they picked over the fields, arresting stragglers and scavenging the remains of abandoned tents. He'd only just managed to fumble into it as troops neared, and he moved on nonchalantly, hoping no one would challenge him. Then he spotted Jacky Biel standing around whilst some other soldiers rifled tents. Cursing, Warboys lowered his head, hoping the gangly shit wouldn't see him. It didn't work.

'Ey up! You pop up and fuck off like a good fortune you do, Warboys.'

Warboys grunted, made to edge past.

'Here, you were a bit heavy handed back there, weren't you?' Biel called after him. 'Started a fucking riot there, you did. But I never saw sign of you when we had to close ranks to push the fuckers back...'

'You want to talk, Biel,' snapped Warboys, turning back despite himself. 'Where the fuck did you go when we charged the walls the night before last?'

'I fell back,' said Biel, patting at his leg. 'Pulled my knee just before we went into that churchyard.'

'Lucky for you.'

'Yah, fuck off Warboys. You ain't no hero. I thought we was rid of you when your old man rolled in on his own last night.'

'What? What did you say?'

'Signed in last night. Reckoned he'd got lost in the Pits.'

'You sure about that?'

'You can't mistake the old git, once he gets a-chuntering about summat. Strolled right in and got given gaol duty, straight away. Fucking tea and crumpets duty that is. One of you two bumming an officer, or what?'

Warboys turned without another word, and rushed for the city gate.

A trudging column congested Blackhaven's main road, troops yawning whilst Warboys shoved his way through. As he sped up the stretch overlooking the Pits, Warboys picked out the stranded bell tower Nouzi Aaranya had taken them past on the way to the *Sunken Pig*. He'd been expecting to have to find it on his own, but if what Biel said was right, he might be saved the bother. Had the old sod managed to escape? Could a patrol have raided the place and freed him?

The AEC loomed overhead, the red and black banner still flying high. Warboys scanned the complex, looking for his dad among the sheds and warehouses separating the surrounding yards. A bridleway led around to the reservoir, where the reflection of moored airships shimmered across the water. There on the opposite bank, a makeshift hangar and landing strip was set up. Finally, Warboys reached the check point. A clerk looked up from his ledgers.

'Name?' sighed the clerk.

'Warboys, W.K.'

'Alright. Go in.'

'Hang about. Do us a favour, mate. I went over the wall with a feller night before last. Went missing in the Pits. Can you look him up for us?'

'Name?' sighed the clerk.

'Warboys, W.E.'

Warboys stood tensely whilst the clerk's hands slid across

the pages of his ledgers.

'I've got a W.E. Warboys in for gaol duty last night. Volunteered.'

'You what?'

'You heard me. The gaol on Riverside. Lots of dissidents to process, you know. Good work for your older VIPs.'

Biel had been right. Warboys wondered if he'd had his senses slapped out of him by the bombs, and the last few days were a hallucination.

He backed away from the office, narrowly avoiding a cart horse, too bewildered to exchange insults with the driver. Tiredness suddenly weighed on him, and he traipsed along the bridleway, watching the airships reflected in the reservoir. Work gangs hung off the backs of carts and yelled across barges. Off duty men loitered on the canalside, others hanging over the balcony overlooking the Pits. Things seemed almost normal.

He saw Bill.

The old man stood against the cornerhouse wall, smoking, casual as you like. Then Bill's smoking hand faltered, and the two started toward one another. Warboys was suddenly taken back to his youth, a tear in his eye, just like the days when Bill had first come into view down the gangplank after a long trip to sea. There he was, the old sod, with his springy hair and his daft 'tache.

They met on the bridleway. Bill's eyes scanned up and down his son, concern giving him a doddery look as he threw an arm about Warboys.

'Bloody hell, son... I'm glad to see you.'

Warboys' frown gave way as they embraced in earnest for the first time he could remember in years. Bill pounded his back. 'Are you alright, son? They treat you alright?'

'I'm alright, but...'

A cart clattered by, full of labourers sending them wolf

whistles.

'Give us a cuddle, darlin'!' yelled one.

'Yah, piss off!' growled both the Warboys, turning in unison. Bill sniffed and backed off the bridleway toward the canalside. He set to rolling a smoke from his tin to contain his shaking, and that was their emotional reunion done.

Warboys stared bewilderedly at his dad. He still looked peaky, and carried bags under his eyes. 'Dad, what happened? Did you get away?'

'No, they... Wait, when did they let *you* go?'

'What are you on about? I've been...' Warboys looked over his shoulder to make sure no one was in earshot before lowering his voice. 'Uparagha sent me out to that bloody festival as a plant. Wanted me to stir up a bit of bother so they could get with their business.'

'Aye, I reckon you'd be good for that.'

'Dad! Uparagha made out as if he was going to keep you. You know, as assurance, like.'

'Funny enough,' laughed Bill, exhaling smoke, 'that's what he told me about you.'

'Fucking *bastard*...'

'We've been diddled, son. They brought me out to Upa-doo-dah not long after he'd seen you. Soon as I set eyes on that black-eyed bastard I thought, I wouldn't trust you as far as I could throw you. But what could I do?'

'So what did he get you to do?'

'Ah, never mind that, son.'

'*Dad!* I'm glad you're alive and that, but you're getting on my bloody nerves already. You said you wouldn't try and protect me any more, so just tell me!'

Bill waited until a barge passed, nodding to the crew who stood ready for mooring.

'He knew the old timers were getting on gaol duty. He wanted me here in the gaol. Wanted a man out.'

'You bust a man out? Shitting hell, father...'

'Alright, shut it. This gaol is like a bloody dungeon. The previous administration had one big room and one record book, everybody stuffed in together, and a lot of sorting out to do. So the Colonel gets in and says, nope, we need 'em processing properly. We need to weed out dissidents, all these Sun-Ivises and such, so he can decorate the square with them for show. So they all had to be sorted and moved. Bloody chaos it was. Wasn't hard to slip this bloke out. I'll not get caught.'

'Who was he?'

'Well, that was something. Posh bloke, it was. Not local. Very civil, and expecting me. Knew what to do and all. I escorted him out and down the lane to our little mate Nouzi—'

'God help him.'

'Yah, he's alright, I tell you. Anyway, this prisoner gent thanked me, gave me a salute, like. Had a little black flower tattooed on the knife of his palm, there. So I looked him up in the ledger when I went back. It was only Jombrey Valego! Do you remember him? Jombrey Valego?'

'No.'

'Mebbe you was at sea, then. Before all this air division nonsense, some showmen did a test flight over Coperny Bay, just for a spectacle, like, on the King's birthday. The first manned floater, they said. No engines or owt, no revolution. Just the balloon and a bucket. It got about twenty yards up before the whole thing dumped into the sea. A right joke.'

'So what?'

'Jombrey Valego was the test pilot.'

'Why would he be in Blackhaven?'

'Well, he was a favourite of the king. He might have escaped south and hid here when Malvy took over. He wouldn't be the only one.'

'Why's Uparagha helping bloody royalists though?'

'I don't know, son, and I don't want to know.'

'You sure you ain't been rumbled, Dad?'

'Positive, son. Here, have a smoke. You must be gasping.'

Warboys couldn't refuse.

'Saw some bloody sights at that festival,' he said.

'Oh aye? What were they doing out there then? Sacrificing chickens? Burning effigies of the Great General? Just having a laugh, mebbe? That'll be illegal next...'

'It was more than that...' He faltered, unsure how to explain what he'd seen. The thought of that emaciated figure brought a shudder. 'Listen though. I've been an arsehole. This Datya business... I've seen enough. Any luck, that Uparagha'll be up and off now, and I just want to say that I'm washing my hands of it all. You were right, and I was wrong. Delusions of grandeur. You were right. And I'm sorry I got you into this.'

Bill scanned him with suspicion that softened into concern. 'I think you might need a bit of sleep son. I know I do.'

Warboys opened his mouth, surprised not to have provoked more reaction, but too weary to object. They walked along the reservoir wall some more until the AEC loomed again.

'I never thought I'd feel so glad to come back to pile of mucky bricks like that. We're lucky to be alive, you know.'

'I know. How's your hearing?'

'Pardon?'

'Silly sod.'

'I'm alright son. Just a bit of ringing left. Here, I hope they've got a working laundry. I must have shit my pants about six times since the night before last.'

He snorted, and nudged Warboys, and they laughed – but Warboys still saw the ghost of fear in his eye.

'You alright, Dad?'

'I'm alright. I was just thinking. It's good you got away. Malvy himself would be down here if it got out that the legendary *Captain* Warboys was compromised.'

'Don't start. Worked didn't it? We survived.'

Bill gave him a playful nudge. 'I reckon it's survival that counts at times like these, eh?'

'Can't enjoy much without a drop of survival.'

Warboys leaned over the wall as they walked. The river ran in a trickle along the gorge, with the rest of the city clamouring at its edges as it opened up toward Conlo Bay.

'Feel that bloody breeze,' sighed Bill. 'It feels different, does the Eastern sea. You can feel the dust in it.'

'Listen, Dad. I mean it. I'm sorry. And I'm going to get us out of this.'

'Yah, give over. You ain't got a thing to do for me, kid, 'cept live to tell the tale. You'll soon get to ponderin' on your bloody uncharted territories again. Then you can go find your own bloody wonderland, eh? Had mine. Lost mine years ago when your mother died.'

Warboys saw that Bill's eyes had moistened up some, and it started to pinch at his own.

'Don't start that again...'

'No, listen. We got each other through alright. Fact is, we're here now. And I'll tell you what, if we can get through this, it might mean those bairns back home might not have to. You can give them that at least.'

Warboys slapped his arm gratefully about the old man's shoulder and they staggered back towards the AEC together, in search of some sleep.

18 THE LAST WONDER

The landing boat came scraping into the shingle of the cove, amidst the clattering of carts and the yarping of seagulls overhead. Warboys vaulted over into the surf with the tow line.

'Right, you land-lubbing wankers!' screamed the pilot, slapping down into the waves. 'You got yourselves a half hour! Then get your arses back o' the queue for the next load!'

Warboys stood panting as more soldiers tumbled over the bow. Bill staggered, gasping as he waded up the beach, turning about to survey the object of their labour.

Framed by the jagged pincers of the cove, the *Tower of Havery* was a hazy grey slab across the sea. After an abrupt collapse of resistance following the Gata, the Colonel had executed several known ringleaders of the Sons, and officially outlawed Sun-Ivis. With Uparagha nowhere to be found, a death sentence was formally placed on him, should he ever turn up. Posters were plastered around to these effects.

Meanwhile, Malvy's war engine was readying to sail south. A convoy of tugs and barges were heading out to load the *Tower* ahead of the mass troop movement down to occupy the peninsula.

'Looks like we'll be off soon, son,' Bill gasped. 'I never thought I'd set sail again.'

'Yeah, alright. Come on, before you start ruminating on the meaning of it all. Let's go see what slop we've got for our dinners.'

A line of sleepers lay like stitching down the beach, leading up to the blackened track that ran away up through

Blackhaven toward the AEC. Along the cliff side, where an old harbourmaster's hut perched, a path ran along the cliff. Two queues formed, one at either side.

'Ey up. It's Barney and Klattersen again.'

At one end, Klattersen, a dour chef with the 45th, fried chipped potatoes in a great cauldron.

'Smell that bloody grease,' snarled Bill.

'It's nice is that. Sticks to your ribs.'

'Yah. Too bloody greasy to stick to owt. Drops right through yer it does. They use his vats on the steamer axles.'

'Give over.'

The two of them craned to compare Barney's stall. Barney was a rotund local, only too happy to sell out to state forces.

'Floured fish again,' said Bill. 'That'll do me.'

'Suit yourself,' said Warboys, and they each parted their ways to line up, idling in their queues, smoking and swearing and letting off wind.

They met again in the middle, pulling faces at one another's choices, and walked up the steps to sit up on the cliff top. A warm breeze waggled the clover heads on the cliff edge, and, up above, seagulls rowed over scraps, diving out of sight only to curl up and around into the cloudless sky. The sun glistened in the bay, almost eclipsing the *Tower* with its shimmer. It was easy to forget the ashen malevolence of Blackhaven lying just behind them.

'I tell you what,' said Bill, breaking a piece of fish away in steaming white flakes, 'it could be nice here. We've got these Modern Endeavours all wrong I reckon.'

'You reckon?'

'Aye. See, imagine it was a nice sunny day and we weren't at war.'

'Go on then. And the Princess of Halshaed is fetching me a pint in her knickers.'

'Imagine you was off work that day, though. None of this bloody mess and engines all over the place. You might roll your trousers up and go for a paddle.'

Warboys nearly laughed his chips out. 'You what?'

'Yeah! It could be lovely here. After the war, I tell you. It's the future.'

'That fish you're eating must've been through an oil slick. It's gone to your 'ead.'

'Shame Barney and Klatters can't get on. This stuff would be nice together.'

'You'll eat owt, you... Here, give us a bit...'

'It's not bad together, is it? Here, we should undercut these daft buggers. *Warboys and Son*. Set up a stall here for when the ladies and children come for a paddle. How's your hand at frying?'

'Here he goes again with the fucking taters!' laughed Warboys.

'Well, it was never the taters' fault, was it? We could go to your mother's grave to ask permission, like.'

Warboys turned, laughing around hot potato. 'You're serious, aren't you?'

'Well it'd be a way of making amends, wouldn't it? Times like this, you've got to think on the future.'

Warboys rolled his eyes, smiling as he thought about it. 'Here, Dad, maybe we could grow some veg out here on the cliff an' all.'

'Nah, you'd never grow owt on this cliff. Too wild. But some of them plots in town would do it. Once you cleared all the rubble and dead bodies out, like. Aye, maybe some nice peas to go with the fish and taters.'

'Peas? In this wind?'

'Well, maybe we could mash 'em up or summat, so they stuck to the plate. I don't know. You can handle that part. If you're good for owt, it's mashing up 'elpless veg.'

'Fish and chips and mashed-up peas. The last wonder of history. That's us sorted after all this is over.'

'Aye. Now you're seeing sense.'

They chewed and looked out over the bay happily for a time. Then Bill looked over his shoulder and his eye caught on something. His humour suddenly dropped.

'Here, look. There's our little mate up there.'

Warboys looked around and frowned. Up behind them, where bracken ruffled on the clifftop, crouched Nouzi Aaranya. Warboys felt a jolt of fear to see him. It had been nearly a fortnight now since the Gata, and Warboys had tried to put it behind him. The Janizar were supposed to be gone. He looked around, wondering if anyone else would register his presence – but Nouzi didn't look like much, and no one seemed to bat an eyelid.

'What the fuck's he doing here?'

'Better ask him to come and sit with us,' said Bill, beckoning him over.

'Don't!'

'Come and join us, son! Have a chip! A chip! Here!'

Warboys slapped at Bill's arm.

'What are you throwing him chips for? He's not a fucking seagull, is he?'

Warboys was on his feet and ready to square up to the kid as Nouzi Aaranya shuffled down the cliffside to join them.

'Let the lad sit down, son...' cajoled Bill, adding under his breath, 'You don't want to have a big discussion about how we know one another, out here on the bloody cliff, with the duty sergeant listening, do you?'

Realising the guile in the old man's hospitality, Warboys sat. He checked to see if Nouzi might be armed and ready to cut some bastard's arms off all of a sudden, then scanned the cliffside for officers who might be on the look out – but no one seemed to notice nor care.

'Come on, Nouzi lad!' said Bill. 'Never mind faceache here. Come and sit down.'

The Janizar knelt, bowed low to accept Bill's offer of a chip, and chewed with great consideration before lowering his head.

'Sat Nam, Shah. Thank-you.'

'No need to bow, son. Just sharing.'

'You are most hospitable. They say this is the Modern World, eh? But sometimes it seems I have left civilisation far behind.'

'You're not wrong there, son. Bit of fish?'

'Ai. Thank you.'

'What the fuck do you want?'

'Here, go easy, son. We didn't expect to see you again, is all. What can we do you for?'

'Yeah. Tell us.'

'I came to pass on my regards. To thank you – *both* of you. And to apologise.'

Warboys' screwed his face up in disgust. Bill just smoked with squinty eyes, assessing the boy as he spoke.

'My old teacher Sukhanava used to say that civilisation was built on three fragile stands. Said that it could be all gone in three strokes. One – buildings fall, materials burn. But walls can be built. Wood carved, cloth spun. Two – blood is let, bones broken. Life lost. Not so easy to recover, but bones mend, wounds heal, seed is sown, Maia gives birth ever again. The third is most difficult. Honour is lost. Sense. Place. Purpose. *Kaarya*. And this is harder even than life to replace, when a son may forget what his father knew in his blood.

'BOOM! BOOM! BOOM!' shouted the Janizar, making three chops with his hand. 'Malvy's great modern inventions come over, like storm clouds. Three strokes, eh? And something has changed forever.'

'Hark at this!' said Bill, nudging at Nouzi, drawing a smile from that pallid face. 'He's a bit of a philosopher, this one. You know what, you got a good point there kid. And Lord knows, no-one has lamented the state of things more than me.'

'That's the bloody truth, an' all,' muttered Warboys.

'So I thank you both, for your dignity and good conduct in desolate times. For your... patience.'

Here he met Bill's eye and bowed again, and Warboys, recalling that Bill had led the prisoner to Nouzi Aaranya's care, wondered what had been said between them. 'And I apologise for the way in which you were deployed, nai? The way you were *deceived*. Not my decision.'

Bill cleared his throat and seemed to relax some. 'You could learn summat off this kid and no mistake. Talks sense, good manners...'

Warboys groaned and pulled a face, wouldn't look at Nouzi Aaranya, and had the odd sensation of being chided in the Blackwater tavern once again.

Nouzi Aaranya shrugged. 'I hope Third Boom hasn't taken too much from me, eh? I hope to hold on to more.'

'It's like I say. You've got your Maia, and all the world ahead of you. It's how you'll go on what matters, eh? And you've got to thank Heaven for small pleasures, eh? It's a nice day! We've got our fish and chips!'

'Ai. Maia lives, and I live. Is good.'

'Ha! It's love, here, see? That's what makes the world go round, three bloody booms or not. That and what you learn on the way. This bugger here, when he was about your age, he used to want to be a bloody knight in shining armour.'

'Dad!' moaned Warboys, collapsing back into the grass in despair.

'Used to catch him reading these fancy pamphlets. Where did you get those bloody things anyway?'

'I nicked 'em off the butcher's boy.'

'Disgraceful you are.'

Warboys shrugged. 'Look, I liked 'em at the time. Good stories. Adventures. Treasure, foreign climes, warriors and damsels and all that shit. Then later on... you know, you get to that age and you're more interested in the exotic centrefolds, like.'

'Aye, I caught him at that a few times, an' all...'

'Yeah, alright, shut it, then. You forget about all that... that *adventure*. I had an idea in my head for years that I'd travel, see the world, just like in them pamphlets. But I'll tell you what happens...'

The Janizar looked warily at Warboys' wagging finger. Bill looked amused by it, and more than a little curious. 'Go on then. I've been trying to figure it out all these years. What happens?'

'You get out there, out to sea or whatever it is. And it's brilliant at first. I remember seeing this bloody line across the horizon, like Hagen's silver coast all over again. But then what happens? You *get there*. You get there, and it ain't silver at all. It's a shithole, same as the one you came from.'

'It's Port Ness!' laughed Bill.

'And then you look up, and there it is again. That fucking Silver Coast, never any nearer.'

'You're a bit philosophical today son!' laughed Bill, slapping his back. 'Are you feeling alright?'

'Why do you get to lament the Modern World all day every day, but when I do it, it's funny?'

'Ha! Cos I've been there, son! Done that. And distance has a way of putting a bit of drunken sheen on all that heartache.'

Bill laughed with tears in his eyes whilst Warboys sat frowning, then slapped Nouzi Aaranya on the back again.

'Here, though, this kid'll do better than us old duffers. He's got his Maia, hasn't he? So you'll be off back to her, soon, will you?'

'Ai. Kaarya. I will do my best.'

'That's it, son. That's all you can do in the end. You keep on, look forward, summat'll always turn up.' Bill stood. 'Right, well, I'm just off for a piss before we go back to work.'

'Why does he always have to *announce* it?' muttered Warboys, sitting back up. He watched Bill go out of earshot and turned to Nouzi Aaranya. 'Right. You. What the fuck are you really doing here?'

Nouzi Aaranya shrugged.

'As I said. To pay my respects.'

'Well we don't want them. Gata's done. I thought you were fucking off home now?'

'Ai. Sekhet has gone alone to the Eldask.'

Warboys recalled the sight of Uparagha getting an earful from the walking corpse on the Tor, and held back a shiver.

'Aren't you his bodyguard, you lot? Why don't you go with him? Or has he sacked you all for being arseholes?'

'Nai. He is most encouraged.'

'Oh aye? Uparagha tell you that, did he?'

'Ai.'

'Funny that. Cos I seem to recall I saw that Sekhet having a right go at Uparagha. I wouldn't trust what he says. He's a liar.'

'Listen, Captain. There is one more thing.'

'Oh, here it is. What?'

'By night, stay away from the AEC.'

'What? Why?'

'I can't say.'

'Is that it?'

'Ai.'

'Right. Well, some advice for you. I wouldn't hang about here. Cos if the Colonel finds you, the set of you will go against the wall. And I tell you what – I won't be crying, mate.'

Nouzi Aaranya looked at him, bright eyes blazing the colour of the sky, and for a moment Warboys didn't know whether to duck or feel sorry for him. The Janizar stood slowly. Bill came waddling through the grasses, fastening himself up. Across the cliff, all hands were rousing to go back down to the shore. Bill patted the Janizar on the back.

'Nice to see you again, kid. Come back for some fish and chips and mashed peas after the war's done, eh? Bring your Maia.'

'Ai.'

There was a commotion then as an officer with escort came marching down onto the sand, barking for the foreman, who scanned the idling soldiers until his eyes fixed on where the Warboys were sitting.

'Better make yourself scarce, son,' muttered Bill, patting Nouzi Aaranya's arm.

'Yeah,' said Warboys. 'Get on.'

The Janizar nodded, a token bow to each of them, and nipped off through the grass. No sooner had he gone, the officer and his men were climbing up to meet them. Bill began rolling a smoke, whilst Warboys yawned in a show of nonchalance.

'Warboys!' barked the officer. 'Which one of you men is Warboys?' Warboys opened his mouth out of habit, to deny all knowledge, then the officer referred to his warrant, and called 'William Eadgar Warboys!' and Warboys realised for once that it wasn't *him* in trouble.

'Dad? I thought you said you were safe!'

Warboys pulled at Bill's sleeve as if to make him flee, but the foreman was already pointing him,. 'Don't worry, son,' he breathed, as the officer came blustering up to confront him. 'You get on.'

'William Eadgar Warboys?' barked the officer.

'That's me, sir.'

Bill looked down at a paper smoke that he turned over

between finger and thumb. A pale resolve formed in the old man's face. The officer looked Bill up and down, then gestured to his henchmen with a tip of his head. 'Arrest him.'

The two soldiers moved to pluck Bill from the cliffside, but Warboys shouldered in to block them.

'Here, fuck off! What do you think you're doing? What's this about?'

'I'd stay well back if I were you, volunteer,' said one of the officer's henchmen. 'Unless you want to be arrested with him.'

'What's he meant to have done though?'

The officer read ceremoniously from his warrant paper, 'I am arresting you for suspected treason. Gaol-breaking. Aiding and abetting the Sun-Ivis movement as a rebel and enemy of Aaland State.'

The henchmen moved again, and again, Warboys put himself in their way. 'You're making a mistake! Dad. Tell them.'

Bill prised him off gently.

'Stay back, son,' he gasped. 'Don't get yourself in any bother.'

Warboys saw that peaky, resigned look on his face, and it rankled.

'Just tell them!'

'Don't mind him. I'll come quietly, sir.'

Don't give in to them, you old sod. Don't be so bloody honest.

With a solider either side of him, Bill was turned to march up the cliff path.

'Where are you taking him?' demanded Warboys, marching off after them.

'Since the gaols can't be relied upon, this one will go to the AEC for interrogation by the Colonel himself.'

Warboys gulped at the air, each breath beginning to form a plea, an argument, a threat, each one strangled by futility. He thought of clocking one of Bill's captors over the head and making a run for it, but there was nowhere to run, and he knew Bill wouldn't have any of it. Behind him, his foreman was demanding that he return to his position. Like a gnat biting at him. White hot anger clouded his vision as he turned, came face to face with the foreman, fists forming in rage, ready to lurch at the man.

'William Konrad Warboys!' came Bill's special stern voice, stopping him dead. Warboys turned to see his dad frowning at him, just as he had when he'd smashed somebody's shed windows, or been lairy to his Nana. It sapped the fight from him.

'Calm yourself down, and stop behaving like a bloody idiot! Get back to your post, and leave me to it. I can fight my own battles.'

Warboys stepped down, let the foreman clap a hand on him. He watched as Bill's frown disappeared, and the soldiers turned and marched him off toward the AEC.

'Back to your posts!' yelled the foreman, distracted by nosey onlookers. 'All of you!'

Warboys looked around, realising the commotion had attracted a crowd .

'Fuck you lot looking at?' he snarled, glaring at them all. There, with smugness lathered all about his face, was Jacky Biel. 'He'll be up against the wall for that,' smirked Biel.

Warboys strode up and locked eyes with him. The foreman's orders went unheard.

'What would you know about it, jug ears?'

'Oh, I know enough. I should keep my head down now, if I was you, Warboys.'

'Is that so? I'll knock that fucking conk off your face if you—'

'Oh no, no you won't, Warboys...' Biel's eyes darted slyly aside, and he lowered his voice. 'See, if I was to tell *all* I knew, *you'd* be going with him.'

'You don't know shite.'

'You two been rubbing shoulders with these Sun-Ivises since

we came across the Yew. The pair of you disappear off into the Pits, and next thing I know, you're agitating at that festival, whilst the old man is freeing prisoners. You're on the take, you are. I don't know how, but I'll have some of it, Warboys. You owe me.'

'A real fucking stalwart you are, Biel.'

'Aye, y' don't deny it though, do yer?'

Warboys' ears rang. For a moment, he stood dumbly, lacking even the wherewithal to plant Biel. The foreman called again, but Warboys looked out across the beach and couldn't bear to take a single step more. He might as well shoot the old man himself if he turned and took part in that grimy work-queue. He had to do something. He turned away without a word, shouldered past the foreman, and marched off, breaking into a run towards the town. Down he went, through the gates towards the Pits.

A gang of cocky kids trailed him as soon as he was down the stairs. He crossed a few alleys recklessly, over towards the bombed out district, heading towards the Sunken Pig. Then there was a sound behind, and he turned to find Nouzi Aaranya, hand on dhas.

'Hui, Captain. I saw what happened.'

'See what you've done now? This is how you pay your fucking respects, is it? Getting him arrested?'

'Captain, I am sorry this—'

'Don't give me that shit again. You know they'll execute him for this, don't you? What am I supposed to do now?'

'I did not want this. He is an honourable man.'

'You come apologising to us, well now's your chance to do summat about it. Take me to Uparagha. Take me *now*.'

Nouzi Aaranya considered this, then conceded with a bow. 'Ai. This way.'

19 OUR MAN INSIDE

'You ripped us off!' shouted Warboys, bursting into the taproom of the *Sunken Pig*, spearing the air before Uparagha with his finger. 'You fucking ripped us off, and now he's got to pay the price. What are you going to do about it?'

Uparagha simply stared back, nonplussed at being addressed this way. Before he could answer, Goro loomed from the alcoves, stamping his foot like a bull about to charge.

'Hui!' he bellowed. 'This is Janizar, eh? This is our *Yin*! You don't presume to speak to him so! Stinking *kitava*!'

'Was I talking to you, you ugly stripe of shit? Get back before your fucking nose pots the window.'

'Captain...' warned Nouzi Aaranya, moving to pull Warboys back. Goro's eyes looked ready to burst out of his head, and with a guttural bark he fell into his stance, gripping the handle of his dhas. Nouzi Aaranya stood protectively before Warboys.

'Out of my way, runt!' growled Goro.

'Goro Chai!' barked Uparagha. 'Stand down. The Captain addressed *me*, eh? Stand down. *Inshie!*'

Goro snorted, slapped his dhas ruefully, and stepped back. Uparagha let out a long, slow exhalation, cast a scrutinising look at Nouzi Aaranya, then gestured to the bench.

'Mr. Warboys. Sit, please.'

Warboys did as he was told.

'You owe us,' he said.

'Eh? Do I? I let each of you live, nai?'

'You know exactly what I mean.'

'Perhaps I was not clear in terms, eh?' That knifelike smile split Uparagha's face, without a trace of humour in the eyes. 'This western parley is not as adaptable as our native *haastya*.'

'You know exactly what you did.'

Uparagha's smile dropped.

'I do not owe you, Mr. Warboys. But we are not without honour. My brother here seems to think this old man is worth dealing for.'

'Ai. Is honorable man, his old man Bill. Knows kaarya.'

Uparagha's eyebrows raised, impressed.

'There is hope for the modern world yet then, eh?'

'Look. I need summat done, I can't do it on my own, and I'm not far behind him. We're fucked. I don't know why you lot are still here, and I don't want to know any more, but I'm out of my fucking depth here, and if my dad goes to the wall, I'll see you brought down.'

'No need for threats, Mr. Warboys. As it happens, we can help each other. Your old man is in the officer's block of AEC, nai? Up above the main silo.'

Warboys hesitated. Uparagha had skipped so quickly from being threatened to negotiating that it threw him.

'That's right...' he began. 'It's where the top brass interrogate the most dangerous prisoners.'

'Dangerous old man, is he?'

'He could knock you out.'

Uparagha took a moment to absorb the comment before going on. 'Well now. Amongst these prisoners are some of my friends, nai? Sons of Sun-Ivis, being readied for execution, like your old man. Also, there is *Ganika* – you call it... *serving girl* in your barracks. Of the two moons, eh? You know the one?' He grinned, cupping his hands before his chest to indicate what he meant.

'I know her,' said Warboys. 'Olga. You can see her in the

kitchen window from the drilling yard. Everyone knows Olga.'

'Ai. She is ours.'

'Your what?'

'Olga is with the *Sons*. Keeps an eye on the Colonel's plans for us. So we knew when safe to move the Sekhet around for Gata. But *Gata* is done and they keep her. And between us, Mr. Warboys...' He leaned across the table, eyes sliding aside. '... we think the officers make use of her, nai?'

'I'm surprised the officious bastards can take their eyes off their maps to be honest.'

'Hui, Mr. Warboys, when the two moons rise before us, we all pause a moment for heavenly glory, nai?'

Warboys frowned, not in the mood for laughs, and wondered why the enslavement of his allies seemed like such bawdy fun to Uparagha.

'One must look after Maia, eh? After the Mother and the Sister?'

He shot an acerbic glance at Nouzi Aaranya, who lowered his head with a wince.

'Alright,' said Warboys. 'So you want to get her out, and the others?'

'Ai.'

'Easily said. It's all sealed off up there.'

'You know the interior well?'

Warboys saw Nouzi Aaranya listening intently now. 'Aye, I've done a few night patrols, reported into that top office. Even if you got a few men to sneak up past the hundreds of troops below the silos, you'd not get through there. They've got another gate that locks from inside.'

'Ai. So we make it much simpler. You have shifts in the barracks, nai? The watch on the AEC?'

'It can be arranged.'

'Ai. Good. Now. There is an old chute for emptying the chaff down onto the barges in the canalway. When your engineers surveyed the factory, they identified a possible way in through the chute, and had it blocked off inside with a closing hatch. All you have to do is unlock that hatch, eh?'

Nouzi Aaranya, looking increasingly uncomfortable, opened his mouth as if to object. Warboys saw a spark in the ink of Uparagha's eye, a moment of almost palpable outrage – and Nouzi Aaranya hung his head in shame. Warboys wondered what the hell was going on between them. Uparagha went on.

'Tomorrow night. Silo caps are up on top level. Olga is our man inside, eh? She has access to silo caps.'

'What, so they're going to come down through the bloody silo?'

'Ai. Tough, is Olga. All our Sons, and your old man, down through the chute and away into the canal.'

'They'll break their bloody necks!'

'Nai. Olga has set ropes on the inside. They can monkey down, nai? Down the sides and out like the chaff.'

'And that's it?'

'Ai. Simple. No confrontation. And after, you can lock the hatch again. Or say rats chewed it, nai? Say Modern World eroded fixtures! You choose!'

'I won't say owt, because we'll be off. I don't fancy waiting about for Malvy's justice. I want to get out of here now. Out of the army and out of Blackhaven.'

'Ai?'

'Aye. Me *and* the old man.

'Ai. Agreed. Is easy to do.'

'You're on, then. Tomorrow night it is. We'll do it on the last watch. Someone'll always swap the dogwatch.' He thought a moment, remembered Jacky Biel's threats. 'But I'll need a half dozen bottles from your stocks to oil some tongues. I'm already in the shit for abandoning my post.'

'Ai. Agreed.'

The landlord came over with the bottles, looking unhappy about it. With that, Warboys stood, straightened his coat, and went to rap on the door to be let out.

He stepped warily out across the cluttered street, through the obstacle course of planks and rubble. A shadow flickered over the broken boards to his left and he turned to see Nouzi Aaranya peel from the dark.

'Still got you following me, has he?'

'Ai.'

'Got a knife there for me, have you? In case I run and tell?'

'Ai. Would be stupid not to. You outlanders know no *kaarya*.'

Warboys stood there a moment, open mouthed.

'Why would you just *admit* it? Are you soft, or what?' Warboys backed away, feeling a collapsed chimney stack for a handy brick, a stick, a rivet to throw, a fucking dead pigeon would do it. But the Janizar just stood there.

'Well... is it going to be now?'

'Nai.'

'Right. Well fuck off, then.'

'Ai. Are you going to do it?'

'Do what?'

'The job?'

'I haven't got much choice, have I? That's if I don't get arrested myself before then. What's it got to do with you what I do?'

'Captain. I did not want you involved in this.'

'So you keep saying. This is the trouble at the AEC you wanted to warn me about, was it?'

'Ai.'

'Anything else I should know?'

The Janizar hesitated. 'Only that I will do my best to help him. You have my word.'

'I don't want your word. What do you care? He doesn't know

any better than to be kind to fuckwits like you. You let me mind my own business.'

Nouzi Aaranya said nothing.

'Can I go now?'

'Ai.'

Warboys rounded a jagged chimney stack to get away, then hurried back to the AEC.

20 DOGWATCH

The sky smouldered like coals over the *Tower of Havery* as the sun set the next night. Warboys leaned on the wall overlooking the reservoir, all the while observing who came and went. He'd managed to grease his way back into service through happy co-operation with the duty sergeant, who hated the dogwatch as much as he enjoyed a bottle or two.

Five men at a time made up the active patrol. At intervals, they changed position, and the first man would come back off the perimeter walk, go in through the makeshift barracks to do a quick check inside the AEC before making a report to the duty sergeant on the top floor. He'd then sign off and hand the keys over to a new man, who would go back down and swap position with the next.

Warboys looked out toward the coast. He hadn't much time to plan. When he'd gotten Bill free, they would go up to the next village on the coast, and get a boat. After that, he didn't know. The old man would be miserable as hell to be a fugitive, but at least he wouldn't be dead. The clouds hung low over the *Tower*, reflected in the reservoir below. Time was nearing. Warboys went to turn in.

Nerves kept him awake. He lay in manufacturing bay B2, lined up like a casualty, watching the angular struts that cut the light into squares. He listened to the mutter of card games in the next bay. Some poor bloke talked to his auntie in his sleep. Fear struck as Warboys thought of Cait and the kids back home, hoping there wouldn't be trouble for them when he went on the run. He hung his head, regretting the day he'd clapped eyes on that godforsaken manual. For the first time in living memory, he suddenly wanted back on those potato fields.

Hour by hour he monitored the fifth patrolmen, counting the metallic footsteps as each man trudged by with the lamp and keys. Some paused on the way, trying to scrounge smokes. Finally there'd be the tinkle of checked-off keys upstairs, before the next man was roused.

He worried how Bill would react. What the old man would say when he found out they'd have to make a run for it. Hoped to god that the dutiful old sod wouldn't refuse to run. And what if they'd knobbled him already? What if he couldn't walk? Warboys ran through the escape route over again – out under the *Sunken Pig*, up the coast to the next village. Find a boat. Find a boat where? He had no idea where.

He thought about Olga. Many a time he'd been on the walls or perimeter and seen her up on the second floor window, bending over, giving passing soldiers an unintentional eyeful. She seemed a simple sort, enjoying the attention from afar – not a bad lass. There was a dearth of female company in Blackhaven, and he'd wondered once or twice if he might get her to meet him in the pantry or some such. He wondered if she'd be grateful for the rescue. Lazily imagining the *two moons* rising and falling before his eyes took his mind off his worry for a time, and at last he slept.

'Here, Warboys. Dogwatch. You're on. Nowt doin'.'

Warboys awoke in a chill sweat, knotted up in his coat as a lamp swung over him. The keys were all but thrown at him by his predecessor, who dropped to his bedroll with a groan. Warboys teetered to his feet, and gathered his wits. Massaging the concrete pattern out of his cheek, he staggered out onto the gantry to start the shift, past the old belt line that ran over the bays of sleeping men. The outside gate clanged coldly, and an unforgiving wind cuffed him about the head as he went outside to relieve the next man. His breath billowed in grey plumes, and shaking fingers struggled to make roll-ups, which he then smoked too quickly. He read insults that had been chalked on the walls by the locals.

A yawning kid came out to replace him, and Warboys in turn trudged around to relieve the rear gate, clapping his hands for warmth. He waited. A grey fox streaked past by the bins. Grey mist hung over the sea, cloaking the *Tower* and the bay. The reservoir began to glow with the threat of a brightening sky. Warboys relieved the next man, passing the outlet chute that cut out through the wall of the AEC. Across the reservoir, one of the airships floated over the hangar roof, whilst lamplight fell on the balloons of two others in dock. He wondered if one was the *Hildegaard*, and longed to be able to haul the old man up and away on her again, so he wouldn't have to do this. Wandering around to the chute, he peered over the walkway and down into the water. Rusted rungs dropped down to a slipway on the water's edge. Wallflowers had long since choked the outlet; Bill would have a job fighting through that lot on the way out.

The yawning kid appeared suddenly to relieve him, and shot his nerves so much he couldn't speak, even to swear. He couldn't quite calm down after that. He made the rest of the circuit, until he came back to the AEC entrance.

'Owt doin?' asked the solider there.

'Fuck all mate. You?'

'Nah.'

The gate chimed. Warboys took his route around the warehouse floors, around the silo housing toward the chute. There was no one here. He climbed a rusted ladder up to the neck of the silo, and carefully turned the squeaky wheel to open the hatch. Old debris could be heard dropping through. The chute seemed narrow, and he worried again about how Bill would manage, or that he'd get stuck. He took a quick look about him before having a little listen at the pipes. There was nothing above the sound of his own heartbeat. It was done.

He made his way up the stairway. The walkway echoed all the way up and through the work bays where the snoring masses lay.

'Here, Warboys, is that you?' came a slurred voice. He recognised Jacky Biel, and could smell the booze on him. 'Nice drop of liquor, this is. I'll have some more of this before I'm done with you.'

Warboys recoiled, wanting to kick the bastard's head in for him, but held himself. 'Yeah, alright. Get some sleep.'

'I'll be seeing you, Warboys...'

Warboys left Biel cackling to himself, and rattled up the metal stair to the top floor office, where the sergeant sat poring over a ledger, a flask and lamp on his desk. The officer's mess lay beyond the gate, along with the servants' quarters and cells. Redundant factory signage still hung in place over this door, instructing Warboys that the other side of the corridor also led to the SILO CAPS. He wondered where Olga was now, if she was ready. Was the old man charming her some? Maybe they were already in the silo. Warboys gave the sergeant a nod, receiving barely a breath in return. He signed the ledger, turned around and went. The stairwell echoed all the way down. He found B2 and shuffled along to give the next man a nudge. A lanky VIP named Murk roused himself.

'Cold out,' muttered Warboys. 'Wrap up warm.'

Murk blundered into his boots, having nothing to say in reply.

'Here, wait on. I'll come out for a smoke.'

Warboys went out after Murk, lit up another smoke with

shaking hands, and made a show of yawning and wandering casually away, around the back wall to the chute. He peered down towards the weeds where the old man would come out. It was going to be a tight squeeze.

There was quiet. He leaned against the pipe, sniffing and smoking and spitting like any loitering soldier might, whilst inwardly, his heart thumped. He pressed his ear against the metal, listening for some hint of the escapees.

'Come on, old man,' he muttered.

From inside he heard a small, strange whistle from inside, as if the building itself were sucking breath.

Warboys frowned.

A sudden, thunderous boom tore the air. The entire AEC jolted from its foundations, knocking Warboys to the floor. The uproar made fuzz of his thoughts, resonating through every bone in his body, leaving him barely sensible as bricks and debris began to rain down. A cold echo rang around the city. Glass and debris rained down over rooftops, plopping into the reservoir.

'What the fuck was that?' croaked Warboys, edging back to see a hideous crack snaking up the length of the building. Distant dogs barked. Patrolmen screamed from the outhouses and watchtowers, and more dull, explosive thuds sounded from inside. Metal creaked. Warboys dithered – then a yell came from the front yard, and the fire bell began to clang, sounding pathetic in the wake of the explosion.

It was *then* that Warboys heard a rattle from the outlet pipe, a soft fumble against the metal, a grunt as a body fell down through the pipe. Warboys' heart leaped and he leaned over to see someone fall from the chute, a ripple swelling out from the water below. Warboys dropped himself down the rungs, straining to see as more debris fell.

'Dad?'

He leaned over to see as a dirty figure hauling itself onto the slipway.

'Dad?'

Nouzi Aaranya's lightning eyes looked up at him, bright against grime-caked skin. Warboys met them and a sense of dread overtook his body, tightening his bowels.

'What the fuck—'

Nouzi Aaranya wasn't supposed to be here. Warboys wracked his mind for some missing nuance, something that could explain this – but, as the Janizar dragged himself up and began edging along the wall and away, Warboys knew he'd been had again. There *was* no breakout. There never had been. He'd let the bastard *in*.

'Oi!' yelled Warboys, furious, unshouldering his Entwick. 'Oi! I'm talking to you! Where is he?' Sweat drenched the small of his back as he trailed Nouzi Aaranya along the wall, finding the bastard's head in his sight-groove.

A second, thunderous eruption snatched Warboys' head aside, took the floor from beneath him. He lost sense of which was up or down, saw the crumbling AEC spin past; then there was a chill shock as he somersaulted into the reservoir, pursued by more bricks and debris. Seconds later, he floundered to the surface to see a great mushroom shaped blackness blotting out the dawn. The godforsaken outlet pipe fell away from the wall, narrowly missing him as it slapped the water. A whole section of the wall followed, sliding down like melting ice. He saw a brick spinning towards him, felt a prang on the head, and slipped under again. From below, the water's surface shimmered with fire.

Someone was pulling at him, hauling him from the water, up onto a horsewash. The AEC still blazed opposite. Warboys' head throbbed so badly he could barely make out Nouzi Aaranya standing over him.

'What have you done?' he slurred, fighting to get the words out.

Nouzi Aaranya was deathly pale. 'We found unexploded bomb in the Pits,' he croaked, trying to be all hard faced and Janizar-like, but failing, losing his hand to the twitching again. 'Upa wanted me to return it, eh? You made it easier.'

Warboys rolled onto his elbows, snatched at the rifle that was still strapped over his arm, and tried to get onto his knees.

'Where's my Dad? Where is he?'

Nouzi Aaranya began to back away. 'I tried...' he gasped.

'Where is he?' screamed Warboys.

'Hui!' barked Nouzi Aaranya, a sudden, counter aggression borne of fear. 'Don't question *me, kitava!* You were only required for distraction! This was just for the ships, nai? Uparagha wants your ships!'

With that, Nouzi Aaranya staggered back, pale and wide eyed as if he'd just woken up.

'I have to go now,' he murmured. 'To the hangar...'

He turned and ran up the horsewash. Warboys stumbled after him, and saw him swallowed by the great rolling clouds of dust that rolled out from the AEC.

He looked around, and his rifle sagged. All across the city fires had been started, adding to the smog that billowed from the barracks. A fire fight echoed somewhere nearby, and Warboys turned to see a crowd of Sons breaking from cover to converge suddenly on the hangar yard, piling over the fences, charging the place like madmen. He staggered closer, saw Janizar join them – Uparagha among them, blade raised as he sailed over the fence, beheading an engineer. As they stormed the complex, Warboys spotted Nouzi Aaranya again, and he snarled, expecting to see the little shit join the rest; but Nouzi turned and headed pointedly away from the hangar, leaping across rooftops, down and away toward the Pits.

Why is he going down there? wondered Warboys, just as nausea hauled him down. He fell, gasping and faint, feeling blood tickle his brow.

The next thing he knew, a familiar shadow crawled across the smog, and he looked up to see the three airships loose from their moorings, quivering and unmanned over the city. One was fully ablaze, another shaken by an onboard struggle. Warboys watched a man fall flailing to his death as the three rose into brooding clouds. The burning *Lucidia* went aimless into the wind, whilst the other two – *Tabitha* and *Rosamundt* – made a shaky turnabout to head north, rising fast. The firefight became a rout as reinforcements surrounded the hangar, shooting down the Sons as they ran for the Pits. The bastards had been waiting for the AEC to go up, to cause a distraction and draw troops away.

He'd been the cue for Uparagha's insurrection.

Finally he peeled himself up to turn and gaped in horror at the sliding pile of blackened bricks that had been their fortress. Half the AEC had now slopped down into the yard, and the silo tower still blazed.

Shit, thought Warboys. Bill.

'Dad!'

He ran towards the AEC.

21 FRESH AIR AND GREENERY

An unrecognisable hell reigned where the courtyard had once been. The charred silo tower spewed smoke, blotting out the light and choking the yard. The innards of the building lay in an avalanche of cracked bricks, splintered boards and shattered glass. Makeshift fire-fighters formed bucket lines, stretcher-bearers rushed to and fro with ashen bodies, and a rescue squad laboured to clear away rubble. The dead were already lining the courtyard.

Warboys walked into the devastation, towards the main building. A whole wing of the factory had split, the boards and joists concertinaed across the yard. Here a recovery gang hefted at a beam. A scrawny, grease-smeared engineer was crawling into the gaps in an attempt to pull survivors out.

'Who's under there?' roared Warboys, storming in to set his shoulder against the beam to help. 'Did the cells come down? The cells on the top floor? My dad was in there.'

'Aye,' grunted a staff fireman. 'That second bang brought the bloody lot down. Fire hit the ammunition stores.'

The scrawny engineer staggered out backwards, hauling a limp figure with him. It wasn't Bill. Warboys set back to his toil, and helped pull out two more dead. Another came out alive, but with his leg all wrought and bloody, as if a starving dog had had it away off the grill. The next came gasping, his eyelashes heavy with dust. Warboys passed him on to the stewards before he went back to the wreckage. Heat and sweat clagged the dust on him, seeming to make cement around his limbs.

It was half an hour later before they found the next one. The engineer fell out of a hole they'd forced, filthy black dust clogging about the fresh red gleam of cuts on his back.

'I can't get him,' he gasped. 'There's a bloody great beam right across him. Right *through* him, mebbe... can't tell.'

'Who is it?' asked Warboys, leaning down to peer into the gap.

'Old feller. Saw his hair, first. Put my hand in it, screwing up through the rubble it was...'

Warboys peered into the hole, and saw those limp, dusty legs sticking out.

He recognised his father's boots.

The strange thing was that, despite his raging effort, his determination to save the old man, now it came to it, he could barely even stand. He sat back and watched, stunned, reverting to boyhood as the rescuers did their work. A winch set was brought in, and several men gathered to guide out the great chunk of masonry that weighed down the beam pressing on Bill.

'Is he alright?' he dared ask. 'Is he breathing? Can you see?' But for a long time no-one answered. He stopped asking.

Gradually, he saw the rescuers lag, saw shoulders drop. Heads shook, and regretful looks were cast over at him. Warboys avoided their eyes. They'd managed to widen the hole enough that a surgeon and his assistant could gain access. Warboys edged closer, watched the surgeon's backside, saw his assistant passing him things, their faces set in stone.

'Cracked ribs,' reported the surgeon, seemingly to himself. 'Lung's collapsed...'

The surgeon withdrew and nodded to his aide, who plucked a square bottle of amber liquid and passed it on into the hole.

'Drink this, Mr. Warboys,' Warboys heard him say. It seemed odd to Warboys to hear Bill addressed as *Mr. Warboys* like that. The smell of alcohol hung in the air as Warboys edged closer, and the surgeon turned to him.

'You're his son, aren't you?'

'Aye. Can you do owt for him?'

'I can leave you that bottle.'

'What? What are you on about?'

'There's not much we can do. That beam is all that's holding him together. He's not got long.'

Warboys gaped around at the rescue team.

'Can't we just pull him out?'

'It'd break his neck, mate,' said the engineer. 'I'm sorry.'

'I'm not sure his neck isn't already broken,' sighed the surgeon. Warboys' eyes swelled with the threat of a sob. The surgeon noticed the cut on Warboys' head and added, 'Look, wait here. I'll send someone over to dress that for you... the priest'll be round in a bit.'

Warboys patted the surgeon reassuringly, but couldn't look him in the eye. 'Yeah, cheers mate,' he chirruped. 'You get on, don't worry about him. I'll sit with him. He'll be alright, the old sod...'

Alone now, Warboys crawled into the hole. The air was thick with dust and heaved in his lungs. Bill lay there like a dusty plaster cast of his former self, the left side of his body still obscured by the beam.

'Dad?' He lay a trembling hand on Bill's head.

'How long have I got?' coughed the old man, weakly.

'Here, just rest, Dad.'

'What do I want to rest for?' he snapped. 'I'll be dead in a minute.'

'Don't talk like that, Dad...'

'They're not sendin' me one of them field parsons are they?' His eyes strained weirdly in his battered old head, looking as if they might come out on stalks. 'You'd better not let him near me. I aren't being sent off by one o' them morbid bastards!'

'Dad, just rest, will you?'

'*You* rest! I ain't dying near one of them buggers. It's like going for a shit with the mayor watching!'

'Well what the bloody hell do you—'

Don't start, Dad, it was on the tip of his tongue to say.

Don't stop.

'Can't you get me out of here? I could do with some fresh air and greenery. I 'ate this place.'

'I can't, Dad. We can't move you.'

Warboys sat back, bricks jutting into his back, listened to the worn lungs whistle as they pulled weakly at the air. He dared not move, in case he obscured the sound of Bill's breath.

'Here. Where's the boy?'

'What? Dad, I'm here. I'm here, Dad.'

'Not you, soft lad. Nouzi Arry-anya. He came looking for me. Did he get out alright?'

'Aye. He did.'

'Good.'

Warboys bit back anger, resentful that the Janizar should be spoken of here.

'There's a bucket down there, feller,' came someone's voice from outside. 'Give him a clean up for the parson if you like.'

Warboys looked at the bucket, nodded dumbly, and reached for the old tin bucket. He squeezed the cloth out, and set about smearing the ash down Bill's face. He rubbed at what seemed to be a clot of ashes, and tore a great scab away from his head.

'Ow! Bloody hell!' cried Bill, lifting his head up. 'What y' doin' to me?'

Bill stared with uncomprehending eyes at his surroundings, hair sprung out like some ragged old jack-in-the box. Then a flush of agony coloured his face and he deflated back into the rubble. Warboys held him steady, nothing but a whistle left in his thoughts.

'I'm cleaning you up, Dad. For the parson.'

Bill frowned. 'You'd better clean my arse then, cos I'll turn round and dig before I let him come near me.'

'Dad...'

A throat cleared outside, and the black figure of the parson closed over the hole, crossing his hands about the place as if he was counting his haul, and not a drop of brandy about him.

'Get me away from him,' croaked Bill. 'I'll bloody jump if I have to.'

'Jump?' Warboys snorted, a laugh that might easily have been a sob. He stuck his head out, met the parson's eye and shook his head. He held up the surgeon's bottle. 'Thanks mate, but I think he's alright with this.'

'Are you sure? Is he... sound of mind?'

'Course he's not. But listen. Been beyond the known world and back, has this old bugger... You can push off now, mate. Ask not what Aaland does for you, and all that...'

Warboys withdrew into the hole.

'Here. Have another slug of this.'

'Nah. I've given up. It's bad for me 'ealth.' Bill wheezed with laughter a moment.

Warboys hung his head.

'It's my fault, this.'

'Yah,' began Bill, building up a few breaths as if to make a final speech in condemnation of Malvy's Modern World. It didn't come. Gunfire echoed from some distant ward, innocent sounding crackles and pops.

'Like taties they was,' came Bill's voice, barely a whisper now. 'A ton o' taties pushin' us down. I can smell the soil an'all... Have they found her yet?'

'Dad, you're in Blackhaven. You—'

'I'll wait here for her...' he gasped, and his chest rattled alarmingly. Warboys wanted to call for someone, knowing there was no one left to call.

'It was lovely to fly with you, son...' breathed Bill.

'What?'

Warboys sat and listened to Bill's breath fade.

'Come on, old man. Any minute now you're going to wake up and give me a right good lambasting...'

There was no response. Bill wasn't breathing. Warboys dared not touch him, dared not go to him.

'Mr. Warboys...' came the engineer's voice. 'Is he gone?'

Warboys waited, built up to speech. Nodded.

'He's gone.'

'You'll have to come out then, mate. There's others still trapped. We'll shift him, but... best you look away.'

Warboys crawled backwards, eyes fixed on the Bill's dusty old 'tache, and sobbed as he was pulled away by the rescuers. Had his back slapped and his hair ruffled as he was passed to the back and out of the way.

There he staggered and fell to his knees, grimaced at the crunching noises of the removal, the crumble of more masonry. Then they forgot both Warboys and moved on to the next victim. The stewards claimed Bill, now a shape under a dusty sheet. Warboys trailed along with them a while, saw other ash-stained stewards on the road, leading across a yard toward the makeshift infirmary. He faltered, lost the bearers in the haze. Warboys sagged into the rubble, unable to watch them lay the old man out in formation with the rest. He could suddenly recall no meaning nor point to anything that comprised him, and let the smoke and dust blot everyone out, making a nothingness of the world.

He came to in a shiver of sweat as the unwelcome row of the senior officers came into earshot from the yard.

'What damage, Captain Ikes?'

'Sir, three ships were hijacked in the raid. *Lucidia* was caught in the fire and is almost certainly destroyed. *Tabitha* and *Rosamundt* are lost sir.'

Warboys found he lay in a crater of rubble not twenty feet from the officers. He kept himself low. A chill sweat broke all over him. He was for it now. He'd been on watch for the bombing. He didn't know what Jacky Biel had already said and to who.

'*Lost?*' roared Linnaeus. 'How could this happen? How can three state ships be snatched from under our noses by these savages?'

'Sir, they had the pilot in tow, sir... the one who escaped the gaol.'

Linnaeus responded with words that degenerated into a canine growl.

'What about the old ship?' he snapped. '*Hildegaard?*'

Hildegaard. Warboys felt the name warmly, like that of an old friend. He hesitated to listen.

'Still in repair, sir, right where she came down in the field after that storm. We commandeered the farmer's barn to make the repairs, sir.'

'How many on guard there?'

Another minor explosion boomed from within the factory. Captain Ikes hesitated. 'A skeleton crew, sir. Two guards, four engineers—'

'Right. Get men to that hangar, and get the Hildegaard up there.'

'What men?' cried another voice. 'There are no men, and even if there were, the gates are all held with firefights!'

Warboys suddenly thought of Nouzi Aaranya's pale, frightened face. That shivering little shit who had lapped up Bill's kindness, then *murdered* him. He recalled the thin layer of resolve laid over the kid's face as he'd turned into the Pits, and imagined caving it in. But a thought intersected his anger

– *why* had Nouzi Aaranya turned back to the Pits? He'd left, claiming to be heading to the hangar. Why then turn away from Uparagha as the others had stormed the hangars and left on board the hijacked ships? He'd been twitching again, though. Little shit probably had another one of his funny turns and gone off to bang his head on a wall.

'Who was on watch?' demanded the Colonel, making Warboys press low to the ground. 'I want the names of all the men on watch last night, and I want them brought to me.'

A small task squad left with an officer to locate the guard roster. Warboys felt a stab of panic, bitterly surprised at the life he still felt in him as he began to edge away through the clutter. He looked up. The great, blazing silo tower glared at him like a fiery eye, and the explosion echoed inside him again.

He broke from cover, head down as more officers passed by, crossing into the yard to report. He ploughed away through the complex. Fucking *bastards,* he thought, suddenly wracked with rage at what had been done to him. Rage at the Janizar, and Aaaland State alike. He came to the gatehouse, his mind churning. When the whistle of another explosion sounded above, Warboys ran out through the checkpoint, and ducked off the main road to avoiding a sergeant who was rallying for aid on his way to the AEC. Firefights echoed from all the city gates. There was no way out of the city now.

Except, he suddenly realised as he looked over his shoulder at the Pits, there was.

The Sunken Pig.

Perhaps Nouzi Aaranya hadn't flaked out. Perhaps he'd been assigned to take the last, least important ship. Nouzi was the runt, after all. And the *Hildegaard* was sitting prone on that farm outside the city.

A tear threatened to well in Warboys' eye as he remembered his flight aboard the Hildegaard. He and Bill clingning to one another like cissies, with that silver coast spreading before them.

It was lovely to fly with you, son.

No. He'd not let them take Hilda.

The soldiers tramped past. Warboys gripped the battered old rifle with the streak of blue paint, and turned into the Pits. He might be caught and shot for a traitor yet – but he'd take that fucker Nouzi Aaranya with him.

22 PANIC

Warboys moved low and swift trough the deserted streets of the Pits, making towards the bell tower. From there he headed in the direction of the city wall, until he came to the cobbled approach to the Sunken Pig. Crouching behind a crumbling wall, he tookstock. An abandoned carriage had been lodged in the road, and hooded sentries skulked up on the battlement, making a narrow shooting range of the street.

Common sense told him he had come as far as he'd get. But anger drove him recklessly out. The sound of his own breath blocked out all else. His vision blurred. He charged, willed the sentries to shoot him dead if they would.

A sentry looked over at him, not sure what to do about a lone soldier charging a twenty foot wall. He shot late and awkward, a fraction of a second after Warboys slammed into the carriage. He heard them up above, muttering from one tower to the other, sensed them shifting around to try and get another shot at him. Splinters frayed from the wood of the cart not six inches from his head. Warboys yanked the stop from the wheel of the carriage, and let the cart roll across the cobbles, moving with it to the cover of the tower wall, beneath the view of the sentries. He quickly climbed up the decrepit wall, gripping weeds and roots to haul himself over the parapet. On top, the scrawny sentry was dithering in the doorway to the stairs, still reloading. Barely an adult. He lunged with the butt of his rifle, but Warboys barged into him, caught his hood and shoved him back over the wall and onto the cobbles below. The second sentry had vanished from his post – probably to raise the alarm. Warboys raced into the doorway, and all but tumbled down the spiral stair.

He came to the vestibule where he and Bill had been separated, and hesitated before several doorways. He detected the sour, malty hum of the pub, and followed it. Pushing open a door, he found the private lounge, where he'd drunk with the enemy. The old rugs were as tacky as guilt on his boots.

Footsteps thundered somewhere above, and Warboys heard someone – the second sentry, he didn't doubt – yelling, 'They're coming! They're here!' He tensed up, ready as dust fell from cracks in the ceiling. Warboys sank into the shadows as several men clattered through the lounge door and over the bar, barely checking the place before they disappeared into the cellar. They were frightened. He waited a moment, and stepped out. Just as he did so, one last man stumbled through the opposite door, and Warboys came face to face with the landlord.

This time the landlord's hands were busying with a rifle, but caught dead in Warboys' sights, he held it high.

'Where is he?' Warboys demanded. 'Nouzi Aaranya?' As the barman looked at Warboys, his eyes narrowed in spiteful recognition.

'He's in bed with your old lady.'

Warboys fired. The landlord slapped on the bar as he fell dead to the floor. Warboys strode over the body, quickly pocketing a big brown bottle that was standing on the bar. Behind there he spotted the cellar trapdoor, still open. Unhooking a lamp, he slid down the ladder into the cellar. Tell-tale ripples still disrupted the flood water beyond the racks. He found the grating and plunged ahead, into the icy cold water, along the escape tunnel that had once led him out to the festival.

A sentry stood in the dim light below the exit, his breath clouding over the water.

'Who's there?' he called. 'That you, Sim?'

Warboys fired, shot him in the gut, then climbed over him to escape the tunnel. Wind shoved at him as he emerged onto the knoll. Another storm rolled out above, black and brooding, and looking back beyond the black slab of the city walls, Warboys saw the fiery glare of the AEC tower, churning out swathes of smoke to join the thunderclouds.

Warboys scaled the hill to see the second sentry bounding away through thick grass, making for the moors. He quickly reloaded, raised his rifle and fired. The shot snapped in the sentry's leg and brought him down in the grass. Snarling, Warboys slid down the hill and charged after him.

'The Janizar! Where is he? Nouzi Aaranya. The blue eyed boy. Where is he?' Warboys cocked his rifle and applied it to the man's bowels.

'He's gone!' sobbed the sentry. 'Long since!'

'Gone for that barn, hasn't he? Hasn't he? Gone for that last ship!'

Warboys felt himself boiling over and kicked the sentry in the face without waiting for an answer. The heel left an imprint on his head.

'How many are with him?'

'Three. Only three.'

'Where is it?'

The sentry pointed weakly over to the west. 'Over that hill till you come to a stream. Follow the drystone down.'

Warboys stood back, moved as if to go, then leaned back in and thumped the kid a few times with the stock of his rifle. He lost himself in the violence a moment, noticed a bead of saliva drop from his bottom lip and stopped. The sentry lay still. Tears welled close behind the rage. The sky shattered, filling with heavy globules of rain, and Warboys started across the heath toward the hangar, with rain and fire at his back like a lash.

The storm erased the landscape before him. A leftover tangle of festival bunting caught Warboys' boot as he gained the summit of a hill, and from there, beyond the rising moors, Warboys could see the dark line of the Eldask. In the murk at the bottom of the valley lay a drystone wall, leading down to a cluster of farmhouse buildings. Loose earth slithered, leading him on.

He followed the wall, hesitating as he saw a soldier leaning on the stone. The soldier wasn't moving and, as Warboys crept closer, he saw bloodcaked arms folded across a fatal laceration. Another lay behind the wall, his face submerged in a puddle. Nouzi Aaranya's handiwork.

The Hildegaard's Hangar came through the haze, the largest barn in an isolated farmyard. Outside, an adapted plough-cart sat end-up, laden with chains that rattled in the wind. Two more soldiers slumped around it, and nearby there lay a hooded Son, curled up dead against the wall. Warboys trod carefully past. Another rebel had been left propped against the barn door, and the faint, bilious stench of the Hildegaard puffed from within, exactly as Warboys remembered it from his jaunt over Salt Row.

The rattle and clunk of something like block and tackle sounded inside, heavy breath and winches being wound. Warboys stepped carefully through the open door. Swaying lamps cast erratic shadows of pillars and beams.

The Hildegaard was adrift, nudging against her makeshift scaffold. Her stern was jammed in the barn doorway, and she bobbed with the weight of whoever was on board. Warboys walked into her shadow and saw the ballast nets slung under the hull. He circled around warily. He raised his Entwick, and advanced on the port side.

Nouzi Aaranya was at the array, between pipes and gauges and levers, haplessly winding at winches, intermittently clasping at his twitching hand. The little fucker had no idea how to launch her, and looked to be losing his mind again.

Just as Warboys levelled his Entwick, a rebel came splashing around the barn door, carrying a coil of rope and a gaff hook. Warboys whirled about, and had fired before he knew it. The shot tore open the new arrival's throat. He staggered sideways, teetered on one leg, then slapped down into the mud.

The Janizar moved before Warboys could turn back, darting around the array and out of sight, tipping the ship. Warboys pulled himself on board; his added weight sank her a moment, so that she dipped under the archway of the barn. Warboys steadied himself, crouching against the gunwale as the wind drew her out. Rain rattled on the balloon, and the wind set the deck-lamp swinging.

'I only want the ship, Captain!' called the Janizar. Warboys could hear the shudder in his voice. 'I only want to earn my way to Maia.'

'Nope. I saw her first.'

He set to reloading.

'I can cut you down before you are ready to shoot again.'

'You're not *that* fast.'

A roll of thunder sounded overhead. The hull tipped heavily to starboard, showing the ground rolling past.

'Captain. There is *kaarya* between us. So I am allowing you to leave. Please go now.'

'Kaarya, is there? You killed my Dad!'

'I tried to save him!' yelled Nouzi Aaranya, his voice cracking.

'Fuck as like, you did. You ate our fucking chips, then killed hundreds in their *sleep*!'

'Nai! After you opened the duct, I climbed in and set the bomb, so that the powder room would not be immediately affected. So that I would have time to...'

His voice faltered whilst Warboys cocked the bolt of his Entwick.

'I went upstairs to open the cells – to help him out. But your old man Bill wouldn't come. He insisted on staying to help fight the fire.'

'So you just *let* him?'

'His kaarya is his own.'

Warboys opened his mouth in anger, but he knew damn well it was true. *He came looking for me*, Bill had said. He could see it now, the strung out kid trying to talk the old man about, the old man refusing to come, staying to *do the right thing*. It brought an unwanted tear to Warboys' eye.

The Hildegaard struck the end of her anchor line and pitched sharply, dumping both men across the deck. Warboys stumbled towards the Janizar, who sprung up from his knees, dhas flying clear to snap the rifle away. Warboys let it go, following through Nouzi's face with his elbow, feeling the satisfying pain of bone smashing into bone. Nouzi Aaranya slithered but kept his footing as the Hildegaard pivoted again, pitching Warboys back onto his arse. He saw the glint of dhas, and flinched, expecting to die. But the Janizar had stopped. His blade wavered, whilst he sagged against the stove, faltering again. The Hildegaard strained at the anchor line like a hooked fish. Warboys glanced and saw the rifle against the gunwale, only just out of his reach.

Warboys rose on one knee, his hands up. Nouzi Aaranya stood hapless behind his shaking blade. Mournful about what he'd done, how he'd failed. Wound up to hell. He'd tried to help Bill. But Warboys couldn't extinguish his anger. He wanted revenge. Fast as a bucket of knives, this kid, but he'd defeat himself, if you let him. He affected calm.

'Alright then,' he said. 'What happened?'

'I tried to bring him away,' muttered the Janizar, scanning the deck as if to fathom some proof of his account there. 'But he wouldn't come, eh?'

His blade shuddered, dropped some. He looked up at Warboys forlornly.

'Alright, mate...' cooed Warboys, mildly, whilst underneath, white hot anger pulsed. More than anger. Panic. 'I can see you didn't mean it. Got a lot on your mind, I know...' Warboys shuddered with self-revulsion as he caught this vile part of him emulating Bill's charm, with the old man not yet cold in the earth. 'Got your Maia to think of, haven't you?'

'Ai,' said Nouzi Aaranya, his eyes shining with tears as they lowered.

Warboys snatched up the Entwick, and Nouzi Aaranya looked up just in time to see him fire. The Janizar's shoulder jerked back, his heels shimmying all the way back as he crashed into the aft deckrail. For a split second, the pitiful blue eyes gleamed, earnest in acceptance of betrayal, then failure. Then his feet flipped over and he was gone.

'Stupid fucking *kid*...' spat Warboys, but regret arose instantly in his chest. Panic, because now there was no one else left to blame. It arose in his throat as he looked back and saw Blackhaven in the distance, glowing like Hell itself.

He found the anchor line and hacked it loose. The ship pitched, and Warboys staggered back as she was snatched away by the wind, rapidly leaving the glow of the city in the distance, rising until there was nothing to see but rain and darkness. The ascent made his stomach feel as if it was dropping out through his arse repeatedly, and he plastered himself to the deck in terror. Clinging to a jackpin, trying not to see the kid's face, so *pitiful* as he'd fallen to his death, Warboys' existence was reduced to desperately *holding on*.

There was nothing else for it.

Part Three

So the Janizar Arja wrought his blade from the last of his brothers and fell weeping, for despite their betrayal, despite his victory, he felt a vast sorrow. Not knowing which direction to now turn his blade, he gazed upon his reflection in the sullied edge, and found the face of a stranger.

— *"The Tale of Arja"; Translation from an anonyous source on behalf of the Black Flower Archive.*

23 THE RED LANTERN

Vapour rushed over the deck, soaking Warboys to the skin. Belaying pins and choppers, catpaws and mallets, bottles, boxes, tins and packs all slid along the deck, creaking on the way like a bunch of moaning old codgers. For a time he slithered with them from one side of the midship to the other.

The Hildegaard listed sharply, swinging him over to the stove. The stink of bile and sweat there was repugnant, but it was *warm*. He hadn't realised how cold he was, and clung there a moment.

Then there was a *belch* from below, loud enough to rattle the timbers of the ship and reverberate through his trousers. He jumped up in fright, struck his head on something with a ridiculous gonging sound, and stumbled onto the deckrail. Below, the greyness rushed past, and fear of the fall stabbed at his toes from a thousand feet below. As he teetered there, the wheel span unmanned. Levers and pulleys wagged as if they were all enjoying the sight of him there, swaying like a nancy. There was another rollicking belch below, followed by a fine, fizzing noise. The piping above the stove creaked, and the ship lurched up into cloud.

Warboys tucked his Entwick under his arm and shuffled toward the stove-thing. He reached for the hatch and hauled it open, expecting to be pounced on by some exotic beast. Instead, a cloud of stink gushed out, and it was all he could do to hold onto the contents of his stomach. Cursing, he peered into the innards of the box, and gawped at what he saw.

Hilda was *alive*.

Where he'd expected to find some sort of furnace, some boiler-and-pipe mechanic, there was what looked like a butcher's offal tray, a box of bad guts with dark, fleshy ribbing. Bilious liquid sloshed about, bubbling around the remains of some half-digested mush. He stepped back, frowning, and found what he supposed was the engine hatch, forward of the hold. He pulled it open to the aroma of a hot barracks after a hard drilling. Writhing pink expanses of flesh worked below, like great slugs housed in a kind of split-pipe canister. Through watering eyes, Warboys saw that the squirming slug things *were* the engine; threaded airscrew axles were housed between two of the great slugs, and as the ripple of their muscles flowed up and down their bodies, so the axle span. Various barbs were poised over sections of these engine slugs, attached to cables leading back to the levers on the array. Like spurs in a horse, he supposed, perhaps to speed or slow the things. A faint squelching noise was the only sound they made.

'Fuck-ing Hell...'

The *Hildegaard* dipped again, and it was all too much. He slapped the hatch lid down and threw up through his fingers, sinking back down to the deck. A headache weighed him down, the warmth loosened him, reminding him he hadn't slept for two nights. In a moment, he'd get up and try to steer the bloody thing properly, plot a course and all that.

In a moment. Five more minutes.

He slept.

~ ~ ~

Nouzi Aaranya fell.

He had sometimes wondered what it would be like to drift away, to death or to Maia. It sometimes seemed there was little difference.

One of his arms wouldn't respond, having been numbed by the shot. The other caught the ballast nets slung below, and was almost wrenched out of its socket as he swung down under the keel. Clouds tore open below to reveal the dark, mountainous woods of the Eldask, spread in all directions. The wind buffeted the Hildegaard, and each dip seemed to burn the wound. He managed to force his legs up, and stuffed himself inside the keel netting, next to a stained, piss stinking ballast tank. He gasped for breath, faint with pain and shock.

The airscrews whooshed behind his head. Lightning flashed, and he could see the trees gathering in lines hundreds of feet below, marching over the mountains toward home.

Another flash, and he saw the tiny pinprick blots of the hijacked *Tabitha* and *Rosamundt* away to the west, fighting the northerly wind for their course. But the Hildegaard was losing them fast. The wind had her, pushing her north over the Eldask, towards Gienha.

He was heading home, to death, or to Maia.

Panic set in, and dizziness overcame him.

~ ~ ~

Nouzi had been twelve years old the first time he and his brothers had gone to pay tribute to Maia.

Cushioned by plump blossom trees, the mirror-like surface of Adharza Lake reflected the Asta Jana Aasvina. Eight skinny boys – Kai, Sila, Hanu, Goro, Hazar, Nasnim, Nouzi and Upa – looked keenly across the lake at the triangular apex of the distant *Samagat*.

'You can fight, eh?' growled Sukhanava, as he paced behind them. 'You can hunt, and kill.'

He paused pointedly by Kai – still the tallest among them – and straightened his back with his stick. 'But not all trials need show muscle and blood. At the end of the hunting season it is customary to let fly the lanterns, in offering to Maia. This will teach you the temperance you need to balance fighting spirit. Now, sit.'

They collapsed all too readily. Upa stifled a yawn and felt the Master's stick about his ear. He pulled faces at Nouzi whilst Sukhanava gave out sheets of thin, coloured paper and a board to each boy.

'Paper folding. Make *Rohi* lamps. When night falls we will light them and set them to fly over the lake to Maia in heaven. Remember – temperance!'

And with that, he left them to it.

Nouzi had done paper folding before. He remembered Maia's soft hands pressing and folding before him, creating dainty models of birds and frogs. He set keenly to work, smoothing his bright red sheet over the board to begin, whilst groans arose from the others.

'Avai,' moaned Kai, scratching at himself in irritation. 'This is not *temperance*, eh? This is aggravation. Hunted day and night by the old man's dogs, and then this! He insults us. I think he is seeing how much we will take. I think he wants us to challenge him!'

The others murmured to echo agreement, as they always did; since leaving the nurseries Kai had declared he would be their leader – their *Yin* – and had waged a campaign of intimidation to this end. Then Nouzi heard Upa mutter, 'Why don't you go and tell him that then?'

Kai stiffened and looked up. Nouzi dared glance at Upa, saw the crescent birthmark creased by his ill-conceived mirth.

Kai sprung up, strode over and kicked Upa to the ground. 'What was that, half-wit? Eh? Did you talk to me?'

'Nai,' he said.

'Ai, good! Because I won't take insolence from you, End Born!

Put you in your place I will, eh?'

Like Nouzi, Upa had long been bullied. They called him *End Born*, because of the birthmark on his face, shaped like the waning moon and thought to augur weakness. Upa recovered himself and stooped over his board, his face flushed with anger. Nouzi Aaranya tried to catch his eye.

'Hui, Asekna!' snarled Kai, seeing him. '*Bed-wetter*. 'Don't you pull faces at me you stinker!'

'I wasn't...' began Nouzi, as Kai's palm caught him soldily across the face, knocking him down. Hanu and Sila sprang up like monkeys, eager to see his face boil over. But Nouzi waited, said nothing, and Kai went back to his mangled paper. Nouzi composed himself, lowered his head and folded.

Heat shimmered over the lake, where bright, metallic dragonflies cut erratically through the air. There was peace, all but for Kai's huffing and puffing, his testy crinkling of the paper.

'Huzhat! This is shit, eh?'

Nouzi concentrated closely on the lines of his folds, making it an offering to Maia Devu in heaven. Soon he had a fine, red lantern. Symmetrical, multifaceted, spacious, lighter than air. His face beamed a little with the thought of the gift.

Kai huffed again.

'You know what I read in the *Datyas* about the lanterns?' began Upa, not looking up from his own folding.

'Did I ask you to speak, fatty?'

'It is said that the Janizar's lantern, when sent to Heaven, is an augur of his future success. That it is alike to his seed to Maia. The seed that travels the furthest, so augurs him to Maia. That's what I read.'

Nouzi saw Kai stiffen as he took this in, and felt his glare. He concentrated on tweaking his lantern, as if hoping to fold himself away from notice. But Kai was up on his feet. He came looming, looking the lantern over before snatching it up, throwing down the crumpled green mess of his own half effort in exchange. Nouzi looked up, ready to object, but stopped. Kai flushed with satisfaction at his catch, the others all jeering like a pack of dogs. Nouzi felt tears burning behind his eyes, whilst they laughed and lay about to wait for Sukhanava.

'Jaluka!' muttered Upa, glaring at Kai. But Nouzi said nothing, knowing he could only try to salvage something from Kai's crumpled green papers.

Sukhanava returned at dusk to assemble them by the lake. Nouzi choked in fury as he stepped up, the water like a black mirror, the crumpled green mess like shit in his hands. Sukhanava inspected the lanterns, his eyes catching a moment on Nouzi before making his address.

'So to Maia!' he commanded.

Nouzi watched Kai launch the red lantern. It lofted wonderfully, leading the others over the lake, their reflections forming a shimmering procession into the dark. The green lantern arose last, catching fire almost immediately. It fell blazing to the lake, whilst the red one soared on toward the Samagat.

Sukhanava patted Kai on the shoulder before dismissing all but Nouzi. Kai's smug expression enraged him, and he glared after him, knowing he'd regret it later. Sukhanava waited until the others had gone. 'Impatience, Nouzi-Chai. Impatience lets the wilderness into one's being. Chaos. Diffusion of *Manas*!'

'Ai!' barked Nouzi. He couldn't argue, whatever the truth. Sukhanava pointed to an isolated tree near the water's edge. 'Without food nor sleep, sit there the night, as the creator sat beneath the *Bodhi* tree, where enlightenment seeped into his senses. And there learn patience.'

And so Nouzi sat under the tree in his undergarments, watching the lanterns drift away into the dark, suffering the limb stinging agonies of injustice that only a child understands. He thought he might actually die of frustration at one point – until Upa came quietly through the undergrowth, and sat beside him without a word, until the morning came.

Year after year Sukhanava's tour of trials ended at Adharza for the tribute, and each year, Kai claimed Nouzi's lantern, each time sabotaging Nouzi's efforts. And each time Nouzi was sent to sit under the Bodhi tree.

One day the Asta sat at the *Paradha* – a circle of standing stones in the forest, etched with Datyas specifically for the education of Janizar. Each boy read from his own panel, whilst Sukhanava strode between them, stick folded behind his back ready to lash them mercilessly about the head for lapses in concentration or posture. They read the *Heroics*, tales of great Janizar of the past, whilst brightly fluttering finches twittered and broke across shafts of light, daring them to be distracted and brave Sukhanava's stick. Nouzi read the tale of Arja, who willingly walked into the wilds to find himself in the trap of his corrupt Asta, only to escape and pick them off one by one. Then the Janizar Kalandra, and his vendetta with a pack of wolves that spanned two years and seven days. He wearily wondered how likely it was that Arja or Kalandra had been the ones being beaten and having their lanterns stolen. He began to idly fantasise about beheading his brothers.

There was a frightful shrieking from above, and all looked up to see a hawk snatch a small garfinch from the air. An explosion of feathers littered the paradha as the hawk perched on a stone and began tearing the finch to shreds.

'See, Jana Aasvina!' said the old Master, seeming pleased. 'One moment we are in the light, the next... *Pfft!*' He flicked his fingers apart in gesture. Hanu and Sila began sniggering, repeating this.

'Pfft!'

'Pfft!'

Sukhanava's smile dropped, and a sharp crack about Sila's ear ended the fun. But Nouzi and Upa stared awed at the hawk, sharing a look as she wheeled off low through the Paradha with her prey, and smiled broadly at one another.

'Pfft!'

There were cages set in the streams nearby, used to snare crayfish for the camp. Nouzi and Upa often used these as an excuse to stay away from the others. On one such occasion, Nouzi and Upa sneaked back to the paradha, using their nets to catch a finch, which in turn they tied to a branch overhanging the stones. After much waiting, the hawk came and took the bait, and another gleeful explosion of feathers left them with great joy.

'Hui, she is like that *sarpa* in the story, eh? Cakora, the winged beast that shadowed the lands of Yev. '

'Ai,' agreed Nouzi. 'Cakora.'

Cakora became their lifeline. Over time they trained her to sit on a long arm gauntlet, to wear a cowl and swoop for offerings, to discern between prey and feather-dummies. And in their togetherness and enthusiasm, they began to think of mischief.

Eventually the time came when Sukhanava ended their vigil in the wilds and sent them to make offering to Maia. Again, Sukhanava ordered the lanterns built, and again Nouzi worked devotedly, made an offer of himself with the finest blood red tribute to Maia. Again Kai came to help himself to the lamp, barely even bothering to be aggressive about it by this time.

They convened again, at dusk on the shore of Adharza Lake, and the lanterns were lit and sent up. Kai stood smug as the red one soared clear, as if he were king Janizar and was already buried in Maia-Devu.

Then a dark arrow shot across the sky. Cakora tore right

through the lantern, tearing strips of paper away until it rolled over and caught fire. Kai, powerless to object, saw his pride fall burning to the lake, and the two runts of the litter were almost bursting as they stamped and smirked and punched one another in delight.

Sukhanava turned in surprise, his mouth taut. He looked over the two smirking runts, at the seething Kai, and back to the lake. And then, for the first and only time that Nouzi could remember, Sukhanava laughed out loud.

'I always wondered,' he began, hoarsely, 'how year after year, red paper could seem green. I thought my eyes were failing, eh?'

The Master dismissed everyone but Nouzi and Upa. They waited for the others to leave, braving the hatred in Kai's expression as he passed.

Left alone with the master, they tightened their buttocks ready for a whipping. Yet to their surprise, Sukhanava simply sat. Warily, they lowered themselves beside him and were quiet for a time, listening to his measured breath.

'These are times of peace,' he said after a time. 'In times of peace, the warlike man turns the spear first against his brother, and then on himself. This is why I teach temperance, peace as well as war, because a predator without prey lives in fear. Some take this lesson better than others, nai?'

'Ai!' they barked, confused, but pleased to be there despite all the days they'd cursed Sukhanava's cruelty.

Sukhanava breathed again, corrected Upa's posture, then stood, arms behind his back, rigid as ever. 'You must show me that hawk of yours some time, End Born,' he said, before walking away, and as the two smiled broadly at one another, Nouzi almost forgot to watch his red lantern, now high enough to meld with the stars.

~ ~ ~

Nouzi Aaranya felt the world sway and opened his eyes to see the Eldask stretched in all directions like some crumpled blanket on a vast unmade bed. The pain in his shoulder came a moment later. The ship banked, swinging the Janizar like a fresh caught fish. The airscrews wailed, and the flukes slapped from side to side. The Hildegaard was drifting rudderless.

Suspecting that Warboys had been thrown overboard, Nouzi Aaranya braved the pain in his shoulder and crawled from the net, up onto the ratlines and over the rail. There he saw Warboys slumped against the stove, and rolled quietly over onto deck. Biting back a cry of pain, he held himself still and assessed the captain. Warboys' hair was caked with blood, but he was still breathing. After a moment Nouzi Aaranya dared to approach, and snatched the rifle away.

I ought to cut his throat now, he thought. *If I were true Janizar. Cut his throat and throw him overboard.* He looked into the direction of the wind, toward the great front of stormcloud that reared up ahead, and knew that the Hildegaard was closing on the boundary, where the temperate winds hit the humid air of home. Beyond there lay Gienha, the Samagat, and Maia. But due west, *Tabitha* and *Rosamundt* were little more than smudges. On board those ships were Uparagha and his brothers, a core of the Sons, under the guidance of the pilot Valego, heading toward the White Spur Coast and whatever Upa was planning next. He was duty bound to deliver the ship to Upa at White Spur. To be derided by his brothers again, whilst Upa decided his fate.

Or...

Or, he could let the wind take him directly toward home. He could cut free from his brothers, claim the airship as a personal capture, and offer it to the fathers. Forget his brothers. It wouldn't be the first time he'd left them for Maia. Perhaps the Sekhet back in Gienha would be impressed enough to allow him to return to her. He could drift like a lantern, straight to her, as he had always dreamed...

His eyelid began to twitch. He imagined that great black triangle of the Samagat waiting to swallow him again. Spots clouded in the corners of his vision.

He cursed, suffered a moment of desperation. An impulse told him to throw himself overboard.

Instead, he turned away, breathed, steadied himself. Focussing on Warboys, he scoured around, found some rope to restrain him. Then he approached the controls. A strange chaos of wagging instruments and dials sprouted from the deck, seeming an unweeded wilderness of machinery. But a wheel, he understood. Setting himself fast, Nouzi Aaranya turned hard to port, nosing into the wind after the hijacked ships. He held hard to course, away from home and Maia, and forced himself not to look back.

24 BARNACLE

There was light invading Warboys' bedroom, a breeze through the stale, sweaty air. A figure loomed in the light, the old man banging about at the crack of dawn. Another job down the yards, probably. Warboys winced, feeling a weight over him, not daring to move in case it was a hangover waiting to ambush him. Bill pulled at his sheets, calling him a lazy bugger – was the old sod actually *tipping* him out of bed?

'Fucking hell, alright! Just five more minutes, Dad...'

Light prised open his eyelids. Warboys felt the motion of the *Hildegaard,* then the weight dropped – not a hangover, but deep and aching loss. The recollection that the old man would never pull him out of bed again. He took a sharp breath. The clouds had broken to reveal meek patches of sky, and the brightness of it all seemed to Warboys to be in poor taste.

The slick deck reflected a figure sitting cross-legged to the fore, with his back to Warboys, working one sinewy shoulder that ran with blood as he gouged at it with a knife. The pronounced outcrop of Nouzi Aaranya's cheekbone showed as he turned to acknowledge Warboys.

'Sat Nam, Captain,' he said, flatly.

Despite himself, Warboys felt relief to see the kid alive. For a split second, he closed his eyes and breathed thanks. Then, remembering Bill was still dead, and realising his hands had been bound, relief burnt away into anger.

'Bastard!' he growled. 'I sent you overboard! What the fuck are you doing on my ship?'

'Hui, Captain,' came the boy's unhurried voice. 'Rest, nai?'

'I'll rest you, you fucker. Why didn't you just cut my throat whilst I was asleep?'

'I didn't come to kill you, Captain. I came for the ship.'

'Fucking untie me.'

Nouzi Aaranya said nothing, and went on gouging at his wound. Warboys cursed. Looking up, he saw numerous gashes and welts in the gasbag. The needles on the array – altimeters and pressure gauges, or whatever the bloody hell they were – shuddered erratically. Levers with severed wires wagged loose, and sulphurous gas hissed free. In the bright of day, Hilda didn't look so good.

Warboys saw Nouzi Aaranya flinch. Blood dribbled from his shoulder as he worked out a sliver of metal.

'Looks nasty, that. I hope you bleed to death. Where are you taking me, you fucking barnacle?' He looked around at the pale sky, trying to see over the deckrail. It was colder, fresher, wherever they were.

Nouzi Aaranya sniffed, waited for a moment of turbulence to pass. 'Captain Warboys. I am sorry.'

'Fuck off. Don't talk to me about it. Not all of us get to come back from the dead.'

'He deserved a better death. He was an honourable man. He told me that—'

'Told you *what*? Have a little conversation, did you, whilst the fucking building was falling around you?'

'Nai, Captain. We spoke, he and I, before he was released from the Sunken Pig. He told me—'

'No! Listen. Don't you dare talk to me about him. Never.'

'Ai.'

'I'd sooner you *did* cut my fucking throat before you talk about him again. You hear me?'

'Ai.'

The Janizar bowed with a shame and humility that made Warboys feel sorry for the kid whilst also wanting to slap him. Nouzi Aaranya bandaged his shoulder, and neither said a word for a time. But Warboys was restless.

'You wanted the ships all along, didn't you? All that about the festival was a load of shit.'

'Nai. To guard the Sekhet and ensure *Gata* was our first duty. But Uparagha... for some time, he has had his own thinking about where our kaarya lies.'

'I'll bet he fucking does.'

'Ai. Upa offered freedom for Valego the airman, and Valego trained us. He captained the *Tabitha* from its dock.'

'What are you going to do with them?'

Nouzi Aaranya shrugged. 'There is a place called White Spur, where we can practice.'

Warboys wondered where he had heard of the White Spur Coast, then remembered that the pirates in his old adventure pamphlets used to go there. It was an uninhabited, rocky strip, supposedly on the border between Aaland and Andamark.

'Practice for what?'

'Upa did not say.'

'He's not told *you*, you mean. You're just the errand boy, aren't you?'

Nouzi Aaranya said nothing.

'Are *we* going to White Spur, then?'

'Avai, I don't know. You shot my navigator.'

Warboys swore in exasperation, then laughed bitterly. Then there was a noise so familiar that Warboys barely registered it at first. A gull's cry.

He watched a pair of herring gulls circle by, sudden, unwelcome memories of the harbour, of piled up lobster nets, of Lily Warboys in her workshirt, soiled knuckles, waiting on the wharf-side. Bill gone.

A pull of descent grew in his gut. He sat up, frowned, listened. A long, low undulating rush sounded from all around, in and out of the wind.

'That's the fucking *sea!*' he growled, and stood carefully, his wrists still bound, his neck craning to see overboard.

'Ai.'

Sure enough, the western sea churned below, stretching into a featureless expanse where pale grey sea met pale grey sky. Not a ship nor the shadow of land could be seen in any direction. The bizarre, whale-like shadow of the Hilda shivered over the waves below, proving that they couldn't have been more than a couple of hundred feet up.

'You fuckwit! What have you done?'

Nouzi Aaranya stood, hand on dhas as if expecting to see some beast hovering off the starboard side. 'Eh?'

'We're sinking! We're going down! This ain't no sailing ship, boy! If we hit that water we're fucked. You're going to have to untie me.'

'Nai. You would try to shoot me.'

'I won't have to bloody shoot you. You'll drown!'

Nouzi Aaranya paced uneasily from one side to the other, peering over as if he might find proof of something other than salt water with which to dispute Warboys' claim.

'Nai. Tell me how to do it.'

'Untie me!'

'Nai!' barked the Janizar, his hands hovering over valves and dials. Warboys strained at his leash, also trying to make sense of the levers and rigs as best he could.

'Have you ever been out on the sea before, mate?'

'Nai.'

'Well you're going to be *under* it soon. Untie me.'

'Can you fly this machine?'

'Not like this I can't. Come on!'

Nouzi Aaranya turned suddenly on him, and the *dhas* flashed clear to cut him loose. Warboys staggered back into the deckrail, and shot the Janizar a glare before stumbling over to the array, massaging his wrists.

Most of the meters seemed to be loose, indicating low pressure. A wide, plate-sized dial bobbed tightly in the red, over a thick pipe that jutted out from the stove. It wound up to a soft pipe that was bound into the gasbag. They needed lift. A likely looking brass valve was set half way down. Warboys gripped the valve, but it wouldn't shift.

'This one. Help me.'

Nouzi Aaranya looked around, found a gooseneck and rammed it through the rungs of the valve so they could pull it.

There was a sigh from the Hilda as the meter fell flatly out of the red, followed by a great bubbling sound that shuddered the decks. The balloon creaked overhead as it tightened. Warboys heard a leak hissing somewhere. His stomach clenched as they hit the curve of ascent, beginning to pull up...

But it was too late.

They were thrown to their knees as the buoyed Hildegaard hit the water. A shower of white foam slapped over the deck. Greedy waves streamed over the gunwales and sloshed down into the hold, pulling the aft back down to the sea.

The Hilda's flight was finished.

25 PONTOON

'Bail out!' yelled Warboys, clambering over Nouzi toward the pressure valves. 'Get below and bail out!'

'Eh?'

Warboys shoved him toward the hold.

'Throw the bloody water out! Find a bucket or a pump! Do it with your fucking hands if you have to!'

Warboys slithered back to the array, found another valve set to the aft and hauled at it, trying to get some lift before the hold filled up. Before him, the Janizar floundered in knee deep water, heaving out with a fire bucket.

'Avai, Captain! Help!'

'I'm trying!'

The valve gave, and something shuddered below. Nouzi Aaranya sprang up from the hold as a great cloud of stinking gasses erupted, and the aft started to level. The balloon swelled, and water poured out through the scuppers as the gondola began to pull away from the water.

The rigging strained.

'We're too heavy! Keep bailing!'

A line frayed and snapped. Other rigs began to creak alarmingly, and Warboys skidded around the array, seeing now that another set of pressure needles bobbed dangerously. He eased off the red lifting valves and stepped away, arms raised as if to placate her. The balloon held taut on her rigs above, just about holding the gondola upright in the water.

'Is it right?'

'I don't fucking know, do I? Seems to be keeping her from sinking for now... but we'll never lift off carrying all that water.'

The wind turned them, sending them sidelong into the waves. The balloon swayed like a metronome, inviting a tide athwartships.

Nouzi Aaranya threw down his fire bucket.

'Avai, the thing is picked with holes. Maybe if we cut a big hole through the hull to drain faster when we lift?'

'Are you soft? I don't even know if she'll fly.'

'Eh, well, it can hardly be said that she *floats,* eh?'

'Listen, I'm not giving up a decent hull, even if it is holed. Maybe *you* could go over for ballast, eh? I seem to remember I already cut you loose once.'

'Ballast!' yelled Nouzi Aaranya, delightedly. 'Ai! *Guruta*! Is there some to cut loose?'

'Don't know. Help me look.'

The two hurried around, finding a few sandbags to cut loose, but little else. Nouzi Aaranya waded around in the hold, dragging boxes and barrels out, whilst Warboys went for the engine hatch, bracing himself for the stench. The flooded engine slugs shivered in the cold.

'Hang about. She's *alive*, ain't she? This thing's like a bloody big gut.'

'Ai. So?'

'So it must have a back end...'

He climbed down below, finding the fat, gristly base of the stove. On two wire frames, two separate organs sat mounted: one a pulsating, veiny balloon of a thing, surrounded by spurs lined with red cords – he guessed this was the gas bladder that fed the balloon – the other, a swollen, blue veined bag that pressed against the hold. Foamy liquid was visible through its translucent membrane, and the spurs poised over this were lined with blue cords.

'Right. Red is the fartbox, blue is the pisspot.'

He stumbled above decks, and over Nouzi Aaranya, who was frantically casting folding chairs, gaff hooks, barrels and god knew whatever else across the deck.

'Just watch what you're doing with that shit!' he barked, as he passed. 'We might need some of it.'

'Ai, captain!'

Warboys found a blue lined lever and hauled it back and forth, finding a squashy resistance, as if he were pulling a cask ale. A vile stench of ammonia bubbled out from the aft, yellowing the foam that slopped onto deck. Warboys pumped away, emptying a good few pounds from the Hilda's bowels, his distant neediness for a pint tainted as he went. The ship rose, but another wave slapped the side and sucked her back down. The airscrews died, flapping listlessly in the current.

Warboys swore, gauging the darker clouds on the horizon. 'She won't take a slap off a haddock drifting side-on like this. We need to get her stable somehow...'

'We can make a Sambhuya!'

'Eh?'

'A *Sambhuya!*' grinned Nouzi, seeming to be enjoying himself a bit too much for Warboys' liking. 'Our teacher Sukhanava taught us how to... to steady our canoes for heavy loads in the lakes. Is like... two logs together.'

'A pontoon, you mean? It's a good idea. It's a bloody good idea. In fact...'

Warboys scoured the Hildegaard, finding one of the welts in the balloon. He saw that it, like the engine was a living thing, and realised that the welts had *scabbed over* – it wasn't a hollow envelope, but a many celled organ, much like a lung. If he looked up close, he could see tiny threadlike veins under the envelope.

'Look at this. She's got to be watertight, hasn't she?'

'Ai.'

'Right. We're going to vent some of the lifting gas. Then we can sink the balloon into the sea, get her out of the wind, and rig up the gondola alongside it, see? We won't fly, but least we won't sink.'

'Ai. Good. *Sambhuya*.'

Buffeted by waves, the two struggled together to de-rig the Hilda's envelope. Numerous times they fell into the sea, gasping with exhauston as they dragged themselves back aboard. It took them the day to do, and by the time they'd finished, the Hilda's great balloon lay strapped beside the gondola like a belly up whale. With a few hours more work they made a pair of flimsy runners on arms, meshed and nailed together with whatever tools they could find, and strapped them to empty canisters, barrels and crates for buoyancy. It would have to do.

At last light, still wet and dripping, Warboys managed to get a fire going in a tin bucket on the foredeck and, by its heat, felt exhaustion overwhelm him. All day, there had been sign of neither land nor sail in any direction. And what was more, a quick inventory of the hold revealed that there was nothing to eat, and very little fresh water. Warboys looked over at Nouzi Aaranya, who stood on the port runner, looking out to sea as if he was waiting for his medal.

'Oi! Numbnuts!' he said after a time. 'Stop posing and get here.'

Nouzi Aaranya sprang into life, running along the arm of the pontoon, flailing like a kid balancing on an alley wall.

'Ai, Captain?' he barked, landing gracefully on the remains of the deck.

Warboys passed him a flask of water. 'Rest. You're no good knackered.'

'Ai.'

Warboys watched him sit down, then rummaged around the clutter on deck and found a small tin medical box.

'I'll clean that shoulder of yours properly, before it gets infected.'

Nouzi swivelled obediently, and hauled off his shirt. He was very faithful, thought Warboys, spotting a claw hammer within arm's reach on the deck. *I could knock his brains out right now,* he thought. *Probably should.* But the anger wouldn't work, wouldn't stick to the kid, somehow. He took a shaky breath.

'We aren't friends. But we're going to have to stick together, you and me,' said Warboys, knowing he was instructing himself as well. 'Men that don't pull together at sea die at sea. We save our differences until shore, right?'

'Ai.'

'If we're lucky we'll come across some schooner on the freight line. We're going to have to frame ourselves a bit if we're to have a chance. And that means you do what I say, right?'

'Ai. Have you experience in sailing, Captain?'

'I do. I'm a chartered seaman. Well, I've got a half a chartership, anyway.'

'Is okay. You only have half a vessel.'

'Less of your backchat.'

'Ai.'

'Cos if I have to shoot you again, it'll be between the fucking eyes.'

'Ai.'

Once Warboys had finished, Nouzi Aaranya turned and pointed to the scabbed wound on Warboys' head, where the brick from the AEC had hit him. Just before the kid had pulled him out. Had he saved Warboys' life? He didn't like the idea.

'Can I stitch this for you, Captain?'

'No, just leave it.'

'Sukhanava taught us stitches. Told us once that he'd stitched himself to a yak to cross the mountains.'

'Just leave it, alright?' snapped Warboys. 'Be quiet now.'

'Ai.'

Warboys turned away, suddenly desperate to go for a long walk. The ramshackle setup suddenly seemed so precarious against the vast, rollicking ocean. So often he had bemoaned his dad's voice. Bemoaned his comments, his advice, his warnings and worries, dismissing it as endless droning. Now there was only silence, an empty horizon, and he understood how *little* Bill had said, when he thought about it. How much tolerance and patience Bill's silence held. He could almost imagine the old man's quiet, that palpable sense of *pride*, even now, after what Warboys had caused. A fit of grief began to overwhelm him, so he pretended to look for something in the hold.

'Hui, Captain, are you...' began Nouzi Aaranya, appearing over the hold. He stopped, saw the tears in Warboys' eyes, and conceded a polite bow before leaving him alone.

Warboys wished Bill were there, with a story about how *he'd* survived at sea. Wished badly to be lectured, advised, lambasted. He shut his eyes and crouched in the hold, cursing himself until the shaking stopped.

26 KAARYA

With sight of neither sail nor land, Warboys paced up and down the deck whilst the sea rose and fell in deepening troughs. Each dip drew a pang of hunger, reminding him again that he had not eaten for days. What was more, the water level was rising steadily again in the hold, even despite their efforts at patching it. Warboys began to feel the weight of that empty horizon. There wasn't a family he knew in Kingstown who hadn't lost men to the sea.

And yet, Nouzi Aaranya worked quietly, stitching happily away at the balloon, as if they were just waiting for a delivery from the butcher's boy.

He was getting on Warboys' nerves.

'Alright there, happy crack?'

'Ai.'

'A strong wind'll put us over, y'know. Belly up and jiggered.'

'Ai,' shrugged Nouzi Aaranya. 'Kaarya.'

Warboys grunted. He needed to occupy himself.

'Just you keep the stove guts fed and watch that pressure gauge whilst I go down and try and plug some more holes.'

'Ai!' barked the Janizar, with a bright little bow. Warboys lit a lamp and went crawling down below with a knot of torn rags and a tin of caulking.

As he worked, he heard Nouzi Aaranya cantering around above, as if they hadn't been awake and grafting to stay afloat for the last two days. Warboys lugged a mire of grief with him, and the kid was tap dancing across the surface of it, as if he never had anything to do with Blackhaven.

'You might want to save some strength up there, kid.'

'Ai.'

Soon the Janizar added to his pacing by mumbling some sort of recital, so Warboys passed up the spare bellows to see if Nouzi could make use of them as a bilge pump. It might shut him up anyway. But Nouzi Aaranya soon found a way to make it work, and the vigorous, squeaky pumping replaced the muttering in getting on Warboys' nerves.

Despite their efforts, the water level was the same by dusk. Warboys came above covered with the greasy, saline film of the engine's sweat, and saw Nouzi stripped to the waist and pumping away in the dim light, showing no sign of tiring.

'Going to pump all night, are you?'

'Ai.'

'You know there's still a load of holes in the hull.'

'Ai.'

'Are you going to pump out the whole western ocean, then?'

'Ai!' barked the Janizar, and carried on, whilst Warboys again scanned the featureless horizon.

'Is this your idea of fun?'

'Kaarya lays a certain path, nai? Our job is to walk it well.'

'Is bilge-pumping part of Janizar training, then?'

'If kaarya lays it before us, ai.'

'Kaarya!' spat Warboys. 'My arse. Just sit down for a minute, will you?'

The Janizar dropped into what he called his *sanyas* posture – a cross legged sitting position, like one of the gurus out of the sideshows in Coperny's Tigertown district, eyes closed, full of calm.

This also got on Warboys nerves.

'Fucking *kaarya*. What is it, anyway? Can you eat it?'

'Kaarya is duty,' announced Nouzi Aaranya proudly, even as

Warboys rolled his eyes. 'Kaarya is purpose. Kaarya is destiny.'

'If you can't eat it, it won't do us no good out here on the briny.'

'We are meritorious through duty itself, nai? All work is purpose, however demeaning.'

'Oh well,' said Warboys, facetiously. 'That's all right then. You know, it might be survival can't be done. Might be our days are numbered.'

'Ai.'

'You don't seem worried.'

'What is there to do with worry? If this is what happens, we act, eh? We act or die. We act *and* die. Kaarya.'

'Easy talk about death, coming from you, that. I'd shut my mouth if I was you.'

'Ai. But you asked me.'

'Is that how you justify it, then?' asked Warboys, remembering his truce, then ignoring it. '*Kaarya*? Is that how you justify murder?'

The Janizar shrugged. 'How can there be murder between soldiers, eh? I am Janizar. Some Sun-Ivi people are born to farm, or to clean refuse. Janizar are born to fight. That is our kaarya. The cleaner is as worthy as the king. Both pave the Way.'

'The *Way!*' scoffed Warboys. 'The way to what? What the hell are you Sun-Ivi people about, anyway? Fucking *Lines*, and Datyas and monoliths and lightning bolts. What's it all for?'

Nouzi Aaranya wagged his finger to answer, so keenly that Warboys immediately regretted it.

'Our creator was named *Iv*. He walked the earth in the land of Yev, in what you call *Asiat*, three thousand years ago. They say he was warrior in early life, like Janizar. But seeing only death and impermanence, he renounced the world, became as Sekhet, and learned to listen for whispers of truth. *Datyas*. He began to record them in stone, and they showed him the *Mahagat*, the great conjunction. The flow of all life. All things have a flow, Captain. In water, wind and breath. But by nature, this flow is chaotic. It tangles and knots. Obscures our being. Grows wild, like the unweeded wilderness. Like a blocked stream, where clear water cannot flow. So Iv set out to *cultivate,* and so wield this flow.

'Iv taught others. Created Sekhet. This was their casting, nai? Their kaarya. To cultivate the flow, they planted, tended trees and waterways. They watched the stars, set the *yasta* – the standing stones – to channel the Lines. They learned, even, to channel lines through themselves, becoming one with them. And so, the Sekhet irrigated the ancient world with the Lines. As they grew, they assigned half their number to serve as soldiers and guards – and these became Janizar. And over generations, Sun-Ivis set Lines and moved on, across the world. Long before your ancestors, the Andwyke was the last place we came to.'

'So Blackhaven Tor isn't the only place where this happens?'

'Nai! Flow of Mahagat is everywhere. Wherever stones have been laid, Lines are established, Gata is formed. Even where stones have long since crumbled. All lead to the Mahagat's core, gathering power now from all those laid.'

'But what are they gathering it for?'

Nouzi Aaranya looked excited.

'To enact Zirisa-Mai. Great journey! Final blossoming!'

'You what?'

Nouzi Aaranya only shrugged.

'Iv believed that this world is a flawed, half existence. The Sekhet seek the next.'

'But what does that mean? Are you talking about the end of the world and all that sort o' shit?'

Nouzi Aaranya shrugged with dramatic mystery.

'You're taking the piss now. I'll slap you one.'

Nouzi Aaranya straightened up.

'Avai! It matters not! Think not of the aim, but the *worth* in the work itself, General-Captain. Ai, *you* should meditate on *kaarya*.'

'Listen mate. I'm a roughneck out of Kingstown. Your sermon is falling on deaf ears. We're all just trying to survive when it comes down to it.'

'Seek more than survival, Captain. More than subsistence.'

'Can't do much without a drop of survival.'

'*Embody* your work, and you exceed material limitations.'

'Oh, for fuck's sake. I wish I'd never—'

'Cast me out to sea, and Janizar is not taken from me. It is skin and seed, nai? I will find a way back to Maia. I am helpless not to.'

'Is that right? Will that be before, or after the end of the world?'

'Both!' snapped Nouzi Aaranya, defiantly.

'I thought you might say summat like that. Well, you'll be lucky to see *land* again, son, never mind mother bloody Maia.'

'Janizar has a *nature* of unrest. He finds no peace but in his action. He seeks the test and overcomes it. In times of peace, Sukhanava used to say, the warlike man turns the spear on himself. Proves himself, earns his right. To the Janizar, the fight always comes.'

'What fucking fight? What are you on about?'

'It will come, I will overcome it, and I will go to Maia once again. Or I will die.'

'You're a fucking lunatic. Has anyone ever told you that?'

'Ai.'

Warboys gave up. He watched a murk on the horizon and *almost* wished it would come their way, so that the kid's resolve might get a licking.

'Fuck me, I'm hungry,' moaned Warboys.

'Ai,' agreed the Janizar, softly.

27 INHERENT NATURE

Nouzi Aaranya spotted fish shoaling beneath the Hildegaard early the next morning, and sprang to life, giddy at the prospect of catching them. Warboys helped fashion a crude net from some ratlines and wire, which they trawled from the runners. But whilst Warboys readied to sit and wait, the Janizar fashioned himself a spear and went stalking out onto the runners in his pants, trying to spear a big one.

'You'll never get one,' groaned Warboys, watching him hover there like a big daft heron.

'Ai. I will.'

'Bet you don't. You'll just scare them off.'

For a good few hours Nouzi stood there, looking more perturbed, until at last he tucked his spear under his arm with a flourish, and cantered back up the arm to the gondola.

'Give up?' asked Warboys, watching him run right past.

'Nai,' snapped Nouzi. 'Idea.'

He hauled the blue lever to expunge Hilda's solids. The Hildegaard's waste clouded the water, and it wasn't long before the aft was seething with feeding fish. Warboys stood to aft and watched the waves jostle with glistening sprats and herring, which in turn attracted mackerel and some others he didn't know the names for. Nouzi Aaranya edged out, and cast his spear to bring in a good sized mackerel, its flanks glistening with electric green bars of colour. He grinned triumphantly back at Warboys.

'Hui, Captain! See! The fight always comes!'

'Yeah, alright. Whatever you say. You won't get another one.'

Nouzi caught another three before the shoals dispersed. Another few pounds of small fish came up in the trawling nets. These tiny slivers of wriggling baitfish, shrimps, even a few jellies, made good live feed for Hilda. She made bellicose work of them whilst Warboys built up the fire with wood scraps and oil, almost shaking with anticipation.

'You see, Captain?' beamed Nouzi. 'You *can* eat kaarya!'

Warboys admitted nothing. But as they sat and ate in silence with relieved, oily faces, he dared wonder: could the Hildegaard herself save them?

The haul of fish proved to be their last. Two more days passed with no sails sighted, and Nouzi Aaranya couldn't catch a thing, hauling net after empty net aboard to no avail.

'But there are shoals all about!' he insisted. 'I can see them!'

He stood out on the runners, peering suspiciously into the water. Warboys was about to tell him to shut his face when he noticed that the engines were whirring quietly along.

'Here. How long has she been running like that? You haven't fed her any more since that last catch, have you?'

'Nai. There is no more feed to give!'

'Well, that's funny, because she's going at full steam.' Warboys went to examine the pressure gauges, and frowned. 'And, she's filling up on gas again! I only vented some yesterday, just to steady us.'

Warboys hurried to peer down at the submerged airscrews, and saw them churning away below.

'I don't understand it. She should be choked up by now.'

Nouzi Aaranya hauled another net in, crouching to examine it carefully.

'Hui. Look at this.'

Warboys tottered along the pontoon arm to see another

empty net – but this time he caught sight of a fine pinkish white filament entwined with it, just before it slipped off into the water. The two peered down beneath the hull.

'Hui, look underneath!' exclaimed Nouzi, pointing excitedly. 'Your ship is feeding herself!'

Warboys scowled into the waves. Sure enough, he saw the flash of several small fish catching the light. They appeared to be suspended, either injured or dead among more of these pink strings, which seemed to be trailing from the keel itself. The fronds gathered at the rear where the waste was ejected, and extended almost out of view, perhaps twice as long as the Hildegaard herself. What was more, strange, translucent, feather-like projections spread from some of the thicker tendrils, angled like fins to direct the motion of the airscrews.

'Bloody hell! She's... grown! And she's... swimming!'

'Ai. And robbing our nets, eh?'

Warboys stared into the water a minute, then went back to look below deck. It had happened so steadily that he'd not noticed, but the engine bulk had expanded beyond that of the slugs, plugging the gaps with fresh sprouts that had then wormed their way out into the current.

Hilda had sealed herself.

'Have you seen anything like this before?' he said, as the Janizar appeared at his shoulder. He'd done so much clinging to Hilda for survival that he'd barely questioned what she was. *A living ship.* The revelation rang with renewed alarm.

'Avai, Captain. No-one has seen anything like this before! A ship that lives and grows!'

Warboys scanned his face suspiciously.

'You *must* know something. This is built from from instructions in the Datyas. This is Sun-Ivi.'

'Nai, Captain. I have never seen anything like this in the Datyas.'

'Read them all have you?'

'Nai, but... there are no *engines* in our society. Sun-Ivis is simple, lives by natural flows. There is nothing like this in Gienha.'

'Well, she hasn't just grown on a tree, has she? She's alive... sort of... but she's been *designed* by somebody to be an airship.'

The Janizar hesitated, and stared off a moment, considering. 'They say that kaarya is in blood, as well as action.'

'So?'

'Sun-Ivis exists to gather flow of Mahagat to its core. Maia is secluded, and Janizar are selected so that the Fathers can control Iv's bloodline, and maintain caste purity. The Samagat, where Maia dwells, and where we Janizar are conceived, born and raised, and where the seed of our creator is to be fenced and herded – is the very hub of the Mahagat. The *flow* through Samagat – this directs a particular *alignment*. Determines kaarya, nai? The Sekhet speak of humours, influences, flows in the body, as in the land. The Datyas map skies and land, but also the minutiae of life. Scripture teaches that all things have an inherent nature. All casts have their own purpose, their own aptitudes. Kaarya tells us how we are. *What* we are.'

'So everything has its own in-built instructions. So could someone get an eel, or a slug or summat, and tamper with them?'

'Nai.'

'Why not? You're casted, aren't you? Bred to a plan?'

'Is not the same. The castings are the result of these alignments being influenced by Sekhet over time. Through Samagat, and over generations.'

'So where did Hilda come from then?'

The Janizar shrugged, as if he didn't care. But Warboys' mind raced. Was this a *designable* life form? The Hildegaard *herself* – now living and reproducing, and one of the few prototypes remaining – was of unspeakable value. *That*, surely, was what the fuss about the Datyas was all about.

'I don't know if I like this...'

He felt giddy, a sense that the world as he understood it was collapsing away beneath him. He knew he didn't have the vision to comprehend the potential he was floating on, but he could sense some catastrophic possibility looming, and for all that he'd idly yearned to storm the world with some discovery, he suddenly felt hunger, thirst and exhaustion above everything.

'Avai, Warboys!' said Nouzi Aaranya. 'What do we do now?'

Warboys looked back to the ripple where the airscrew turned under the water. She was taking them out west, deeper into the ocean. Could have been for days. He swallowed. Where the hell would a living, feeding ship take them to?

'Shitting hell. If she's feeding... she'll go for the shoals. The gulf streams. We'll be miles away from Hagen's Strait now!'

Warboys rubbed his head and cursed inwardly, trying to reach a decision. Could they try to steer her somehow? Should they kill the engine? No. She was all that was keeping them afloat.

'There's still a decent chance we might spot a trawler if we're headed for the streams. We'll just have to sit it out.'

'Ai. Take the path given, nai? Kaarya.'

Warboys didn't answer. He felt suddenly sick to make such a bold, nerve-wracking decision of sitting back and doing nothing. The thought filled him with groundless unease – and yet, wasn't that what he'd done all his life? Somebody somewhere was having a right laugh.

But it wasn't him.

28 TO HEAVEN

Warboys fought restlessness and agitation, hunger and nausea. He craved a smoke. He struggled to sleep, now acutely aware of the sinuous thing below him, stealing all his food. In restless fits he saw Bill's dusty waxwork face, and the burning silo tower glaring through storms. He scowled on waking, as the sun broke cheerfully from the clouds, withweather so suddenly clement, Warboys thought that the pastel skies might be taking the piss.

He needed distraction. Nouzi Aaranya was there on the foredeck, boiling a panful of Hilda's piss.

'So what about Maia then?'

'Hui,' said Nouzi, after a long pause. 'What about Maia?'

Warboys shrugged. 'What happened? You might as well tell me now. You're always banging on about her, but you never say anything I can make sense of. Tell me about her. The last time you met. How did you leave it?'

Nouzi Aaranya set aside his pan, and looked out to sea for a long time. Warboys sighed, figuring that was that.

'It was the day of my making,' began Nouzi. 'On that day, twelve years after leaving the nurseries, we were due to return to the Stylite to be Named. To become Janizar.'

~ ~ ~

Dappled sunlight broke from between heavy leaves, and lush pink blossoms burst all about. Nouzi, Jana Aasvina, emerged from the humid, cloying cocoon of the jungle. After months of retreat, of meditation and calm, he knew that the ordeal had finally come. He washed himself slowly in a stream.

He found Tetso the Stylite, still perched atop his stone, seemingly unmoved in all the twelve years since Nouzi had last come before him. His matted tresses looked to have taken root among the moss and lichens, and his eyes gleamed as he arose, dropping with surprising dexterity from the pillar, like a lizard, to all fours. Nouzi dropped to his knees as the Sekhet arose and surveyed the newcomer.

'Nouzi, Jana Aasvina. I have sensed you. Sitting in the woods! Waiting, like the *sanyas*. Did you find it, child? Did you find the echo?'

Nouzi Aaranya lowered his head. 'Forgive me, Shah,' he murmured, 'I don't understand.'

The Sekhet grinned, the gleam of blackened teeth joining that of his eye. 'Avai, my child. There is yet time.'

Tetso's hand slapped down on Nouzi's scalp. 'Thus I Name you *Aa-ra-ny-a* – the Wilderness Born. You are Janizar Named. The lines grow heavy around us now, and Zirisa-Mai, the final blossoming approaches. You are among the last, and most important of your kind. Do you accept kaarya?'

'Ai!' he barked.

Tetso hovered over him, looking up at the blossoms, not moving, as if he'd taken root again.

'Is that it?' Nouzi Aaranya dared ask.

'Ai,' grunted the Sekhet, withdrawing his hand.

And with that, he was Janizar. Nouzi *Aaranya*. The name reverberated a time, and he muttered it to himself, tested it. Soon though, his heart began to pound in his chest at the thought of what came next. Silence bloomed, until Nouzi Aaranya almost forgot the Sekhet was there.

Then Upa arrived. Nouzi immediately noticed his face. Where the crescent birthmark had scarred him, now a sharp black tattoo scythed savagely through his eye. He strode with a comfortable power, very obviously leading the others, leaving no doubt that he had succeeded in his takeover. He was Yin, now, and in following, the others had effectively conceded this. Seeing this, Nouzi Aaranya held a thin veneer of calm, feeling the buzz of his own audacity at having dared to arrive before the Yin.

'Wait a minute. Why did you go to the Stylite on your own?'

'I had parted ways with my brothers some months earlier. To retreat into the jungle and meditate on what was to come.'

'Fuck off. What's the real reason?'

Nouzi's head dipped for a moment, as if weighed down by the memory.

'Things happened between us. It was for the best.'

'Alright, cagey. Go on.'

'I had not seen Upa, or any of them for three months...'

Nouzi Aaranya looked up and met Upa's eye, and saw there was curiosity there, a hint of warmth still that made him want to go to Upa, to smile and embrace him. But as the others lined up alongside Upa – Goro, Hazar, Hanu, Sila, Nasnim, their presence seemed to sour the old friendship. With them at his side, Upa's aspect seemed changed. He seemed colder. Threatening. More *Janizar*. Unsettled, Nouzi Aaranya looked away.

'Hang on – that's only seven. Didn't you say there's always eight in an Asta?'

'Ai. There was another. Kai.'

'Where was he?'

'He was dead. As I told you, Captain. Things happened between us.'

'Tell me then! Don't miss the good bits.'

'Avai, Captain! Kai has no place in *this* tale! Let me continue!'
'Alright, alright! Bloody hell!'

Tetso the Stylite bade them sit, and waded around, his tresses swaying as he Named them all. He came last to Upa.

'Upa, Jana Aasvina...' The Sekhet leaned to place a thumb on Upa's new tattoo. 'You who they called *End Born*, the last, the weak, the waning moon... I Name you Upa-*ragha*, the eclipse of the heavens!'

Uparagha bowed low, and backed away.

'Well then,' croaked the Stylite. 'Stand, and turn now back to Samagat, for Maia awaits your seed.'

Nouzi Aaranya stood dizzily, feeling his short life suddenly flicker before him. The way back. The moment of his making.

'Janizar!' roared the Sekhet. '*Navaii!*'

Janizar! Prepare yourselves!

They left the clearing and before them, in the last light, Heaven – the great *Samagat* – loomed on other side of the valley, its perfect pyramidal lines silhouetted in a lilac and orange sunset. Nouzi Aaranya walked at speed, afraid to meet Uparagha. Servile *Nemayanda* in bright, patterned robes awaited them at a splitting of the paths that overlooked the valley, offering water, and token weapons.

Nouzi Aaranya heard his brothers' sussurations as he took his dhas in full view of the others, and waded off through the foliage to his starting post. His intent now stated. He knelt, and waited.

'Su tembe tu Devu-Mai!' came the Sekhet's call, rolling through the jungle like a thunderclap.

Bow then to Maia in heaven!

Nouzi Aaranya's mind clawed to recall Maia, finding only fragments, half remembered snippets painted over by lust and fear and dark imagining.

'Su tembe tu Astava!'

Bow then to your brothers!

Jealously, he sensed them – out of sight but near, at their own starting posts, the remaining six Brothers of Jana Aasvina. And among them, the one he feared the most – this powerful Uparagha, once Upa, his best friend, to whom Nouzi had made long and earnest confessions of his own love and desire for Maia. Who knew this day was *everything* to him.

'*Inshie!*' came the Sekhet's final call.

Begin!

Nouzi Aaranya scrambled down the rise and ran low, squinting through trees slanted like spears into the earth. He breathed deeply, calling for the keepsakes of training that would see him through. A line of monoliths led toward Heaven, and he followed it as fast as he dared.

He heard footfalls, twigs crunching, leaves swatted aside. Sensed his brothers flanking him. Scarlet birds scattered through the thicket, and Sila's distinct war-howl roared somewhere close, almost shocking him from his feet. He dropped his hand to his dhas, making ready. Laughter echoed.

'Hui, look at him, running like a savage! Hiding in the forest all this time has foamed his mind!'

'Hui, *Aaranya*. We don't race for Heaven any more. Where do you think you are running to? You've been reading too many *Heroics*, eh?'

An arrow hissed by, thumping into a tree. They were playing him, driving him the way a wolfpack might. He stopped, looked about, saw their sniggering shapes loitering in the trees.

'Hui!' he called, scaring himself. 'You are more like monkeys than Named Janizar! Come out, if you dare!'

None came forth. He sniffed, spat, made a show of contempt, and turned. Then Goro loomed from behind a stone, colliding with him. Nouzi Aaranya bounced away. Face to face with Goro like this, he felt his bowel squirm. Goro had been Kai's eager henchman over the years. He'd beaten and bullied and kicked him. Stolen from him, pissed on him, mocked and denounced him at every opportunity. Nerves sung in Nouzi Aaranya's joints, whilst Goro seemed even more mountainous.

'What are you playing at? You should concede now, *Wilderness Born,* and later, perhaps even *you* could dip your khus.'

'Ai,' came Hazar's voice, as the others emerged to surround him. All but Uparagha. 'Perhaps the Stylite should have named him *Seventh Helpings,* eh?'

'Ai. *Slippery Khus.*'

Goro issued a phlegmy snort that was as close as he ever came to laughter. Nouzi Aaranya saw the sneering, presumptuous arrogance of his face and in a sudden, almost involuntary lash of anger twelve years fermented, his dhas flicked clear.

Goro's leg barely twitched as the blade's tip seared under his kneecap. His eyes opened in panic – then Nouzi Aaranya lunged into a hefty kick that bounced Goro off a tree and down into the leaf litter, where he clutched his knee and gargled in pain. Hazar and the others stood back in surprise.

'What now, then, Goro?' roared Nouzi Aaranya. 'All of you? Were you given instructions for this? *Kitava!*'

Hazar looked at him curiously, and nodded.

'Avai, stand down brother. You have proved your point, nai? Walk along with us. Uparagha waits ahead.'

'Hui, *reason,* is it, Hazar? Now? *Courtesy?* After all these years?'

He spat. For a moment all past humiliation welled up, his dhas felt potent in his hand, and the prospect of revenge threatened to obscure his purpose.

Nai, my brothers! he thought to say, whilst he caught his breath. *All of you! I've beaten you, eh? Because you scrape and coddle for favour. You've come here tonight just to subsist. To please Kai, once. Now to please Upa. To please any who bully you. You have forgotten kaarya; I have not. I have never forgotten Maia. This is the day for which we were made, eh? And I will go to her, or die.*

He thought to say all of this, then turn his back and leave, calm and capable. The statuesque Janizar of the Heroics. Instead, he doubled up against a tree and threw up his guts.

'But for Maia's sake you live!' he eventually managed to cough out, before staggering away. His brothers stared after him with flat, stupid expressions.

Was that statuesque? Well, it would have to do.

'Ha! You're a real professional.'

'Ai. I was very afraid.'

'I bet Uparagha was, as well. To leave the others behind, waiting for you like that.'

'Nai, they had conceded to him, letting him reach Maia first. They were tending their bruised pride by turning on me. As it ever was.'

'I wouldn't be so sure. I think he knew they'd get in your way.'

Nouzi Aaranya paused a moment.

'Hm. I never thought of it that way.'

'He was your friend, wasn't he? He'd have known more than anyone what you wanted. He must have counted you a serious threat.'

Nouzi Aaranya considered this.

'Get on with it, then.'

'Ai. I guided myself on, along the line of standing stones. No one followed.'

The trees receded, and the line of monoliths marched on into an open glade, where ragged patches of purple-flowered emberweed rolled and beckoned toward the pyramid, looming just over the camber of the hill.

Awe streamed down Nouzi Aaranya's cheek in a helpless tear.

He saw Maia in fragments. A nostril. An elbow, a length of black hair.

He ran, bounding through the emberweed toward the Samagat, wondering if Upa – Upa*ragha* now – had beaten him to Maia. Then, passing the last cluster of stones before the entrance, and seeing the gate was open – he nearly fell over his rival.

Uparagha was sitting sanyas there, waiting, with his back to the entrance. The warm glow from the gate outlined his hair, and the solid stock of his shoulder. He looked up calmly, as if Nouzi's defiant run were a stage play he had been idly enjoying.

'Sat Nam, Nouzi-Chai. I have missed you.'

Nouzi Aaranya stumbled, feeling his knees sag under the weight of Upa's inky stare. He felt a longing to drop and sit gratefully down with his old friend. But he held stance, hand ready on dhas.

'Is it done?' he demanded. 'Have you been to her?'

'Nai, brother. I will not go.'

Nouzi Aaranya stared, uncomprehending. Uparagha took a deep breath.

'After you left for to your retreat, Nouzi-Chai, our brothers and I sought Maia in the slums. Dipped our khus, nai? Many times. They say that in the outlands where we are to be sent, she is on every street corner smoking papered leaf. It doesn't matter where we find her, in what skin. In Maia there is a profound lesson. She shows you the hole in yourself. Shows this, Nouzi Aaranya – we are simple, pathetic engines of *want*. Cessation of desire is brief, nai? But then the moon turns, Maia is gone, and pulls at you again, like the Earth hauls at the moons, and the moons haul at the sea, and we crave again, on these strings, played by the Fathers like puppets. You and I have already suffered, eh, Nouzi Chai? *We* know loss. The Fathers raise us as Warlords, offer us Heaven as a counterweight for the dross we endure. But Heaven is not enough. *She is not real.*'

Nouzi Aaranya heard this last whisper with a chill in his heart, and waited politely as his nerves would allow.

'I accept you as Yin. But I mean to go on.'

'Ai,' nodded Uparagha, sagely. 'Of course you do! We each have *kaarya* of our own.'

He arose then, hands raised, moving close in to Nouzi Aaranya, who felt swallowed in his bulk, half expecting attack. But Uparagha only planted a kiss on his cheek.

'You are beautiful, Nouzi Aaranya,' he whispered. 'Remember. *She is not real.*'

Nouzi gaped as Uparagha bowed to concede, and stood aside. There was the faintest trace of a smirk on Upa's face as passed, and Nouzi Aaranya wondered a moment if he was missing something, if he should just stay and be safe.

And that was it.

He meandered across the clearing to the gate, struggling to accept the fact he'd arrived. In the gateway, his dhas fell from numb fingers with a clang.

The runt had become the victor. He was going to face Maia.

'What, just like that? He let you pass? What was he playing at?'

'He wanted to be Yin. He didn't want Maia. He knew I did, and as Janizar, an Asta is obliged to provide seed before leaving for duty, nai?'

'Cosy. So why'd he have to undermine you like that, then?'

'Avai. Upa always had his own view of things, eh?'

'He's a twat, you mean.'

Nouzi Aaranya took a breath.

'So what happened?'

The wind howled in the gateway, chilling the sweat in his back. A nascent chord of panic chimed inside him. He noted it, repressed it, reasoning with himself.

This is the moment of your making.

A gloomy tunnel sank away before him. As he moved, the lamplight picked out the Datyas etched on the walls, making them crawl like insects in the corner of his vision. He'd expected a long forgotten familiarity to filter back. He'd expected home to piece together, like Maia's face before his eyes, to know again that comfort and love that had become a legend over the twelve years of his exile. Yet the place seemed alien. He barely noticed the faceless, wasp-waisted *Exhis* – the sanctum guards who peeled from the shadow of the vestibule to escort him.

He shuffled forth, following the Exhis dumbly, gaping up at the great archways as they led him down more corridors to a vast bath-house. Here he was attended, unclothed and examined, whilst staring at the luminous mural of the Mahagat that sprawled overhead. The whole universe was mapped there, with the Maia constellation at its core. He recognised *that* at least – he'd climbed to see her every night during his hiatus in the jungle.

He was offered the *Hookah*. The smoke rushed around his blood in a stream of silk, pooling in his skull, erasing his wounds, dissolving his limbs. Long harboured desire suddenly flooded him. He felt himself swell to the far corners of the room, sniggered deliriously as he sensed his erection standing hot in the cold air, the greatest standing stone in creation.

His mind tried to summon up the fragments he recalled from her face. The subtle delve beneath her cheekbone, the variegated green of her eye. Soon he would look upon her in full flesh, and remember.

The Exhis took him through an archway to the threshold of the bedchamber, then left. He paused there, awed at the vast, circular comfort space, veiled and laden with blossom and soft pillows. The distant chime of panic sounded again, deepening in his chest. He struggled, but pushed it down.

A gentle draft rolled down to kiss his skin, and then Maia was there before him.

He dared not look. His eyes dropped down past his bobbing khus toward his feet. One moment he felt nauseous and near to sobbing, the next he fought a stupid grin as he snatched glances at the shadowy contour of her breasts. The indent of tendons on supple shoulders. The dark, rich aperture between her lips. And then, for real, her hand sliding into view, taking his.

He *touched* her, at last. Twelve years later. Smooth, warm and delicate fingers folding over his again.

Then, at last, he looked up.

She's not real, came Upa's whisper.

The panic arose in a sudden surge, a thundering, irresistable cacophony in his chest. Biting snakes of fear went straight for his eyes, and then, where Maia's face should be, the air melted. Flickers of imagined fragments broke free like a flock of crows. Terror overcame him, utterly. He lost Maia's hand again as numbness encroached, his arms prickling with bites that possessed his movements.

Half blind, paralysed and suffocating, he saw Maia's face squirm, her eyes streaming out like a smear of paint on a canvas.

'Bit of a bugger, that,' said Warboys.

Nouzi Aaranya's eyelids flickered, breaking him from his tale. For a long time, he didn't speak.

'That was the first time the terror came, and it has plagued me ever since. That is how I *left it*.'

Warboys saw devastation in his eyes as they turned away

and out to sea.

'I don't blame you,' said Warboys, after a time. 'I mean, there's no wonder it bothers you. They set you against one another like that... then you have to go back in there after all that time. Hell, even the hookah would be enough to curl your mind. But...'

Nouzi Aaranya met his eyes warily, and Warboys tried to think of some kind wisdom to impart, the way Bill would have done.

'It's like I say. The Silver Coast. Beautiful at a distance, not what you thought you wanted when you're on top of it. Then you suddenly realise you don't know what you bloody want.'

'Nai,' objected Nouzi. 'I *know*. I know more than ever. What would Maia be if we could possess her, eh?'

'Give over. Any lad in that situation might have panicked. There's no shame in doubting. We're only human.'

'I don't doubt Maia.'

'Look,' began Warboys, taking a breath. 'You think this woman is the be-all and end-all. Wait 'til you get shacked up with her. Just the bloody beginning of your problems, mate. Me and my Cait, one minute she's tossing me off behind the engine sheds. A right pair of cushions on her. Now *this* is wonderland, I thought. Next minute, I'm shitting myself because she's somehow talked me into getting engaged.'

'Is not the same.'

'*Is* the same. Worse in fact. I spent the next week running from the Garron brothers. Prize fighters, the pair of 'em. No forgiveness there. You think I was born with my nose this way?'

Nouzi Aaranya studied Warboys uncertainly; then his expression soured.

'Hui, Warboys, you belittle me, eh?'

'I didn't mean—'

'You belittle everything because you know no kaarya! You westerners are lost. *Kitava.* You throw yourselves into your war machines and your industry, your money and your *modern world*. But the machines run you, nai? The factories and mills and ships run *you!*'

Warboys scowled at him. He'd been trying to be kind. Reassuring. But now the kid's back was right up, and Warboys felt his own temper rising.

'You're just being pig headed. Gods or machines, revolutions or whatever it is, there's always some idiot chase to waste your life on...' Nouzi Aaranya stood and walked out onto the runner to be away. '... I'm trying to *help* you, you little shit! You keep your feet on the ground. You keep going and...'

Warboys felt his father's words forming, then wilting in his throat. 'Ah, *balls* to it.'

They said no more, kept to themselves, and the day died in a pink rose on the horizon.

29 THE FACT OF DEATH

Warboys saw the shark first. Its fin broke the water behind Nouzi Aaranya, who was out on his usual spot on the runners.

'Here. Look there!'

The Janizar turned around and let out a cry of horror, bounding back to the gondola and all but into Warboys' lap.

'Avai! It is *Sarpa*! Demon! It comes gaping, to swallow us!'

Warboys coaxed him back to the gunwale so they could have a look. The mottled body glided along behind them, with a white maw wide enough to swallow a man whole. It was a big bugger as well – a good twenty feet from nose to tail.

'Don't worry. It's a basker.'

'Eh?'

'A basking shark. It's just trawling for the small fry, look. No teeth. He just trawls, look...'

Nouzi peered over and seemed to see the sense in it.

'Hui. I'll stay here.'

'Fair enough. He'll follow us a while I reckon. They sometimes sit in on a boat's wake, feeding off our stream, like. I told you, didn't I? Hilda's following the streams.'

'What does basker taste of?'

'You'll be bloody lucky.'

For a long time they watched the shark trailing after them, until dark and cold distracted them. Warboys was just lighting the fire for the evening when the ship suddenly jolted and began heaving backwards. Warboys shared a look of pure bewilderment with the Janizar.

'What the hell..?'

They saw the basker break the surface again, slapping at the surface with uncharacteristic aggression. It made a close circle around the Hildegaard, which seemed to trail around after the thing. It was only as the shark thrashed and rolled over that they saw the pink coils eating into its flesh.

'Avai! Hilda is trying to eat the basker! What do we do?'

'What can we do? Do you fancy going down there to cut it loose?'

'Nai.'

'Thought not.'

'Leave it. It's a big bugger. It'll pull away.'

The basker pulled on, and a gentle bow wave built against the Hilda. Nouzi Aaranya watched the shark with a determined fascination.

'Maybe it'll pull us to an island somewhere. With a pub.'

Nouzi Aaranya wasn't listening. The shark hauled on toward the featureless horizon, and in the steady motion of the tow, Warboys felt a strangely familiar sense of gloom befall him.

Here he was again, over the wrong side of thirty, drifting at the mercy of the tides, no aim or direction, and nothing but loss and regret. And here he was again, with a part of him feeling a little bit grateful that someone else had taken the reins. There was the basking shark, taking on his dad's role, doing its best to find the streams, pressing on, pulling his useless weight along. He tried to sleep, but the steady heave of the basker brought an awful sense of unease.

By the morning the shark had tired, lolling near the water's surface. More tendrils had entangled it, a veiny mass pulling it closer to the Hilda. Warboys saw it and felt a stab of fear beyond what a dying fish should evoke. He tried to distract himself, but couldn't help think of Bill struggling against the increasing weight of the tower, nor his pale, drained face when they stormed the walls at Blackhaven. And all the while, Nouzi Aaranya pointedly watched the last throes of the shark.

Warboys finally snapped.

'You're sick, you. Why are you staring at it?'

'Hui, Sukhanava used to make us watch things die all the time. We watched wasps suffocate in jars. Followed speared pigs that staggered and bled. Once he made us watch a paddy field worker impaled on his own fork. *To fear and turn one's head away from the fact of death,* he used to say, *is to fear life itself.*'

'Bunch of fucking lunatics, the lot of you. Leave the poor thing be, can't you?'

An oily soup clouded the water, and Warboys felt the impending death hanging over them.

'Nothing in life stands still. All is flow. All things die and decay. Rain runs ever away to the river, as I will always go to Maia.'

'Yah. We're all adrift, you and me. Lost at sea, with no more than that fucking grey nowt out there.'

'Nai. Even *you* have purpose, Captain.'

'Don't talk to me!' he snapped, rising to his feet. 'If I'm not fucking fed up of *you...*'

He clomped up and down the deck, heart thumping, half tidying up whilst Nouzi sat with a perturbed expression on his face. Eventually Warboys clambered over onto the balloon to seek his own company, and sat himself down by a fluke, glowering at the sea.

And he couldn't help but think –

Had they buried the old man yet? Would they send him back to Coperny, or tip him in a hole with the rest? He might never know. Bill might be rotting in the courtyard of the AEC still. Some bastard might have robbed his boots. The Sons of Sun-Ivis might have taken the place back, and left him to the dogs. If

Blackhaven had been held, perhaps he was in the hold of a ship, waiting to be delivered back to Coperny.

For a while he watched the water, and began to see shapes bobbing there. Frightened himself with a sudden, vivid imagining that the old man would rise from the water in sopping wet kecks and climb aboard. *It's only the basker*, he told himself, but still pulled his toes away from the edge, and hugged his knees.

Stop it.

In the corner of his eye, Nouzi Aaranya edged urgently out onto the runner to look at his portentous shark.

'Hui, Captain! See! She is releasing it!'

Despite himself, Warboys turned to look, some perverse stab of hope in his heart. Little more than the bones remained – a fully formed skeleton with a gaping skull, only a few tattered strips of flesh clinging to it. The Hilda's tentacles released it to the current, and Warboys looked on in horror as the ghostly form spiralled down, fading into the gloom below.

He turned away.

Probably Cait had already received a letter from Captain Zander of the 45th, and was already rifling through Nana Warboys' house. Hard cow that she was. Probably plotting to sell the allotment on. He frightened himself again with the thought of the old man rising from the soil, pushing up his marrows and turnips as he arose like one of the Sekhet.

Stop it.

There was a sudden thrashing from the water, and a sinuous tremor shook the whole vessel. Warboys turned to see the gondola tipping, lifting the runner clear of the water with Nouzi Aaranya on it. There was the buzz of the airscrews spinning freely in the air, and Warboys recoiled at the sight of the mass of tendrils hanging out of the hull, now as thick and as plentiful as the roots of a tree.

A great pink tendril curled from the water, squirming like a trodden earthworm, at least as thick as Warboys' thigh. He saw the look on Nouzi's face – that same bewildered expression he'd had when Warboys had shot him overboard – just as the tendril smashed clean through the runner and dragged him under the waves.

The whole ship shuddered as the gondola rolled over again, now half flooded.

Warboys slid down onto the deck and waded around, his mournful gloom igniting into panic, realising he was desperate not to let the boy die. Not to send him over the edge again. He suddenly knew that it was Nouzi Aaranya, for all that he rankled him, that had been keeping him afloat all this time. Not the Hildegaard.

The boy.

He snatched up the Entwick, hoping it wasn't too waterlogged. The ship rolled back again, bubbles rising from all around. A splash came from the far side of the balloon.

'*Wahbwa*-!' came a brief gasp, suddenly silenced. Warboys threw himself over to the starboard side to find only bubbles. Time seemed to stretch out.

'Fuck this,' gasped Warboys. Sliding back down onto the flooded deck, he aimed down at the engine. He fired. The ship convulsed with pain, shaking the gondola furiously. Wood splintered below as the engine casings cracked under the strain. Nouzi Aaranya surfaced off to starboard, gasping as Warboys collared him and hauled him out onto the balloon. Intermittent spasms came from below as the Hilda's tentacles writhed in pain, then sagged, and sank away.

For a time, neither could speak.

'Hui, Captain. Have you killed her?'

'I don't know, mate. Let's just stay away from the edge til dawn, eh?'

'Ai.'

They huddled together meekly, and waited for movements below. None came. Nouzi Aaranya's breathing quickly steadied. Warboys sighed in relief – not just for the stillness, but for the boy.

By dawn, only the Hilda's balloon was visible above the waves. Residual gas bubbled occasionally from the gondola, which had sunk fully beneath the balloon, where the sinuous undercarriage was picked at by shoals of fish and small sharks. Warboys and Nouzi Aaranya lay like drying fish fillets, feeling the tugging and biting below.

'Well, that's it, kid. I reckon we're about f—'

There was a solid thump, and Warboys rolled over, frantically clawing at the balloon as he slid off into the cold water. He held his breath, ready to swim, fearful of sharks or tendrils – but, at waist depth, his feet landed. He stood gasping, bewildered. He padded with his feet, then turned and saw a low sandbank rising from the water some thirty yards away.

'Here, kid... it's... land! Land!'

In the poor light, the bank was almost indistinguishable from the sea. But as dawn drew on, the shimmering expanse of sandflats spread as far as he could make out, carved into ripples by the tide, dotted here and there with the coiled remains of sandworms. They were beached – but, except for the bank itself, there *was* no land.

At low tide, Warboys waded up onto the mushy sand, squinting into the distance, carrying a rope fed out by the Janizar. And there in the shimmer of the flats he saw shapes moving.

'Here, look! Are they ships?'

'Nai,' croaked Nouzi Aaranya, standing to look, shading his eyes with his hand. 'Hui, Captain. Men. Perhaps thirty of them.'

'Who are they?'

Nouzi shrugged and went to find his dhas. Warboys watched as the crowd came closer. They were an ill-clothed bunch, carrying rakes and buckets and sand-sieves, looking something like the cockle pickers who worked the estuary back home – except most of these men were caramel skinned, Tugels by the look of them, and they in turn were shading their eyes to peer back at him and Nouzi.

'Do you recognise these, Captain?'

'Well, wherever we are, it ain't fucking Coperny Bay.'

A distant shout echoed across the flats, and they saw guards armed with rifles emerge from the group, apparently ordering the pickers back to their work before marching stoutly towards the Hildegaard. Warboys clambered up to retrieve the Entwick. Nouzi Aaranya tensed visibly.

'Go careful now, kid. Let me talk, alright?'

'Hui. You need rifle to talk?'

'I hope not. But you never know.'

'Ai.'

They waited, squinting across the sandbank to await the new arrivals. There was nothing else for it.

30 COMPANY POLICY

The armed guards arrived, half a dozen men wielding old fashioned Imperial matchlocks. Nouzi Aaranya stepped forward, hand on *dhas,* but Warboys collared him. The lead gunman was a bearded, hunched westerner with mottled skin. He gave Warboys a nod, his eyes darting around keenly.

'What's that, then?' he said, pointing at the Hildegaard. Warboys couldn't place his accent, but he spoke Parley, at least.

'That's my ship.'

'Funny lookin' ship. Yours, is it, you reckon?'

'Aye.'

'Why's it marked like an Aalandic ship, then? *A.S. Hildegaard,* it says.'

'Listen. Nice to meet you and all that, but you couldn't give us a hand with her first, could you, before she drifts off again?'

'Aye, I reckon I might.' He whistled, and all but one of his colleagues swapped their old matchlocks for grapples and towlines. Whatever they were doing out on the flats, these people weren't averse to a bit of salvage on the side. Warboys' thoughts raced, wondering what best to do. He might be about to have the most important military invention in history nicked and stripped by idiot scavengers. Of course, if he went and made a fuss, he'd reveal what she was, and almost certainly lose out.

Best play it all calm, like.

'Right. Thanks. What's your name?'

'Mr. Quinky,' replied the leader, and pointed to a flaxen haired Jurman beside him. 'This here's my associate, Mr. Flakstav.'

Warboys waded back toward the balloon, ready to rig up the recovery ropes for the gang. Nouzi Aaranya scampered up onto the balloon after him.

'Just play along, kid,' muttered Warboys. 'Keep your head.'

The two helped rig tow lines and grapples all about the Hildegaard. With a great deal of heaving, Hilda was hauled up onto the sand, where she lay glistening like a beached whale. Warboys circled the wreck, wondering if she could be restored. The growths on the hull were all but gone, picked away to stubs in the sea. The stove still bubbled, and certainly stank, and there was still pressure in the balloon – but, otherwise, it was hard to say if she was even still *alive*, if that was the right word.

'Funny lookin' ship,' repeated Quinky. 'Ready for the breakers, is it?'

Without warning or permission, several of Quinky's gang scaled the gondola and started rummaging around.

'Here, now wait—'

'Hui, kitava!' roared Nouzi Aaranya, suddenly aggressive. 'Off! Off there! Avert your eyes from her, eh? Deal with us! Listen when we speak!'

The salvagers halted and stared, stunned by this outburst, and Nouzi Aaranya spat with contempt. Warboys shot the Janizar a warning glare.

'Listen,' he began, holding up his hands, but Nouzi turned on him.

'Avai, you are a captain of Aaland, nai? Why do you tolerate these scavenging *charya*?'

Warboys faced him, speaking through clenched teeth.

'I wasn't going to *say* that though, was I, dickhead? We don't know who these people are, do we? Fuck's sake!'

'Why care who they are? *Kitava*. Who we are is our concern. Why don't you tell *him* how to proceed, eh?'

'Will you just shut up?'

Incredulous at the boy's sudden arrogance, Warboys looked closer and noticed a certain glaze about the boy's expression. *This* Janizar was all front. This was the Janizar that cut Iren Samsta's fingers off. He was scared, out of his element, and the hard man Janizar facade was how he coped. 'Just... calm down, play along. Now is not the time to fight. Alright?'

Warboys stared to impose his point until Nouzi Aaranya shrugged petulantly. He turned to Mr. Quinky.

'Whereabouts have we landed, mate?'

'You're not landed yet. This is only sandflats. It's low tide now, but it'll all be sea again in few hours. You're lucky we're out here a-cockling.'

'We're grateful.'

'Oh aye? For what?'

'Well... we could do with food and shelter, like.'

'Food and shelter I can do. But I reckon you can give over that rifle now, and him those blades.'

'Listen, Quinky mate. You'd better let me have a word with your Gaffer before you—'

Quinky turned his matchlock on Warboys' face, and cut him off.

'Alright, *Captain.* Do as you're told now. And your cabin boy.'

Warboys let the Entwick drop, and held up his hands. Warboys saw the other guards start, and turned in time to see Nouzi Aaranya forcing Mr. Flakstav down onto his knees, his arm locked behind him.

'What are you doing?' yelled Warboys, as several matchlocks were trained on them.

'He tried to take my dhas!'

'Just give him it, dickhead! Stand down.'

Nouzi Aaranya let go of Flakstav, who crawled away, massaging his shoulder. 'Ai,' he said, sniffing, 'but I *give*, eh? You don't take. This is *respectful.*'

He handed his dhas over. Mr. Quinky cleared his throat and spat. 'Bring them.'

Warboys tried to speak again but Flakstav's rifle butt struck his cheek and knocked him sappy. He looked up to see Nouzi Aaranya take a blow from a Jonah stick before two other guards seized him. He took it quietly, didn't fight back.

'You don't speak now,' said Quinky, 'less I speak to you. Maybe the gaffer'll speak to you, and maybe he won't. Either way, you come with us, and you work, and you get food and a bed. Elsewise, you go back in the sea. Company policy.'

'What about my ship?'

'Reckon on her as a down payment on your life. You got a new ship, now. The good ship *Endurance*. Come on now. Tide's coming.'

They were dragged up, herded together with the cockle pickers, and marched across the flats. Warboys looked ruefully back at the Hilda, glaring at the crew hanging back to pick her over. At least she wouldn't drift off.

They traversed the featureless flats until the triangle of a sail emerged out of the haze. A sloop waited by a makeshift jetty of pallets and boards, along which crates of fresh cockles were being loaded.

Warboys and Nouzi were sent to the foredeck, packed in by the rest of the cockle gang. Foreign smelling sweat steamed off musky bodies as they pressed in. Warboys saw the kid's eyes scanning across the different shaped eyes of the Tugels, and a solidly built hulk of almost blue-black colour who pressed in beside him. He began to twitch. Fearing a breakdown, Warboys nudged Nouzi Aaranya reassuringly.

'Just hold steady, kid. Bear with it.'

Nouzi Aaranya stared bewilderedly at the Tugels, who engaged in their nasal, whining patter, waving their arms about as if swatting flies. Then he turned and stared at the black man, until the black man noticed and stared back down at him. Noting the hefty size of the man, Warboys nudged at the Janizar.

'Stop staring.'

'Avai, Warboys. He is like the colour of ink. I never saw a man like him.'

'Fuck's sake...' cursed Warboys, letting his head drop. 'Listen mate, don't mind him, he's just a bit... *foreign*.'

'Ha!' laughed the man. He grinned broadly, an alarming set of teeth offset by the wrinkles of his smile. 'Ain't we all, nowadays?'

He laughed, a grinding bass sound, and offered his hand to Warboys.

'I am known as Joe Bonboas. Welcome to the crew of the *Endurance*.'

'Right. Nice to meet you, Joe. Warboys is the name. This is my... this here is Nouzi Aaranya.'

'Well met, Nouzi Aaranya.'

Nouzi Aaranya was so busy staring at Joe, he hardly seemed to register any of this. Warboys shrugged apologetically and wound a finger at his temple by way of explanation.

'So what landed you here then Joe?'

'Same as all the rest. I am hearing of General Malvy's great new land of opportunity, and coming to Coperny to steal all your native jobs while you fight down south!'

He laughed again. 'No, my friend. I was aboard the whaler Clara-Kee a time.'

Warboys eyed Joe's barrel chested build. 'You were a harpooner then?'

'Aye,' laughed Joe. 'But the quarry has changed some! Oh my glory days are behind me!' he laughed again. 'I found myself stranded at Junkers, and these here—'

'Junkers? Are we near Junkers?'

'Aye. It lies a day or two's sail due nor-west of here.'

'Hui, Warboys,' muttered the Janizar, still staring at Joe. 'What is this Junkers?'

'The Junker Line, kid. It's a floating port, a flotilla a couple of hundred miles out from the west coast of Aaland.' Warboys knew Junkers well, having sailed to and from it several times as a stop off on the way through to Port Nyssa during his commission on board the *Call of March*. 'They call it the crossroads of the world. We get there, we can get anywhere.'

'Aye,' laughed Joe. 'If you can get there.'

'How long have you been out here?'

'A month now.'

'Don't they let you work your way out?'

'These Tugels,' began Joe, pointing toward the gang of caramel skinned men and women in broad sleeved tunics, most of whom had their hair in neat plaits, 'are all one family. Kuo, they call themselves. Been here a year.'

'Fuck off!'

Joe Bonboas grinned, and Warboys began to think he might have a tic rather than an overpowering sense of humour.

'They don't question our captors about it. It is a cultural thing...'

'I daresay the captors haven't mentioned it either, eh?'

'Aye,' laughed Joe. 'That, too, is a cultural thing. But lately, their Senior has been growing more tense. I see him watching, and whispering.'

Joe nodded toward Senior Kuo, a wiry patriarch with a greying plait and weathered robes.

'Many are being exploited,' said Joe. 'Malvy is offering citizenship to any who will work, whilst the Empire has left a mess of her colonies, as well as many freed slaves who did better under labour. More and more come to Junkers every day, stowaways looking for a place in Malvy's new world. But Junkers is a cutthroat hive, and they come like baby turtles hatching on

Bestour Beach. More every week, promised passage to Aaland. I couldn't rightly say, Mr. Warboys, whether any make it to discover the fabled land of wonderment or not.'

'Who's running this game, then?'

'The foreman is a drunk brigand by the name of Adnam, back on the Endurance. But the real gaffer is a man named Jayman. He owns the Endurance, and takes the profits, be it seafood or salvage. I don't know Jayman's face, but he has a lot of money on Junkers. And not just from cockles.'

'So we're going back to the Endurance now? Is she going back to Junkers tonight?'

Joe laughed. 'Oh, no, Mr. Warboys. The Endurance doesn't *sail* anywhere.'

Joe pointed to fore. The sea below was becoming shallow, rising up to a shingly bank where a great heavy, turreted lump of a ship lay beached and askew, seeming at distance to be balancing on the sea's surface.

'Here she is, my mates!' laughed Joe, in mock pride. 'The HMS *Endurance*!'

Warboys looked up. The *Endurance* was an old prison hulk. She sat at a tilt on an isolated bank of shale, her bloated flanks so blistered with barnacles that she seemed more like some great dead carcass than anything man made. With no land anywhere to be seen, she was the only feature on sky or sea.

'An Imperial ship, she was,' said Joe, as they drew near. 'Sailed out of Lutarch in Cory in 1798, and south through all the Arrican colonies. All manner and colours of men have lived and died on those old decks.'

Warboys could barely muster a mumble in reply.

'Aye,' said Joe, 'abandoned at Junkers after the Andwyke, she was. Meant to leave her for scrap, but she came to be under the ownership of Mr. Jayman, who lets her out for cockle picking. She ain't going nowhere now.'

'Huzhat, Captain! I don't like that!'

'Easy, kid,' muttered Warboys, scanning the hull. He noted the tiny, barred port hole slots, the dark, rotten old boards lined with the rust of wars a hundred years finished, and couldn't help but feel dread.

The sloop came to a floating jetty that ran alongside the hulk. The guards ushered them up and out, along a badly scaffolded staircase that had been bolted to the hull. Blocky cabins and sheds quartered the deck, where the smell of spoiled fish smothered the air.

The cocklers laid out the catch before being escorted below. Adnam, the foreman, awaited them on deck, a slovenly figure in a long coat. Mr. Quinky whispered a while in Adnam's ear, whilst he scowled at them with the veiny eyes of a long term drunk.

'Listen, mate,' began Warboys, hoping to draw some thread of negotiation with the man. But Adnam cut him off.

'Don't *mate* me. That an airship out there, is it?'

Warboys sighed. He took the man for an angry little crook and fancied sticking the nut on him – but refrained.

'It is.'

'Captain of Aaland, are you? You don't look like no airman. Ain't much of an airman sinks a fucking airship.'

'Never said I was.'

'Fuck you doing out here with an airship then?'

'Listen. There might be a big deal to be had here. Let me talk to your gaffer on Junkers. Mr. Jayman, is it?'

Adnam scoffed.

'After my commission, are you now? Fuck off.'

Adnam thumbed at Quinky.

'Get these twats below. You're salvage, you and your ship, just like the rest of 'em.'

Warboys opened his mouth to object but saw the raw

contempt in Adnam's eye and turned away. They were thugs, the lot of them. It was hopeless to argue. These men were slavers, and out here it was easier to shoot him than ask questions. At least, if he'd managed to plant a seed of curiosity in Adnam's mind, then maybe he wouldn't just strip the Hilda down straight away.

Quinky ushered them on. The hold yawned, dank and dark, lit by dim, stinking oil lamps. Nouzi Aaranya shuffled along like an old lady, and Warboys tugged his sleeve to move him along.

They went down through three identical decks to the bottom, where the guard unlocked a rusted gate and led them down a long, narrow corridor lined with barred cells to either side. The air was thick and soupy. The meagre glow of an oil lamp picked out piles of blankets, sacking and a few buckets.

'It's a cell,' said Nouzi Aaranya.

'We're on a prison hulk, mate,' scoffed Quinky 'What did you expect? Captain's cabin?'

'No,' said Warboys, ushering the Janizar inside before he started off again, 'this'll do. It's nice, this is.'

'You'll get a bullet in your arse if you cheek me.'

Warboys was about to laugh this off when he saw that Quinky had swapped his matchlock for Bill's Entwick.

'Here, you cheeky fucker! That's my old man's rifle! What do you think you're doing with that?'

'Consider it a rental,' growled Quinky. 'Unless you got more to say about it?' Warboys stayed there, boring into Quinky with a murderous glare, until Joe Bonboas' hand on his shoulder eased him back.

'Make yourselves comfortable!' Quinky laughed. 'You'll be out on the flats in the morning, so get some kip.'

Nouzi Aaranya sat sullen on his bunk, huddled away from everyone, and waited for the guard to leave. 'Avai, Captain. I don't like this.'

'Listen. We ain't got a choice. Just play along for me, alright? I'll get us out.'

'To where?' gulped Nouzi Aaranya, looking suddenly daunted.

'Well... to Junkers, of course. Where else?'

Nouzi Aaranya shrugged.

'Why?'

'We'll get the Hilda back. Or we'll find a ship or summat, I don't know. What's the matter with you? Use your initiative! If we get to Junkers we can get back to our bloody...' Warboys hesitated, saw a blazing tower, a great cone of smoke rising and smothering everything. 'To our lives, like...'

He swallowed. 'Anyway. Just keep your chin up. There'll come a time, and you'll have to be ready, alright? But until then, just play along.'

Nouzi Aaranya's eyelid flickered. Warboys looked around, tensing at the thought of an episode this tightly packed in with all these men. 'Listen, don't worry. You weren't supposed to take your own food in the Blackwater Tavern but I used to sneak patty butties in under my hat. Nowt's impossible.'

Nouzi Aaranya said nothing. Warboys peered out into the gloom, saw the bleak slits of light barely penetrating the ship, and suddenly wasn't so sure.

31 THE PATH LAID

Warboys found himself grafting. It was their third day working with the gang, raking up clusters of cockles for sieving. He looked up from his work to see clouds swell across a plain blue sky, doubled in the mirror of the flats. Quinky and Flakstav stood around smoking, and beside him, Nouzi Aaranya busied about like an eager squirrel digging for his nuts.

'Enjoying yourself, are you?' said Warboys, as he set his rake into a new patch.

'Ai. I think of *meritorious duty*, Captain. Kaarya, nai? I think of my path to Maia, paved in cockle shells.'

'Don't start all that again.'

Warboys hauled in another load, and heard Quinky's laughter. Noting the old blue flecked rifle, he called out.

'Here, what's the rifle for anyhow? They get a bit savage out here, do they, these molluscs?'

'Yeah, summat like that, mate. Best you get back to work, eh?'

'Dickhead,' muttered Warboys, bending back to his rake. 'I'll 'ave 'im.'

Beside him, Nouzi Aaranya raked with quick, martial strokes, as if the sands were his enemies, the rake a spear.

'Oi!' came Quinky's cracked yell. 'I told you once. Don't cross that line!' He pointed at a ragged boundary rope beneath Nouzi Aaranya, lying right across the flats between two scuffed old bouys.

'Ai, but I can see tracks of many cockles beyond here. Better grounds that way, I think.'

'I don't care what *you* think. Tide comes in with a vengeance, and you don't want stranding. Besides which, there's other gangs that work these flats, and there's boundaries between us and them, right?'

Quinky pointed to a crowd of tiny figures on the far side of the flats, barely visible through the haze. 'See that lot over there? That there is Mr. Dassler's cockle gang, see? There's money for him and Mr. Jayman both in these sands, so we stay out of one anothers' way. So keep this side o' that line!'

'Ai!' barked Nouzi Aaranya. His gaze lingered on the distant figures for a moment, and Warboys thought he saw a flash of mischief there. But, twirling his rake about him as if to deal death with it, he obeyed, withdrawing over the line to set his rake into the sand

'Here, slow it down,' said Warboys. 'You're just making the rest of us look bad. Always got to keep a bit in reserve, you have.'

'Hui, Warboys, you are a shirker. I work the path laid.'

'Well you're a mug. Listen. A bloke on the early shift told me last night that he saw a big salvage tug going past. Reckoned they had summat big and round in tow.'

'So?'

'So? It'll be the Hilda, won't it? I reckon they've towed her off to Junkers.'

'So? Is about fucked, anyway.'

'Mind your language. At least if we can get away to Junkers, we don't have to worry about getting her there.'

'Ai. But we are slaves, nai? Cockling. *Play along,* you said.'

'Are you daft? You'll be all cockled out by the time you get to her. You'll get there, to Mrs Maia, and you'll have no cockles left.'

Nouzi Aaranya grunted, unimpressed, and dragged the next full box away toward the sloop.

Joe Bonboas waded up.

'He's a fast worker, your boy. Where did you get him? I'll get to Coperny one day, and I could use one of him for sweeping my shop floor.'

Joe laughed a deep, infectious laugh.

'Aye, well this lad will sweep your floor, then he'll sweep the bloody *pattern* off your floor. Afore you know it, he's dug you a tunnel to the Asiat and lined it with flower boxes.'

'Oh? I'll give you three bits.'

'Throw in a paper smoke and you've got a deal.'

Joe laughed again and slapped his hand into Warboys'. Quinky barked at them and they set back to work.

Then Warboys turned to look for Nouzi, only to find he'd vanished. 'Where's he gone now? He's like a whippet out of a trap, that boy...'

Warboys spied Nouzi Aaranya's footprints crossing onto the forbidden side the flats, and looked up to see him sprinting directly toward Dassler's gang.

'Oh, shit...'

~ ~ ~

Nouzi Aaranya cast himself to Maia.

He'd turned to collect a new load, and seen a stark nothingness ahead of him. Clouds passed, leaving a plain blue sky, reflected in the flats. Nothingness above and below, neither firmament nor foundation. He suddenly knew he was lost, without his brothers, with no purpose but to collect molluscs. He remembered that Sukhanava said: *This is why I teach temperance, peace as well as war, because a predator without prey lives in fear.*

He understood that now, as a low chime of terror rumbled in his bowels.

He tried to breathe, calm himself, find peace. But he looked into the mirror below and felt himself falling away from Maia. The chime arose, singing in his chest, and he knew he had to *act* before the terror overtook him.

He saw the figures on the flats. Their rivals. And he cast himself toward Maia, the only way he knew how.

Within shouting distance of Dassler's gang, he raked a patch over, and then squatted down to haul the cockles into his sieve, waiting for them to notice him, then doing it again, adding a provocative monkey-walk.

'Muy!' came a yell.

'Oi!'

'Muy! Albay n mueno!'

'Oi! You there! Fuck's he doing?'

Dassler's cockle gang were hard looking men, pale and sinewy with sandblasted skin. One had a face like a bruised plum, wielding a cutter, whilst another scarfaced lout spun a steel-tipped Jonah. Nouzi stood as the guards pushed through, rifles at the ready.

'Here, he's one of Adnam's!' said a guard. 'Listen kid. Understand me? This is Mr. Dassler's patch. You just leave what you got there and fuck off back over the line, and I'll promise to count to five before I start shooting.'

'Nai. I have cockles for Maia. I'll take these, and I'll have yours as well.'

He nodded over to the patch Dassler's gang had been working, where crates were stacked high. He held the guard's glare, seeing his face redden. He felt the chime, held it back, let it spring him tightly.

'Right lads,' coughed the guard, 'chop his fucking hands off!'

The two brutes lunged. Nouzi Aaranya sprung from his crouch, cracking his sieve full of cockles on scarface's nose. Nouzi kicked him between the legs, snatching the Jonah away as he doubled over. Plum-face's cutter flashed past Nouzi's face and he spun, rapping the stick against plum-face's head again and again as the victim stumbled, sank to his knees, and finally fell flat in the sand. A man with a spear lunged, hesitated, and Nouzi Aaranya threw the Jonah, bouncing it off his forehead. One of the guards cocked his rifle and edged forth.

'Fff—' he began, raising his rifle to shoot.

Nouzi sprang forward, driving the spear into the gunman's sternum with a thump. In the same movement, he snatched up the rifle and turned it on the stunned gang.

A shot sounded out from behind, and Nouzi Aaranya looked over his shoulder to see his own gang. Quinky and Flakstav bore down, their own rifles raised. Warboys came forward, staring at him warily.

'Stand down kid!' he called, seeming to recognise something in Nouzi's eye. 'You're going to get yourself killed here.'

'Aye, right he is!' snarled Dassler's guard. 'This boy here's crossed the line, Mr. Quinky!'

'He has that, Robbo,' replied Quinky. 'No argument here. Let's us just—'

Nouzi Aaranya wasn't listening. He held Warboys eye a moment, saw him shaking his head.

Then he picked a rival guard, and fired.

Warboys saw it coming, but before he could call out, the guard had fallen, and Nouzi Aaranya was charging. A sinewy thug closed on Warboys as Dassler's gang flooded over them. He reacted, felt his Jonah connect with a wet crack, and the thug slapped into the wet sand. Joe Bonboas wrestled in the sludge, and Senior Kuo slashed a bright arc in the air, keeping two more of the rival cocklers at bay. Warboys looked about, wondering where Quinky and Flakstav were, seeing that the bastards had retreated to leave them to it. Warboys ducked a swing from a sinewy Kraeki man who barged into him, sending both into the cockle crates. It went like any streetfight, when the tempo slowed, when both sides quickly sensed they'd had enough. Warboys punched, felt the imprint of teeth in his knuckles, and pulled away from his assailant to see a thin wave sweeping across him, chilling his legs as it came to claim the flats with foamy blankets. There was a sound like castanets as the cockles spilled across the sand, some of them already sticking out lolloping orange tongues to drag themselves away into the coming waves.

'Tide's coming!' he bellowed. Dassler's gang broke and made a run for it, and Quinky called them back. Warboys looked around, seeing Joe Bonboas stagger over, looking ready to retreat – but Nouzi Aaranya raged on as if this were the last battle on earth. Warboys saw him clatter a straggler, who fell face down into the surf before being rolled away by the tide. Then the Janizar gave chase, heedless to danger, surf foaming at his heels as he sprinted off towards Dassler's sloop.

'Oi!' bellowed Warboys. 'Oi! You'll... ah shit!'

Joe gasped, shaking his head. 'He'll go to his death out there today!'

Quinky and Flakstav came wading over to usher them back to the sloop.

'Get your arses back over here, and bring those crates!'

'We're missing a man!' yelled Warboys. 'We've got to go back!'

'He's your friend,' brayed Quinky. 'You go get him, and to hell with both of yer! We can't stay here!'

'Yeah, you'll take the fucking rewards though, if we come back with a double load, won't you?'

'He'll not come back from there today, mate!'

A wave broke over Joe Bonboas' back, showering foam over them both. 'Warboys! We have to go now. He's lost.'

Warboys teetered a moment, then swore and charged off after the boy, picking out what shallows there were left to reach him.

Up ahead, Dassler's gang dithered at their sloop, caught between escaping and dealing with Nouzi Aaranya – who, having claimed Dassler's crates, now pelted cockles after them like some little tyke on the green. Warboys arrived as the guards mounted the sloop, priming their matchlocks. He thundered over, dragging Nouzi behind the crates as a shot sang overhead. But Nouzi didn't flinch. He stood again to throw back a few cockles in retaliation and, again, Warboys dragged him down.

'What the fuck are you doing?'

'Eh?' replied Nouzi dumbly, his lightning eyes flashing against the grime of his face.

'Why are you doing this? Do you want to die here?'

Dassler's lot called the retreat, scrambling aboard the sloop. A wave slammed into Warboys and the Janizar, knocking the wall of crates over.

'Shall we charge them, Captain?' gasped Nouzi.

'*Charge them*? Are you *listening* to me? No, we're not going to charge them!'

'I think we should give chase. Hijack the boat.'

'Are you daft?'

'How else will we avoid drowning?'

'Oh, you've just thought of that, have you? We're meant to be playing at *cockling*, kid. Not waging a bastard war... we're supposed to be getting out of here, and you're going to fuck it all up!'

'A man runs away to find himself waiting.'

'No, don't give me that. You don't have to go this far every bloody time!'

'Oh, but I do, Captain. I am what I do. *Sukaarya*, nai?'

'If it makes you happy to be dead, fine. I'll wring your fucking neck once we're safe!'

The waves blasted them aside, and they clambered onto the

ramshackle crates as the sea came. Dassler's sloop was already well away. Warboys looked up and saw Quinky's sloop coming around for them, no doubt eyeing the crates to which they were clinging. Warboys felt anger boiling as Quinky came alongside, dragging aboard what they could, and leaving him and Nouzi until last. Joe Bonboas hauled them both over the gunwale to safety, but Warboys was so furious that he could not muster even a word of thanks.

'Keep me away from this fucking idiot!' he growled, and shoved through to the stern to sit away from Nouzi Aaranya.

The sloop fought through the waves, and the Janizar sat sanyas at the bow, straight backed and meditative.

Warboys fumed all the way back to the *Endurance*.

32 BAD NERVES

Warboys tramped through the hulk to the cell deck without a word to anyone. He went to his usual spot against the outer hull and sat heavily down, his face like thunder. After rations were denied for the night, all eyes fell reproachfully on Nouzi Aaranya. Senior Kuo gathered his sons about him in a circle, conducting some debate in hushed tones.

'It seems Senior Kuo is reaching the end of his patience,' muttered Joe Bonboas, as he bound wounds next to Warboys. 'The boy is a liability for us all.'

The Janizar himself paced restlessly, forming a gangway for himself.

'He's got wind up his arse,' announced Warboys, loud enough for everyone to hear, 'and it's making his ears cold.'

Hearing this, Nouzi Aaranya marched over to Warboys.

'Hui, Captain. Come and play *Hastaya*!'

Over the past few nights, Warboys had seen Nouzi Aaranya goad some of the younger Tugels into playing a game he called *Hastaya*. It was a kind of play fight, which to Warboys' eyes looked like a sort of violent pat-a-cake that sometimes boiled over into punching and wrestling. A lively trade in gambling on the fights was always short lived, as the volunteers always lost, invariably ending up on their arses, sporting bruises and nosebleeds.

Warboys rolled his eyes. 'Sit down, kid. You don't want to play with me.'

'Enough talk, eh? Play!'

'If I play, will you sit the fuck down?'

'Ai!' Nouzi nodded, bouncing from foot to foot. Warboys stood, rolled up his sleeves, and laid his wrists over Nouzi's. In the corner of his eyes, Warboys noticed the Tugels scramble to vantage points, murmuring wagers to one another.

They began rolling their arms back and forth over one another's, as if a small keg were being rotated in the space between them. Warboys lunged forth for a grab, but Nouzi folded his arms away, landed a dummy strike near to Warboys' head. They resumed motion.

'Alright, I get it. What's this called again?'

'Hastaya,' he began, '*the flowing hands*. An adaptation of meditation technique. Is like a two man *Resadem*, nai? The object is to push a way through the other's defence. Make contact with the opponent's head or torso before the other. Tightens the reflexes. Make striking more intuitive. Develops a sensitivity to the flow of a fight. Allows a man to feel the energies that flow from one to the other, through one man and into another. Feel the *Lines* between us.'

'Yeah alright then, shut it. Hell, I know you've got bad nerves, but what's wrong with a smoke?'

Nouzi Aaranya said nothing, lost to the rolling motion.

'So where does this stop, then? When every cockle has been picked and we're all dead? You think that'll do it?'

Nouzi Aaranya grunted, landing a blow to Warboys' chest, causing him to stagger back.

'Not so rough, dickhead!'

'You're too tense!' scolded Nouzi Aaranya, in an unusual show of irritation. 'Relax your arms!' He slapped Warboys' forearm.

'If you slap me again, I'll slap you back mate.'

'Perhaps if you could get anywhere near me, you might.'

'Keep talking.'

They touched arms again. Nouzi Aaranya exhaled, settled into the motion again, and closed his eyes.

'Arrogant tosser you are. I could have died chasing you today.'

'Hui, then don't follow.'

'Hey, you jumped on *my* airship, shithead!'

Nouzi Aaranya quickly slapped his hands away, jabbing gently at Warboys' throat.

'Come on then. Again,' snarled Warboys. 'Keep going.'

Around them, the faces of the gang drew in. More wagers were muttered, heads nodding and fingers signalling. Joe Bonboas finally broke and had a punt.

'Getting to be a bit of warrior king down here, aren't you? Big Janizar. But compared to those proper Janizar out there, you're just burying your head in the sand. You want to know what I think?'

'Eh, you'll tell me anyway...'

'You're *scared*. Deep down inside, you're shitting your kecks.'

'I don't fear death, Captain.'

'Oh I know that. Proper bullet head, you are. Don't mean you fear nothing at all, though, does it?'

Nouzi Aaranya said nothing, closed his eyes to the flow.

'You were a mess when I met you. Back in Blackhaven, where you were playing Janizar, chasing kaarya, earning your way to Maia, and all that. And it strikes me as funny that I've never seen you so 'ealthy as when we're drowning. When we're about to be eaten by sharks, or shot at, or when you've got fish to catch, cockles to scoop, shit to scrape, knickers to stitch, *anything*, in fact, apart from your actual kaarya...'

Nouzi Aaranya barely managed to slap away a jab from Warboys, and shoved him off. He took a shaky breath as they rejoined.

'See, I think you don't want your real kaarya. You're *scared* of it, and you'd do anything to avoid...'

Nouzi Aaranya's eyes flared up, and he slapped Warboys attempt away in a rather too forceful flurry.

'You would know, eh, Captain Warboys? A man who runs in his sleep!'

'You what?'

'You roll and gasp and sob in your sleep, and you start to run, squirming on the floor like a grounded *catyan*, and you *run from what you did!* You would do well to face your own kaarya before you tell me mine, *kitava*.'

Warboys thought of his dad, and admitted a moment of desolation to himself. Nouzi Aaranya slapped his arms, slipping through the exposed gap. Ready for the counter, Warboys grabbed his wrist in a vice like grip, only to find the limb go limp as Nouzi folded his elbow into Warboys' jaw.

Warboys staggered back. The Tugels waved hands to shift odds.

'Little shit,' growled Warboys, red in the face. 'Again.'

'Ai.'

'Fair enough,' said Warboys, as they recommenced play. 'I admit it. But at least I *know* I'm running. *You* don't really want to go back up there to Maia. If they sent you back up there tomorrow, if beloved Maia in Heaven so much as flashed her arse your way, I think you'd shit yourself. You'd rather run 'til you drown than go back. So don't give me any more shit about *kaarya*.'

Warboys felt a break in the rhythm, and saw the lids of Nouzi's eyes flicker. He took another dig.

'Funny, isn't it, that I woke up on the Hildegaard and she'd turned hard to a westerly course... when I could have *sworn* that the wind would take her north for free. Right into the Eldask, back to Maia. Probably right between her legs if you wanted...'

He'd touched a nerve. That mothlike flicker afflicted Nouzi Aaranya's eye, and Warboys fancied he could feel it in the play.

'But that's it. You *don't* want, do you?'

Nouzi Aaranya's pupils dilated, staring into some distant scene of horror and failure, his guard dissolved. With a fiendish grin, Warboys sent an almighty slap across the Janizar's face, knocking him bewildered to one knee. For good measure, he landed a left hook on his jaw, knocking him flat on his arse.

'Oh, I enjoyed that,' grinned Warboys, wringing his hand as Nouzi Aaranya bounced comically off the hull and up again to his feet.

'I broke contact!' he yelled. 'You cheated!'

Warboys shrugged, doing a poor job of hiding his amusement. Behind them, uproarious Tugels mobbed one another for their winnings.

'Your trouble is, kid, you play too straight. You wouldn't see it if someone came at you sideways, if your enemy jumped on your head, or if opportunity came chewing at your arse!'

Nouzi Aaranya flung his arms in anger.

'Again!' he demanded.

'Piss off!' laughed Warboys. 'I won and I aren't playing any more.'

The gate creaked above.

'What's all this racket down here then?' yelled Quinky. 'Ain't a night without food enough for you lot?'

The Tugels skittered around anxiously as Quinky and Flakstav clomped down.

'Again!' yelled Nouzi Aaranya, oblivious.

'No. I might rip your fucking head off next time.'

'Well then, try!' demanded Nouzi, even as the guards unlocked the inner cell gate and came ready with their Jonahs. 'Play again!'

'No. And the next time you go running off looking for a fight you can fucking stay gone, 'cos I'm not coming after you.'

Warboys saw Flakstav's hand slap down on the Janizar's

shoulder. Then he saw Nouzi Aaranya whirl about. There was a gristly pop as he spun, turning the guard's arm over against itself, then a wet thud as Nouzi's elbow hammered Flakstav's jaw through his tongue. Then Quinky struck the butt of Bill's rifle against Nouzi's skull, and the Janizar fell heavily to the deck. Warboys backed away.

Flakstav staggered, bleeding and angry, his arm hanging limp, then came about and the two guards set about Nouzi Aaranya whilst he lay limp on the deck.

Warboys' heart was suddenly thumping in his chest, pushing anger away for something more urgent.

They'd had enough of Nouzi already. Warboys knew that. They had no cause to nurture the kid. No, it'd be a kneel on the foredeck and a shot to the back of the head for him now.

Oh well, Warboys told himself. *They can do what I couldn't. I'll be rid of him now. Aye. Good riddance to the little fuckwit.*

Then there was a sudden, vivid memory. The earthen smell of the potato fields. The ache of desperation in his joints. The rough arms of the other workers, dragging him away from the foreman's son that first day at work after Lily's funeral. He'd been a boy not yet in his twenties, having lost his mother, lost his way, fired up on grief and anger, and they expected him to stand there picking fucking potatoes. The bastards might as well have tried to light a candle with one of Malvy's bombs. And here was Nouzi Aaranya, picking cockles, his head addled for all this talk of kaarya, and god knows what else had been done to the poor sap in his youth, growing up alongside that set of Janizar bastards, with no women, the dream of a god that wasn't there, and precious little love. Couldn't have been much of a childhood.

A tear welled in his eye as Nouzi Aaranya was dragged through the cell door. Warboys watched, and regret – another thumping explosion in his chest that felt set to echo all his days

– almost crippled him.

Almost.

Quinky was fumbling for the keys to lock up behind him. It was then that Warboys lurched forward.

33 PIRATES

Warboys barged through the half open door, shouldering Flakstav aside and grasping at Quinky. The three of them stumbled over Nouzi Aaranya and hit the adjacent cell bars with a clang. Quinky squirmed away as Flakstav raised a Jonah over Warboys – then Joe Bonboas appeared, slamming the squat Jurman into the bars with another resounding gong.

Quinky was backing quickly away to the stair-gate, keys chinking in nervous hands. Warboys charged him, but halted as soon as Quinky raised the old Entwick. At a stand still, Warboys eyed his dad's rifle. Quinky's gaze lingered over Warboys. Then he pulled the trigger.

There was a click, a small *phut*, and then a silence.

Quinky peered down at the rifle.

Warboys knew that *phut*. The hammer had fluffed in the chamber, but not punched into the cartridge. Just like Bill had warned him.

It'll usually shift with a good hard slap.

'Gives it here,' he said, snatching the barrel from Quinky's grip. He turned it about and slapped the hammer with the heel of his palm. With a scratchy thud, the Entwick shot its load right through Quinky's leg, painting the gangway with a flower of hot blood. Quinky let out a gargling scream, and Warboys stepped back, shaken by the memory of Bill. Senior Kuo closed in and clubbed Quinky down, silencing him. Quickly, the Tugels dragged the guards into the cells, then began arguing among themselves about what to do.

'They'll shoot the lot of us for this,' warned Joe, who then repeated his opinion in Tugelese. Senior Kuo considered this, then gathered the elder men of his family and pointed up the stairway, raising his club to call for blood. With that, the Tugels, arming themselves with what they could, flooded up the stairs to storm the Endurance.

'Brace yourself, Mr. Warboys,' called Joe, over the clamour. Tugels are a mostly a docile lot, but this blood has been a long time coming...'

Warboys nodded and went to Nouzi Aaranya.

'You alright there, kid?'

'Ai.'

'Can you get up?'

'Ai.'

'Good. You remember those fights of yours, that are always coming?'

'Ai?'

'There's one here. Now.'

'Ai.'

Warboys hauled Nouzi Aaranya to his feet.

'Time's come then. Joe. Are you with us?'

'Well, Mr. Warboys, looks like you have left me little choice, eh?'

Joe managed that deep bass laugh again as he picked up a cutter, but Warboys didn't see much humour there this time.

'Let's go, then.'

Warboys, Joe and Nouzi ventured warily up onto the main deck. They heard the Tugels running rampant, thundering charges across the decks, shots firing and steel clashing, shrill Tugel ululations. The butchered bodies of Adnam's crew littered the gangways.

They made it up to the main deck, where Senior Kuo stood guard on the hold whilst two of his sons looted the stores, having already lined up every weapon they could find. Warboys, shaken by the sudden bloodbath, was all ready to find the sloop and leave them to it, but when Nouzi Aaranya stepped out toward the hold, Senior Kuo turned his rifle on them.

Nouzi Aaranya bowed, and raised his hands. 'I only want my *dhas*.'

'And if you please,' added Joe, 'my harpoon. It is a keepsake.'

Kuo barked a command to his sons, keeping the rifle raised all the time. His sons emerged and lined up with him, rifles raised, and Kuo sneered grimly. Joe Bonboas made a terse exchange in Tugelese.

'What's he saying, Joe?'

'He doesn't want us to leave,' gulped Joe. 'He thinks we're going to steal the sloop and abandon them.'

'Tell him that—' began Warboys. Then there was a shot, and Kuo's ear jumped from his head in a spray of blood. As he collapsed, Warboys turned to see Adnam and his guards charging up from below deck. He and Joe dragged the Janizar away to cover, rounding the cabin as the young Tugels screamed and returned fire. Warboys pressed to cover, waiting for the firing to stop. Eventually, Adnam and two remaining guards crept out and ran for the steps down to the jetty.

Warboys took off after them. Down below, Adnam was already boarding the sloop. He was about to give chase when a guard rose up on the steps, lifting an old shotplug funnel like Nana Warboys used to have. Warboys flinched away as a volley of tacks and glass boomed past. He ducked next to Joe, looking to check on Nouzi. But the Janizar was gone again.

Down on the sloop, Adnam shoved off with a long pole, whilst his two guards fired parting shots. Before long they were out of reach.

'You'll all hang for this!' Adnam shouted, as the sloop drifted around the stern of the Endurance. 'Jayman will have you chopped up for sharkbait!'

Warboys ventured down the steps, despairing, sensing the escape had failed by a hair's breadth. Then he looked up and saw Nouzi Aaranya mount the aftcastle and charge along it, leaping recklessly after the sloop.

The Janizar flailed in the air and hit the sloop's mast, tipping one of the guards overboard and nearly keeling the whole vessel. He tumbled down through the sail in a ruffle of cloth and limbs, and slapped heavily down onto the deck. The last guard closed on him. Warboys raised his rifle and fired hopefully. The shot missed, only serving to make the guard duck – but then Joe Bonboas appeared at Warboys' side, grunting as he hurled his harpoon in a high arc. It speared the last guard straight through, hammering him into the deck. Then Nouzi Aaranya scrambled up, and his blade was on Adnam.

'Don't kill him!' yelled Warboys.

An angry cry came from behind, as the surviving Tugels came upon their dead Senior, and began to wail with rage.

'We had better leave, Mr. Warboys,' said Joe, wading eagerly into the water. Nouzi threw a rope, and Warboys and Joe hastily boarded the sloop.

'Impressive shot,' said Nouzi Aaranya, as Joe retrieved his harpoon.

'Impressive jump,' grunted Joe, making haste to set sail as Tugels lined the jetty, gesturing after them. A shot zipped overhead.

Once a fair distance away, Warboys strode over to Adnam. A scattering of hastily gathered treasures lay around him.

'The Hildegaard. Where is she?'

'The who?'

'Don't play silly buggers. My ship. Where is it?'

'Mebbe it flew away.'

'I'll fly you away in a minute. Gone to your gaffer, has she?'

'Any salvage I get, I report to Mr. Jayman. He had it towed off to Junkers soon as he could.'

Warboys effed and blinded under his breath.

'You won't get her back now, mate.'

'Don't fucking *mate* me now. You ain't in a position to talk all cocky.'

'I'm not. But Jayman is a big man on Junkers. Big money. Got a small army he has. You'll not get her back.'

'Well, we'll just have to see, won't we?'

'You're pirates now,' spat Adnam.

'No we bloody ain't,' snarled Warboys, catching Joe's doubtful look. 'We're... between jobs.'

'You're finished, is what you are.'

'Alright. I'm fed up of you now.'

Warboys stood Adnam up, and pointed him back toward the surviving guard, the one Nouzi had knocked overboard. The guard was now being hauled from the water by bloodthirsty Tugels, whilst the others awaited him on the jetty with cleavers at the ready.

'Don't worry, look. You and your mates are always welcome back on the good ship *Endurance*!'

'You can't just leave us here!' spluttered Adnam.

'I can.'

Warboys pushed Adnam into the water. He arose roaring in protest.

Joe and Nouzi exchanged looks before shrugging and conceding to Warboys lead. Joe took the tiller, and gave them to the wind.

Nouzi Aaranya sat quietly, watching the sea long after the Endurance had faded behind. Warboys went to sit with him, slapping a hand on his shoulder.

'Alright there, kid?'

'Ai.'

'Captain. I'm sorry. I was foolhardy, eh?'

'Yah. When I was your age, I'd have done worse. And I'd have done it on badness an' all. Thing with you kid, is you just do what you reckon you have to. However fucking tapped in the head it might be.'

'Ai. Well. You have my thanks.'

'Shut your face. We're all right. When we get to Junkers, you can buy me a pint.'

34 THE JUNKER LINE

It was after dark the following night when they saw a line of lights strung for miles across the blackness of the open sea. Nouzi Aaranya sat poised on the bow, staring intently.

'Is it land?'

'No. That's the Junker Line.'

Nouzi Aaranya tried to make sense of the mess of flagpoles, masts and scaffolds jutting up from the surface of the sea. But as they came closer, the structure came into view – a great flotilla of vessels, moored together to make a strip several miles long.

Walkways of board and rope spanned between a ramshackle host of vessels, from mastless old warships, to Imperial galleons, Aalandic tallships, hulks, barges and decommissioned steamers.

A central gangway cut through the clutter, winding away into the distance, and from it, voices blew, with the whine of a violin. In the lantern light, people milled to and fro, cast as shadow puppets against sailcloth windbreaks.

'They call that central strip the Great Gangway,' said Warboys. 'A street through the sea, like every dock street from every town you've ever seen, all packed on top of itself.'

Nouzi Aaranya stood back, shaking his head in bewilderment.

'Eh, but how did it all get here? I don't understand what I am seeing.'

Warboys laughed. 'Aye, I had that thought the first time I came.'

Joe Bonboas laid a hand on Nouzi's shoulder.

'It started as a naval blockade, during the Andwyke war. Those sandbanks where the *Endurance* was moored are part of a sunken archipelago that goes all along Aaland's west coast. It makes for a natural barrier, forcing you down Hagen's Strait to get to Aaland's west coast. So the Empire anchored warships across to block the strait, and put an end to the war by choking her enemy's supply.'

'Were you there, Captain?'

'Cheeky bastard, I wasn't even born!'

Nouzi shrugged, as if he couldn't possibly be expected to have such a vast grasp of ancient history. Joe laughed and continued.

'A lot of the old gunships stayed after the war. Some sunk, others were abandoned, and as time went on they retired the ships from Imperial service. Some were prison hulks like the Endurance, and most wouldn't have made it back west, so instead of sending them in to the breakers, their crews moored them together. Trade still came through, and stopped off there on route. And it grew from there.'

'Who rules here?'

'Money, mainly,' said Warboys. 'Junkers ain't a country, nor a state, and there's no kings or generals. If you've got money, you can get what you want, and no questions asked. If you ain't, well... you end up raking for cockles.'

The sloop was soon cutting in amongst the rabble of boats and floating jetties that trailed out from all sides of Junkers. Nouzi helped haul in to a berth. There were no guards to contend with, but Joe gave a one eyed man a coin to watch the sloop.

'I don't know if I should go here...' Nouzi told Warboys.

But Warboys just sighed, scratching at the savagely spiky growth that had grown around his face and neck over the past few weeks.

'Junkers is packed with Imperials, Aalanders, colonials,

every bastard going anywhere comes through here. No-one's going to notice *you*.'

Nouzi let Warboys haul him onto the floating jetty. Water slopped about their ankles as they made their way up a ramp to the Great Gangway. The row of themasses grew to a roar, and the breeze brought the smell of burning coal and cooking fat, lavender, citrus and rotten fish.

'Hui, Captain. What will we do here?'

'We're going to see if we can get the Hildegaard back.'

'Why though? She is wrecked.'

'She might be wrecked, kid. But is she *alive?* That's the question, ain't it? And this fuckwit scrapper Jayman won't know he's got the wonder of the modern world, will he? We might be able to blag her. I don't know. I'm not going to let her go for nowt though, that's for sure.'

'What *then?*'

'I told you, it's the junction of all the world here, kid. We can do anything.'

'Avai, Warboys. I told you. I am for...'

For Maia, he wanted to say. But something stopped him. Their confrontation over the game of Hastaya had stayed with him. Warboys had shamed him, brought the truth of his fear out into the open. His brothers had never absolved him of disgrace in any form. And yet, be it by courtesy or ignorance, Warboys had overlooked his dishonour. Here, in Warboys' company at least, he felt he had no claim to make. Far from making himself sick at the lack of kaarya, Nouzi Aaranya – to his shame – felt *relief.*

'Let's just see if we can get her back, alright?' Warboys was saying, as slovenly as ever. 'We'll be in a better position then.'

As soon as they joined the great Gangway the hawkers were at them, selling smoking weed and sweet Cercan oranges, handing out tickets for labour and tokens for cheap drinks. A sour, beery hum rolled past. The crowd rocked as one on the sway of the waves, like shoaling fish. Unshaven men eyed purses from beneath lampposts made of decommissioned masts, and bunting and flags were strung over in an array of colours, nationalities and principalities. Trinket stalls encroached onto the walkway, people shimmied this way and that, and Nouzi Aaranya stared like a frightened cat.

'Just calm yourself a bit, kid,' muttered Warboys. 'You don't want to look like a fucking sap, now. You're no more outrageous than any bugger else here.'

Nouzi Aaranya cleared his throat, puffed up his chest and tried to play Janizar. But when a battalion of whores swanned past, he clung fast to Warboys. A flame haired woman from the far north caught his eye and winked, loitered a moment, propositioning him in a language he didn't think he understood.

He managed to look away just in time as her face smeared away in the corner of his eye.

'Just go easy, will you?' laughed Warboys, pulling him out of his shock. 'We'll get to that.'

More of them came, coffee coloured women from the far Asiat, and coal coloured, goose shaped women with vast backsides from the south sea islands.

He avoided their faces.

He looked to see Joe and Warboys' eyes lit up with glee as they tracked the women shamelessly, and caught one another's eye, laughing together.

'Aye!' agreed Joe. 'Just go easy for now, eh?'

The Gangway rose steadily, coming to a kind of pier-head junction slung over the old HMS Muldark, that overlooked the Line. The undulating street zig-zagged into the misty distance, sparked by pricks of lamplight.

'Right then,' began Warboys 'I for one am fucking rasping for a pint. Will anyone join me?'

'Aye!' roared Joe.

'What about you, kid?'

'Hui, Warboys, I thought we were looking for the *Hildegaard*.'

'Yeah, well... this *is* looking. You don't wander up and down *looking* when you could just ask at the bar and save yourself a bit of bother. Junkers is about five bloody miles long and counting.'

'Ai,' Nouzi Aaranya swallowed. 'I'll come.'

'Too fucking right. You owe me at least six pints.'

'Ai.'

Nouzi Aaranya tucked tightly in behind as Warboys led them towards a crook in the Gangway. A bar with black awnings was cut right across the dismantled forecastle of an old galleon, as if she'd sailed right into the walkway, smashed open and started trading that very morning. A carved dog reared over them, and a sign hung from the bowsprit, declaring the place open as the *Dog's Head*. A caged Tree-panda chewed cigars in the doorway, and shanties boomed from somewhere within her smoky holds. Sailors yarped and smoked, perched in old cannon slots and portholes.

Nouzi watched Warboys at the bar, easily engaging one of the singers, who wore a grey dress jacket marked with the insignia of the Aalandic Navy.

'Here, mate, you lot off down to the Wyvern, then?'

'You what mate? No!' roared the ensign, throwing a pally arm around Warboys. 'War's over!'

Nouzi Aaranya could not help but smile at the joyous mix of cheers and boos from the raucous sailors.

'What do you mean?' asked Warboys.

'There's been a ceasefire!'

A chorus of cheers. The galleon tilted and a beer slid off the bar and smashed. Double cheers. 'Bloody hell! What happened?'

'Malvy ran out of south to march across!' said another, less drunk ensign. 'We got the land army in over the islands and breathing down their necks on the mainland. Fucking Air Force over the bastards like bad weather. Unification, he's calling it! There's to be a victory parade in Coperny!'

'What about Blackhaven?'

'Oh, it's taken, mate. Naval supply port now.'

Nouzi Aaranya reflected a moment, wondering what had become of all the Sons of Sun-Ivis now that their leader had abandoned them.

'Hear that?' cried Warboys. 'War's over!'

Nouzi Aaranya saw Warboys' smile falter.

'Hui, Captain. Is this not good for you?'

'I reckon it can't be bad,' he shrugged. 'Shame some had to die for such a daft squabble though, eh?'

Nouzi Aaranya sensed Warboys was thinking of his father, and felt his spirits drop some.

'Ai.'

They were quiet a moment. Nouzi Aaranya wanted to console him about Bill, but didn't dare. Then Warboys said, 'Have a pint', and Nouzi Aaranya was confused.

'Captain, I don't want to—'

'Shut your face and drink this.'

'Ai.'

Nouzi Aaranya sipped his ale suspiciously.

'Look at that, Joe! Dying men traverse the oceans of the earth in search of that umber draft, and he sips at it like it's his auntie's cod liver oil. Drink up, son! It'll all make sense soon.'

Nouzi Aaranya pulled a sour face whilst Warboys plunged in and out of the throng of drinkers, and soon the Janizar could barely see nor hear anything through the sheer mess of sounds and sights.

'Here, mate,' said Warboys to the Ensign, 'there's a shipbreaker by the name of Jayman somewhere on Junkers. You wouldn't know where to find him, would you?'

'He ain't just a shipbreaker, mate. He owns half the Line. What are you after?'

'Somebody said he might have some parts I need, is all.'

'Well, he's got a little harbour of his own off Sea Gardens. Try there.'

'Sea Gardens? I know it. Cheers mate!'

Nouzi Aaranya felt his skull fizzing with ale, so that it resisted the intake of information. Joe Bonboas was away talking to an old harpooner, and a woman with gaps in her teeth was smiling at him. He hid behind a keg until she was gone, then Warboys insisted on another round before they left. They gave Joe instructions to book cabins – having shared out Adnam's booty between them – and left him talking to a painted man in military issue boots.

Eventually Warboys hauled Nouzi back outside to the pier head. Compared to the stale hum of the *Dog's*, the sea air was like a slap about the head.

'Are we going to Sea Gardens?'

'Yes.'

'What is Sea Gardens?'

'You'll see. Come on.'

'Ai,' murmured Nouzi Aaranya.

35 PHANTOM

The main Gangway forked and they took the lesser path around barnacle-choked wrecks that peeped up between the walkways of the stretch called Sea Gardens. Great forests of bladderack encroached upon the pilings, lending the place a briny hum.

There weren't many folk around here, the general rabble tending to take the main Gangway, along by the oyster bars of Little Jurma. But here, Warboys was surprised to see well-to-do ladies walking arm in arm with suited gentlemen, and private guards plodding up and down the moorings. These were, he realised, the wealthy refugees of Malvy's revolution. The thought made him laugh. He hoped they were uncomfortable.

'Right...' said Warboys, teetering a bit as he turned to instruct Nouzi Aaranya. 'What was I saying? Oh aye. Behave yourself round here. No chopping, alright? And look sober.'

Warboys gazed with envy across a refurbished gunship, its portholes displaying a fancy dinner party within, ladies and stiff collared gentlemen dining by candlelight. Above them, a small plantation of hardy dune grasses lined the deck in decorative barrels.

A pair of shiny skinned South Island kids squatted by a capstan, begging from passers-by.

'How there, mister. We know this place. We seen everyone come and go. What you lookin' for?'

'They reckon there's a man named Jayman, has his own little dock out here.'

'Jayman's is just along here, mister, at the black galleon's berth. And for just a penny-fenyg, I can give you a tour.'

'I'll give you a tour,' said Warboys, giving a good natured showing of the back of his hand. They came to a fenced off wharf, where the ornate black galleon *Orchidia* reared up from the waves like a fortress. It was a much bigger outfit than Warboys had imagined. Her decks were adapted to a townhouse style abode, her cannon removed to form a fine terrace, her forecastle extended into a kind of rooftop balcony overlooking a private harbour where various smaller vessels were moored. A second, secluded harbour lay beyond, ringfenced in a barricade of barges, along which armed guards patrolled.

There, Warboys could see the roof of some large, half cylinder structure, ribbed and covered with canvas. The shape reminded Warboys of his dad's strawberry nets. The clatter of tools echoed across, and there was a familiar tang in the air.

'Smell that? It's her, I tell you! Come on. Give us a peg up.'

'Hui, Captain. I don't think you should.'

'I'm just going to look, alright?'

Whether it was the drink or not, he didn't know, but Warboys couldn't find it in himself to panic. Nouzi helped him up and over the fence.

'Hui, Warboys! The guard will come back!'

'Shut it. Come on.'

The Janizar scaled the fence with monkey-like ease, and they hurried down to a long pier that led across the first harbour to the barricade barges. They waited for a guard on the forecastle of the Orchidia to turn, then peered over.

The cylinder thing took pride of place in another secluded harbour. It was a half-pipe, mounted on two floating strips to form a hangar. And there, sure enough, the AS Hildegaard was intact within, anchored to a narrow barge. Workers milled in and out on walkways, and various other barges, flatbeds and narrow boats moved around the harbour.

'She's up, look! This Jayman is no fuckwit scrapper... They're renovating her!'

Nouzi Aaranya breathed sharply, and fell away into shadow a split second before a light from the Orchidia shone on them.

'Halt there, unless you want to be shot!'

Warboys raised his hands in surrender, allowing Nouzi to move away. A guard arrived down the pier, young, and well turned out with a nice modern firearm.

'Alright there, mate?' said Warboys, jovially. 'Can I interest you in some shellfish?'

Another guard joined the first.

'Get up here, now.'

In the corner of his eye, Warboys checked Nouzi Aaranya's retreat over the fence. He clambered slowly, playing for time.

'What do you think you're doing?'

'Look, I won't mess you about. I've come about my ship. See that beauty you've got in that hangar? She's mine.'

The guard sighed.

'I'm going to set you in front of this nice rifle here, and we're going for a nice walk back to the front gate. Then we'll say no more about it.'

'Can't I at least have a word with your gaffer?'

A muzzle in the back pressed him on. 'I'm trying to be reasonable with you, my friend.'

'So am I! She's mine. That there is the AS *Hildegaard*, lost out of service from Blackhaven maybe a month ago now, along with the *Tabitha* and *Rosamundt*. I landed her in the strait and we ran aground at the sandflats where the *Endurance* is moored.' Warboys took a breath. 'That idiot foreman Adnam stitched us up. So I reckon I'd better come in and see Mr. Jayman.'

'Why didn't you just come to the front gate and say so?'

'The thought never once occurred to me.'

'Well, it's a damn fool way to carry on, breaking in like that.

You could have been shot.'

'Sorry.'

'Alright. You'd better come with me.'

Warboys straightened himself up and cleared his throat. He glanced back to the Gangway as he did, and spotted Nouzi Aaranya loitering outside of the reach of a lamp. He raised a thumb as subtly as he could, trying to reassure Nouzi, then realised the thumb might mean nothing to him. Or something else entirely. He was foreign *and* daft, after all.

Ah well. He'll be alright for a minute, surely...

And so Warboys just shrugged, and walked away with the guard, leaving the Janizar waiting forlornly like a lost beggar child.

~ ~ ~

Nouzi Aaranya watched Warboys escorted away to the Orchidia. It seemed he would not be harmed, so there was nothing to do but wait.

He loitered a while, growing damp and cold, watching the galleon. He sighed heavily. Here he was. *Wilderness born*, on the fringes, hiding away again, without anyone to validate him.

But something in his old conviction had become dislodged. The rumble of voices and footsteps from the Gangway called louder and louder, until he found himself straying back towards it.

Warboys would be alright. Joe was at the Dog's Head. They had cabins there. Why shouldn't he wander a while?

He rounded the corner and stepped onto the Gangway alone. It was a shock not unlike diving into cold water, appalling but exhilarating all at once. The rush of the packed gangways carried him along, a tide of faces and limbs and skin crashing over him. His purpose was forgotten in his fear, hemmed in by this constant stampede of stinking outland humanity.

Kitava, they were called in his native language – *strays.* Without casting or kaarya, they were as dogs unleashed, pissing in corners and mating unregulated. Shouting and screaming and staggering around. Loitering and glaring in idle madness.

Even here, he saw one squatting to shit directly off the Gangway whilst others lay gummed to their own vomit. There was the stink of burning oil and frying fat. Of overbearing perfumes, hoppy, yeasty body odour. Clutter, things everywhere – stuffed animals, carved whalebones. Arrican copper kettles and glazed monkey skulls. Oranges encroached by blue grey mould. Some folk stared, whilst others looked away shiftily.

But most alarming of all – most *alluringly* – there was Maia. *Everywhere,* there was Maia.

A painted woman blocked his path, gap teeth, glassy eyes and black hair. Stains running down from her eyes. His heart began to pound, and he had to look down.

'What do you want, love?' she purred, sidling closer. 'I can help you.'

Nouzi Aaranya looked down at her hands. He wanted to look up, but felt his vision squirm, and shouldered past –

He saw her eyes smeared away in ribbons of smoke – yet he survived! His heart thumped in excitement. He was not in danger on Junkers. Anything was allowed here. The forbidden was available.

Maia stood in twisted parody, on every street corner, behind every bar: Maia's eyes in the grimy, beautiful, multi-coloured faces of the street. Sometimes she'd glare, sometimes she'd wink with eyelashes like black grasses. Sometimes he'd catch himself watching her hips, tilting like a boat in a storm before vanishing among the stinking throng. He saw her naked breasts presented like mangoes from bare windows and doorways, cupped in massaging hands to demonstrate ripeness. He felt surges of panic and arousal all at once, daring to peek for a moment before his eyelids started to flicker.

He'd never walked free like this. Never even visited the slums of Gienha, as his brothers had. He'd left home under Upa's sponsorship, and seen the outlands for the first time at Blackhaven. But Blackhaven was a city at war, not the decadent hive that this place was. There he could always escape across rooftops, into bombed out districts, where Maia hid and wept in dark cellars, unseen. Here the only escape was into the sea. Here, all of a sudden, he wasn't sure escape was what he wanted.

Through a fruit market he went. The sickly rotten sweetness of it dizzied him, the flies and peelings squashed underfoot. The row of hagglers, the bruised flesh, figs and melons and shapely squashes, Maia's mangoes before his eyes again.

He found a corner beside a stall, and caught himself. Breathed. Played his *Resadem*. Picked up the sound of the waves below for pace, and thought of Gienha. The peace of the blossomed gardens. The quiet, dignified business of the workers through the shaded canopies of the markets. Sunlight stretching beneath arches. The gentle buzz of *gomeda* lamps on the promenades. Maia in her proper place above, unseen, in that cold rectangle of darkness always above, always veiled in mist, a distance that calmed and reassured.

That *anaesthetised* him, he thought, bitterly.

Then he saw the dark haired woman saunter around the corner, looking for him with her leaking eyes, pawing at him.

'Come here, love. Are you nervous? I can be gentle...'

For a moment he was tempted to look her in the eye. Perhaps her face would hold this time. Perhaps finally he could see. Touch.

Terror and arousal vied for him, blood rushing from his head to his khus.

Go, and protect Sun-Ivis, he recalled Maia say, on the day he left the nursery. *Protect... me.*

It was too much. He was afraid. He groaned and pulled away, clutching at his hair. 'Off me! You are a phantom! Sarpa!'

And so saying, Nouzi Aaranya made for the safety of the Dog's Head. Fear passed, and excitement arose, the feeling of *survival* in him as he ran, grinning fiercely all the way.

36 THE WARBOYS METHOD

Whilst awaiting Mr. Jayman on the grand decks of the *HMS Orchidia*, Warboys sat ill at ease among opulent surroundings. Orchidia's gundeck had been stripped and merged with the orlop deck to create a fancy reception hall. Paintings hung from wallpapered bulkheads, and the mosaic floor had been laid with the pattern of a dark flower. A proper waiter type brought him a hot ginger brandy to sip whilst he waited – but an armed guard was never far away. Flower baskets now stood where lines of cannon once sat, forming an observation terrace that overlooked the floating hangar. There, a steady train of workers trailed in and out to work on the Hildegaard.

What were they doing with her?

A tautly postured gentleman in a tailed jacket and waistcoat eventually arrived. He had thick, neatly trimmed facial hair from which a small, pointing nose curved. This, combined with the circular flight goggles he wore, put Warboys in mind of an owl.

'Mr. Warboys?' he enquired, removing his hat and goggles to reveal kind, smiling eyes. He peeled off a glove and offered his hand. 'Leonarde Jayman. You are the Hildegaard's captain?'

'Erm... acting,' said Warboys, unsure how to conduct himself.

'I understand you have suffered some inconveniences at the hands of my employees?'

'You might say that...'

Mr. Jayman sat heavily, as if deflated with dismay. 'I see. Let me first assure you, sir, that I had no idea of your existence until now. Mr. Adnam erroneously assured me that neither pilot nor crew were to be found with the Hildegaard. Had I known this was not the case, I would have insisted on your safe and immediate passage here.'

'Would you?' began Warboys, warily. 'Right...'

'I cannot apologize enough, and will of course compensate you for your inconvenience. And let me promise you, Mr. Adnam will be dealt with.'

Warboys thought of the rampaging Tugels, but said nothing.

'First, Mr. Warboys, I insist that you tell me all about what brought you to the Endurance. I understand you left Blackhaven on board the Hildegaard? Was this as part of her crew?'

Warboys cleared his throat. 'No. I was infantry, not Air Force. The rebels attacked the barracks, and hijacked the ships.'

'By *rebels* you mean this new Sun-Ivis movement? The cult of Uparagha. King of the Waning Moon, and so forth.'

Warboys hesitated.

'How do you know about that?'

'All news comes through Junkers, Mr. Warboys. Malvy is never shy about announcing his victories, nor denouncing his enemies – he has recently outlawed Sun-Ivis nationally with his latest crude declaration. Ha! As if one could merely switch off one's nature! But do go on.'

'Well, I ended up chasing one of Uparagha's men to the Hildegaard's hangar. One thing led to another, and I ended up left on board as she was launched...'

Warboys opted not to mention Nouzi Aaranya for now.

'I take it you are not rushing to report back to active duty, Mr. Warboys?'

'I'm no Malvyite. I was hauled off the street, same as the rest of them.'

'Indeed. That warmongering old mountain goat Malvy has very nearly press-ganged the whole country. But you are not alone in your dismay, Mr. Warboys. There are others who believe that it is not time for Malvy's so called Modern World. His abominable gloating about the End of History! Not now and not ever! Tell me. The rebels that tried to steal the Hildegaard. Would they have been one of Uparagha's trusted? His *Janizar*?'

Warboys shrugged, feigning ignorance, and hiding in his brandy a moment. Jayman's questions were very pointed. And what *was* he doing with the Hildegaard? Something was amiss. Warboys scanned him again and noticed a tiny motif on his jacket. A black flower. He looked down, and saw again the same black flower depicted in the mosaic beneath them. There was something about that insignia. Where had he heard of it before?

Bill. It was the old man who'd mentioned it. The pilot Bill had released from Blackhaven gaol had the same mark tattooed on him. Warboys felt a sudden strike of nerves.

'I'm not being funny, mate... but who are you? You're no salvage merchant.'

Jayman nodded, his lips forming a tight smile.

'Mr. Warboys. You're from Coperny, aren't you?'

'Aye, I am.'

Warboys glanced for the exit, noted the positon of the guard.

'Good man. Whereabouts?'

'Kingstown. Why?'

'Ah. A very underprivileged district, but good people. Good people. Well, sir, you might have heard me by title. My full name is Leonarde Jayman-Bernigny.'

'Bernigny? The *Duke* of Bernigny?'

Warboys recalled the rumours that were doing the rounds in Coperny after Malvy's rise to office: the aristocrats raided, the talk of a firefight outside Bernigny's manor. His mind reeled.

'The very same,' began Jayman, holding up his hands genially, taking Warboys' hesitation for awe. 'Though, you understand, I'm sure, that in these days a royal title is no longer something to declare. Malvy's agents are widespread and numerous.'

Warboys stood up quickly enough to knock the table. His brandy glass spun across the mosaic and he backed toward the door.

'That pilot Valego is your man, isn't he? That's how you know so fucking much about Blackhaven. You're backing Uparagha!'

'No.' Jayman held up his hands to placate him. 'No, Mr. Warboys. Uparagha organised those attacks alone.'

Jayman's eye went to the door to hold off the guards who now loomed.

'Let me out!'

'Please, sit down, Mr. Warboys. Let me explain. You've done me a great service coming here, and I can assure you, I had nothing to do with either the bombings, or the hijacking. I need pose no threat to you.'

Jayman gestured persistently to the chair, and Warboys saw he had little choice. He lowered himself reluctantly, and a butler bustled in to clear up the mess.

'Those ships,' Jayman began, waving away the guard, 'and the technology that supports them, were developed by my organisation of associates *long before* Malvy seized office.'

'What organisation is that, then?'

Jayman's palm pressed proudly to the black flower on the breast of his jacket.

'We are a consortium of... concerned gentlefolk, who wish to stand for knowledge and reason. For enlightenment. Advancement, but all in the right hands, managed well and not squandered for this grotesque levelling of the workers that Malvy has unleashed. Say one thing for the monarchy, Mr. Warboys, the worker knew his place!'

Warboys raised an eyebrow at that, and wondered what Jayman thought *his* place was.

'Long before he made his revolt public, the general committed treachery of the highest order. He sent his personal guard to capture our facility on Havery Moor...'

'Sesaw told me that Havery Moor was theirs, and that *your* rebels raided it.'

'Lies, Mr. Warboys. Havery Moor was ours, and always had been, under the king. Great breakthroughs were made there. We were very close to mastering the craft. We had actual manuals, Mr. Warboys! Can you imagine?'

'You're talking about the Datyas,' said Warboys flatly, wanting to bring Jayman off his perch a little. For a split second Warboys thought the amiable wrinkles in Jayman's eyes ironed out, then he composed himself and sat back, slapping his thighs as if awed by Warboys' talent.

'You are a sharp one, sir! I see you've taken a few steps into our world already. What, might I ask, do you know about the *Datyas*?'

'I know Malvy's aeronautics people are after them. They're some sort of working manual for growing and raising those engine slugs.'

'Amongst other things, Mr. Warboys, yes. Amongst many other things. As a matter of fact, we believe they originated with Sun-Ivis.'

Warboys nodded, and let him talk.

'Not this new movement, you understand. Not Uparagha's rag-tag rebels. His own race. The original, ancient people of Sun-Ivis. They have been a great source of interest for my organisation over the two hundred years since Aaland was colonised. There are still some, Mr. Warboys, who will tell you they never existed – but we know different, no? Their achievements reach back beyond the beginning of what we understand as civilisation. They were stargazers, Mr. Warboys. Information gatherers. Since history began, Sun-Ivis collated catalogues. Star charts. Measurements. Formulae. Things never before dreamed of in Western scientific discipline, all just tucked in along all the usual mythical rot. Most remarkable among these was a catalogue of living things. Not just an index of genus, as such, but something much more fundamental. What we call the *building blocks* of organic life, if you will...'

Jayman paused to let this sink in, and Warboys strained to make sense of it, recalling Nouzi's talk of kaarya.

'And yet, these wonders stayed lost amongst the scripture of the Datyas, misunderstood and used by no-one. Not even, it seems, by Sun-Ivis itself.'

'Why, though?' said Warboys. His mind reeled yet again as he tried to reconcile everything he knew. Did this indexing and mapping have anything to do with what he'd seen at Blackhaven Tor? What were the Sekhet aiming for?

'Perhaps we will never know, Mr. Warboys. It was a latter day offshoot of their people who were the first to speculate, to *use* this information to enact, and experiment, rather than just catalogue. But, of course, they were deemed rogue, beset by inhibited minds, the Malvys, the likes of which oppress you and I to this day. A fugitive came to us, and at great cost, time and endeavour, the rare fruits of their work began to be recovered by my organisation. We came to the brink of the great aviation technology you are familiar with, only to be seized by Malvy's revolutionary dogs. Manuscripts burned. Samples destroyed.'

Warboys sipped his brandy, frowned and nodded.

'Those airship engines – what we call the *digestive fission and floatation unit* – have been sent off to common war without thought for the wider world. For science. For civilisation. A *devastating* loss to progress. That is the *real* hijack, Mr. Warboys. The hijack of this very country! Malvy recognised early that those ships are artefacts that will determine the course of history. Now, several unsuccessful attempts were made to reclaim the units—'

Warboys' jaw tightened as he remembered the Hildegaard drifting over Kingstown, his and Bill's arrest in Coperny. All because this black flower mob had tried to hijack her. He said nothing.

'—and we have since been monitoring their whereabouts closely. So, when I heard of the situation in Blackhaven, I was naturally intrigued when this unsavoury Uparagha character rose up and stole the ships – but I can assure you once again, sir, it was he who approached *us,* and only *after* the hijacking.'

'What about Valego? He's your man, isn't he? Surely you knew Uparagha was breaking him out?'

'No. Valego is a dear friend. He fled Malvy to the south, but was betrayed to the authorities there, and gaoled to await sentence. Uparagha's intimate links with the locals allowed him to identify Mr. Valego and his talents, and his release was arranged...'

Warboys felt a bitter taste in his mouth at that. *His release was arranged.* A simple arrangement, a task for staff, and never mind the lives burned up in the process. He wondered if Malvy's violent cancellation of the aristocracy was a bad thing at all.

'Uparagha then demanded that Valego provide rudimental training for the purpose of the strike. But he also extracted the name of our organisation – and, recognising a fellow enemy of Malvy's state, Uparagha has since contacted us to negotiate an alliance.'

'For what?'

Jayman shrugged. 'He sought our backing to consolidate his gains in Blackhaven. To recruit any and all enemies of the state for more attacks.'

'Well? What did you say?'

Warboys swallowed, gauged again the position of the door, and the guard outside – waiting to judge what his host said next.

'My organisation is not itself concerned with warfare. Not *in itself.* But measures must be taken and losses must be expected if we are to rectify what Malvy has done. An arms race *is* coming, Mr. Warboys. The pressing matter of the day is the possession of Aaland. And the key to that is the power of those ships. But whilst warmongers like Malvy and Uparagha look to the short term victories to be gained from the ships themselves – *we* look to the long term. The attainment of the advanced craft of the Datyas, the knowledge itself.'

'You haven't answered me. Are you in league with Uparagha or not?

'I agreed to a meeting with him, and attempted to negotiate for the return of the ships. But Uparagha wanted to deploy them to his own ends, and refused to relinquish even one. He came here like some thug for hire, offering to spearhead an attack on Malvy, and expected me to—'

'Uparagha? Is he still on Junkers now?'

'No. Negotiations were strained and difficult, made mercifully redundant after the Hildegaard arrived. I was able to send him on his way. My people saw him leaving the Line two days ago. I believe he had been encamped far north, on the border coast. So no, Mr. Warboys, I am not working with Uparagha.'

'But would you have done, if I hadn't blundered along with Hilda?'

Jayman smiled pleasantly.

'It is immaterial now, surely! We have far better – we have you! Thanks to your great discovery, we have the means of production in our hands again!'

Warboys went from suspicion to confusion in a breath.

'Great discovery? What?'

'Well of course, you see, the ships, once grown and configured, were thought to be barren in terms of spawning. But not only have you brought us the Hildegaard, a first generation motor stem, you've made it sprout! It's the first time it has ever been achieved. Really quite remarkable!'

Warboys managed to iron the confusion out of his face a little.

'Well, you know. I did what I had to.'

'Genius, Mr. Warboys! Really, we're quite flummoxed with what you've done.'

'So now you can work out how to grow them again?'

'And so much more, Mr. Warboys. Please avail me. How did you do it? My crew are hankering after what we've already dubbed *the Warboys method*.'

Warboys flushed a little, not sure whether to feel pride or embarrassment. Jayman called for more drinks, tightening his happy little eyes as he soaked up every word. Omitting mention of Nouzi Aaranya – hoping that it was plausible that he'd survived alone – Warboys told Jayman as plainly as he could what had happened, from the crash landing on the sea, right through to the mutiny on the Endurance. Jayman waved on through the latter, seeming almost bored by it, but his eyes twinkled brightly whenever Warboys spoke of the Hildegaard's workings and behaviour.

'Quite the adventure!' he beamed, standing. 'Let me shake your hand, sir! Not many Airmen would have coped with having to de-rig and sail an aircraft the way you did! The ordeal you describe is quite phenomenal.'

'Well, you know, I do have half a chartership...'

'Imagine what you could do with a full one! Now, if I might impose on you a short time more... I'd like you to spend some time here with the Hildegaard, in the company of one of my clerks and the engineers, to provide a detailed account of your experiences. I would, of course compensate you *generously*.'

'Wait. All this fancy talk of enlightenment and progress and all that. It sounds nice. But you're royalists, aren't you? So this

Black Flower organisation of yours is looking to put the King back on his throne?'

'Alas, King John's line is lost. But my organisation still has roots over the western sea, in the old countries.'

Warboys laughed humourlessly.

'The *Empire*, you mean? I'm not for Malvy, I'll tell you that. But it doesn't mean I want the Empire coming back. My dad fought in the Andwyke...' He trailed off, felt a newfound surge of pride in the knowledge that his dad had fought for his future even before he was born. 'Aaland is still my home,' he managed to add, kicking himself for only just seeing this now, 'and I've got family there.'

'I fully understand your apprehension, sir. But Aaland is already stolen. Already under attack – from Malvy himself. Whether you stand for a cause or not, Mr. Warboys, the world stands at the brink of an arms race. The technology is here. It is now. The question is, who steers it?'

Warboys digested this. He didn't particularly want to help Jayman. But hadn't the horse bolted already? Uparagha had Tabitha and Rosamundt. Malvy still had other ships. Someone else could easily work out the method he'd happened across, and Jayman seemed easy with the knowledge that the Datyas originated with Sun-Ivis. Did it matter any more?

'I offer you the chance to change the world, Mr. Warboys. Work with us, and help renovate and study the Hildegaard. In addition to the substantial compensation I mentioned earlier, I would pay you very generously for your time. I'll pay you a severance fee for your family – enough to relocate them in good time, should you wish – enough to *set them up for life*, as the saying goes. I can lend you resources and contacts to enact that. Otherwise, you are under neither contract nor obligation to stay longer than you wish.'

'Leaving the Hildegaard with you.'

'Of course,' said Jayman, eyes creasing with that genial smile again. And then he sat back to take a sip of his drink.

Warboys kneaded his forehead, feeling way beyond his depth again. Perhaps Jayman was right, and with war coming, was being as reasonable as could be expected in all of this. Perhaps it was all out of his hands now whether he objected or not. He couldn't go back to Aaland. Cait would be better off without him – in fact, the less association she had with him the better. At least now he could finally send her some money. And he'd been lucky enough to land in the care of Malvy's enemies. He didn't think Bill would have objected too much to that. And, of course, there was *the Warboys method*. What would Bill have said to that? Perhaps there was an engineering career here for him. He wondered if Bill would be proud to see that.

He drained his glass, and felt the drink dissolving tired old conflicts of loyalty. *Fuck it*, he thought.

'I accept.'

Mr. Jayman's eyes twinkled.

'I congratulate you, Mr. Warboys. With your consent, the world has taken a great leap!'

Warboys welcomed the gale coming off the sea as he walked out onto the Gangway, feeling as if his brain had been wrung out. Jayman's clerk had met him on his way out and paid him enough to sober him up on the spot. He had freedom. He had money. He had purpose, all of a sudden, here at the Junction of all the world. He had everything he thought he'd wanted, and yet even when he was wrecked at sea on the sunken Hildegaard, he'd never felt quite so *adrift*.

Thoughts stormed about his head so much that he could barely even roll a smoke. He resolved, instead of considering his future position in the world, to get out of his mind drunk, and walked off in search of Nouzi Aaranya. They were going to get blind drunk, him and the boy, and make light of it all, at least for one night.

They were good for that, if nothing else.

37 FREEDOM TO CHOOSE

'Hui, Mr. Bonboas. Are all your friends that colour?'

Nouzi Aaranya had been sitting in the Dog's Head, staring at Joe for some time. He was beginning to suspect he was drunk.

Joe laughed, as he always did. 'Not all of them, Nouzi Aaranya. You, for example, have always looked a bit peaky to me.'

Nouzi Aaranya smiled and sipped at the pint that Joe had bought him. The bitterness was becoming easier to take.

'Hui, Mr. Bonboas. Is your *khus* as dark as the rest of you?'

'No, my friend. It is a made of blue crystal, but glows red when eligible ladies are in range.'

Nouzi Aaranya gaped, and Joe held his eye until they both cracked up with laughter. They were still laughing when Warboys shouldered into the Dog's.

'Good news!' he laughed, enveloping Nouzi Aaranya in a rough embrace, ruffling his hair and jabbing him in the shoulder. 'I found her!'

'Who?'

'The Hildegaard, you knobhead! Come on, drink up! Let's move on!'

Nouzi hurriedly necked his pint, and tumbled after them, out of the Dog's Head, and along to the nearest beer stall, built on an overturned whaling boat lined with tusks and jawbones. An old woman in a black veil served from behind a stack of piled up kegs. Nouzi Aaranya forced himself to try and peer at her, wondering if he could build up to Maia. Her face squirmed and he looked away – but he held himself well. The ale was making him braver. Warboys threw an arm about him, spilling some beer across the walkway.

'Avai, Captain! You are wasting my precious elixir!'

'Ha! Silly bastard! Listen though—' His bellowing was rattling Nouzi Aaranya's brain, yet he still couldn't hear clearly. 'I've got a job.'

'What *job*?'

'Working for Jayman.'

'Avai, Warboys, this man steals from you then pays you off? *Kitava!*'

'It's not like that.'

'Everything here is like that.'

'Listen. There might be something for you, too.'

Nouzi didn't bother to refute him this time, and Warboys went on.

'You can't go back. Not now.'

'Why?'

Warboys leaned against the bar. 'Listen. You don't fool me. You're a stubborn little shit, and I don't doubt you've got the will to do whatever you set your mind to. But you're finished with Sun-Ivis, alright? I don't mean it nasty. It was just never meant to be.'

Nouzi Aaranya considered it. Perhaps it was the poison of the ale, but he couldn't bring himself to object.

'But you *can* find kaarya somewhere else. I'm staying on Junkers to get a bit of cash together before I move on. Why don't you come with me?'

'Hui,' laughed Nouzi Aaranya, looking to Joe incredulously, 'you don't know where *you're* going! How would I follow you?'

'Why not? We could do owt we liked. I'll even...'

Warboys was distracted a moment, staring after some slinky Asiatic girls passing by. Nouzi Aaranya followed his eye and dared a glance, then hid his face in his drink. Warboys noticed this, and studied him.

'You *can* look at them, you know. You're free here.'

'Freedom itself is not purpose,' objected Nouzi Aaranya, more by habit than anything.

'Oh, for fuck's sake! Let yourself off the hook!'

'A man runs away to find himself waiting.'

'See, you're just repeating things your teacher told you now. Did Sukhanava teach you to squawk like a parrot as well?'

Nouzi Aaranya couldn't answer, realsing that he wasn't sure if he even understood what was coming out of his own mouth, let alone believe it. He glared at his pint reproachfully.

'What do you intend to do, anyway? Go back to your brothers? You can't stand them! Why bother? Set fire to some old ladies? Mug a blind man? Fucking Janizar, my arse... You said it yourself. It's all third boom now. All found and finished, this world. You're a decent kid at heart. You don't need them.'

Nouzi Aaranya shook his head blankly, couldn't remember what he stood for or what he was doing. He thought sadly of Adharza Lake, that burning paper lantern tumbling down to the mirror surface of the water.

'Here,' slurred Warboys, nudging at Joe. 'You know what this kid needs?'

'A haircut?'

'No, no! He needs to get his leg over, that's what. You need a lady for the night.'

'Nai!' objected Nouzi, but his heart jumped with more than a little excitement.

'Look. You could at least *try* and enjoy yourself! See what there is to offer you! Alright, there's no god and no honour and no truth anymore, but you do get freedom to choose, don't you? That's what the modern world offers you. Just have *one* night. Just one night. See what kaarya brings, eh? *Come on.* We'll get you a classy one down the *Rosey Blush.* You can stick the rod back up your arse in the morning if you like...'

'Or tonight, for a few extra bob!' laughed Joe, joining the appeal, ruffling him about the head.

'Ai!' he barked, and grinned. 'Freedom to choose! Let's go! One night only.'

'You're up for it? No more moaning about kaarya and and all that?'

'Ai! Up for it! Let's go!'

Warboys slapped his back, and the three of them stumbled on. Warboys insisted on a quick drink first – but this extended to several Andam pipe brewed ales, some Imperial wines and a few *Wodjak* spirits from Dusja. Nouzi Aaranya felt so drunk that the swaying of the sea threatened to push him up out of his own head. Warboys whistled and called after passing girls, and Nouzi Aaranya joined in, calling bawdily after them even though his own mangled, mimicked words were a mystery to him, and the Maias were still just smears of fabric and grease in his eyes.

They found a stall where an old Tugel called Ulao made fireworks, framed by rows of innocuous, neat looking paper tubes with red tails.

'I want some of them fucking bangers!' announced Warboys gleefully, striding over to buy. He set some off on the Gangway for a laugh. The hot explosions were still flashing in Nouzi's eyes on their approach to the notorious schooner *Rosey Blush,* where a gangway led onto a dark, gently lit stairway.

'Come on, kid. In you go.'

He went stumbling over the threshold, into the dark, sniggering as he went. Warboys left him in a plush cushioned corner, and his and Joe Bonboas' muffled laughter slopped around the cloying hot reception room. There were *women* – with strained imitations of Maia's voice, flat like foreign wind instruments. He steeled himself, ready to be able to look at them. Warboys went to speak with the staff.

'Have you got a... here, Nouzi mate. What sort of bird is your Maia?'

He could only murmur in response, looking at his toes.

'Ah, never mind. It'll be a dark haired girl I reckon. Asiatic maybe. With a big backside. In the master suite! Aye! The captain's cabin for this boy!'

A man with a painted face came to usher him through, requesting that he remove his dhas. Warboys stepped in and offered to keep it, shoving him onward. Velvety curtains opened to a corridor that was like a yawning gullet. Voices whispered. The smell of some acrid smoking weed wound around him from behind a curtain.

The usher led him on. The dim wall lights fluttered – or was it his eye? The beams of the ship reared over him as he stepped into a cabin. A distant chord of panic struck somewhere under the waves of foam and beer and scum in which he'd marinaded his mind.

The usher was gone. The door closed.

She was there before him, kneeling on the bed, curves of skin cast in shadow, dark hair adjoining the black around her eyes, falling in coils over her breasts. He felt his khus surge into rigid life.

He knelt before he fell, trying to compose himself and sit sanyas. A ridiculous world-renouncer with a throbbing erection. She was laughing, saying something, and he couldn't understand, didn't know if she was speaking a language he knew or not. He saw her shadow crawling over him as she stood and closed the door, narrow waist and blooming hips. She knelt before him and he closed his eyes in fear, felt her breath making his eyelid flicker. Her hand stroked his khus through his clothes.

His heart thumped as, with eyes screwed shut, his mind assembled fragments again: the variegated green pigment of her eye, the freckles across the bridge of her nose, the creases in her bottom lip.

He opened his eyes and looked at her.

There was nothing there but a squirming mess. He'd been a fool. It was happening again.

He saw Maia's eyes bleed out of her face like a streak of dark paint on canvas, and lost himself to the terror.

~ ~ ~

Through his stupor, Warboys felt his arm jerk as the dhas was pulled from under it. He awoke frowning. Quick footsteps faded aross the boards, and a draft blew across his nose. He realised he had slept, and arose slavering on the chair arm in the *Rosey*, confused and hungover.

Joe was nowhere to be seen. The curtain near the exit billowed. Fighting drunkenness, Warboys bounced from one side of the corridor to the other as he made his way down to the so-called master suite. The door was ajar. Warboys pushed it open, and found Nouzi Aaranya's girl, a crease of irritation in her brow as she bent to pick up cushions and blankets.

'Has he finished?'

'Finished?' she snapped, waving her hand away down the corridor dismissively. 'Gone!'

'Oh.' Warboys looked her over a moment, and she drew the sheet over herself. 'Well, I booked you for an hour. Any chance of—'

'Finish!' she yelled. 'Gone!' She shoved him out and slammed the door. Warboys stumbled up the stair to the gangway. It was deserted, and the awning rattled with rain. He heard the sound of vomiting and walked about to look over onto the *Rosey's* aft-deck. There, Nouzi Aaranya bent double in the dark. Warboys rolled his eyes.

'Don't tell me you threw up on her.'

There was no answer.

'Nouzi mate, are you...'

It was then that Warboys caught a glimpse of silver in the boy's hand. He was holding his dhas, reversed in his grip and poised to be driven into his own stomach.

'Oi!' roared Warboys. 'No!'

He scrambled across the deck, slipping on the boards. He lunged and snatched at Nouzi Aaranya's arm just as the dhas was thrust home. The blade shot out through Nouzi's coat, glistening and red.

'Oh, fucking hell! You silly bastard...'

Cold fear impaled Warboys' own gut as Nouzi Aaranya fell sideways to the deck, coughing up vomit. Warboys dithered, tore the shirt away to see blood blooming across a laceration that ran from the middle of Nouzi's gut to his side. He'd managed to pull the strike aside when he'd grabbed Nouzi Aaranya's arm – but the dhas had still skewered him, and stuck fast.

'I just wanted to see Maia's face, Captain...' he gasped. 'But there's nothing there. Nothing there...'

'Alright, kid. Just calm down. I'll sort you out.'

'I don't want to be here any more.'

'Just shut up. Shut up! I'm going to sort this.' Warboys cast about the blur of the Junker Line for aid, and remembered Jayman. Surely, Jayman would have doctors and surgeons.

'Just hold on, kid. I'm going to sort this...'

Part Four

We may speak of trials, of hardships along the way, but what it truly cost to get here we may never know, for the journey has changed us irrevocably, and we can never again recover those same men who first set sail.

— *Hagen's journal, 1625*

38 WET SHAVE

Warboys weathered his hangover as he waited on board the *Orchidia* for the boy to wake. For long hours he scratched at his hair and watched the cabin walls. Went out to look over the balcony at the glistening kelp. Rolled smokes. Picked the boy's dried blood from under his fingernails.

Eventually the lightning blue eyes opened a slit, strikingly intense against his washed out face.

'Alright there, kid? You're safe. You're in a cabin on Mr. Jayman's ship.'

Nouzi Aaranya frowned and tried to sit up, then gasped as he plunged, in pain, back to the bed. Raking at the bedshirt that had been put on him, he felt a trail of stitches now lining him from gut to ribs.

'Easy. Just rest for now. Jayman's surgeon stitched you up. That blade of yours slid under a rib and out the other side, and missed all your giblets on the way. Made a right fucking mess, but the wound was fairly clean, like, so... I caught you in time. I think you'll be alright. Lucky for you I was there.'

Nouzi Aaranya closed his eyes and said nothing. Warboys swallowed. 'I tell you what,' he smiled, 'I've never seen such a shower of shite as what they line up as Janizar these days...'

The kid didn't see the joke. He closed his eyes to sleep, or to *pretend* to sleep. Warboys' relief immediately soured, and he resisted the urge to slap him, turning to walk out – *angry*, and not knowing why.

He turned about in the doorway and came back.

'Why? We didn't survive all that at sea for you to come and off yourself! Tell me – *why?*'

Nouzi Aaranya tested his lips, his eyes moistening as he whispered.

'It happened again, Captain. I thought I was free, but the terror stays with me. I understand now, why it happens. Upa tried to tell me. You tried to tell me. It is a lie I have lived for all these years. There is no Maia in heaven, watching. There are just women, hidden and painted. There is no *Deva*. That is why I could not see Maia's face. Even here in the outlands, there is no god, nor kings nor laws. No boundaries nor countries. No pure blood. And what is left, Captain? If all is *choice*? Choose beer. Choose boat. Choose Maia. What is *real*? If Maia is not God, if the Sekhet are not law... then truth is not truth and death is best.'

'Truth? What did I tell you? Kaarya, destiny, all that shit. We can all go chasing our silver coast... our bloody, bastard wonderlands... but there's *nowt* without survival!'

Nouzi Aaranya looked at him earnestly. 'Then what is the *point?*'

'You just... you keep...'

Warboys couldn't find the answer. Bill would have known what to do. Bill would have smoothed it all over. Bill would have known not to force the kid. He turned and kicked a table, toppling a lamp, which blinked out. He stopped in the doorway, breathing deep. He backed in and picked up the lamp carefully, avoiding Nouzi Aranya's eyes.

'I've got to go and work now,' he said. 'There's a full staff on board if you need owt. Just ring that bell for the quartermaster.'

'Ai.'

'I'll be back later.'

He left, sad and frustrated with himself, flicking his dog end out over the balcony into the bladderack below. Half way up to the main deck, he turned about and crept back, popping his head back around the cabin porthole, just to check the kid was still breathing.

~ ~ ~

Joe Bonboas was already smoking on the wharf when Warboys alighted the Orchidia. The two walked on toward the Gangway together.

'I tell you Joe, it's like having a baby.'

'Ah, you've gone soft on him, Warboys.'

'No I haven't. I just want him to get better so I can wring his fucking neck for him, that's what.'

'You love him really. It is touching to my heart.'

'Piss off. I'm serious. I've had to hide all my sharp things, put my rifle out of reach. And then you think about where we are! Junkers ain't a play pen, is it? He might go off the end of the fucking pier!'

'In which case, you can't do anything, can you? Give him time. He will be alright. We all have our dark nights, and we face them alone.'

'I've had plenty of rough nights, Joe. But I've never woken up dead before.'

Joe Bonboas laughed, and Warboys shook his head.

'Nowt bothers you, does it Joe?'

'Oh, more than you know, my friend. I was there when the slavers came. I have seen some dark sights. But then, this is why I laugh, eh?'

'Alright. But what am I meant to do with him now?'

'Nothing. Let him work it out.'

'You don't fancy staying a while? Maybe I could find you a job with Jayman.'

'No my friend, I told you. I have to open my shop. My partner awaits me in Coperny.'

'In that case...' Warboys fished out an envelope and handed it over. 'Can you take this for my Cait? The address is on there. A bit of overdue alms, like.'

'There is a sizable amount here, my friend. Are you sure?'

'I trust you.'

'Consider it done.'

'I'd appreciate it, mate. Here though, I can't see you stood behind a counter somehow. What are you going to sell? Harpoons?'

'Haircuts.'

'What? You're joking!'

'No!' laughed Joe. 'The world always needs a haircut, my friend. I'll give you a discount. The closest wet shave in the Andywke.'

'You're not coming near me with that harpoon.'

Joe laughed.

'Good money is it, in barbering?'

'Respectable. I want to try and be there in time for this rally they are talking of. Many haircuts needed, just in new recruits! He is a showman, this Great General. He prepares a world famous show of might, knowing his rivals and enemies are watching. And there will need to be haircuts, Warboys! More haircuts in any one place than has been known in history!'

'I was there, you know, at his first public address. Seems like a long time ago now.'

'Aye, well, they say this one will declare Malvy's United Andwyke to the world. The North South Rail is finished, and they are going to send the first cross continental train, the *Unification* – from the Wyvern up to Andamark, passing through Coperny at noon sharp on the day of the rally. His *Eyrie*, as they call it, is finished, and there will no doubt be a great display of floating balloons to delight his public.'

'That reminds me, I meant to go and see that barmaid again after work...'

'Mr. Warboys, you are an incorrigible bastard! I have a prospective captain to court back at the Dog's. I expect to be away tonight. Pass on my regard to the boy if I don't get chance.'

'Aye, I will do. It was nice knowing you, Joe. Good luck to you.'

'Remember Mr. Warboys. I'll be there in the arcade off Blyte Row if you ever need a trim.'

They shook hands, embraced, and Joe went his way.

Warboys turned to walk back towards Sea Gardens to report for duty.

39 ENTWINED

Nouzi Aaranya dozed, dreaming of Cakora crossing bright skies, hearing the undulating whistle he and Upa had used to call her. Something cracked on the porthole, and disturbed him. Gradually, the sound of pattering rain invaded his dream, and he opened his eyes to find himself still aboard the Orchidia. The lamp burned low, picking out droplets on the porthole as they formed rivulets down the glass.

The Cakora whistle sounded again.

Nouzi frowned, uncertain whether he was awake or not. He moved to sit up, only to cry out at the painful pull of the stitches across his abdomen, and collapse again. He forced his breath down and listened.

The low whistle came again, unmistakably. Somewhere close.

He rolled himself off the bed, and struggled to open the cabin door, coming to overlook Jayman's outer harbour. The lamp-post on the gangway cast shimmering light on the waves. And sure enough, more clearly now, from the darkness surrounding the lamplight, the whistle came again.

Excitement moved in him. *Fear* moved in him. He dressed carefully, retrieved his dhas from where Warboys *thought* he had hidden it, and shuffled along the passageway. The pain bent him over, set him gasping like an old man, but he kept to shadow, careful to move out of sight of Jayman's housekeeping staff. Leaving the Orchidia, he sneaked across the complex and through the gate, where he arrived at the lamp post on the Gangway. Dizziness throbbed in his head, and he cursed, supposing that he had dreamed it all. Had they given him some sort of medication?

Then there was a soft call from the darkness outside the lamp's halo.

'Nouzi Aaranya.'

Just shy of the lamplight, a figure stood. Stray lengths of wild hair frayed his outline, dhas handles jutting from the solid stock of his shoulder.

'Sat Nam, Nouzi-Chai.'

Nouzi Aaranya shifted his footing, feeling strength ebb away as he confirmed the voice.

It was Uparagha.

His stomach turned over, and he surprised himself, feeling excitement, guilt and fear, even as Uparagha ventured into the lamplight's edge. The smiling Yin had caught some sun, and Nouzi Aaranya felt a distracting flush of admiration that made him reflect on what a wasted, bandaged *kitava* he himself must look.

'Upa-Chai...' he began, lowering his eyes as his tears began to well. He strained a moment, knowing it was unthinkable for a Janizar to behave like this, much less in the company of his brothers, or his *Yin*. Had Goro or any of the others seen him, they would likely have challenged him to a death duel there and then out of disgust. But precisely because it *was* Uparagha, he suddenly realised he'd *missed* him – not even just these last weeks, but before that, ever since Gienha, since Kai had died, since *Cakora*, ever since Upa had declared himself Yin. Upa had been his only friend, the only one who knew his spirit. And suddenly he was powerless to prevent his tears.

'Avai, Nouzi-Chai' cooed Uparagha, laying his hands on his brother's cheeks. 'It is good to see you alive, nai?'

'I am *sorry*...' was all he could muster in reply. 'I am always crying to you. I shame you.'

'Nai, nai,' whispered Upa. 'No apology. I've come for you, eh? I've come for *you*...'

This surprising tenderness broke Nouzi Aaranya, who melted into Upa's shoulder, sobbing uncontrollably. *The Janizar who wept*, he reflected bitterly. Was there a story in the Datyas about that?

Uparagha looked warily across Jayman's complex, and pulled Nouzi Aaranya away from the light, past the shellfish stalls to a jetty that sank down below and out of sight of passers by. There Upa took his face again, and looked into his eyes.

'Nouzi-Chai. How did you know we were on Junkers?'

'I didn't. I was trying to get the Hildegaard to White Spur, but we crashed in the sea and...'

'We?'

'Ai. With the soldier, Warboys. We came to an agreement.'

'Hui. Where is he now?'

Nouzi Aaranya was wary of the stern way that Upa posed the question.

'I don't know,' he lied. 'But why are *you* here?'

Upa ignored the question, scanning Nouzi Aaranya's eyes as if to check his bafflement was genuine. 'Why did you bring the Hildegaard to Jayman?'

'I didn't! We were wrecked, and his *charya* brought the ship ashore. Why? Who is Jayman to us?'

Upa's face wrinkled in contempt a moment before a smile lightened his face. 'He is nothing. He has missed great opportunity. Avai! Is kaarya that we meet, then!'

Upa looked Nouzi up and down, lingering on his bandaged midriff with an oddly amused expression. 'It happened again, eh? Your terrors.'

Nouzi Aaranya hung his head.

'Ai. I tried to fall on my blade.'

'*Huzhat...*' Upa embraced him keenly, and Nouzi Aaranya felt the terrible confession slopping out of him.

'Upa-Chai, I don't know if I can follow kaarya any more. I don't know if I can live for her any more...'

He sobbed outright, but again Upa coddled him, seeming pleased.

'Avai, hush! Of course you can. Maia is your great journey, nai? Nothing has changed, Nouzi-Chai. You are feeling ill and sullen, that is all. Do you remember, after Naming when you ran from Maia, from the Samagat, and went to throw yourself from the Edge? Remember I came? I found you? Is the same. You are a great spirit, Nouzi Aaranya.'

Nouzi felt excitement, relief. *Comfort.* Here was his friend again. Here was *kaarya*, when he had lost it. And then Upa went on.

'You *will* go to Maia,' he said – and Nouzi Aaranya found that his heart sank a little again. 'I will send you to such a feat that the Sekhet will demand your seed brought again! There will be Datyas written to tell the tale of Nouzi Aaranya!'

Upa looked so bright and faithful, that Nouzi could not bear to refute it. *Don't promise me Maia*, he wanted to say. *Don't patronise me. I'd come for you, if you but asked.*

'Ai...' he said instead, smiling meekly.

'Hui, *isht.* Our kaarya is entwined, nai? No more falling on blades. We need you.'

'*We*? Are our brothers here?'

'Avai, don't worry about them. *I* am Yin, eh? Be quiet now. I'll explain everything soon, away from here.'

'Are we going *now*?'

'Ai. We must be swift.'

Nouzi Aaranya felt a pang at the prospect of abandoning Warboys. Perhaps he should delay, find Warboys, or leave him a message. But kaarya had determined his next path, and

Warboys would never understand. Best that he and Upa never meet. He let Uparagha's broad smile reassure him as his brother took his hand and led him away.

~ ~ ~

Warboys was taken down to the Hildegaard's hangar to start work. There he was assigned to Tanner, the old chief engineer, who led him out across the pier for a tour of the dock and hangar facility.

The Hildegaard was still moored to her barge inside the hangar. Inside, engineers crawled around, testing her with pressure gauges, or pasting transparent membranes over the envelope. Others scraped below with fine tools. The hull had been stripped of damaged carvels, and all but the beams had been removed, so that engineers in butcher's aprons could loiter on deck, poring over manuals and leering together at her giblets. Splatter marks and greasy footprints spread out from her, and many odd tanks and barrels were attached by piping. She seemed to be growing again, and in rude health – but Warboys felt uncomfortable at the sight of strangers rummaging around in her.

Tanner interrogated him about what he'd done with the Hilda at sea. In response, Warboys trailed about her renovated deck, pointing here and there, recalling times and estimating measurements, talking about the water, the sunlight, and a great deal of other details that never seemed to find an end. A clerk followed them, making copious notes.

Warboys tried to focus, to impress Jayman's men with his attitude, and maybe learn something useful – but he found himself distracted, worrying about the bloody kid back there in the cabin. A break eventually came, and he excused himself for a smoke at the earliest opportunity, so he could pop in and check on the boy.

Extra guards on the complex gate made Warboys suddenly anxious. He rushed on board and found the cabin empty. There was just a mess of sheets and a musky, sweaty smell. The dhas was gone. Warboys' mind reeled as he turned about, suddenly afraid that the kid had gone and done himself in after all.

He left the Orchidia and all but crashed into a pair of guards on the way back down the pier. 'The kid. Nouzi Aaranya. Where is he?'

'Just calm down there, Mr. Warboys. We need to ask you some questions.'

'What are you on about? Where is he?'

'He seems to have sneaked off without an escort. Thing is, sir, one of my lads thinks he saw him outside the complex, down the Gangway. With someone who looked like Uparagha.'

'You what?' Warboys halted. 'What did he look like? Where did they go?'

'Calm down, sir. Mr. Jayman wants everyone to stay here, until we know for sure. Is there anything you can tell us, sir? Who is this Aaranya fellow? Why would this Uparagha character have an interest in him?'

'I don't...'

Warboys hesitated, then moved abruptly to leave. The guard caught hold of him.

'I'm going to have to keep you here, sir. Mr. Jayman asked that you both should stay on the complex.'

'What? Why?'

'He reckons it's for your own safety. This Uparagha character is very dangerous.'

Warboys shrugged, rolled his eyes genially. 'The thing is,' he began, low and confidential, leaning in to speak so that the guard leaned closer to hear.

Then he stuck the nut on him.

The guard staggered back on his heels and landed heavily on his backside. Warboys let himself out onto the Gangway and ran for it. He was shaking as he fled Sea Gardens and cut toward Little Jurma. He passed a stall where fresh cockles stuck their tongues out. He wondered if Nouzi had gone willingly. Devastation turned his stomach as he feared that the boy had just upped and left him like that. A sense of anger. *Betrayal.*

But then again... Was Nouzi even capable of deciding what he wanted to do? Had Uparagha bullied him into it? Warboys saw the pair of South Island kids knocking about near some stalls, and veered towards them. It was worth a try.

'Here, lads. I'm looking for couple of lads that came along here recently. You'd know one of them on account of his tattoo, like a new moon on one side of his face.'

'Cost you a penny-fenyg,' muttered one. 'Reckon you already owe us one for showing you down to Jayman's.'

'You can have ten bob if you tell me.'

'We seen 'em. Went down under. To the jetty along there.'

Warboys paid the kid, and walked to the next jetty ladder, where he climbed below to the cold lower level that ran beneath the Gangplank. Weak light crept between the thin lines of the planks above, blotted out by the shadows of passers-by. A rickety stairway led down to one of the many makeshift jetties that skirted all of Junkers. These minor jetties were always manned by crab fishermen who would taxi folk about the line for a small fee. He called to the first one he saw, and asked after the Janizar.

'Aye,' the boatman replied. 'Took off in my best dory about an hour or two ago. Went out to Cemetery End.'

'That's right up the north end, isn't it?'

'Aye. The cold end, where the line breaks, and the wrecks litter the waves. Need a boat to catch up, do you?'

Warboys thought about it. If Uparagha was here, the other Janizar would likely be as well, and maybe some of those nutcase Blacklanders, the Sons of Sun-Ivis. He slumped against a piling for a moment, and kneaded his forehead. He wondered if he should let it go. Nouzi had always said he would go back to his duty.

Would he just piss off like that? Little shit. After all we've been through. I could just go and sleep it off, then turn up to work for Jayman and forget it all.

No. He had to check. After last night, Nouzi was in no sound state of mind to decide for himself.

'You get me a boat ready,' he told the boatman. He hesitated, recalling that he'd need to get his rifle and kit from the Dog's. Another idea began to form. 'I'll be back in five minutes. I need to see a Tugel about some bangers.'

'Right you are, sir.'

40 THE FALLING TREES

The dory flanked Junkers due north, and Nouzi Aaranya watched as its weathered pilings fell across the sandbanks at the neck of the strait. Here the stripped cadavers of abandoned boats peppered the water, and an old church temple boat, once the sanctuary of some heathen god, lay end up, its holy keel waving ignominiously at heaven. Broken jetty-ends stood alone in the sea, and the first hints of ice in the air blew down from the Andavirke.

'I like Junkers best here,' said Uparagha. 'Here we see the ruin of the world, eh? No pretences. Here is just the wreck and the skies, nai?'

The dory approached a fallen section of the Gangway. Here the line collapsed, splintering into walkways and jetties, a maze of routes and dead ends alike. Fires flickered amongst the ruin. A pair of Blacklanders emerged to pay the boatman, one marked with the crescent of the Sons. They helped Nouzi Aaranya onto a jetty, before Upa sent them on ahead and took Nouzi's arm to lead him into the floating wastes. Crossing a frayed rope bridge, they reached a holed tug boat that lay propped up on another wreck. A collapsed jetty sheltered it from view. Upa settled on the cabin roof. It was quiet, deserted but for the echo of a salvage crew clattering about somewhere distant. A flask and cups were set out ready.

'I have boat and crew waiting further along. But we will sit here a while, nai? Talk away from the ears of the *charya*.'

Uparagha sat to one side of the makeshift tea-set, bowing

formally to invite Nouzi to join him.

'Is no dainty Gienhan set, eh? But in cracked civilisation, I do my best.'

Nouzi Aaranya smiled appreciatively, lowered himself stiffly to sitting whist Upa poured.

'I don't understand. I thought you were going to White Spur. Why are you here on Junkers, Upa-Chai?'

'I came to recruit this Jayman-Bernigny to our cause.'

'Our *cause*?'

'Nouzi-Chai. It is a dated mode of action the Janizar have followed. The world is changing, and we can no longer afford to work alone. I gained an army in Blackhaven. I have loyal Sons. Learned there are many others who would resist Malvy and his modern world, nai?'

Nouzi Aaranya felt a sense of dread. It seemed that Uparagha's rebellious streak had grown dangerously in his absence. That he had forgotten kaarya. But Nouzi's own honour was compromised more than ever now, and he felt no right to object. He let Upa go on.

'Jayman refused me. He cared only for the intellectual value of the *Tabitha* and *Rosamundt*, and thought nothing of their *use*. I was suspicious when he ended negotiation so suddenly, and ejected us; so we hid, and waited to find out why. We spied the Hildegaard – and then *you*. Ha!'

'I apologise, Upa-Chai. I did not intend to damage your negotiations.'

'Hui, no matter. We do not need Jayman, nor his Black Flowers. We still have the ships, and enough Sons to make an attack of our own.'

'Where?'

Uparagha smiled.

'Malvy is planning a rally in Coperny to announce his conquest. Five days from today, his generals and subjects will assemble, and Malvy will claim the entire continent for his Nation State; with his fleet gathered in the harbours, with his airships up above, with his symbolic steam-engine *Unification* crossing the viaduct, he will stitch the lands together for everyone to see. But we will strike, Nouzi-Chai. Ai. All the world will see that Malvy's power is not infallible.'

'Eh? But how? How can we do this?'

'Hui, Nouzi Aaranya! I have planned, eh? We will use our ships to bomb *them*! The strike will take place at noon, when the *Unification* makes its pass over the viaduct.'

'They will see us coming. Malvy still has ships of his own.'

'The pilot Valego showed us many things, Nouzi Chai. These ships are very *malleable*. At White Spur, we practised compression of the airship balloons. Did you know they can be deflated – or *exhaled*, is more correct word – enough to pack into the hold of a flatbed barge? Ai! Not only that, but we can vent lifting gas, is pressurised and stored by canister, ready to aid rapid inflation and lift. I have learned all this! Modern technology! *Rosamundt* and *Tabitha* are to be smuggled into Coperny Bay, out of sight of Malvy's patrol ships, so that they can be deployed quickly, in close range to the target.'

'Can the ships really be lofted quickly enough? Malvy's patrol ships will counter swiftly.'

'Ai. Good, Nouzi-Chai. Our brother Nasnim has been practising. Bombing and plundering ships in the Andam strait, like some fat hunting Cakora! He found us an artillery piece, stolen from an Andam gunboat, to cover our launch. Even so, I too am concerned that this will not be enough. Speed and agility are everything...' A grin opened slowly as he looked at Nouzi Aaranya. 'And that, my brother, is where *your* kaarya lies.'

'Eh? Me?'

'You. We leave soon to meet the barges at White Spur, where the ships will already be packed. From there we sail to Coperny, to join the flotilla amassing outside the harbour. Then *you* will spearhead a crippling first strike that will disable Malvy's new Eyrie. This will double as the signal for launch – and deliver a message to all these so-called Modern men. You will become *legend.*'

Uparagha grinned maniacally, his eyes glistening with pride.

'You want me to take another bomb? To the Eyrie?'

'Ai. You are the swiftest, the most agile warrior I know. You excelled in Blackhaven. This will be another AEC.'

The words set panic gonging in Nouzi Aaranya's chest. A lowly Third Boom attack on a scale he hadn't imagined. He struggled to find a way to question the plan without offence.

'Upa-Chai. Forgive me. Do you think the Sekhet Fathers really intend you to do this?'

Upa merely smiled.

'The Fathers have *commanded* this!'

Nouzi Aaranya frowned.

'Hui, are you sure?'

'Ai. I told them: You Sekhet look long into the forest, seeing saplings sprout, whilst we Janizar dodge the falling trees in the here and now. They have conceded to my authority in this.'

'When? When did you tell them this? You surely haven't been back to Gienha?'

'Nai! I told it to the Sekhet, after he arose from Blackhaven Tor. He conceded! He said, *we feel it coming, Uparagha. This Modern World.'*

Nouzi couldn't help recall what Warboys had said. *I saw that Sekhet have a right go at your friend.* It didn't correspond to what Upa was telling him now. Was Warboys mistaken, or exaggerating, as he was prone to do?

Nouzi Aaranya tried but failed to penetrate Upa's black eyes.

'Why didn't you mention this before?'

'Blackhaven was... difficult for you, eh? I didn't want to ruin your focus... But I explain now, Nouzi-Chai. Just as I explain always to you.'

Nouzi looked away. Upa wasn't telling him everything. But he set it aside. It wouldn't be the first time Upa had patronised him.

'Aaland is unhappy, unstable, nai? We can make it revolt against itself. When Jayman-Bernigny sees what can be done, he *will* join us. Others will follow. The royalists and rebels. The ousted and the slighted. The Sekhet bred us for this, eh? Sent us to war! After this, Sun-Ivis won't have to hide in the Eldask!'

'But—'

'But *what*, Nouzi-Chai?' snapped Uparagha, suddenly impatient. 'Maia? You're going to ask about Maia, are you?' Upa's eyes rolled, and Nouzi Aaranya flushed in shame.

'Nai...' He hesitated, overwhelmed. He regretted the weakness he'd displayed earlier. But display it he had. And now Upa's eyes seemed to stare right inside him. 'Avai,' Upa said, lazily waving a hand, displaying nothing of his earlier empathy. 'After this... she will *crave* your seed, I'm sure.'

Nouzi Aaranya hung his head in shame. He hadn't even been going to mention Maia. Upa was assuming he wanted Maia. And why wouldn't he, after listening to a lifetime of vows and blind devotion? But Nouzi wasn't sure anymore. The shame bloomed privately, all the years he'd dedicated himself to Maia or death. And now he couldn't dedicate himself to either. Lost in thought, Nouzi sensed belatedly that Upa had paused. He looked up to see Upa's eyes sinking down across Nouzi's body as he moved in close, sliding his cheekbone along Nouzi's.

Hot and heavy breath clouded between them, and Nouzi knew he'd be allowed no more questions. Upa stood and pulled him into the stuffy old cabin. The sloping floor threw them together against the porthole. He felt a familiar unease, and for all that he was relieved and enamoured to see Upa, he felt somewhere a stab of irritation. Here he was injured, derelict, with so much needing to be said, and still Upa's khus arose to intrude, first above the truth, first above all concerns. He flexed to let Upa strip him, but the wound bit sharply, and he fell back in pain. Upa knelt over him, his fingers tracing the railroad of stitches across his gut. His eyes gleamed in his silhouette as Nouzi watched, wondering if the Yin would remember, and excuse him from duty this time. Their breath clouded in the air.

But Upa only looked toward the cabin door to check the coast was clear.

'We haven't got long,' he breathed, sending shivers down through Nouzi's *khus*.

Nouzi braced himself.

An odd, silent flash of light came through the porthole, and halted them both. It pulsed silently, like a lightning storm without thunder, painting glistening edges along their bodies. Belatedly, the thunder began: sharp, cracking gunfire, thunderous banging, clouds of smoke in flickering white light. The two Janizar stared in shock at one another, wriggled and parted, hauled up their clothes to spring from the cabin, ready to meet the intrusion.

Out on deck, Nouzi saw the sparks of white fire through the pilings. The two Janizar parted to advance separately on the source of the light.

They rounded the pilings to see a bucket bobbing along in the water. A stack of Tugel fireworks had been stuffed in it, and pushed out to distract them. A rocket screamed out and exploded over the sea, and from its light, Nouzi Aaranya saw a figure emerging from the junk-piles behind Uparagha.

'Oi, dickhead!' came the voice.

The two Janizar spun about to see Warboys, rifle already cocked and levelled. He fired, and sat Upa heavily on his backside. Warboys strode after him, reloading as he walked.

With an unapologetic look at Nouzi Aaranya, Warboys applied his boot to Uparagha and shoved him flat on his back, applying the muzzle to his temple.

'Not so fucking mouthy now, are you?'

Warboys cocked the bolt on the Entwick. There was Uparagha, mastermind of the Blackhaven bombing, a bullet away from revenge. He could shoot him now. Shoot him and be done with it. Shoot him, like he'd shot Nouzi Aaranya. As if that would resolve him of any blame himself. As if that would bring Bill back. The burning Silo tower seemed to flare up in the nearby bonfire, boiling the sweat off Warboys' face. His limbs began to shake with the effort of the trigger.

'Nai!'

Nouzi Aaranya raised his dhas, striking Warboys' arm just as the crack of gunfire tore the air. Warboys recoiled quickly, withdrawing his arm in fear, expecting it to be missing – but the kid had kept his blade sheathed. Hesitantly, he set to reloading his Entwick. Uparagha stumbled to his feet, blood spreading across his side.

'Hui, Warboys!' yelled Nouzi Aaranya, standing between them, looking from one to the other. 'This is not the way to—'

'Shift', grunted Warboys.

Nouzi Aaranya matched Warboys' step to cover Uparagha.

'Run, Upa-Chai. Go to your boat. I will follow.'

Uparagha glared at Warboys, then grunted and rolled off the deck, staggering away and out of sight.

Nouzi Aaranya and Warboys stood gauging one another by the waning flicker of the fireworks.

'You with him now, kid?'

'Ai! When did I say I would not be? What are you doing here?' There was a certain edge in his expression that Warboys did not like.

Silence bloomed between the two. Warboys held his rifle fast. Nouzi Aaranya rested fingers on the handle of his dhas – and the two stood armed against one another as they had the night they'd met.

41 THE DEVIL OFFERS

'I won't let you murder my brother, Captain,' said Nouzi Aaranya, relaxing his stance. 'But nor will I fight you. You are free to leave. Go now. Go back to Jayman, and pay-packet.'

'Don't talk to me like that, after I risk my fucking life to see you're alright!'

'I am all-right, eh? I am with my brother.'

'You're just going to run along after him then?'

'Ai.'

'Just because the Devil offers you sausage rolls, doesn't mean you go round to tea.'

'Who is Denzil?'

'I said *Devil*, not Denzil!'

'Eh?'

'Oh for fuck's sake... Listen. He'll just *use* you. He lied to the Blacklanders to use them for an army, and now they've lost their city. He lied to get me and my dad to help him, and now I've lost my dad. He uses people, and discards them. He doesn't care whether you live or die.'

'A Janizar does not fear death.'

'Fuck off. What's he planning?'

'Why do you care? You don't care about Malvy, or your own country. You don't know duty and honour.'

'There'll be no honour with him, mate. It'll be another dirty, third boom slaughter.'

'Your General will see what *he* has wrought, eh?' shuddered Nouzi Aaranya, that hard man façade slipping on again. 'He will see his displays of power reflected back at him!'

'What are you on ab...' Warboys faltered. *Displays of power.* He recalled what Joe Bonboas had said. *Haircuts.* He felt a prickle of horror crawl up his spine as it suddenly became clear. 'It's the fucking rally, isn't it? He's going for Coperny. The Capital. For Malvy's rally. You remember the AEC, do you? There'll be women, you know. And children. *My* children...'

'Avai, Warboys, you're trying to corrupt me again, eh? Because *you* have no kaarya!'

'Is she worth it? Kill children for Maia, would you?'

'There is no—'

'Because they'll be there. We don't keep them indoors where I come from. Would you kill Bill again? Would you?'

Nouzi Aaranya said nothing.

'What about all that *civilization* you were bleating on about?'

'Is *this* place civilization, Captain? This filthy Junction? Is there any such thing, now?'

Warboys lowered his rifle, blew out an exasperated breath. 'So that's it then. Tea and cakes and a cuddle with Lord Bastard and we're off back to murder? I thought we'd gotten somewhere, you and me.'

'Hui, Warboys, you are like midges in the morning. You should let me go and rejoin my brothers, before they come looking. I am indebted to you, but—'

'Well fucking pack it in, then! *They're* not going to look out for you, are they? Next time your stupid head goes pop! They're going to dangle you in the fire, just like last time!'

'Nai. You don't understand kaarya.'

'Are you still scared of him?'

'Eh? Nai! I fear no-one.'

Warboys saw Nouzi Aaranya's face flush a little. His objection was a little too overwrought. Something was going on with those two.

'What were you doing in that cabin?'

'Eh?'

'Are you bumming him?'

'Nai...' shrugged the Janizar. Then he thought again and added, 'What is *Bumha*?'

'You know what I mean.' Warboys spat demonstratively before translating. 'Are you giving it him up the arse?'

Nouzi Aaranya's face reddened. He began to pace, glaring all the while.

'Hui Warboys, you make grave offenses! Uparagha is my brother, eh? Astava!'

'Is he giving it *you* up the arse, then?'

'Yavyek! You be careful what you say, eh? I don't know much about your western way, but what you speak of is unclean, eh? *Nidhaman*.'

'Why have you've gone all red, then?'

'Eh? So?' Nouzi Aaranya waved his hand in dismissal, then sniffed and snorted his nostrils clear, as if to be done with the issue.

'I've heard of fellers *mistreated*, like,' began Warboys. 'Wouldn't want owt like that to happen to you, is all...' Warboys tailed off, and lowered his rifle. 'Ah sod it. I reckon you can look after your own arse.'

'Avai, Warboys,' said Nouzi, wagging his finger. 'You should show more respect, eh? Thick head! You go now. No execution will take place, eh? No *Bumha*. I am leaving now.'

Nouzi Aaranya turned and went, off after Uparagha. For a moment, Warboys thought of shooting the stroppy little shit.

'Nouzi Aaranya!'

'Nai! Be quiet! I'm going!'

'You're making the wrong choice. Oi! I'll have my say if I have to tie you up.'

'Hui, you can try.'

'I could do it alright, you little twat. Don't you worry.'

'Ai?'

'Cocky little shit! If I...'

To Nouzi's surprise – and to Warboys own – he stopped himself. Took a breath.

'Just listen a minute. Don't let anybody force you to do anything. That goes for the Sekhet. Goes for Maia. Even goes for me. I shouldn't have sent you into that knocking shop. I just... it was just a joke. Not even a *joke*. I just thought it would help. Take the edge off, you know... You're just a kid. I'm *sorry*, alright? Got your looks and fitness and all your bloody life ahead of you, and you live in your head like some shrivelled old nun...'

Nouzi Aaranya swallowed, his voice softened. 'Avai, Captain. It doesn't matter now. Is forgotten.'

'*Listen*, though. I'm telling you. You don't have to go with them, and you don't have to stay here. We can go somewhere else.'

'We?'

'Yes, we. I'm asking you to come with me. Or don't. Go and sweep Joe's shop floor. Go whaling on the Arricas. Just don't go with those bastards.'

'Avai, Warboys, I have a destiny to keep, eh?'

'Destiny! Fuck off. The only destiny we've got is the grave, mate. What's true is this – there's nowt without life. I'll let you go, if that's what you want...'

Warboys pointed his rifle skyward to demonstrate this, and Nouzi Aaranya laughed.

'Very kind. Here I was, powerless to leave, eh?'

'Don't get cocky with me, just 'cos your mates are here. If you go with them, I...'

'Ai? What?'

'I won't let him do it. I can't. Not again. I'll stop him. And you won't get in my way. Not if you're with them. The rally is in five days time. I'll see him then.'

Nouzi faltered a moment, looked quizzically over his shoulder as if to doubt his hearing. Then he shook his head sadly.

'Nai. You won't stop us, Captain. You are roughneck out of Kingstown, nai? Isn't that what you said? You'll do nothing. Because you don't care.'

'Mark my words – you'll regret going with him.'

'Uparagha's kaarya is entwined with my own, nai? I have to find my place with him.'

'Or *against* him.'

Nouzi Aaranya said nothing. He turned and walked away. Warboys ducked to hide behind some pilings to make out as if he'd already vanished – all dramatic, like – but Nouzi Aaranya took a sidestep and saw him.

For fuck's sake, Warboys thought, his arms slapping despairingly down by his sides.

'What's the matter?' he snapped, flushing. 'Did you want a kiss before you go?'

'Nai.'

'Sod you then. I reckon you'll do what you think is best when the time comes. You always do.'

'Ai.'

'Five days!'

Nouzi Aaranya waved dismissively, and vanished into the dark. *Little shit*, thought Warboys, still itching to shoot after him, put a bit of wind up his arse. Not so long ago, he would have done. Now, he just sat down to catch his breath. His hands slid down the old blue flecked rifle, and his head rested on the stock. He began to shake, afraid of the ominous portent of his own promises.

42 THE COMPANY OF MY BROTHERS

Nouzi Aaranya found Uparagha's crew at the broken tail end of the Junker Line, manning a battered steam tug hidden among debris and wrecks. A small crew of Sons attended them, pale, angry looking Blacklanders who bowed respectfully when Nouzi boarded.

Uparagha sat to aft, a thunderous expression on his face. He ordered the crew to set sail, before stripping to have Nouzi Aaranya attend his wound. The bullet had barely nicked his side, so Nouzi Aaranya cleaned and dressed it whilst the crew edged awkwardly around them.

'Hui, he is a tenacious kunapa, this Warboys, eh?' grunted Upa.

'Tenacious, ai, in his way. But not without honour.'

'Honour? Ha! A man who shoots from the dark. He is a thug.'

'I would not have survived without him.'

'Oh? Where is he now, Nouzi-Chai? Your pet?'

'Dead,' lied Nouzi Aaranya, glad that Upa's back was turned. He had only been in Upa's company a few hours, and already he was lying. Lying to flatter, as they'd had to do with Kai. The feeling frustrated him.

'Ai. Good,' sighed Upa, barely stifling a yawn. 'Rest now, Nouzi-Chai. We are some hours away from our destination.'

'White Spur?'

'Ai. Our brothers await.'

Goro. Sila. Nasnim. Hanu. Hazar. For all that he'd been relieved to see Upa, Nouzi didn't relish *their* company. Upa yawned some more and went to doze in the cabin. The tug was too hot and cramped, so Nouzi went to sit sanyas at the stern, watching the waves churn in their wake. Junkers faded as day encroached, and the vastness of sky and cloud sent him into a reverie.

The company of his brothers. He didn't relish it at all.

~ ~ ~

'Runt!' barked Kai, yanking Nouzi roughly out of his tent. The jungle reared up around the stream, where blinding sunlight cascaded down. A warm breeze chilled Nouzi's skin, already tacky with piss, and Kai held him at arm's length, sneering at the runt even as he bared his own nakedness unashamedly.

'Hui, Asekna! You stink! Look at you, steaming like a fresh boiled levny! You woke me up again with your pathetic gasping and moaning!'

Before Nouzi could respond, a solid palm caught him across the face, knocking him down.

'Maybe that will send your stupid dreams away!' Kai was handsome now, tall and muscular, but harsh featured, with piercing eyes. 'Screaming for Maia like a baby every night! Huzhat, you make me sick!'

Nouzi's face reddened. He said nothing.

'We're supposed to be *resting* here, eh? Two weeks pursued through the forest, and when I get the chance to sleep, here you are yelling through the night and pissing all over the place like some kukkura! Get down, kukurra!'

Kai forced him down, and then began to empty his bladder onto him. 'If you move I'll kill you.'

The Asta roused from their tents, waking up indifferent to, or else amused by, the runt's torture.

'Hui, Asekna, you have the wrong type of wet dreams, eh?'

laughed Sila.

Kai finished, and shoved him away before heading to the water to splash his face. Nouzi Aaranya stayed where he was. There was no point in resisting, or aggravating them.

'You're supposed to be Janizar, eh!' said Kai. 'What will you do if you ever come before Maia?'

'He'll piss himself!' called Sila.

Kai stretched languorously. 'What can I do? I try to break your bad habits. I try to toughen you up.'

He plucked a spear from the ground and jabbed it into the skin of Nouzi's tent, again taking the opportunity to complain about the stench. When nothing happened, he peered inside, disappointed to see it empty.

'Hui, where's Upa? Didn't I tell him last night to be up before dawn to cook crayfish for our breakfast? Where is he?'

'He didn't come back last night,' muttered Nouzi. 'After you...'

Kai's stare dared him to end the sentence. *After you beat him, and took him off to fuck him in the bushes.*

He recalled it with a shudder. The week before, Cakora had taken a quail that Kai happened to be stalking, and he'd not let them forget it ever since. Last night, Kai had been drunk, angry about his quail again. Eventually, after dark, he'd hauled Upa across the stream to the woods to *put him in his place.* The sounds echoed again in Nouzi's mind: snivelling and grunting, strangled sobs. He remembered the sight of Kai wading back, flushed and massaging his beloved khus, the way a victor might clean blood from a blade. Nouzi made the mistake of moving too early to go to Upa – Kai saw him, and forbade him to leave camp. He'd lain in a feverish sweat whilst they'd drunk, laughed, and shared a *hookah.* Eventually, he'd slept.

'After I *taught him a lesson,*' Kai asserted, hitching up his khus again. 'Didn't I warn him about that stupid hawk of his?'

Barking a mock challenge, Kai ripped Nouzi's tent from

its pitch, ravelling it about the spear head in one of his showy fighting stances. The others laughed to ingratiate themselves with him.

'Why did you have to do that?'

Kai beckoned him to the bankside, and put an arm on his shoulder. 'Because I want to, eh? I am your Yin to be!'

He underlined this by slapping Nouzi hard about the face, cold eyes challenging him to *take it*.

'I want my breakfast. Sukhanava will be back today, and he'll want us ready. You go find your little friend, eh? He'd better not be off with those birds again. I already had to teach him a lesson about that. Tell him I like the taste of hawk. I'll stuff it with his little *khus*!'

With that, Kai hurled the spear and the tent into the river, where it began to drift away. Nouzi moaned as he watched it go.

'Oh, and don't forget my spear, eh? I want it back. *Inshie*! Go! No beating one another's *khus* up there!'

Nouzi bit back a retort and took his leave, staggering along the bank. He fended off tears by working up to an angry sprint, desperate to separate himself from the rest of the Asta Jana Aasvina. Once out of sight, he charged into the shocking cold of the stream, washing away the piss and tears. Then he ran again. Trees, birds, moss and vine all sailed past.

He found the tent and spear caught in the rocks down where the stream began to froth. Heaving it from the torrent with some difficulty, he strung it up as well as he could. It would never dry in time for the night. Cursing, he took up Kai's spear and bolted off back upstream to find Upa.

The End Born had been working on the crayfish nets all the previous day as the first punishment over the quail. Upa had set the cages upstream in the eddies below the rockfalls, but now Nouzi arrived to find them abandoned, untethered and drifting downstream. Upa was nowhere in sight.

'Huzhat!' he wailed. 'His head is foaming with *spuma!*'

Nouzi waded into the water to retrieve what he could. But fear grew steadily in his stomach, because Kai's orders had not been enacted. There were no crayfish, and there would be no pretending. He knew it was a case of damage limitation at best now. But where was Upa?

Nouzi abandoned the clear up, scouring the woods for signs. Running up the trail that climbed the hill, he halted for a moment at a fork. One way went to the *paradha*, whilst the other way, wind pulsed through the flowery woods from the ridge they called *Dha*, the Edge. The old fear arose as he found himself wondering if his friend had gone that way. Recollection of last night's atrocity – and his own failing – stabbed at him again.

Now, Nouzi felt a deep plunging fear. What if Upa had done it this time? Gone down the path and over the Edge?

He opted for the paradha. The roar of the water faded behind, and under cover of the thickening canopy, the ground cooled. The monoliths stood before him in quiet detachment. As Nouzi crossed into the paradha, he sensed an ominous quiet, a lack of birds and life. And yet, a presence.

'Upa-Chai? Brother, are you here?'

It was then that Nouzi spotted the scattering of long, striped russet feathers, drifting loose along the ground. He recognised Cakora's plumage immediately, and without understanding what alarmed him so, his heart began to pound. He saw the handmade hood cast aside, the claw-scarred long-arm gauntlet, the careworn accessories that he and Upa had so painstakingly crafted, now abandoned. He stepped warily around the monoliths, and there he found his friend.

Upa knelt in the mud, hair dangling over his face. Before him, splayed like a ruined angel among an explosion of feathers, was the body of the wood hawk Cakora. She had been slit open from throat to tail, her ribs like tiny harps, exposed and parted. Flies buzzed over the corpse, landing on Upa's face as they came and went, and yet he stared relentlessly into the remains, his eyes as black as coal.

Nouzi's head thumped as Kai's arrogant voice came to mind. *He'd better not be off with his birds again. I already had to teach him a lesson about that.* The strangled moans from last night jumped to mind, somehow made more horrific by the sight of the slain bird.

'Huzhat!' he cried, finding himself near to the tears he'd already suppressed today. 'He goes too far!'

Upa looked up from his stupor. 'There's nothing there,' he murmured. 'Nothing there...'

'Upa-Chai...' he began, his hand hovering over Upa's face, hesitating to touch him, not knowing what he could usefully say. Anger found him, and he whirled away, beating Kai's spear against a tree until the shaft cracked. The tree shuddered. Leaves fell. Upa did not move.

'I hate Kai!' screamed Nouzi. 'He is a filthy, stupid coward! Kunapa!'

'Hui, Asekna!' came Kai's voice. 'I'm here. What are you saying to me, eh?'

Nouzi spun about in shock. Kai was standing on the edge of the glade. Alone, the way he often was when he went to look for Upa. Nouzi knew he was done for now, whatever happened. Hating Kai more in that moment than ever he had, he snarled at him, clutching the broken spear.

'*Kunapa*, I said! You've gone too far this time! You go away and leave us or I'll give you this spear back! I'll give you it, ai!'

'I don't know what you're talking about, *Asekna*,' began Kai, punctuating his sentence with a lurching, predictable blow that popped in Nouzi's nose, 'but you *never* speak to me like that!'

Nouzi berated himself as he fell. In training, he was well

capable of catching a swing like that and popping the offending arm from its shoulder, but against Kai...

The would-be Yin scanned the place with disgust, frowning at Upa, who still crouched among the flies and bird guts. Kai almost looked confused. Was he so arrogant as to be bemused by the devastation he wrought? He opened his mouth to speak, but Nouzi lurched wildly at him. Kai stepped back, face contemptuous as he bobbed and landed a fist across Nouzi's nose, sapping him before he lunged to catch a hold.

'You're coming with me, pissy,' growled Kai. 'I'm going to teach *you* a lesson.'

Kai hauled Nouzi roughly through the woods, away from the *paradha*, up the hill toward the Edge.

Daylight pulsed in the gaps between thinning trees. They came to the sheer rocky drop, where many weakling Javani had fallen to their deaths. Kai dumped Nouzi on the outcrop, overlooking the sprawl of the forest, the rocky ground veiled in mist hundreds of feet below.

'I've had enough of you, piss stinking runt. *I've* been carrying you all these years, when you should have been strangled at birth! You're a skinny, weak, bedwetting *jaluka*, and you'll never be Janizar. Do you hear me? I tell you now, you'll never make it. You'll never cross that glade, and you'll never make it to the Samagat. Your seed will curdle inside you. You saw the last of Maia when she hauled you from her teat in disgust. So I'm telling you, eh? Here's your chance. They all go from this edge, the weak ones. They crack their heads on the rocks because they know they're not worth anything but a charya's supper. So I'm telling you now, runt – *jump.*'

Nouzi looked out into the wind, his eyes streaming with tears, and wondered, actually, if he cared one way or the other. He thought of Maia and felt a weariness beyond his years. The urge to jump surged in his legs. He turned to Kai.

'Nai,' he said, and spat a great bloody gob at his would-be Yin.

Kai bore angrily down, each blow smearing the jungle across Nouzi's vision. He squirmed under the blows until he fell dazed to the floor.

One of Cakora's feathers fluttered past, over the edge and into the wind. Nouzi looked and saw Upa, coming up behind Kai with the broken spear.

Kai arched at the last moment, but the spear bit into his side. He slapped it away and went for Upa, wrenching him about, bouncing him off a tree trunk, before snaring him in a chokehold. Upa calmly sank his teeth into Kai's forearm, clamping his jaw shut like a dog. Kai yelped, his hard façade faltering as he pummelled Upa's head in panic. The two fell apart. Upa dropped to the floor, and Kai fell on his backside, gaping at the bloody red horseshoe in his arm.

'You're an animal!' cried Kai.

Upa looked at him blankly, his chin running with blood. Nouzi climbed uneasily to his feet, taking up the fallen spear head. He pointed it at Kai. The Yin backed away, cradling his arm.

'You're going to regret this,' he whispered, sniggering hatefully. He turned and marched away. 'I'm going to bend you both over, you pair of runts! And we'll *all* have you, eh? One after the other! You wait! You're going to wish you went for that Edge!'

Kai began calling for the others as he went, making a show of trying to rally them. His cracked voice faded away down the rise.

Nouzi dropped the spear head and fell dizzily to his knees, beathing heavily. Upa panted, his eyes dull and acknowledging.

'We ought to make a run,' he said. 'He'll come back.'

'Sukhanava will be back soon, won't he?'

'Eh? So what? Sukhanava will *encourage* them! *Let the strong root out the weak*, he'll say.'

'We're going to die either way...'

'You stood for me,' said Upa, with a bow of his head. 'You didn't have to.'

'Nai,' groaned Nouzi – but, even as he spoke, Upa's acknowledgement triggered his latent grief, and he could not stifle a wracking sob. 'I'm sorry, Upa-Chai. I'm sorry I didn't come last night.' Upa watched him. Everything seemed lost. A moment passed.

'Hui, Nouzi-Chai.'

'What?'

'We should go after him.'

'What, to beg? Avai, that will make it worse!'

'Nai. We have to finish him. Now. Before he reaches camp.'

Nouzi Aaranya looked up, choking back the tears. He nodded, surprising himself.

'Ai. He won't expect it.'

They arose as one. Nouzi saw that Upa had a knife already, and so took up the broken spear again. They took off in pursuit.

Up ahead, Kai's angry thrashing betrayed his location. He turned and snarled at them, utterly oblivious to their intent.

Upa shouldered into Kai almost mischievously, catching him off guard. The next moment he was working at that statuesque stomach with the dirty knife. Nouzi Aaranya saw Kai's eyes widen, an indignant gargle escaping, as if he were actually *offended*. At the last, it was that *regal* expression that snapped something in Nouzi.

Leaping forward, he yanked Kai's head back and rammed the spear-head into his neck. Blood sprayed the broad leaves of the thicket. Upa followed Kai down, still stabbing.

Nouzi Aaranya pulled Upa away. He saw the gouts of red pulsing out of the various holes in Kai's skin, watched them slow and then cease. The would-be Yin, their tormentor for twelve long years, now lay dead in a mush of rotting leaves.

There was quiet. The two killers panted for breath, slick with blood. A bird chirruped nearby.

'Hui, that's done,' said Upa, eventually. 'We'll take his head back to camp. Let them know this Asta has changed, eh?'

'Eh?'

His level manner shocked Nouzi. Upa knew what to do. He could already see ahead of this. As if he'd expected all this to happen.

'If we leave him, we can't claim his death. Goro will be waiting, eh? He needs to be put in his place. This is how they raise us, Nouzi-Chai. This is our *kaarya.*'

Nouzi was stunned. His eye had already swollen up, obscuring his view, and he struggled to know if the pall of darkness was in his head or not.

'Were you tempted?' asked Upa, without looking at him. 'To take the edge?'

'Ai, I was. Of course I was.'

'Well then. What kept you? What keeps you now?'

'I wouldn't have given him the satisfaction. And...' As he closed his eyes he felt the touch of the wind on his face, imagined it as Maia's calming touch on his skin.

'Maia-Devu,' he said. 'Maia Devu, Maia Devu. Always it will be.'

Upa smirked, and nodded.

'Well then. Put her in mind, and do this with me.'

'What about you, Upa? What keeps you from the edge?'

The End Born nodded solemnly, and looked out over the sunlit valley. 'One day, this whole world will pass over that edge. And when that happens, I'll be the one to push it, nai?'

His eyes reflected nothing, and in an ominous moment, Nouzi sat up and stared at him. A savage grin split Upa's face, his teeth pink with his enemy's mark.

Upa stood, considered Kai's gaping corpse a moment and nodded, as if satisfied. He caught hold of Nouzi's arm and embraced him.

'Things have changed. We have to be strong now, Nouzi-Chai...'

Nouzi Aaranya relented a moment, felt the greasy layer of Kai's blood sliding between their skins. A sense of suffocation overcame him and he pulled away.

'There might be an axe back by the crayfish nets...' He said, starting off. 'For the head...'

'Ai,' said Upa.

Nouzi Aaranya looked over his shoulder and saw Upa, massaging at his *khus* and smiling, his clothes tattered, body emblazoned with Kai's bloody fingerprints. Their eyes met a moment, and without a word, they both knew it – Nouzi would not, *could* not come back. Upa would bear Kai's head back to the camp alone.

Things have changed.

Nouzi Aaranya roamed long into the jungle, grateful to lose himself in the wilds.

43 PROOF OF LOVE

Nouzi Aaranya watched the White Spur coast come into view through the mist, awed by the craggy peninsula of pale cliffs and secluded bays that would go on rising to the north, into the icy Andavirke pass. This in sight, the crew roused. Out on the furthest promontory of White Spur, a small rocky island materialised, straddled by a small circular gun-fort long since disused.

The airship *Tabitha* sat at steady anchor above the fort, erased intermittently by the mist. Below, Uparagha's small fleet was moored. A pair of massive, yellow-rimmed barges formed a makeshift hangar deck with their closed hatches. Around these, other boats and tugs converged. Uparagha's recruits – sea and flight crews alike – gathered across the rocks like a colony of sea birds.

Uparagha came yawning from the hold, smiling blearily at Nouzi Aaranya as he hauled on a jacket.

'See the first of those barges, Nouzi-Chai? The *AS Rosamundt* is already packed inside.'

Nouzi looked across and noticed a slight bulge arching the great hold doors – and a certain musky scent that seemed familiar.

Then he spotted their brothers on the rocks.

Goro, Nasnim, Hanu, Sila, Hazar. Nouzi Aaranya tensed at the sight of them.

'Be at ease, Nouzi Aaranya!' said Upa, patting his shoulder. 'You are Janizar Named, nai? You command respect.'

'Ai.'

The tug hauled in to moor. There was a general hubbub as Upa disembarked, as the Sons of Sun-Ivis – some that Nouzi recognised from the *Sunken Pig*, and others besides – bowed their head for Upa. Nouzi Aaranya followed him, watching these devotees curiously as they skipped across the rocks to meet their brothers.

'Sat Nam, my brothers!' called Upa. 'See here who has returned to us!'

Goro's eyes gleamed with distaste. Nasnim nudged Sila, who looked up distractedly from trying to roll a paper smoke with one hand, apparently having been expecting someone else. A hyena smile broke on his face when he saw Nouzi Aaranya. 'Huzhat!' he guffawed. 'Where in all of Maia's great sump did you drop from?'

Nouzi Aaranya frowned. 'Hui, Sila Astava, I never liked your mouth. Respect Maia-Devu, or... or I'll knock you out, you fucking dickhead...'

Sila exchanged incredulous looks with the others, and burst out with another guffaw. 'Avai, Nouzi-Chai. You swear like a westerner!'

'Did your Warboys teach you that?' asked Uparagha.

'Is modern world now, nai?' snapped Nouzi Aaranya, cheekily. 'He is as good a teacher as any.'

Uparagha smirked, but his eyes betrayed irritation. Prompted by his arrival, the AS Tabitha was now being roped and hauled down for packing into the second barge – but some dispute had broken out amongst the crew. Distracted by this, Upa patted Nouzi hard on the back and marched over to impress himself upon the workers.

As soon as he was gone, Goro swelled before Nouzi Aaranya, blocking the light.

'Listen to me, *kitava*. By Upa's grace, you live, eh? But

remember your place.'

Nouzi Aaranya felt his heart battering his ribs. But he sighed and smiled bitterly. 'Ah, it is good to be in the company of my brothers once more, nai? Set of bastards, you are.'

'Hui! You cannot afford insolence, Nouzi Aaranya. At the Naming, you failed and fled. In Blackhaven, you failed and fled...'

'Nai, Goro. After the Naming, I went past *you*, eh?' He saw Goro was still carrying a slight limp. 'You should get some crutches.'

Goro turned to the others. 'Why do we tolerate this? We should cut his throat! He is an outcast!'

'Avai Goro,' muttered Nouzi, feeling an excess of insolence, even though inside he was screaming at himself to stop. 'I think you have grown even more beautiful than the last time I saw you...'

Goro's small eyes glossed over with anger. There was an uncomfortable silence. Nouzi Aaranya knew he had crossed a line.

'We know why he really brings you back, eh?' hissed Goro, looking to his brothers for support. '*Charanayati!*'

The slave who bends over. Goro paced, watching him to see how he would react. Nouzi Aaranya sniffed, defied the terror in his guts to pace a moment before taking stance.

'Dhassama!' he cried.

Hazar and Sila stepped back whilst Goro bristled. The clamour all about the rock ceased as everyone turned to look.

Uparagha marched over to stand between them. 'Hui! What are you about, eh?'

'I won't tolerate disrespect from this runt!'

'Goro Lautama, we are not squabbling Javani any more. Nouzi Aaranya is our brother.'

'He has never been one of us!'

'He ran us all to Maia, nai? He was the very spearhead of our success in Blackhaven. Singlehandedly, he took the final ship, whilst *you* were ferried and spewed your guts. And he will be spearhead of our next assault. Stand down. Both. Clear the air. We are the leaders of these men, nai? Behave. We have an airship to pack. Now, *inshie!'*

Privately relieved, Nouzi Aaranya straightened himself, and bowed respectfully to Goro. Reluctantly, Goro followed.

'Found your *manas* again, nai?' said Upa as they dispersed towards the barge to pile onto the deflating Tabitha.

'Ai.'

'Be careful with it,' grunted Upa, gripping his arm in a tight warning. Nouzi Aaranya pulled away and set to work, sensing Upa's eyes on him.

Tabitha was eventually packed, the hold doors weighed down with crates and the stolen cannon. The Sons gathered in the turret to court Uparagha before departure. Nouzi Aaranya had mingled with them – but, after a time, he felt sick of himself. Sick of the pretence of acting the Janizar invincible, even as his heart pounded with fear. And so he'd removed himself, as ever, to wander the rocks alone, and was still there long after they'd all dispersed to their ships. He tried not to think of the bomb. Of the AEC.

Is she worth it? came Warboys' voice. *Kill children for her, would you?'*

He heard a soft approach behind.

'Hui, Nouzi Aaranya,' came Upa's voice. 'What are you doing here? You dream of Maia still, eh?'

'Eh, I manage not to piss myself with it these days though.'

Uparagha laughed, then looked off across the sea.

'Nai,' sighed Nouzi. 'I've been thinking about Kai. Cakora. The Edge.'

'Ai?'

'I wish we'd finished Kai earlier. I hated him.'

Upa only shrugged. 'I miss him, sometimes. Kai was very beautiful.'

'Beautiful?'

'Ai. He didn't earn respect by being soft with us. I admired him.'

'It didn't show. You used to aggravate him more than anyone.'

'He used me, and I used him, nai? Is as it has always been. What other proof of love is there than to take your beatings in good grace?'

'Love? How can you say that after what he did? To you! To our Cakora?'

'Ai. It's true. I loved that hawk like Maia...' Upa's eye twinkled almost mischievously. 'But we yield to become strong, nai? We bend over and receive, in order to gain.' That shimmer persisted in his eye, something dirty that he suppressed with a grin.

Nouzi Aaranya was shocked by this flippant reply, but before he could speak, it came. He should have known it would, after his defiant display with Goro. After his *backchat*, as Warboys would have called it. He should have known he wouldn't get away with all that freedom.

Upa checked shiftily to see they were unobserved, then took Nouzi's hand and hauled him toward the barge that held the AS *Rosamundt*. Down under the canvas they went, into the walkway rounding the hold where the airship was crammed. The air was thick, musky and hot with the stinking sighs of the ship. Uparagha stumbled over him, breathless and angry with desperation, knocking over tools, oilcans and sacks of engine grease. They pressed into one another. Nouzi felt Upa's teeth sink into his shoulder, shocking him to the *khus*, and triggering a strange, cold anger of his own. His hand twitched with daring before catching Upa's hair, forcing his head down along his stomach, setting Upa's nose to the track of stitches that led downward. There was a pause. Nouzi's heart thumped. He felt Upa's nose following the stitches, felt breath on his rigid khus – and, for a moment, he feared the teeth again before he felt it warmly enclosed.

He used me, he remembered Upa saying, *and I used him. Is as it has always been, nai?*

Nouzi was angry, and could not think of Maia. He thought of the burning lantern falling to the mirror lake. The hawk split from throat to tail. Then he came, emptying with long, forceful gouts. He braced himself as Upa arose, vengeful and spitting. Sinking his hand into some spilled engine lubricant, Upa greased himself before wrestling Nouzi over.

Nouzi Aaranya's mind fled.

He wondered. If he had gone with Upa, borne Kai's head back to his brothers. If he had fought Goro earlier on, and killed him, would *he* be impressing himself on the others like this? Was *this* the true life of the Janizar?

The hold became sticky with sweat as Uparagha worked at him. Eventually, hot breath blasted past his ear as Upa finished. He pressed Nouzi's face down to the hold floor, a rictus grip on his hair relenting steadily as he recovered his composure and withdrew.

Uparagha plucked at his khus, smearing his hand along the folded bag of the *Rosamundt* before covering himself and staggering away. Nouzi Aaranya curled up on the floor and bit back tears. He could feel no pity for himself. It seemed right that this should hurt. That it should be brutal and cold.

And yet, as he lay there, staring blankly, he thought of Warboys. Warboys was a rough edged kitava, but Nouzi knew that he would not have wanted *this* for him. He felt a shameful heat on his cheeks, and reflected that Warboys had sat respectfully by his bed whilst he recovered – whilst Upa had hastened him off to play khus almost immediately. The image of the unshaven old kitava standing watch over him made his tears well harder than ever. But Warboys was gone, now. No-one to help when his head went *pop*.

He tried instead to find Maia, but all he could see was the dead hawk, an open, harplike mess in his mind's eye.

44 FIVE DAYS

'Five days,' Warboys told himself.

Climbing through Cemetery End, he made it back to the north end of the Gangway at first light. At the first tavern he found, he steadied his nerves and saw the dawn in with a strong drink. Jayman's men were out in force, looking for Uparagha – and, after Warboys' thuggish escape, for him. He gave himself in without fight, and was quickly escorted back to Sea Gardens.

'Mr. Jayman will see you right away,' said the guard.

'Is he even up yet? It's barely light.'

'Mr. Jayman is a sharp overseer. Inspects the hangar at first light, every morning without fail.'

Sure enough, Jayman was down at the hangar, wiping his hands with a cloth as he discussed something with Mr. Tanner. The guard cleared his throat and Jayman turned to see Warboys, a more reserved humour in his eyes.

'Mr. Warboys. I would have preferred you had stayed on the complex. You're lucky to be alive.'

'It was important. Couldn't wait.'

'Where is your young friend?'

'He left with Uparagha.'

'Hm. A shame. But perhaps, if you had been more honest about who you were with, I could have helped prevent this.'

'Listen, I thought the kid had left all that behind. I didn't mention him because I was just trying to protect him. Seems he's gone and let me down.'

'Indeed.'

'Did you know Uparagha was planning an attack on Malvy's victory parade?'

Jayman smiled mildy, as if this were idle gossip.

'Is that so? Well, as I said before, Mr. Warboys, I made it clear I didn't want any part of his barbaric, short sighted plans.'

'You won't do anything to stop him, then?'

Jayman looked the closest to irritated that Warboys had yet seen. 'Would you have me *warn Malvy*? Aid the greatest enemy to mankind that history has ever known? I think *not*, sir. Averse to this callous enterprise as I am, Malvy has brought this on himself.'

'I'm not thinking of Malvy.'

Jayman took a moment to pull on his gloves.

'I think I have made my position more than clear. Now, unless you have changed your mind about *your* position, Mr. Warboys, I would expect you to report sharply back to your duty.'

Warboys looked at Jayman's amiable face and felt a deep loathing for him. He wasn't for war. *Not in itself.* But he'd let other lunatics provoke it for him. He'd smile and drink his brandy, playing with his engine stems whilst the bombs came for all those people – all those potential *subjects* – queuing unawares for Malvy's victory speech. His anger arose. He thought of ripping that neatly trimmed beard off Jayman's face. But he calmed himself, took a breath, and went inside himself, like the kid used to.

Five days, he told himself.

'Aye. I reckon so,' said Warboys. 'If it's alright by you and all, I'll carry on working. For you, like.' If he'd had a cloth cap to grip humbly, he would have done.

'Of course. The offer still stands. Though my guards are here for all our benefit, and I would appreciate it if you wouldn't assault them.'

'I'll buy that guard a drink or summat.'

'Quite. Well, you can take the cabin your young friend recently vacated. Take a rest day. Then report to Mr. Tanner.'

Warboys trudged meekly off to the cabin. It had already been cleaned by Jayman's staff, but Warboys hesitated before the bed, suddenly thrown back to that endless night when Nouzi Aaranya had lain there.

He sank down by the door, and ground down his fear. *You could still run,* he told himself.

Five days suddenly seemed like a very long time.

Warboys watched everything, becoming involved in every job he could. Engineer Tanner received him back gracefully, and they resumed their review of the Hildegaard. During long-winded pressure tests, he weighed in with the rest of the hangar staff, steadying Hilda's drift with barge poles, watching for who everyone was, where they worked, and when. He watched them 'milking' – venting gas to keep the bladders generating healthily – and saw how they stacked pressurised canisters filled with the spare gas.

Tanner listened with interest about the basking shark, and was running with the theory that the saline, nutrient rich water of the gulf streams had offered prize growth conditions. There was some talk with Jayman about the effect of whatever 'derivative genus' the engine stem was reverse engineered from. A catfish? A flatworm? Some kind of mollusc? Jayman talked of samples, and sometimes stored cuttings in glass jars for his 'associates.'

Warboys didn't pretend to understand all of this, but he watched, and learned a few things about how to fly the ship, about the different balloon compartments fore and aft within the main envelope, and what all the vents and valves did, how the heavier air displaced the lifting gas for a more sophisticated type of ballast. Funny to think of how he had floundered and misunderstood, venting piss and caulking guts. Funny to think that, for all she'd meant to him on that gloomy evening in Kingstown, he'd had no idea what she really was.

Hindsight was a sickeningly useless thing, he reflected now. Nouzi Aaranya's words echoed still.

You'll do nothing, because you don't care.

Four days.

The next day, miniature launches were performed in the shelter of the hangar, but what little excitement the flight tests brought was bludgeoned into boredom by ten times the amount of boring pressure and volume tests. He found himself feeling the old despondence about work.

The nights were hard, and the cabin unbearable. His pay was more than enough to drink and eat what he liked. He had more than enough money for women. And not those Gangway slappers, either. Proper, exotic, polite ones that you could choose the size, shape and colour of.

He went for a walk to have a look at one, but barely got past the fruit market, where he saw some melons and had a sudden memory of Cait, how things had begun behind the engine sheds all those years ago. How he'd fucked off and left her to it over the years.

He bought a bottle instead, and found himself hanging about, smoking in the doorway, as if he were still listening to the stupid kid breathe. Warboys shook his head, sighed heavily and flicked his dog end out into the bladderack below.

Three days.

He pressed his head down into the bar, feeling pins and needles in his backside whilst some old codgers set the world to rights. The horizon rolled up and down past the portholes, empty and grey. The rum he'd drunk burned nicely, high up and rivalling his conscience, where it suited him best.

He could just stay. He could work for Jayman, or get a berth somewhere else. He had enough money now to be comfortable, for the first time ever. He didn't have to graft if he didn't want to. No more queueing, if he didn't want it. No more mud. He could just wait until this coming war they were all talking about came and went, and buy himself a nice little cottage by the coast. Watch that dreary grey horizon roll up and down, counting the days 'til he keeled over, drunk out of his mind if he wanted. He didn't have to do anything anymore. He was free.

You'll do nothing, because you don't care.

He stood, far drunker than he realised, and fell heavily on his arse. Moments later, the landlord had him thrown out onto the Gangway, where he sat until he was soaked by fine drizzle.

Two days.

After work the next day, he went to find Ulao, the old Tugel who'd sold him firecrackers. With a little goading and a lot of money, Ulao showed him how to take the charges apart, the way they stacked inside their tubes by layers that banged or screamed alternately.

He returned to his cabin and dismantled Bill's old Entwick, laid out the parts for a thorough clean. He hoped that the kids, if that's what he could call them, could have some sort of life. Was the baby born yet? Had she really called it *Shandy*? Did children growing up under Malvy's government have fun? Did they go wading down the horsewash to collect cockles and winkles? Was that planned in the revolution?

He reassembled the rifle, leaving the stock detached to suit his purpose. He tore a hole in one of his pockets. He thought of Nouzi Aaranya, and for a moment wished to be back there with him, on those sand-flats, in sight of that damned silver coast.

Stupid fucking kid.
One day.

Warboys awoke in the cabin, the thrill of fear in his chest. The porthole beamed, white as the major moon. He thought of all the mornings he'd lain in bed, anxious at the thought of daily graft. The fear of his father's footsteps coming to drag him up to face responsibility. He knew now. It wasn't the graft he feared. It never was. It wasn't even about his mother's death, if he was honest. It was the complacency, the meaninglessness of it. The fear of failure, of *accepting* failure. It was never money or work that lulled and bored and disillusioned him – it was the lack of purpose, of being part of a herd, of not being decisive, not making a stand in the world. Being washed away in it.

He went out to the balcony as the horizon brightened. That godforsaken silver coast again. That bloody bastard wonderland. Chase it or die. Chase it *and* die. He was the son of pioneers and adventurers, and he understood now. The kid was right. He did know *kaarya*.

He stood, slung his newly cut down rifle under his coat so that it fit down his trouser leg, and took a great swig of rum. Once it had burned up some of his doubt, he limped out toward Sea Gardens.

Today was the day.

45 ANCHOR LINE

Thick fog rolled in from the sea, blotting out the Gangway. Warboys turned in at work, finding the guard was at his post on the gate, as ever.

'Alright there, Ned?'

'You're early.'

'Aye, well. Thought I'd better show willing.'

'You carrying a bit of a limp there, Mr. Warboys?'

'Oh, I took a bit of a fall last night, is all,' snapped Warboys, afraid that the rifle would show. 'Here, do you fancy a pint later? Just to say sorry for that little misunderstanding last week. My shout.'

'Aye, go on then,' said Ned. 'Nice of you.'

Warboys made his way along to the hangar, careful with the way he walked. The complex was swamped in grey.

Mr. Jayman was already on the hangar walkway, engrossed in conversation with Mr. Tanner about the day's agenda. The day shift hadn't yet started, and the night staff were signing off.

'Morning sir,' chirped Warboys, as he passed.

'Good morning, Mr. Warboys! Bright and early this morning, I see?'

'Early, sir. Not so sure about the bright!'

Warboys shared a laugh with Jayman. *Give the posh bastard a bit of worker's banter to keep him sweet.*

He slapped his hands together and surveyed the place. The Hildegaard loomed over them as ever, still anchored to the narrow barge, which was itself moored to fore and aft. Warboys scanned her quickly. If he knew his stuff, he'd say Hilda was ship-shape and tipping the meter at just below launch pressure.

Jayman and Tanner were still engrossed in conversation. He had to be quick. The day shift was due any time. He meandered at the aft, near the racks where the milking canisters were lined up. He made a show of stamping his feet and blowing on his hands, shaking out small packets from the hole he'd made in his pockets, and out of his trouser legs. He bent as if to double-knot his boots, and sparked a match to light the fuse in the bag, hoping to hell he'd packed it to smoulder the way Ulao had shown him. There was a brief hiss, and a twine of smoke, which he wafted at frantically before kicking the packets under the pallets. He waited a moment. The pack was either smouldering away as he intended, or it was duff. He looked around. Jayman was just winding up his meeting, and the day shift were arriving down the walkway.

More pressure tests were announced, just as Warboys had predicted. He leaned on his bargepole and waited dutifully for instructions. The minutes crawled. He lined up with the others, holding the Hilda steady with shaking hands.

He recognised the sulphurous smell rising first, and braced himself, hoping no one else would notice. Soon a milky white cloud arose from around the gas canisters. There was a hiss, a jet of flame, and the hangar quickly filled with sulphurous fog.

'Leak!' yelled one of the engineers. 'Canister leak!'

At this, Warboys turned clumsily with his bargepole, knocking over one of the canisters, which fell with a clatter through the billowing flame and smoke. The crew backed away in fear, some dithering in the smog, others making to flee.

'Hold your positions, men!' came a commanding voice, as Mr. Jayman arrived in the hangar, leaping boldly onto the barge to climb aboard the Hilda with Mr. Tanner. 'Leave the canisters! Evacuate the Hilda, quickly! The ship! The ship is everything!

Get the barge out!'

Men went to untether the barge and set to shunting her along toward the dock. Warboys fell into step, hauling the balloon with his pole. The fire sucked at the air, scorching Warboys' back. By the time they got to the mouth of the hangar, the rack of canisters was engulfed, and the roof was ablaze. The doctored Tugel crackers had done a fine job.

The Hildegaard emerged, in plain view for anyone on Junkers whose attention had already been grabbed by the clouds of smoke. Just as she cleared dock, a canister rocketed from the hangar, bouncing from the roof supports once before knocking a man off the Hilda's barge and into the water. Another burst from the canvas, and the flames roared yet more with the influx of air.

Whilst all eyes turned in horror to the blaze, Warboys jumped aboard the barge. Looking up, he saw Jayman peering over the rail, white with anger. Only one man remained on the docking barge, cowering on the port side, leaving it to turn listlessly in the dock. Warboys shoved past, pushing him into the water. Finding the windlass, he loosened one of the Hilda's two moorings, and she began to lift from the barge. He scrambled up the rope and clambered on board as she lifted, landing right in front of Tanner and Jayman, who watched him rummage ungraciously in his trousers for his rifle. Eventually he shook out the Entwick, and managed to turn it on them.

They froze. Jayman remained calm, raising his voice over the chaos that unfolded below.

'Mr. Warboys, what exactly are you doing?'

'Changed my position. I want my ship back.'

Then Warboys' trousers, left compromised after the extrication of his rifle, promptly fell down.

'Your...' began Tanner, pointing.

'I know...' replied Warboys. An awkward moment passed

whilst he tried to look like he still meant business whilst frantically hauling his trousers up and buttoning the fly.

'I thought we had settled all this,' said Jayman. 'If we could just—'

'If we could just shut our well-to-do cakeholes, I'll have my ship back, please and thank you and fuck off your majesty. Mr. Tanner. Cut that last anchor line.'

'But, lad...'

'Are you sure you want to do this, Mr. Warboys?'

'Quite sure thanks, you bastard.'

There was a racket from behind, and Warboys peered over Jayman's shoulder to see a small army of guards, levelling rifles at him from the deck of the *Orchidia*. Their captain called keenly for Jayman.

'Here,' said Warboys, 'come and give them a wave.'

He moved Jayman around to starboard, to show him off.

'Hold your fire, men!' called Jayman, calmly.

The guards dithered. Warboys saw Mr. Tanner hadn't moved, and was still frozen in fear.

'Mr. Tannner?' said Warboys. 'How are we doing with that anchor line?'

'Don't make me do this, lad...'

'Alright then. Get yourself off then, mate. It was nice working with you.'

'Eh?'

Warboys sidestepped, caught Tanner's overalls in his fist and dragged him over the deckrail, where he fell with a splash into the sea.

Jayman watched, all the creases of humour gone from his little eyes. The Hilda strained at her anchor line, as if eager to be free.

'One last time, Mr. Warboys. I plead with you to see sense. *You* can decide the course of history!'

'Nope.'

Warboys heard a row below, then the tell-tale tug of the anchor line being wound in. The bastards had swum out to the barge.

They were winching him down.

He had to move, now. He looked around to locate the anchor line. Then the ship tipped, and Warboys saw Jayman stepping forward and falling, disappearing below.

'Fire!' came Jayman's command, cut short by a splash as he plunged into the water below. Warboys cursed as gunfire rattled in the hull, sending splinters flying. The envelope thudded and popped with bullets. He dived and hauled the crank loose.

The Hilda rose to meet the wind.

'Fire! Fire at will' yelled Jayman, treading water below. 'Board her! Grab the anchor! Grab the lines!'

Jayman was desperate. He'd have her shot to pieces if it meant keeping her. After all, he'd regrown her from a sorry state once already. Bullets popped all along the starboard side, and Warboys could only lay flat, waiting to be borne away. But the Hildegaard seemed to just hang there. The airscrews weren't moving, and Warboys could feel tremors through the deck as the engine twitched in pain. She twirled listless around the Orchidia's masts. Warboys feared the engines were dead.

'Prime the cannon!' came Jayman's frantic yell, as the Hildegaard drifted clear of Sea Gardens.

Cannon?

Hilda began to sink toward the Gangway, scuffing a sausage bar and tearing strings of flags from old masts. Jayman's men charged out after her, scattering passers-by. Warboys stood and threw himself against the array, looking for something to get her going. More shots pinged past as Hilda cleared the line and sank toward the floating jetties. The water twinkled between the boats, waiting to suck Hilda down again.

'If only you had a face, Hilda love, I could slap it.'

He patted at his jacket, and found the bottle of rum.

'Here, try this.'

He poured a shot for Hilda, saw a spasm start in her stomach, feeling it echo through her deck and into the airscrews. She dipped sharply and, in that moment, Warboys thought he'd finally killed her. Then she inhaled tightly, and the airscrews blustered into life with a wet, flatulent sound. Hilda arced up into the air, trailing flags and hanging lamps. The Junker Line dropped away behind, and soon Warboys saw the mess of the jetties spreading out like the roots of a tree.

Then a distant bang and flash came from the fog-smeared *Orchidia* and Warboys could only clench his arse cheeks together as the shell approached, then whistled by, not ten yards off the starboard side.

'Missed!' said Warboys, raising his fingers to Jayman in a triumphant *V*. He swigged more rum, exhaled heavily, and turned to survey his ship.

'It's just you and me, now, missus.'

She was peppered with shot, and limping some, but she'd fly. He pottered about, setting the instruments, pleased with his new knowledge. He patted Hilda's stove, swigged some more rum, poured another shot for Hilda. Flatulent objections began bubbling up almost immediately, and the airscrew whirred with renewed urgency. The Junker Line faded fast below, a crooked strip of clutter lying jagged across the sea.

'I tell you what, Hilda love, it's a good job we're a bit drunk, or we might not know what we were doing.'

Warboys set a westerly course toward Coperny, and increased altitude, until the clouds drenched his hair and the sea was like black puddles in amongst them. He still wasn't too keen on the height. But there was nothing else for it.

46 MEET THE FOUNDER

Sunset cloaked the mountain, bathing the founder's statue in a fiery glow as night encroached. Through the seemingly endless queue of sea traffic that awaited port, Nouzi Aaranya stared at Coperny in awe. The monstrous mass of the city growled through the dark, wreathed in smog, ceaselessly spewing ships and noise. To his eye, the mountain looked like a great crippled titan, all but overwhelmed by the urban tide that slopped up against it. He looked through the forest of masts, towers, turrets and chimneys, the wink of glass and gaslight. Listened to the seething of machines, horns, bells and voices. The grand new viaduct now spanned the city and, even as daylight faded, the streets teemed with life. Up on the side of the mount, a pair of perfect ovals floated at anchor outside Malvy's new Eyrie.

His target.

'Nouzi-Chai' laughed Uparagha. 'You've been staring since we arrived three ours ago.'

The *Yin* had ingratiated himself with the crew of the tug, and he and Hazar had played seemingly endless games of cards with them. 'Is a mess, nai? Would be good to burn it and start again.'

The players murmured agreement.

'Is that the plan, Upa-Chai?' asked Nouzi. He joked, but since their encounter in the Rosamundt's hold, Nouzi had fallen into his old role on the edge of the Asta, letting Upa and the rest scheme without him. Was he to find his own way into the Eyrie? Upa had witheld the finer details of Nouzi's mission, and even now showed no urgency, lounging around like any one of the hundreds of other crew-members waiting for port.

He was getting on Nouzi Aaranya's nerves.

'The plan is, my friend,' said Upa, after bowing out of the game, 'for you and I to climb up there. At first light. To meet the founder!'

Nouzi Aaranya looked up to the founder on the mountain's peak. Hagen was just a silhouette now, and he seemed somewhat dishevelled to Nouzi Aaranya, as if shrugging in apology for the mess below.

'Eh? Up there?'

'Ai.'

Again, Upa did not elaborate. Nouzi pondered on this for a time, then lost himself in staring at the city once again. It made perfect sense that Warboys should have been born here, with his fumes and row, his stubble, confusion and vexation. There must be thousands like him in there, lost and aimless in life.

Did they deserve to die, though?

Just before dawn, a small fishing boat pulled in beside the barges. Uparagha rose, flexed, and came to nudge at Nouzi Aaranya.

'Hui. It's time.'

Away from the Sons, the five Janizar gathered. Uparagha bowed formally to those staying behind.

'Sat vaa, my brothers. Good winds, nai? Be swift, and remember – once the payloads are delivered, come for us at the summit. We will withdraw to watch the smoke rise, nai?'

Goro shot a dubious glance at Nouzi Aaranya, then dipped his head to speak. 'If the first strike should fail...'

'It won't,' snapped Nouzi Aaranya, angry that Goro seemed to sense his doubt.

Uparagha angered him still more when he shot a placating look at Goro over his head, as if he was a child. 'If by any chance the first strike should fail, look to the founder for the signal, nai?'

The others bowed low, smug and knowing with one another. Nouzi Aaranya went with Upa to board the fishing boat, hefting a pair of packs with them – one containing the bomb.

'Sat Vaa, Nouzi Aaranya,' sneered Goro, holding his eye in contempt. As the boat pulled away, Nouzi made an obscene, slack wristed gesture, and enjoyed Goro's indignation a moment before turning away.

A pair of fishermen declaring themselves Sons of Sun-Ivis piloted the boat away from the main shipping lanes, around the bay and along the coast for a good hour or so. Cursing Malvy all the way, they condemned his rally vociferously. As dawn began to glow in the east, they came to a cove north of Coperny Mount, where foothills plunged from coastal cliffs. Here they saw the humpbacked shape of the mountain's north-western face, which showed little hint of the urban sprawl that hid beyond it. Waiting on the tide until the water receded, Nouzi and Uparagha waded to shore through squelching kelp and rock pools. One of the fishermen led them into a cave. Upa lit a lantern to lead them through.

'Watch your footing, Nouzi Aaranya. Is treacherous.'

The fisherman led through chill, shimmering caves thick with icy mists, following an old smugglers' route. At last, the guide wished them luck, and left them at a pothole that led out onto the foothills.

Dawn was bursting brightly over the mountain by the time they emerged to begin the climb up the north face. For hours they rose through biting winds. Below, the great grey western ocean rolled toward the mount in endless foamy white strips.

By mid-morning, the rock face eventually tilted over to a more forgiving angle, and here grasses and shrubs grew.

Eventually they could walk. An overgrown path wound up toward the summit, where Hagen waited with his back to them, mottled with lichens and moss, and striped with seagull shit.

Uparagha set down his pack and saluted up at the founder. Then he strolled over to the edge of a sheer outcrop to look down over the city, before beckoning to Nouzi Aaranya.

'Hui, look.'

Nouzi edged forward. Through grimy smog, he looked down on the Capital of Malvy's new world. He had looked down on Gienha and seen its harmonious lines. Here, structures erupted over one another, seeming random but for the alluring hint of pattern suggested by repeating rows of terraces. His eye darted around as if to find the overall design, but were snatched away by rails cutting here, canals cutting there, until his head ached with the effort.

Through the roar of the city he could hear a band, and saw the red bunting lining the main streets near the harbour. Every surface seemed to teem with life as they gathered to await their great general's address. *How many Maias below?* he wondered. *How many children?*

The viaduct reared over the crowds, carrying that silver rail northward. Along there, the steam-train *Unification* would come. He scanned the harbour, so choked with tallships and tugboats that the water was barely visible between, and eventually spotted the yellow rimmed barges that they'd left behind. His gut turned over as the reality of his mission sank in.

Uparagha beamed. 'Is quite something, nai? Ha!'

'Ai,' croaked Nouzi Aaranya. 'What now?'

'Down, Nouzi-Chai! Look down, down, down!' Uparagha gripped his collar and angled him towards the barely visible roof of the Eyrie, which jutted from the face of the mountain, maybe two hundred feet below. Moored alongside it were the dark ovals of Malvy's airships.

'The *Eyrie*. Your target.'

Uparagha strode happily to his pack, and drew out the bomb. Nouzi Aaranya recognised it all too well. A small, tapered wooden cask with a handle on the top.

'So arrogant are they, these new masters of the sky, that they do not think to look for danger *above*, eh?'

Nouzi peered down at the air-station.

'Set your ropes for climbing. Shortly before noon, shimmy down and set the bomb off in the main hangar, by the canisters. Exactly as you did in Blackhaven. This will cripple them, and be the signal to launch *our* ships.'

Nouzi Aaranya swallowed, feeling a sudden terror at the prospect of what he was proposing to do. He looked at the rock face. He doubted a monkey could scale that face in the time needed to avoid the explosion. He wondered again if Upa had counted on his return from the AEC. Sensing his apprehension, Uparagha ruffled Nouzi's hair, and planted a rough kiss on his cheek. 'You always were the bravest among us, Nouzi-Chai. You can do it. Only you.'

'Ai,' he said, biting back anger.

'Think of Maia, eh?'

'Ai.'

Uparagha went joyfully off to rummage in the packs, and hauled out a tin, which he prised open, unleashing a foul solvent smell.

'Hui, what's that for?'

'For the founder. To keep them looking up when the ships launch. I thought it would be a nice touch, nai? Welcome everyone to *our* wonderland, nai?'

Whilst Upa began to splash the solvent over the statue, as happy as a finch in summer, Nouzi Aaranya shook. He doubted his capability. He doubted his conviction. He wondered if Maia might await him after he blew himself to ash. Or fell. Or was shot dead. But, all the same, he held himself, sat sanyas readying himself for descent and death.

The hours passed, and amidst the racket of the gathering crowd below, a clock began to chime eleven. Nouzi clenched his eyes shut, feeling a surge of panic with every strike. He felt his eyelid flicker as the task loomed.

Eleven came and passed. Eventually Uparagha nudged him. His heart jumped, thinking it was finally time. But Upa was looking out over the harbour, where two of Malvy's airships – *Enid* and *Nancene* – had left the Eyrie.

'Hui! Where are they going?'

Nouzi Aaranya watched the ships come about in a broad pincer movement, and belatedly he noticed their target – a third ship intruding across the brightly coloured harbour.

'Hui, Upa-Chai...' began Nouzi Aaranya, at first thinking the third ship was *Tabitha*. 'Why have they lau...'

He trailed off. The barges were still sealed. The third ship wasn't *Tabitha*, nor *Rosamundt*. He looked again. The new ship had an unsteady sway, and was trailed by seagulls. It had a grimy sheen he suddenly realised was *very* familiar.

'Hui! Isn't that the Hildegaard?'

'Huzhat! It is like a turd flying down a twinkling summer stream! What is Jayman playing at?'

Uparagha went in his pack and snatched up a telescope. 'Huzhat!' he exclaimed, sounding more exasperated than Nouzi Aaranya had ever heard. 'It's *him*!'

'Jayman?'

'Nai. Look.'

Upa threw down the telescope in disgust. Nouzi Aaranya picked it up and looked for himself.

The battered old ship drifted over the harbour, corralled between the slicker shapes of the *Enid* and *Nancene*. A foreboding bloomed inside Nouzi Aaranya, for there, leaning over the Hildegaard's deckrail, shrugging pugnaciously at the captain of the *Enid*, was Warboys.

47 A BLOODY HERO

Warboys saw Malvy's ships dovetail to either side of him, and cranked the Hildegaard up a notch, determined to get as close to the hangar as he could. He hoped to fuckery that their curiosity would outweigh the temptation to shoot him down. He also wished the flock of seagulls on his tail would bugger off. They'd latched onto Hilda's stench some miles back, and they were making him look unprofessional.

He was too nervous to look over Coperny much: the finished viaduct lent a skewed familiarity to the mess of the harbour, which again swarmed with crowds. He looked overboard and saw Hilda's shadow spreading across the harbour, and being joined by two others.

Above, the AS *Nancene* flanked his port side, whilst the *Enid* came below to starboard, both swinging about with ease. Nancene pulled in not thirty feet off, looming nearly twice the size of the Hildegaard. There was a full crew, including a pair ready with rifles. They looked more bemused by him than anything else. A goggled bombardier in a fancy cap leaned on the port rail to bellow at him through a horn.

'Ahoy there!'

Warboys said nothing, and pulled to starboard. It was all he could do not to crash the ship, let alone banter with this fat idiot.

'Ahoy! Slow down, there! You'll hit the mountain!'

'Alright, alright! Hang on!'

Warboys eased up, and slowed to a drift. The flock of seagulls shot by.

'Identify yourself!' yelled the captain of the Nancene. 'What ship is that?'

'This is the AS *Hildegaard!*' he yelled. 'Taken from Blackhaven. I've brought her back!'

'Alright... Prepare to be boarded!'

Grapples came rattling over the deckrails, and Warboys gulped.

Ah well, he thought. *The right thing. Here goes.*

~ ~ ~

Nouzi Aaranya set down the scope and shot a wary look at Uparagha, trying to hide his excitement.

'What is *he* doing here?' Upa demanded.

Nouzi Aaranya felt himself wondering the same thing.

'You told me he was dead.'

Nouzi avoided Upa's searching look, playing for time. 'Ai, well. He was looking very old.'

Upa was not amused.

'Did you lie to me, Nouzi-Chai?'

'Does it matter?' he shrugged. 'What can he do, now?'

Nouzi Aaranya watched the trio of airships as the Hilda was escorted back to the hangar. He wanted desperately to know what Warboys intended. Had he meant what he'd said? Was he coming to stop them?

'What did you tell him?' demanded Upa.

'How could I tell him anything? You don't tell *me* your plans.'

Uparagha gave a sharp look.

'Never mind. He has done enough bringing that old wreck in so brazenly. Has proved a point, nai? Taken the edge off our surprise – and drawn those ships out of dock.'

'Perhaps.'

'I'm not happy with this.'

'Ai. He has that effect.'

'You seem amused.'

'Ai.'

Uparagha grunted, unimpressed. 'Ai. Well. It works out well. He has at least herded those two patrol ships back to the hangar. Go down there and set the bomb. Kill him, along with the rest.'

'Now?'

'Now. Time is near, in any case. Warboys will die before he can convince them to act. Your time has come, Nouzi Aaranya.'

'Ai.'

Nouzi Aaranya walked to the edge to secure his climbing ropes, feeling the life of the city blaring up at him, and losing himself in the craft of the knot-tying. He barely noticed when Upa began to pace, eyeing him impatiently.

'Hui, Nouzi Chai. You take too long. Are you ready?'

Nouzi Aaranya came out of his trance, and stood. He inhaled deeply, and steeled himself for what he was about to do.

~ ~ ~

'Look how easy it was for me to just pull in here, right over town!' yelled Warboys, rubbing at his head. Despite his protests, he'd been marched off to an interrogation room in the Eyrie, where a flight deck officer in a stiff charcoal jacket had questioned him. At Warboys' insistence, Anders Sesaw of the Aeronautics Divison had been fetched, and now listened with a puzzled frown. 'It was easy! And if I can do it, anybody can! That's what I'm trying to tell you!'

Anders Sesaw patted his lovely hands on a stack of reports he'd been leafing through.

'Mr. Warboys. Following the enquiry after the attack on the AEC, you were identified as part of the patrol. You then went promptly missing from action, and evidence was later gathered to suggest that you had been involved with the insurgents at the Gata festival, and that your late father, William Eadgar Warboys, was responsible for the release of Jombrey Valego, a known enemy of the state – who was identified as part of the hijackers' group. A statement given by one of your own squad stated his belief that you are an outright traitor.'

'Fucking Jacky Biel,' growled Warboys, knowingly. 'I should have run that fucker down...'

A watching deck officer sniffed at him. 'I should watch my mouth if I were you, son. This doesn't look good for you!'

'Alright. I know. But you have to do something!'

'Mr. Warboys,' Sesaw interrupted. 'You haven't told us how you know what you claim. Why you came to be aboard the Hildegaard – *again*; what you know about the Blackhaven bombing, where you've been for the last month, or what you've been doing with military property.'

'I'll talk. Once it's safe. But you have to listen. The Sons of Sun-Ivis have got the *Tabitha* and the *Rosamundt*, and they're going to attack during the rally.'

'Alright. So these *Sons*, they're the crescent marked yokels from Blackhaven?'

'Yes.'

'Who've got wind of some folk legend of an ancient Sun-Ivi religion, and now they're invoking it against the State?'

'No! Well, yes, but their leader Uparagha is for real. Janizar. Real Sun-Ivis. Sun-Ivis is still alive, in the Eldask.'

'Mr. Warboys,' scoffed Sesaw, 'I'm an accomplished philologist, and I can tell you, the lost Asiatic civilisation of Sun-Ivis is an obscure rumour even among scholars. I—'

'Well you're shit philosogist, because I'm telling you that—'

'Philologist!'

The deck officer cut in.

'*Whoever* they might be,' he began, with a sharp glare at

Sesaw, 'what are they planning?'

'An air strike, I reckon. Look, I've got family here. Just clear the streets, can't you?'

'Clear the streets? Even if what you're telling me is true—'

There was a knock and another officer appeared in the doorway. 'Sir... the City Warden has received your message. He's asking for... clarification.'

The officer sighed and moved into the doorway, leaning back to look at Warboys. 'I'm going to bear in mind what you say, and advise precautions. But I'll echo what Mr. Sesaw has said. Whether an attack comes or not, you've got a lot of explaining to do.'

And with that, he left the room. Warboys looked up at Sesaw, who stacked his papers and stood to go.

'Will he clear the streets at least?'

'Well, the steamer is near, and the streets are packed, so what they'll do at this late stage I don't know. At any rate, your arrival has meant the fleet is on alert, Mr. Warboys. We're preparing ships to stand watch. If any other unscheduled craft come within five miles of Coperny, we'll know about it.'

'Alright,' sighed Warboys, setting his head hang. 'Then that's as much as I can do.'

'If you're right about all this, you could be a bloody *hero*.'

'I doubt it.'

'On the other hand... if you're found guilty of some of the charges levelled... you'll be up against the wall and shot whether the attack comes or not.'

'You're a real comfort, you are. Can't you get me a smoke or something?'

'Unfortunately, no naked flames are allowed on the hangar deck. A formality.'

Warboys sighed, and sank into the table. The door closed, and he was left alone to await his judgement.

48 CAKORA

Nouzi Aaranya hesitated, looking from the cluttered harbour to the open sea.

'Tell me the truth.'

'Eh? What do you mean?'

'If we strike here today... with these painted fool *Sons* you have running around calling out our people's name... it won't be the end. Malvy will return fire. His ships will swarm over the Eldask. His troops will come, and plunder everything Sun-Ivis has worked toward... The Sekhet have not survived all these years by waging open war. I don't believe they ordered this. Tell me the truth.'

Uparagha sighed, a long and testy exhalation.

'You are right, Nouzi Aaranya. The Sekhet know nothing of this. This is *my* war.'

Nouzi Aaranya turned around, horrified.

'But... you spoke with the Sekhet, after the Gata... Did he not oppose this?'

Uparagha sneered.

'He lies dismembered across the fields beyond Blackhaven Tor. I cut his head off myself.'

It was an unthinkable crime, so casually confessed. Nouzi Aaranya felt suddenly dizzy, and the city below seemed to swell up, ready to receive him.

'*Huzhat*... they'll invade! Thousands of them... They'll break the Samagata...'

'Ha! Good! That's what I want!'

'You promised me a way to Maia! Not the destruction of everything we are!'

'Avai! I offered you your purpose! What you choose to dream is your concern. Find Maia in the wreckage, nai? Soon she will be a whore in every trinket shop doorway.'

'Why? Why are you doing this?'

Uparagha sneered at him in disgust.

'Why, Nouzi Aaranya? *Revenge* is why. I want revenge on our Sekhet Fathers. They breed us Janizar from their own bloodline, only to make slaves of us, generation after generation. They set us against one another, so we can have the privilege of sacrificing ourselves for their *cultivation*. Let *them* finally suffer the consequences of their precious work!'

'But what about Maia?'

'I will not be dulled by the promise of Maia!' growled Upa, his face creasing with hatred. 'I stared long into the darkness, Nouzi Aaranya! Long into the nothingness! Now it is *their* turn!'

Nouzi Aaranya's eye watered in fear. The words chimed in his chest, wrung some memory from him.

Upa, staring into nothingness.

There's nothing there...

He felt the shock again of his own despair, when he'd staggered from the *Rosey Blush*. And suddenly, he remembered Cakora's feathers loose and drifting off into the wind. He recalled Upa's odd smirk when they had last spoken of her. Kai's mystified expression when he found them with the dead hawk.

And with that, came realisation.

'It wasn't Kai who killed Cakora, was it?'

Nouzi saw the sickly smile on Upa's face and shook his head in disgust. 'I should have realised it. Kai's face... I should have realised it! Kai didn't slay that bird... It was *you*.'

Uparagha sniggered.

'Hui, Cakora was my lesson in love, eh? I was watching

her that day. Watching her movements, the light between the feathers, and it suddenly struck me how loathsome I was. How *attached.* What was there in this thing that could string me to it with love, I thought? What good is this doing me when Kai is coming for me again? And so I decided to cut it open and find out. What was there inside? Eh? Nothing. *Nothing.* A gaping hole. Nothing in it! Nothing there! Like Maia. *Not real!*'

Nouzi Aaranya felt colour draining from his face. The terror began to congeal, forming spots at the corner of his eyes.

'The Fathers are right. The End *is* coming. Not *Zirisa Mai,* though. The real end is this *Modern World.* Soon the Fathers will awake from their transcendence and find a steam railway burning up their precious gardens. They want the end of the world, eh? I will bring them it in droves! Plunder, pillage, fire and *rape!*'

'You lied to me, Upa-Chai. You lied, all along...'

Nouzi Aaranya teetered by the edge, felt the weight of his life dragging at him. A tear streamed down his face, now his doubts were confirmed. Uparagha's expression softened, and he approached, raising a tentative hand to touch Nouzi Aaranya's chest.

'I had to, nai? I understand. We are broken beings, we Janizar. I *know* how she eats at you, Nouzi-Chai', he purred. 'I know how you have strung yourself along all these years...'

His hand moved up, fingers burying in Nouzi's hair. That hot, needy breath again. '*They* have strung you along. *She* has strung you along. You and me, and all the Janizar before us. Forget Maia. Do this for me, eh? For us both.'

Nouzi Aaranya wiped his tear away, and pressed his forehead against Uparagha's. Upa planted a kiss on his cheek. Nouzi pulled away, his fingers moving sensuously down Upa's cheeks as he stared deep into the ink of Upa's eyes.

'Nai,' he said, curtly.

And then he stuck the nut on him.

Uparagha staggered backwards in shock, and went sprawling to the ground. Nouzi Aaranya paced uneasily over him, his head ringing.

'Big wanker! Offering me to the Edge, eh? You're no different than Kai!'

'I never claimed to be different,' croaked Upa, padding at his bloodied nose. 'I am *better*, because I survive him.'

'You're worse, because you're a liar! You lied to get me to help you kill him, so *you* could be Yin. You used me to make your third boom attack! Stand up, *kitava*! Arsehole! Shithead! Stand up and take stance! Dhassama!'

Uparagha rolled up onto his knees, snorting clots of blood. A distinct whistle sounded from a distance, and the two looked southward to see a white plume of steam puffing along the north south rail, approaching fast. The *Unification*. A cheer came from the city below.

'Avai, Nouzi Aaaranya. You are wasting my time, eh?'

Uparagha snatched up his lamp, which he smashed against Hagen, lighting the fuel. Flame spread across Hagen's outstretched arms in a silky blanket.

'The backup signal, nai?' he grinned. 'We knew there was always the chance you would fail again.'

The thunder of cannon fire resonated from below, as the stolen artillery was unleashed from the barges. Nouzi stood firm as the mountain shuddered below his feet. He drew his dhas, catching flame along its edge.

'Dhassama!' he insisted, stomping forward.

Uparagha grunted, drew his dhas with a flourish, and took stance.

'Good, then. I'll send her a lantern in your name.'

'Tchi!' yelled Nouzi Aaranya. 'Inshie!' And the two sprang toward one another.

49 BOMBS AWAY

Warboys' head sank, mashing his nose into the table. He could just about hear the roar of the crowds from outside. He heard the hangar staff shouting – in excitement, it seemed – and supposed Malvy was about to make his address.

There was a distant *bang*.

Warboys looked up and frowned. He heard a whistle, rising to a roar. The floor jumped beneath him, pitching him and his table over. He looked up, seeing plaster and dust showering down from a great crack in the wall. The door had split open, its frame now a shattered rhombus. He wondered, with a dead weight in his gut, if Nouzi Aaranya had delivered another bomb.

Dust belched from outside. Warboys edged to the door to peer out onto the metal walkway, ducking away as men clattered toward the hangar entrance, an officer screaming orders after them. There was another dreadful whistle, and the room juddered again. Warboys panicked, suddenly thinking of the AEC. Bill's last moments would have been something like this. Quick moments, fast decisions before death. Fear drove him out onto the walkway.

He stepped out unchallenged. The walkway creaked in its fixings. Through the gaps, he could see the city, hundreds of feet below. A burning airman burst through the main hangar door, and toppled over the balcony before Warboys could act. He watched him plummet for what seemed an age, feeling the scorching heat pulsing out of the hangar doorway.

'Oh, shitting hell...'

Shielding his face, Warboys entered. The hangar was wreathed in flame from deck to ceiling, and he recognised the sound of gas canisters fizzing. The blaze forced him up to the observation platform. Below, the harbour front clamoured with people. Screams echoed, the ineffectual barks of soldiers trying to clear checkpoint-choked streets. Warboys scanned the bay, trying to make sense of what had happened. The stricken AS Nancene drifted over the city, her balloon ablaze, the crew in panic as she sank away inland.

He saw the AS *Enid* come about, her crew roused to look for survivors in the hangar. Warboys raised his arms, and heard a distant *bang* sound out again. Looking down over the harbour, he saw a curl of smoke bloom out from a yellow rimmed barge out near the harbour walls. Then he understood.

It wasn't a bomb. The barge was mounted with a cannon. The bastards had their own *artillery*. The Eyrie was sheltered from the sea, but Malvy had never counted on fire from his own harbour. Warboys threw himself down as the whistle rose into a roar. The *Enid*'s gondola burst into fragments, scattering men and debris into the air. The balloon rolled, shedding its burning rigs like an orange skin, and plummeted, trailing black smoke.

That was it. Malvy's defence fleet done for.

A burst canister rocketed over Warboys' head. Fire crawled along the observation deck toward him. Rather than be trapped, he rushed through the fire for the door, back down towards the cells.

He looked down over the harbour as he ran. A gunfight echoed as naval ships converged on the barge – and then Warboys doubted his eyes as the barge yawned open, tipping crates from her deck as something swelled up from the hold. He halted, open mouthed as an airship balloon popped roughly out, and in seconds there was the *AS Tabitha*, crewed, painted with Uparagha's crescent, and rising rapidly toward the viaduct.

A second barge burst open, and the larger AS *Rosamundt* swelled up from within. *Rosamundt* trailed, bearing the fire of naval troops as she lifted sluggishly. Warboys could tell she was carrying a hefty payload. He scanned across the dockside, seeing the city troops in chaos, the wharves still crammed with onlookers. To the south, the steam train *Unification* was arriving, bang on time, and now Tabitha and Rosamundt gained rapidly on the viaduct.

Warboys staggered along the walkway, back past the cracked cell door. He squinted into the smoke, fearing that he might see the kid loitering there. Or parts of him. He wasn't sure there *was* any way down now. He staggered along, scouring for a service duct, perhaps an escape ladder. He barged desperately through a service bay door, and it was then that he saw her again, tucked away in disgrace, but *intact*.

The AS *Hildegaard*.

~ ~ ~

The two blades flashed, chimed twice, then Nouzi Aaranya slashed across Upa's chest. Upa gasped and span a wild, whirling strike for the throat. Nouzi Aaranya flexed away, but lost his balance, lashing out as he staggered, his dhas cutting away some of Upa's ear. They parted, took a breath, and lunged again. Snarling, Uparagha whipped at him with lightning slashes, forcing Nouzi Aaranya further and further back, until he lost his footing. Nouzi snatched out at Upa's arm as he fell, yanking Uparagha into the burning statue. Upa writhed away, an oily flame clinging to his collar, and let out a roar as he snatched up the tin of solvent, coming in a windmill swing. The tin buckled Nouzi's guard and caught on his skull. Seeing the burning figure of Hagen disappear out of sight, he rolled backwards, over and over down the incline.

Nouzi Aaranya clawed at grass and soil. Too late, he glimpsed his climbing rope and plunged over the edge, hurtling towards the rooftops far below.

~ ~ ~

A gristly noise came from the *Hildegaard*'s engine as Warboys emptied rum into the hatch. Bubbles shook in her guts, boosting her forward with great, flatulent bursts of objection, out through the hangar arch and into clear air. He saw Hilda's shadow flickering over King's Row far below, past the dock offices, past gaping people scurrying around the streets. Belatedly, he realised that people were looking up *past* the Hildegaard, to where Hagen's statue blazed, spewing coils of smoke into the wind. The sight horrified him at some base level – the wonderland, founded, now burning for all to see.

Warboys didn't muse for long. The ominous ovals of Tabitha and Rosamundt swelled before him as he headed on an intersecting course toward their portside flanks. Within seconds he was close to ramming distance of *Tabitha*. He didn't know if airships *had* ramming distances, but it was too late to worry about that now.

As she loomed close, Warboys saw several crew members lying dead or wounded already. The surviving crew dithered, their attention split between the target and the dirty old ship now steaming toward their port side.

Warboys saw the Janizar Sila steady among them. He picked up his Entwick especially.

'Have this, you monkey-faced twat!'

Sila ducked as the shot pinged off their stove – then the Hildegaard shunted Tabitha's tail end. Their crew was thrown to the decks with the impact, and Tabitha spun about, airscrews straining against the backward motion, left dead in the air as

Hilda bludgeoned on. For a moment, at least, Tabitha was stalled.

Rosamundt moved steadily on, looming starboard below to overtake the Hildegaard. Shots drummed on the Hilda's hull. Warboys could see the brute Goro on her aft, urging his pilot on.

'Oh no you fucking don't!' seethed Warboys, hauling the wheel about as the Hilda picked up speed to come around again. Rosamundt's shadow crawled over onto the wharf, still rising, not ten streets away from the viaduct now.

Hilda gained rapidly, close enough that Warboys could hear Goro's guttural command, and the clunk of the bomb chute being loaded.

'Come on, Hilda! Shift!'

Shaking the last of the rum into the intake, Warboys drove Hilda forward, rocking back and forth as if he would shove her along himself. Shots peppered the aft. One hit Warboys leg, and he stumbled, only to see the *Tabitha* had recovered, looming against the bright sky once again.

'Hui!' bawled Goro. 'Steady there... steady... *dhassama!* Bombs away!'

Warboys saw the first bomb drop. A shadow rushed up to meet it on the canalside. A geyser erupted with a boom, carving a moored schooner up into two halves.

'Steady course!' roared Goro. 'Ready payload!' Warboys saw Goro leave the array, and turn back aft. He stooped quickly to collect and aim a bow. The shot looped erratically though the air, curving in the side wind. Warboys ducked as it filled his vision, and there was a crack as it pranged itself through a pressure gauge, only inches from his skull. Looking up, he saw Rosamundt rising sharply, and hauled the wheel to catch her slipstream. The Hilda rushed forward, and Warboys wheeled frantically back the other way, rum-trumps rollicking in Hilda's guts as she rammed the port side of the heavier ship. The gondolas swung up and locked together with the impact, sending both Warboys and the enemy crew sliding athwartships.

Warboys clawed his way back to midships, peering nervously at the furious Sons crewing the Rosamundt – now just a few strides away. He jammed the Hilda's airscrews into reverse. It would slow them, but the Rosamundt was still drifting over the viaduct. A screech of brakes sounded and, from the south, he saw the *Unification* hurtling down the track toward them.

Goro appeared at the gunwale, ordering his crew to maintain course. Then, meeting Warboys' eye, he drew his dhas and set to slashing at Hilda's enmeshed cradle rigs.

'Oi!' yelled Warboys, raising the Entwick to fire. But the Hilda sagged with every cut, the shot went high, and Goro barely flinched. He cut again, and the Hilda's gondola dropped hard, tipping down under Rosamundt's hull. Warboys clung on for dear life as he was tipped downward, seeing the shadow of the two tangled ships rising over the viaduct.

The scream of the steamer came closer.

'Hold steady!' growled Goro, frustrated now. 'Hui! Ready with the chute, kitava!'

So saying, he jumped down onto Hilda's slanting deck. Warboys fumbled to reload, and raised the Entwick, but Goro was on him in a pace. The dhas flashed up and cut the rifle aside, searing across his arm, then finished with a curt jab that drove its point into Warboys' chest.

'Fuck...' gasped Warboys, sagging down to the deck. Goro sneered, looming over him, the blade raised to finish.

Then the underside of the Rosamundt's hull swung over onto the Hilda's sunken deck, and cracked the Janizar on the head, knocking him back against the Hilda's deckrail.

Warboys caught the Rosamundt's ballast rig and dragged himself under her keel, off the Hilda and out of Goro's reach. He gasped for breath, feeling the cuts throbbing all over him. He yearned for the strength to clamber up onto the Rosamundt and knock them all out.

'Bombs away!' came a yell from above.

There was the click and clunk as the chute deployed. The bomb – a small tapered beer-keg thing, with three triangular flights at the narrow end – dropped from the chute, caught in the ballast net that Warboys had stetched out, and settled next to him. He seized up in panic. A sprung dial on the top twanged as its trigger coil edged around.

He had seconds. He stared in horror. Then he heard Goro's voice –

'Come here, kitava!'

Warboys clawed for a hand hold as Goro reached from the Hildegaard, caught his ankle and hauled him across. As he went, he snatched at the bomb. The Hildegaard see-sawed to present Warboys to Goro, and Warboys was tipped forward like a cadaver from a coffin. The Janizar's small eyes widened as the bomb came to him, delivered in his victim's hands – and, as he backed away toward the deckrail, Warboys gave a shove to go with it, tipping him backwards over the rail.

Momentum almost carried Warboys over as well. He didn't hear an explosion go off, because everything was subsumed by the noise of the *Unification*. The awful wail of brakes eclipsed all sound, and Warboys turned around to see the black, riveted front filling his stern view. The collision caught his breath as both ships were hooked out of the air by the train, and everything was erased in a sudden hot whiteness. Warboys clung on as Hilda rolled, felt a twang as the knackered rigs tore away from *Rosamundt*. Then there was sky again. Hilda breeched like a whale through the cloud, and Warboys' stomach lurched as she tipped to what passed as level for the slashed and mangled rigs. The train ploughed on through the Rosamundt, which had collapsed around the front of the engine cylinder like a rotten fruit. Rosamundt's gondola shattered, barrels, bombs and crew bouncing along the sides of the railway. The brakes screeched on, and the train teetered as she slowed. With a steady creak, the carriages halted. Steam gushed out. Warboys heard shouting.

The Hildegaard drifted backwards in the bow wave of the steamer for a moment before starting to sink. Warboys dropped and lay bloodied on the deck, watching the viaduct disappear upward as the Hilda fell like a leaf. The angular shadow of the dockside buildings stretched over him, and he heard voices, men, women, children, just before the Hildegaard came to a crunching halt on the cobbles.

50 AIR FORCE

Warboys heard voices. Northern accents, the sudden sense of *home*. Hands reached over the rail, faces appeared. Then there was a soldier's voice, calling them all off as he approached the gondola, a proper infantry greencoat with scruffy big sideburns.

'Are you alright in there, sir? Are you hurt?'

Warboys couldn't quite sit up.

The soldier climbed aboard and helped him. Warboys strained to stand – only to find a whole street looking at him.

'Good fucking job, mate!' yelled a clothcap, echoed by many other voices, familiar seeming men and women he'd never met before. He felt a bit of a fraud, and looked to the soldier, who gave him a nod to confirm the plaudits. A round of applause broke out from the street, and although he reckoned it might be nice to sit back and think about it afterwards, right then it made him feel a bit of a twat.

'Forceful bit of flying, that was!' the greencoat said. 'Ey up, sir. You're bleeding, look.'

Warboys looked down at himself and saw he was soaked through to the skin with blood.

'Yah,' he muttered, swallowing his fright. 'It'll be alright.' He staggered over onto the street to scan what narrow stretch of sky could be seen beside the viaduct. 'What's going on?'

'We got a tip off before the attack,' gasped the soldier. 'The rally's been cancelled. We've moved hundreds, but we're still trying to clear all the wharves...' He turned, remembering his duty, and shooed the audience off. 'Here! Come on you lot. It's not safe yet! Get yourself off! Move along!'

'Where's the *Tabitha* gone? The other ship?'

'Think she pulled about for another go, mate,' said a clothcap, thumbing at the air as he departed.

Warboys saw a sharklike shadow cross the street as the airship *Tabitha* glided over the viaduct, toward where the *Unification* had halted. There was the distinct clunk and thump of the payload, and bombs dropped out: one, two, three.

'Get down!' screamed Warboys. 'Get d—'

Thunderous booms erupted, and the train jumped up like a happy salmon. A great slab of the viaduct dropped off and crushed the dock offices below, and a wave of cobbles rolled up from the street. Bricks and debris rained down. Warboys ducked as some bounced against the Hildegaard, searing the envelope. Then he heard a great moan, and looked up to see the train carriages slip off the viaduct like a titanic necklace, slamming through rows of buildings several blocks long. A great cloud of dust billowed from beneath it all, and after a weak few retaliatory shots in Tabitha's direction, silence ruled. Warboys staggered after Tabitha, until she slipped out of sight between buldings.

'Ah shit.'

He moved back toward Hilda, but dizziness overcame him and he stumbled. The greencoat was there to help him on to the deck.

'What are you going to do, Sir?'

'I'm the bloody air force now. I'll have to bloody stop them, won't I?'

Warboys set about knotting the hacked up rigs the best he could, shifted the gas into a different pocket to get some lift going. The balloon began to swell, bobbing back to life. She lifted awkwardly, the gondola tilting alarmingly as she went.

'You sure she'll fly, sir? Is there summat I can do?'

'I could do with moving her out into space for take off.'

'Right you are, sir!' And, with that, the greencoat mustered bystanders to take the tow ropes and haul the re-inflating Hildegaard along the cobbles and up. The greencoat patted the keel as she lifted.

'Best of luck, sir!' he yelled. 'By the way. What's your name?'

'Warboys. William Konrad Warboys.'

'Right, well. Good luck, Mr, Warboys. You do us proud.'

Warboys shared a meek salute with the greencoat. The Hildegaard rose, her gondola see-sawing dangerously. Warboys spotted the *Tabitha* above as he turned to set the airscrews and rose to pursue. He lifted his coat briefly to see scarlet patches soaking him, and felt dizzy. Specks pulsed before his eyes as he felt himself drifting up even faster than the ship.

~ ~ ~

Nouzi Aaranya snatched at the rope, gasping as it seared his palms. He swung heavily down into the rock-face, and fell, clawing at rocks that slammed him left and right. He snatched at an outcrop, arm nearly wrenched from its socket, and somehow managed to steady himself. His boots braced against the rock.

Below him, Coperny was a swamp of smoke and screams. He looked up. Cursed. The rope was some way away. It would take a good few minutes to climb back. As he scrambled up, he saw a dark shape rising through the smog, and felt a shock in his toes the likes of which he hadn't felt since the basking shark. The *Tabitha* rose up and over him.

He heard Sila's voice, and clambered as fast as he could, reaching the summit in time to see Tabitha drifting low over the mountain top. Whorls of flame spun from Hagen's arms as Tabitha overshot, struggling against the wind to come about and cast anchor. Uparagha trailed anxiously after her whilst

Sila yelled down. Only one navigator remained, gripping the wheel frantically against the wind.

It was done. They were escaping.

Nouzi Aaranya staggered to his feet, throwing himself down the slope to slam into Upa's back. They fell heavily, Nouzi Aaranya pitching over into the ground. Beneath him, Upa's head struck a rock. They grappled, and the Tabitha came about to hover unsteadily a little way down the hill. In the chaos, Nouzi saw Sila mounting his deckrail, training a rifle on the fight.

Upa rolled, caught Nouzi about the throat, and drew a long gutting knife. Upa's lips pressed into his ear, his voice suddenly tender as the point of the knife pierced his skin.

'Nouzi Aaranya, you are persistent as the hawk. And now you can—'

The light was blotted out for a moment. A gunshot sounded, and Sila fell back from the deckrail. The Hildegaard rose over the mountain top, banking uneasily as Warboys appeared at the bow. He finished reloading, fired again on the Tabitha, and Sila's dithering navigator cringed away from the wheel. Tabitha slipped into the wind. Uparagha faltered, moved away from Nouzi to give chase – but then the Hilda came swooping down, blocking him from the drifting Tabitha. Up above, Warboys reloaded and aimed again. Nouzi Aaranya rolled to his feet, unsure whether it was Upa or himself that Warboys was aiming at. Then Upa, caught between the two once again, gave Nouzi a vengeful glare before breaking into a sprint toward the Hildegaard. Warboys fired. Nouzi Aaranya saw the back of Upa's coat jump out – but it didn't stop him. Uparagha sprang savagely, reaching out for the Hildegaard's trailing ratlines.

51 KAARYA, AND ALL THAT

Uparagha slammed into the Hilda's starboard railing, his weight tipping the gondola dangerously. She banked and spiralled, sinking down below the edge where Nouzi stood. He flanked her along to the very end of the rock, where the city roared below. There, he took a breath, turned for a run-up, and threw himself off the edge, flailing at the Hilda's trailing rigs.

Wind rushed in his ears. He found himself praying to Maia in earnest.

His arm jarred against a knot, his shoulder almost wrenched from its socket again. He was swinging on a rope, some fifteen feet below the keel. The ship dipped, and began to descend at greater speed. Smoggy clouds parted to reveal chimneys and steeples, and the Hildegaard veered down toward seemingly endless blocks of terraces. Nouzi's flailing boots kicked off a chimney pot, then came skidding onto a slate roof. The rope fell slack as the ship swept down past him, and the Janizar found himself tottering along the roof arch to keep pace with the ship, holding the rig like a lead as she sank lower into the street. Uparagha was still clinging to the deckrail. Warboys pale and bleeding on the deck. Fear stabbed at Nouzi Aaranya, and propelled him over a chimney pot. He came careering toward the edge of the building, and dived off, swinging hard on the rope, trying to weigh the ship down. His boots clattered against the cobbles as he swung around a lamp-post, and set his weight against it, trying to jerk the Hildegaard to a stop. He was dragged into the post with a clang, and fell face down in the mud, dazed and exhausted. The Hildegaard pitched, ploughed across the green, and veered to a halt.

Dogs barked. Voices called out from the battlement of terraces. Nouzi looked up to see a boarded-up pub. The sign creaked. *The Blackwater Tavern.*

Uparagha tumbled from the Hildegaard, crawling to his feet with a boar like grunt, and stumbled away down an alley. Nouzi Aaranya climbed to his feet as the balloon lolled down, dragging the gondola over to tip Warboys out onto the mud of the green. Warboys cursed, ghastly pale as he turned to spot Nouzi. The rifle's muzzle made uneasy circles in the air as he raised it to Nouzi Aaranya.

'Are we alright, you and me, kid?' he rasped. 'Cos I've got another round here for you if not.'

'Ai! Ai. Don't shoot. You were right, Captain. He was lying, using me for his own gain. You were right. I made the right choice.'

'Thank fuck for that,' said Warboys, and collapsed into the grass. Nouzi Aaranya ran to his side as people gathered at the edges of the green.

'Avai, Captain! Captain!'

'Stop slapping me.'

'Can you move?'

'Fuck knows mate,' Warboys groaned. 'I don't know. Shit... Is he dead yet, your mate?'

'Nai... the *strength* of him, Captain! He would have gutted me...'

Nouzi Aaranya felt his eyelid flickering.

'I should have known,' he gasped. 'I didn't want to see it. He was my only friend.'

'Alright kid, just calm down. Listen. You've got to finish him off now. Kaarya and all that, alright? You don't want that fucker popping into your mind every time you go to the outside lavvy.

Go after him... take the rifle... and for god's sake, *shoot him*. Shoot him before he opens his mouth. Then get yourself gone.'

Nouzi Aaranya smiled haplessly and shook his head. 'I can't,' he whispered. Warboys saw his eyes glaze over, his hands starting to claw.

'Oi! Listen now. It ain't real. If you go after him flapping like a chicken, he'll wring your fucking neck like one. You aren't a chicken, you're a Janizar, alright? Look, there's a charge in ready for you. Put it between his fucking eyes, for god's sake...'

Nouzi wobbled as he rose. At great pain, Warboys managed to sit up and get a hand on his arm to steady him. 'Look here. *Look.* Watch... your cocking bolt tends to get stuck here. It'll usually shift with a good hard slap. But you have to be quick, or it'll go off in your face... are you listening?'

'Ai.'

'The sight groove is wrong. Bears to starboard... to the right, alright?'

'Right, alright. Ai.'

'Good. Now take it and piss off, will you? Do it for me. Do it for... Bill.'

'Bill,' repeated Nouzi Aaranya, feverishly. Nodding uncertainly, he shouldered the Entwick.

'Aye, Bill. That's right, take a deep breath... in... out... and *go*.'

Warboys watched Nouzi Aaranya cross the green into the murk of the alley, and gasped in pain. Just before he vanished, Nouzi called back.

'Warboys?'

'I'm 'ere! What?'

'For Bill, eh? And for Maia.'

Warboys laughed. The daft sod might have marched on in the name of cheese at that moment. And yet, Warboys found himself choking up with a kind of pride.

'Aye. For Bill and for Maia.'

'Ai!' nodded Nouzi Aaranya, with a gleam in his own eyes. Then he was gone into a haze, and Warboys could not tell whether it was smoke or his eyesight failing.

Tears swelled. It was not so much that he was injured beyond his understanding, that he might be on his own deathbed, nor even that Uparagha had escaped him again. It was that sense of having to let the kid go to it on his own. It came to him with great clarity that he had done all he could. He had passed the rifle on, and had to watch the boy walk on. And it washed over him again, how Bill had suffered him over the years, how much patience he'd had to urge him on despite everything, and how his efforts had ended sadly in the passing over of a paint flecked old rifle. He understood now.

And, besides all that, the bastards had shut down the Blackwater Tavern.

A tear streamed down his filthy cheek.

Funny how things turned out.

52 A BIT OF PACKUP

Nouzi Aaranya followed Uparagha down the alley. A cat gawked at him from some bins before skittering off, and the passage led onto a street smothered with smoke. He stepped out, jabbing the Entwick before him like a spear.

Civilians, still clearing from the Dock front, emerged out of the mist, having been evacuated from the main street. Droves of young men, women and children. All those who might have died. Some cried out as Nouzi Aaranya ploughed through. Passers-by stalled, muttering about him. A shop front showed him his reflection – a dirty, wild eyed young foreigner with a dead man's gun, heading against the flow of people. Soldiers' voices barked in streets unseen, still working to herd civilians back to their homes.

He found fresh blood on the pavement, and followed. Finally slowed by his wounds, Uparagha had slumped in the doorway of a boarded up church, plastered with red and black propaganda.

Nouzi Aaranya waited politely for a woman to pass before raising the rifle. Uparagha looked up at Nouzi Aaranya with eyes like black buttons. The woman wailed, went crying for help, and a man swore and nudged his friends. The crowd veered away, loitering at distance. Nouzi Aaranya remembered how Janizar back home sometimes confronted one another and took to blades in public. That was at home, though. That was Gienha. That was before the booms.

'Hui!' he grunted, doubting the feel of his fingers as the Entwick stubbornly cocked. 'Uparagha!' He felt he should make some sort of announcement. His voice echoed, and the crowd halted to watch, hushed. 'King of Waning Moon!'

Uparagha forced himself onto his hands and knees, and opened his mouth to say something.

'I would have gone with you,' said Nouzi Aaranya. He fired with no further warning. The archway sprayed with crimson, and Uparagha fell flat with barely a gasp. A man swore through his teeth. A woman screamed. Some ran.

Nouzi Aaranya breathed deep. The murmur of the city arose, voices and wind, sulphur and tobacco. The tramping feet of soldiers, coming closer. He focussed himself, shouldered the Entwick, and strode across to Uparagha, drawing his *dhas*. A boy's voice with Warboys' accent could be heard saying, 'He's round here, mate! In front of the church! Here!'

Nouzi Aaranya lifted Uparagha's head by the hair. A disbelieving crowd gaped as he held it still for a moment, and inhaled again to ensure balance before the *dhas* came down in a flash of dirty daylight.

~ ~ ~

Warboys heard people coming toward him. Women gasping. Daft lads muttering, daring one another to come closer.

'Is he one 'o these Suneyevs out of Blackhaven then?'

'I dunno. What does one look like?'

'Here! I know him! I swear I know that bloke. It's that bloody feller! What's his name...'

'Fucking hell! It's me dad!'

Warboys squinted up as Edgear leaned over him, seeming a lot bigger than he had all those months ago.

'I thought I told you to keep off this bloody green!' croaked Warboys.

'Did you come down in that thing?'

'Aye. She's alright, isn't she? What do you think?'

'You're bleeding.'

'Ugh! Fucking right he's bleeding! Look!'

Caitlin Garron's voice sounded shrilly from across the Green, and a collective of mothers called their lads in and away from trouble. *It's Warboys!* kids were calling. *Warboys!*

'What you on about, *Warboys*?' bawled Cait, as she stormed into view and stood gaping at him. Wilyam followed, his wild ginger hair sprung in shock.

'Just thought I'd drop in, like,' Warboys gasped. 'See how you are.' Cait saw his blood-caked clothes, and sent Wilyam off to fetch old Marta Biel. Next thing, Marta Biel was scowling at him past her family nose, and some kids were climbing up the *Hildegaard*'s rigging. A fearful moan came from the crowd as the balloon suddenly inflated and Hilda began to drift down the row, leaving a small fat boy forced to charge for the deckrail, his face a picture of panic as he dove overboard. The *Hildegaard* lifted of her own accord and drew away the crowd in a procession, bending lamp-posts and terrifying cats.

I ought to have warned them about that sort of thing, thought Warboys, as he watched her drift off toward someone else's life.

Edgear and his mates carried him across the Green and in through the back of Cait's house, where the sound of a bawling baby rose to meet them. He smelled sour milk and cabbage. The lads dumped him in the armchair by the fire, opposite the mother-in-law who was leaning over a cot, where little arms and legs snapped up in frustration. The old lady still managed a glare, as if he'd fallen in drunk from the pub and not just saved half the populace.

'Alright there, Gertie?'

Gertie Garron turned and pulled out the baby, pink and kicking, wrapped in wool.

'Who's this, Shandy love?' Gertie Garron cooed. 'Who's this?

It's your daddy! Such as he is...'

Warboys looked at the screeching thing, and Cait's eyes moistened a little.

'She's got my nose,' he said. Cait rolled her eyes. '*I* haven't even got my nose anymore...' He trailed off. The baby looked... *nice*. It surprised him. She flailed her arms, as if to lambast him. He wished Bill could see her.

'He can't stay here,' snapped Gertie. 'Trouble'll come looking for him. Always does.' This triggered a sharp tongued discussion between the women that he couldn't be bothered to follow. Wilyam stood in the doorway staring at him, as if Warboys were an angel embodied.

'The dragons got me after all,' he said, smiling drunkenly at the lad. 'You should see the state of *them*, though.'

His eyes closed.

~ ~ ~

When Warboys awoke it was growing dark. Cait was standing sentinel, peering out through a gap in the curtain. She looked at him, the lamplight warm on the line of her jaw.

'Keep quiet you,' she said, sharply, taking a puff on her smoke. 'There's been a patrol past. They're out looking for you.'

'Where's your old lady? Gone to roost in the loft, has she?'

'She's took the bairns round hers. Marta Biel's gone to fetch a bloke she knows can stitch you up properly.'

'Right.'

'We heard about Bill. Got the letter last week. I'm sorry.'

Warboys couldn't think of anything to say.

'What are you doing here, Will?'

'I just wanted to... Listen, I've had it, alright? I just wanted to see you... see you all alright, like. Baby looks... smashing. You've pushed out a good one there...'

Cait shot him a look.

'Look, Cait, if I could do it all again… I'd see us right.'

'Why are you saying that? What have you done?'

'You might as well just turn me in. I don't want trouble for you.'

'Why? What have you done? Will I get a reward?'

'I've got some money for you. I'm sending it with a friend.'

'Oh aye. I'll believe it when I see it.'

Warboys didn't bother to argue. He smiled at the thought of Joe Bonboas strolling around Kingstown. That'd give them all summat to talk about.

There was a banging at the door.

'Open up!'

Cait hung in the dark, that grim face of hers on, and Warboys suddenly yearned for the simple days, when she worked the bar at the Five Cats, the merciless way she used to drag him off into the alley out back, and it was up against the wall and quick, before the landlord caught her skiving.

'I know you're in there. Open this door or we'll kick it down!'

Cait peeled back a sliver of curtain and flushed red. 'Fucking Marta Biel! Wait 'til I see that old bastard…'

Warboys heard her thumping up the stairs, the squeak of the front window.

'Stop banging!' he heard her yell. 'I've got kids in bed!'

'You'd better open this door now, love.'

'Or else what?'

'You're harbouring a criminal.'

'No I aren't. Fuck off.'

The window clanged. Cait's footsteps thundered back down,. She scowled at him. Just like the good old days.

'That'll do it, then,' said Warboys.

'They're not having you. I know what happens. Folk get dragged out of their homes at night and never seen again. You've got responsibilities.'

He took a breath and prepared to get up and give himself in before Cait got herself arrested. Then he happened to look up toward the back window. A pale face had appeared, eyes blue like lightning.

'Cait, love. Just keep them talking a minute, will you?'

Cait opened her mouth to reprimand him some more; then more banging – on the window this time – angered her into action. She thundered up the stairs to shout from the window again.

With some effort, Warboys unfurled his limbs and doddered to the back door. Outside, Nouzi Aaranya stood in the yard like some rascal calling him out to play.

'Hui, Captain.'

'What are you doing here?'

Cait's voice could be heard like a volley of gunfire as she gave the soldiers what for. Warboys sidled out. He pushed the door closed. Nouzi Aaranya lifted something, and Warboys turned to see the slack jawed, mangled head of Uparagha gawping sightlessly at him.

'Fucking hell!' exclaimed Warboys, stumbling away into the wall. 'Dickhead! As if my nerves aren't shot enough!'

'I did it. I beat him.'

'I'd have taken your word for it! What do you want me to do with that, now? Put it on the fucking mantelpiece?'

Nouzi Aaranya looked deflated. His arm sank. 'To prove myself to the Sekhet, should they find me.'

'Fucking lunatics, the lot of you.'

'Hui, is just the way we do it, eh?'

'Not here we don't. Come on.'

Warboys leaned heavily on Nouzi as they went quietly through the gate and out onto the green. Sunset and smoke cast a dirty glow on the clouds. 'Get me away.'

'Where are we going?'

'For a bit of fresh air and greenery.'

Shoulder to shoulder, they struggled out across Kingstown Green, leaving the clamour of Cait and the soldiers behind.

~ ~ ~

'Here we go,' announced Warboys, as they arrived at the allotments. The clouds of smoke had thinned now; late sun illuminated the cabbages and cauliflowers, picking out shiny discs in the tops of the water butts.

'Alright there, Stan?' called Warboys, to a doddery old fellow in a flat cap, working away at his scallions, indifferent to bombs and foreign invaders. Stan raised an arm to acknowledge him without looking up. Warboys smiled, and nudged Nouzi. 'He's here day and night, is Stan. Gardens is his *kaarya*, like.'

Nouzi Aaranya looked feverishly around, perhaps expecting some attack. Warboys couldn't muster the words to reassure him – for he felt his own heart racing as he rounded the plots towards Bill's. On the one hand, he had a lot less blood to go around now. On the other, he was dreading the slug-eaten, overgrown jungle he was sure to find.

But when he came upon Bill's plot, his eyes almost burst. Lush cabbage leaves waved like a welcoming crowd. Cauliflowers sprung from the earth, carrot leaves gushed like verdant geysers. All perfectly maintained as if the old man had never left it. A trellis arched over the path, woven with runner beans. And there a shiny new plaque had been mounted.

This plot is maintained in memory of
William Eadgar Warboys,
by his loving family and friends

'Bugger me,' said Warboys. He felt a tear form and was forced to go behind the shed to take a moment. 'I need a smoke.'

Whilst he hid there and rolled one, he sensed Nouzi Aaranya lowering himself into sanyas position, as if he were in some kind of shrine. Warboys sniffed.

'How's this for cultivation, then?' he called out.

'Ai. Is very beautiful.'

'You know what? It *is*, isn't it? I never appreciated it before, but it bloody is.'

'Ai.'

Warboys emerged, leaning against the shed. Inhaling, he stared thankfully to the sky. His eyes came to rest on Uparagha's head, which sat in Nouzi Aaranya's lap like a crystal ball.

'Here, I'll get you a bag for that.'

He doddered back into the shed and started rummaging around.

'Avai, is alright, Captain... don't trouble yourself.'

'No, it's no bother. You want a bag for a thing like that.'

Warboys went off to look in Bill's shed, finding it open. 'Never lock it, you see, and they'll never think you've got owt worth nicking. Here.'

A canvas bag flew out, and Nouzi stood up to tip the head inside. He wiped his hands on his jacket. 'Ai. The most valuable things cannot be stolen, eh?'

'That's it. The old man was right about you. Apart from the moths in your skull, you got a good head on your shoulders. Same can't be said for your mate there... Oh! *Yes!* You lovely old bugger!'

'Eh? What is it?'

Warboys emerged from the shed with a bottle of beer in each hand. 'Sly old sod! Look at this! There's a full crate in here! Now I know what this gardening lark was all about. Here. Have a drink with me.'

'Avai, Warboys. You look deathly pale. I think you need medicine, eh? Not beer.'

'Shut your face. Here.' Warboys passed him a bottle, then collapsed into a wheelbarrow, and held his drink aloft.

'To Bill.'

'Bill.'

They drank in a peace, and the sun dipped below the surrounding chimneys.

'Bloody hell,' sighed Warboys, lowering his bottle. 'I can feel that. Say one thing for blood loss. You get your money's worth out of your booze...'

'On the night of the gaol break,' began Nouzi, quiet and tentative, waiting to see if Warboys would stop him, 'I went in to speak with your old man. He was as gracious as ever. He spoke about you.'

Warboys drank, watched, made no move to stop him.

'He spoke about the day of your birth. How proud he was. How the world changed, seemed harder, but more worthwhile. He knew he had to strive then. He knew *why*.

'I would have died for the idea of Maia. In many ways, Uparagha was right. And in some ways, his actions were not his fault. The Fathers breed us and abandon us, then send us out to fight their war, steal Maia from us and hold her as a prize. But *their* Maia is a dream, eh? A notion. Life is the first thing. You were right.'

'We all have our moments. So what are you going to do next?'

'I'm going to find Maia.'

'For fuck's sake...' muttered Warboys, eyes rolling.

'Nai, but listen...'

Warboys bit his tongue, let the buzz of alcohol and blood loss erase his exasperation. Let the kid talk.

'I won't follow ritual if it doesn't suit me, and I won't die for a dream anymore. Not for anyone. I'm going to stay alive, and find her. In the flesh, eh?' He swallowed, rallying himself to believe the words. 'In the flesh. But I'm going to do it my own way.'

Nouzi Aaranya took another swig, eyes watering.

'Well, good for you. You keep going, and summat turns up. Always does. Kaarya, ain't it?'

Nouzi Aaranya swigged at the ale, seeming to find conviction there.

'Ai.'

'What else did the old man say?'

'Eh? Oh. He said you were such a big fat baby that he could hardly hold you up, and the amount of times he dropped you might account for your behaviour in later life...'

'Alright...'

' ... and he said your head was so large and thick that...'

'Alright! Stop there.'

It had grown dark. There was a clamour approaching. Hobnail boots on cobbles, commanding voices.

'Listen. You'd better be off. They'll be here soon. Don't get caught. Here, take a few of these...' Warboys teetered to his feet, and dropped a couple more bottles in the bag with Uparagha's head before Nouzi Aaranya could object. Then he tottered around to a small apple tree and plucked a few to add to the bag for good measure.

'There you go, son. A bit of packup for you.'

'Captain. They'll hang you. Come with me.'

Warboys exhaled a long, satisfied puff of smoke.

'Nah. What was it you said? A man only runs away to find himself waiting.'

And with that, he raised his bottle again. 'Here's to survival,' he said, and took a long swig.

The clamour came closer now, a bright searchlight over the allotment, picking out the military cap of some sergeant, the muzzles of Entwicks bobbing beyond the trellises and beanpoles. Warboys turned to warn Nouzi Aaranya, but the kid was already gone without a trace.

How can he do that and I can't? wondered Warboys, idly. Tipping the dregs down his throat, he slumped back into his wheelbarrow and watched the searchlights picking out the overlapping outlines of the cabbage and cauliflower leaves.

Acknowledgements

This bloody book has taken years and years to think of, write and get published.

It is dedicated to Emily, to Thomas and to Ivy, as proof that you can get anywhere, eventually.

Love and thanks to my wife, my Mam and Dad, family and friends who supported me throughout, directly or indirectly over the years; who read, encouraged, listened, tolerated; sat next to me whilst I was somewhere else; who let me loiter in their houses and sheds; who became cross-eyed gawping at millions of cover variants.

Special thanks to Chris Skerrow, for dragging himself through the very early drafts and finding encouraging things to say; to Jamie Adams, who did a favour for a stranger and met Warboys years before he met me; to Rob Dinsdale – my agent, but also my SFF genre-pal – for his honesty and enthusiastic dedication to this project, even despite the odds; And to Russ Litten and Shane Rhodes of the mighty Wrecking Ball Press, for taking a straightforward punt on me.

Lastly, "The Regulators" – whoever and wherever you all are now – I remember you.

I owe all of you a pint.

Shazam!

Biographical Note

Lee Harrison was born in Kingston-Upon-Hull, where he now lives with his family. Fantastical stories and daft thoughts helped him hide from real life to survive the 80s and 90s, until *Indiana Jones and the Temple of Doom* inspired him to study Religion at Lancaster University. This blew his mind. He negotiated his return to Hull with a couple of grim short stories and was published by *Route* before returning to his fantasy master-plan. Even though he is a sort of writer, he refuses to mention pets, preferring instead to point us towards the glorious host of noble and biologically diverse animals that still perform an actual role in the Earth's ecosystem. He has no spare time.